THE DARK OF
SUMMER

THE DARK OF SUMMER

E.M. PARSONS

CUTTING EDGE

ISBN-13: 978-1-952138-13-3

Published by
Cutting Edge Publishing
PO Box 8212
Calabasas, CA 91372

CHAPTER ONE

July in Pennsylvania is hot. It's hot and it's dusty, and the cars kick pieces of melted tar, tire-plucked out of the highway dividers, against the windshield of the cars behind—or onto the limp pants of a walking man.

It's hot. And in the lake country, north of Meadville but not yet north enough to be Erie, it's no time or place to be walking a secondary road with a city suit and no money and no place in the whole wide world to go.

Zack Webster stepped off the hot pavement as a roar from behind signaled an approaching car. He didn't turn, didn't raise his thumb. He'd tried that. People are not too damned anxious to pick up a tall stranger, over thirty, wearing a dirty white shirt and a loosely knotted tie, carrying a suit coat over one shoulder. Especially one whose face is craggy and not used to smiling; whose eyes are dark and deep-set, seeming always to be in shadow.

The car went by without stopping. As he'd known it would. He looked ahead.

As near as he knew he was on a State road near some lake called Conaghton, or something like that. Same name as the town he'd left hours before: the town where his bus ticket had run out of juice, where his trail would begin to be harder to trace.

He turned with the thought, looked behind.

The gesture was instinctive, and he snorted at his own self-indulgence. This wasn't Europe and Wilson Agnew was only a U.S. Senator, not an SS Commander. He shrugged heavy shoulders in a habitual rolling motion, began doggedly plodding on down the pavement.

A hayfield off to the left kicked the sun around in waving light-shafts. There was a farmhouse over there. On the right was tight brush, unrelieved. Another car swept by. Swim suits streamed from the door handle, and the people looked sunburned and happy.

Somebody should be happy. Somebody in the goddam world. Zack switched his coat to the other shoulder. Hot. Well, he'd been hot before.

He thought of Wilson Agnew and of his own big fists shattering that pigeon-smugness, that patrician elegance. One hand clenched as he walked and his eyes narrowed, a glimmer sneaking in.

He almost smiled.

A truck rounded the bend ahead, lumbered down toward him. He watched it, fascinated by the hulking shape, the growling sound. The sound kept him from hearing the car coming up from behind. There was a blast of horn, a flash of anger in the face of the truck driver, and Zack twisted, fell away in time to avoid by inches the fender of a speeding convertible. The horn blared. A curse word drifted back.

Zack caught himself against a close-growing birch, spun quickly to get his balance. His coat lay in the dust of the road shoulder. One shoe sole flapped as he moved, torn loose in the evasion.

"Son-of-a-bitch," he said, but there was no heat in the words. He just said it, and picked up his coat.

Then he saw the convertible stop down the highway. It was an old one, a '55 or '56 Ford. There were four people in it, two couples. He watched, incuriously at first, then with more attention as the car began to back, weaving swiftly on the steaming pavement. He brushed his coat aimlessly. All he needed was a fight with some vacationing jerk who wanted to impress his girl.

The Ford came back rapidly, reverse gear howling, and stopped right beside him.

"Hi," a girl said from the front seat. "You all right?"

Zack watched the men; one, the driver, was petulant but he didn't look deadly. The other, an easy-smiling, thin guy in the back seat, echoed the girl's question.

"You okay, man? That was pretty close."

Zack nodded. He pulled his soiled handkerchief from his pocket, mopped his face with it. The little girl in front, the one with the streaming hair and wide mouth, pushed open her door. She wore brief shorts and a white halter. Her skin was lightly golden, and contrasted with the red-leather upholstery.

"Come on," she said. "The least we can do is give you a ride."

The driver said, "Put him in back, Andy, for Christ's sake. One time use your head."

"Don't be icky, Frank," the girl said. She moved on the seat, gestured. "Come on. We can't eat you. At least not without an invitation."

She laughed, and everyone else did, too, except the driver—and Zack.

"Don't mind Frank," she said. "He thinks he's the reincarnation of Rudolph Valentino and sometimes we have to muzzle him. Get in."

Zack looked over the car. The driver stared ahead glumly; the man and the blonde girl in the back nodded agreement every time the girl—what was her name, Andy?—opened her mouth. Hell of a name for a girl. He nodded abruptly, making up his mind, and slid onto the hot leather of the seat. The driver took off and the door slammed. The wind felt good. Zack stared straight ahead, conscious of his rumpled appearance, the three-day beard.

The girl smiled up at him, shrugged. "Isn't it just wizard?" she said, for no reason Zack could see. "The day, I mean."

Wizard. Zack grunted, folded his coat on his long legs. He didn't look at the girl directly, but she was impossible to ignore.

She was very young, pretty except for the big mouth and the way her eyes grooved deeply at the corners, and she came only to his shoulder, sitting down.

The driver leaned forward, spoke past the girl. "Where you want off, Jocko? We don't stay on thirty-eight except to the turn-off.

"Anywhere," Zack said. "Anywhere it's easiest."

"Oh, now wait, friend man." The girl put a small hand on his forearm, turned slightly. "You must be going somewhere. We're not much help if you're going far, but we'd like to take you as far as we can."

"Anywhere. Just anywhere."

"Well, if that isn't the most—"

"Andy, will you for Christ's sake let it alone?" Frank leaned on the horn harder than was necessary as he whipped the Ford around a pick-up truck. "The guy knows where he wants to go. Can't you for one time not try to run the whole goddam world?"

"Pish," the girl said. She didn't seem offended.

"Don't forget we have to stop off at the par," said the other girl, the one in the back seat. She leaned forward between Zack and the little one. "Hello. I'm Carol Normer and this thermometer type playing with my leg is Dale, my husband."

"Thank God he's your husband," Andy said. "That's the only way you'd get him to play handsies."

Zack nodded acknowledgement, feeling heat behind his ears. He used the handkerchief on his face again. The little girl, Andy, leaned her softness on him in turning to the rear seat.

"See, Dale? Your old lady is a lecher. She wants right away to make this perfectly wizard man know she's available."

"With you around, Andy, an early claim is no guarantee," the man called Dale said. He caught Zack's eye, deepened his grin. "Pay no attention, big fella. These theatrical people, you know ..."

"Oh, yes," Andy said, recapturing Zack's arm. "We are of the theatah." She smiled with exaggerated archness, made a long face. "It's a summer thing on the other side of the lake. Called the Cow Shed, and appropriately named, thank you. I'm Andrea Manning and this churl at the wheel is Frank Bonino—the closest we could get to Tony Curtis for sixty a month and beans. If you stay around this area, why don't you come over and see us?"

Zack nodded, saying nothing. He looked at his watch. Three-thirty. Most of the day gone, a lot of daylight. And he'd done nothing constructive. Nothing but wander disconsolately along a summer road feeling sorry for himself and cursing an unkind fate.

He saw the girl looking at his watch, flipped his coat over it. It was a good watch. Much too good for a hitchhiker.

The timepiece had been a gift from Fay Temple. Fay. There it was. The name. Or, more properly, the NAME. Fay—of the golden eyes and precise walk, the Smith accent and lazy sense of the rightness of things; the perfect assurance that social Washington was her particular oyster and would open to her loveliness, her charm.

Zack had been on the verge of being appointed Special Investigator for the powerful Senate Subcommittee on Unions and Employment Practices. Of course Wilson Agnew had taken care of the appointment. And everything else, too. The business he'd worked so hard to build up, the name he'd established. Even his war record came under fire. The years in the OSS, the seven jumps behind enemy lines had helped him in the super-patriotic milieu of post-war Washington, D.C. Then had come the affidavit from Joe Springer charging Zack with misappropriation of special funds during a behind-the-lines operation in Italy. Joe Springer, of all people. Joe, whose faulty Italian had gotten him snatched by the roving Nazi patrol, whose life had been saved by Zack's intervention.

But, then, Wilson Agnew had connections everywhere. He operated on the theory that a man walks quiet when his shoes are full of razor blades. And he always provided the blades. Zack had no doubt that Springer was miserable over the affair; they'd become good friends and the stocky ex-Captain could only have acted out of the shadow of serious threat.

All of Agnew's gambits had hurt. But the destroyer had been Fay's denial, her refusal to support and stand by him.

"Darling," she'd said that night, the night he was to tear out the roots of ten years' work, smash in blind rage the life he'd carefully, dedicatedly built. "Darling, you can't expect me to throw myself away. You know what I want, what I must have. I love you, Zack, but why must you be so wrongheaded?"

"You mean why don't I suffer that bastard Agnew's dirty tactics in silence. Why don't I wait and hope and keep my nose clean and maybe he'll forgive me." He'd growled then, the old hunted feeling returning. "Well, I'm damned if I will. It was my job to get the evidence on Agnew. His lousy organization stinks up the government and you know it. The Committee knows it—everybody in the world knows it because I proved it! Me. With records I schemed for and conversations I waited months to get on tape."

"Zack, you can't fight Capitol Hill. You know that. You're politics-wise enough to realize you're licked. Fall back and regroup, darling. There's time. All the time you need."

"Time! Time has nothing to do with it. Agnew is a crook and a snake, and I'm a son-of-a-bitch if I'll let him push me around because he's a United States Senator. And maybe that's the best reason why I shouldn't let him get away with it."

"Zack, you can't beat him." She said it calmly, her strange, golden eyes looking at him but also seeming to consider some deep thought of their own. "He's too powerful. The court order closed you up. The paper Springer signed put your best weapon, your fine war record, out of commission. Nobody will hire you now."

She'd been right—as always. And she no longer wanted to marry Zack Webster.

Somehow the shock was much worse in that he'd never considered that Fay might turn aside from him. How could she—with her breeding, charm, loyalty and serenity? But he had to admit—later, when the sobering thoughts had come—that these were attributes he saw in her. He had no idea how anyone else considered Fay Temple. What was the need? For Zack Webster, two college years and one rugged war removed from Mechanicsville, Pennsylvania, she was everything in a bucket, painted gold and crusted with diamonds. If Fay Temple wasn't constant, nothing was.

The wild trip to Agnew's, the fight—all that had been easy after the scene with Fay. And now he had not only the Senator's wrath to face, but the cold actuality of a bench warrant in issue for one Zachariah Colton Webster, charging Assault w/Intent to do Great Bodily Harm.

The convertible stopped. Zack became aware that the girl beside him was shaking his arm. He looked around. Her face was inches away.

"Hey, fella," she said. "This is the lake. We go around to the other side, but I don't think that would help you." She studied him a moment; the others had not moved but were evidently waiting for him to get out. The girl's hand tightened on his arm. "Your face was terrible just now. All ridged and hard. I'd hate for you to think of me like that."

Zack pulled his arm away, swung open the door.

"What is this place?"

They were parked in the circular drive of a rambling, weathered hotel sitting just a stone's throw from a lake of startling blue. Off to the left were buildings and an amusement park; a green quad and a boardwalk separated the hotel from a busy beach.

Dale, the thin man, said, "I work here. In the lounge. If you stay around, drop in and it'll be worth a drink."

Zack got out, started to close the door. The girl, Andy, stopped it with an outstretched leg. A very nicely tanned and rounded leg.

"Wait. You haven't told us your name. Are you going to? It would be very rude of you to let us almost kill you, then rescue you and not even get a name."

He raised the handkerchief, swabbed his face. The girl's cool eyes—what the hell color were they, anyway?—followed the soiled rag, then lifted to his face.

"Zack," he said, because he could think of no other. "Zack Webster."

Pennsylvania was a long way from D.C.

"Zack," Carol Normer said from the back seat. "Nice. Fitting, too. Hard face and big shoulders. Kind of Zackish …"

Andrea Manning said, "You can't get mad at me, Zack, because I'm too small. So—do you need any money? I mean, are you broke? I could let you have enough to—"

"Oh, for Christ's sake," Frank Bonino said. He raced the Ford's engine with an impatient toe. "Will you let the guy go? What are you—hot for him or something?"

Zack's hands twisted the handkerchief. He pushed the girl's leg out of the way, shut the door softly.

"This lake," he said. "Is it a resort, or what?"

Andy knelt on the seat, bringing her head almost to a level with his.

"Conaghton? The Pearl of the Pennsylvania Poconos? You mean you've never heard of lovely Lake Conaghton, where the Abbots and the Codges …"

"… play around in private lodges…" Dale added, singing it.

They all chorused: "And the virgins don't stay virgin very long."

Everybody laughed. Even Frank Bonino, his handsome head thrown back, good teeth gleaming in the sun.

Dale got out of the car, after kissing his wife. He was tall— about six and a half feet, straight up. He grinned across the car at Zack.

"These people are nuts. I don't know why I let my young, tender, impressionable wife mess around with them."

" 'Cause you can't stop me, sweetheart," Carol said.

Andrea Manning bounced on the seat to attract Zack's attention. "Zack, I can't wait. So tell me. Are you gonna stay around here? Are you? 'Cause if you are, I want to know it so I can protect you from the female cannibals hereabouts. Their fertility dance is a frightful thing. Do you water ski?"

Zack shrugged, wanting to get away from the group now, look over the new situation. The lake had possibilities. Transient haven; pleasure the main commodity. Yes, it might be just the place to drop out of sight.

"Do you and are you?" the girl insisted.

Zack swung the coat to his other arm, lifted his soggy handkerchief and wiped at his face. He said, "I want to thank you all for the—"

That's as far as he got. Because a pair of cool, strangely slippery lips had fastened on his; two slim arms went around his neck. Andy Manning kissed him briefly, then pulled his head down till the lips touched his ear.

"Didn't mean to startle you," she whispered, "But you'd better quit waving that handkerchief around. It's covered with blood."

CHAPTER TWO

The Hotel Gableton was a sprawling, frame three-story, dripping weathered shingles and surrounded—at least on the two sides Zack could see—by an old-fashioned veranda, climbing vines and all. It was big. There was no sign, other than the small bronze marker on the grass where the drive angled off from the road leading down to the beach. Double doors were open to the July afternoon; the lobby seemed very dark and cool, shading to dimness just beyond the door. Subdued music drifted out; a few wicker chairs held uninterested types on the front porch.

"You work here?"

Dale turned from watching the convertible disappear down the beach road, nodded. His long face was very tanned and tiny lines split whitely at the eye corners.

"This is it. Beautiful Hotel Gableton on sparkling Lake Conaghton. American plan, rooms seven-fifty and up. Reservations until September first. Act now."

Zack crumbled his handkerchief, stuffed it into a coat pocket. "Seems dead."

"Well, it ain't Coney Island. But the park over there gets a lot of evening action. Roller skating, plus all the junk on the midway. You can't see from here, but they've got the whole bit—concessions, rides, you know."

"How about work? Could a guy catch on without too much trouble?"

Dale looked at him for a long moment. Then he nodded toward the lobby. "Let's go in. I don't go on until five. We can sit at the bar and talk it over. I'd say the chances were pretty good for a guy like you."

"What is there to talk over?" Zack pulled away from the thin man's hand. "Who do I see?"

"That's why I said let's go in. Couple things you should know first if you're going to work around here."

They started inside.

Zack rolled his cuffs down, fixed the links. He buttoned his collar, knotted the tie up close and donned his wrinkled coat. Not much help. Not with three days of whiskers and dust beaten into the skin. He felt very grimy.

Dale led the way past the circular desk nestling under a curving stairway directly in the front as they entered. The lobby was smaller than Zack had thought: potted plants and darkly upholstered, overstuffed chairs were dotted about. There was a blond man behind the desk busy with an overstuffed woman in flowered shorts. He nodded to Dale, examined Zack briefly.

The bar opened off the lobby at the bottom of the stairs. It was better lighted, had no outside windows. Just a half-bar to the left, tables and booths everywhere else; decorated tastefully in contrast to the rest of the hotel. The wallpaper was black with dark-red abstract figures; a gold mirror behind the bar reflected the room softly with shimmering highlights. A jukebox sat at the left of the door against the wall. In the far right-hand corner was a six-inch riser that passed for a stage, holding a piano covered in white leather, studded with gold nails. The place was almost empty. But cool and restful after the harsh sun, the dusty highway.

Zack walked all the way to the end of the bar, took the last seat facing the door and the room. Dale followed, eyes narrowed against the changed light.

"What'll it be?" he asked, settling his six-foot plus on a cream-leather stool.

The bartender drifted up, polishing a brandy snifter. He nodded at Dale, looked at Zack, then looked back again in a double-take.

"Tie straight?" Zack asked softly.

The man blushed. He was bald, about forty. The red-and-white jacket covered a slight paunch, a white shirt and a gold silk tie.

Dale laughed. "Don't stare, Rube," he said. "This is my friend, Zack Webster. Zack, Rube Ziegler. He holds the plank till five."

The bald man mumbled something, looked away from Zack's hard eyes. Dale ordered and the man left gratefully.

"I look that bad?"

Dale swiveled on the stool. "Nah. Not really. Your beard sort of accents those grooves in your face. I guess the lighting helps. You're a hard-looking guy."

"What do you think about me?"

"None of my business, man. That's the way most folks around here will look at it, too. This is a resort. Mind your business, have your fun. You know how it is. Secretaries save all year, take two weeks at Conaghton. They know nobody is peeking from behind the curtains and they figure for once they can do what they want to. You mean it about a job?"

The drinks came. Zack looked at his bourbon; his throat tightened. He hadn't had a sip since early morning in the bus station. He deliberately let it sit there, the desire mounting in him. Self-denial had been so long a part of him that even now—years after the hiding, killing, pretending in Italy and France—the abnegation, the deception was an almost unconscious practice.

"I mean it," he said. "I have no money." He looked at the thin man. "None at all."

"About the drinks, don't—"

"Not the drinks. I need some quick cash—just a little. Then I'll try to get a job around here, maybe stay the rest of the season."

"Andy offered you money. She likes you." The man grinned, sipped at his amber drink. "At least it looked to me like she did."

"Knock it off. Here's a watch." Zack stripped the Philippe from his thick wrist, held it out to Dale. "Go ahead. Take it. It's yours for ten dollars."

"Ten—Aw, now, Webster, that watch is worth a hundred dollars. I couldn't—"

"Several hundred. Ten and it's yours. And the name of the man to see about a job."

Dale seemed embarrassed. He turned the dull-gold watch in his fingers, moved his eyes away.

"Yeah, the initials say Z.W.," Zack said. "So look and get it over with. It's not hot. You want it or not?"

"I couldn't do that, Zack," Dale said. "Look, suppose I let you have ten? You pay me when you get paid. I know Kinchloe will hire you. They always need men. Especially good men."

"Buy it or not. I don't want it. The watch is yours."

He picked up the drink then, his face showing nothing. They were too far down the bar to see the mirror, but a line of glasses reflected silvery images in each. He sipped the drink, then downed it.

"Okay, Zack," Dale said. He slid a bill across the bar. A twenty. "It's a beautiful watch. I'll take care of it."

Zack snorted harshly, crooked a finger for the bartender. "I don't give a damn what you do with it. It's yours. You want another?"

"No. I have to stand back there all night. It gets a little drunk about midnight."

"This joint livens up, does it?"

"Wait'll about eleven. Then it romps. No dancing, though. And that cuts the take. I keep telling Johnny that, but he says we make more with a music room. Maybe he's right. The pavilion down the beach has open-air dancing for free every night until eleven. That's where the young set goes. We get 'em later."

Zack downed his second bourbon, shoved the twenty at the bald barman, who still wouldn't meet his eyes. "Now, about the job …"

"Oh, yeah." The tall guy turned on the stool, bony knees brushing Zack's leg. "Well, look. The best way would be for me to see Johnny Kinchloe before I go on. Then you could talk to him or—"

"Taking the boss's name in vain again, Normer?" a voice said.

Both men turned. A dapper blond stood there—the same man who'd been on the desk as they came in. He looked like a hotel manager and like nothing else in the world. His thin face was untanned, closely shaven; eyes of pale blue glittered in the artificial light. He wore a lightweight worsted suit, a white shirt and a small-figured tie. The corn-colored hair was cut neatly and combed straight back. He smiled thinly.

Dale said, "Johnny. Just talking about you. Have a drink and I'll introduce you to Zack Webster."

"I'd be charmed. But right now I want to talk to you about something else."

"Johnny, Zack wants a job. I thought you could find a place for him."

The man's hand cut a short arc through the air. "Not now. I said I wanted to talk to you. Come along."

He turned, started off. Dale flushed deep red, looked at Zack. He called after the man: "If you want to see me, Kinchloe, it'll be right here."

Kinchloe stopped, came back slowly. His eyes looked at Zack with more interest.

"Oh?" he said. "Well, then, all right. I want to know if you've been to the Ship today. At any time."

"You checking up on me, Johnny? Why should I tell you where I go when I'm not working?"

"Don't be an ass, Dale." The cutting motion again. The man stepped close, angled his shoulder between Zack and the other man. "It's Marie. She left at noon and I haven't been able to trace her. You know how I feel about that. You know I won't stand for her jeopardizing my career."

"Aw, for Christ's sake, Johnny. What are you asking me for? You know how Marie is. Maybe she got hung up with somebody in town. Doesn't she take the receipts into the bank every day?"

"Listen." The little man had forgotten Zack, who sat, not moving. Kinchloe gripped Normer's arm. "I won't have it. I've told the bitch about it before and I want to know. Were you at the Ship?"

"No," Dale said. He turned back to the bar. "We went to Meadville, bought some junk and saw an early movie. We haven't been to the other side. Frank and Andy took Carol to work just now, so none of us have seen Marie. Now, will you talk to my friend about a job?"

Kinchloe relaxed his grip, stepped back. He didn't look at Zack. "He can talk to Marie. When she gets back. I've got to get back to the desk."

"How do you know she'll be back?"

The little man smiled, shrugged his coat straight and ran both hands over his hair, patting it. "She always comes back. That's the one thing I can depend on." His eyes flicked to Zack, then away. "It's ten to five. You better get ready for work."

He left, moving rapidly, shoulders squared and not bobbing, hands held easily at his sides.

Zack grunted. Dale stared at the bar for a moment, then smiled weakly. "Local jazz," he said. "Well, I gotta get behind that board. Stick around."

Zack said, "Wait, Normer. How about this Marie I have to see? Will she be around?"

"I don't know. Neither does Johnny. You see, he's got a bug. An itch, like. He wants to be the youngest manager of a first-class Miami Beach hotel there ever was. And Marie makes it hard. Not with the work—she's a help there. But she's a—well, Andy put it pretty good back there in the car. She's a cannibal." He grinned down from his standing height. "Beautiful as hell, too. She shoots at every male in sight. But she's all right otherwise— good businesswoman. That's why Johnny tolerates the rest of it. The Hotel Company runs a couple of concessions, a beanery on the beach and some french fry booths. She takes care of all that. Don't worry about the job. Get a room and freshen up. We'll take care of you tomorrow."

"Yeah, okay." Zack picked his change from the bar, got off the stool. "I don't know whether this is such a good idea or not."

"What the hell," Dale said. "For the summer you can't beat it. Lots of booze, lots of women." He glanced at Zack. "And, like I said, nobody asks questions."

"Who else might be hiring?"

"See Samson Coy. He has a little office under the Beach Club. That's that joint we saw. You go around the side, down toward the water. A dock goes left under the Pavilion. You turn sharp right and you see a hole-in-the-wall office where the fishy Mister Coy hangs out."

"He run the park?"

"Some of it. The Park is split up all kinds of ways," Dale said. "Coy has the beach. The only decent one on the whole lake, incidentally. And he has the roller rink and several of the little things. Booths and such—couple of rides. He's a big man."

A very young, very much made-up girl in toreador pants came over to the jukebox, stood hipshot reading the selections. Dale moved to the trapdoor in the bar, lifted it.

"Come around later, why don't you?"

Zack followed him, then leaned on the plank when the lanky guy had lowered it.

"Can't afford it. Listen. What kind of guy is Coy? What should I do?"

"Just tell him you want to work. He's always short. But I'll tell you now, he pays nothing. And call him Samson." He grinned, thin face breaking into a good smile, white teeth flashing. "That's the kind of a guy he is. Even his wife calls him Samson."

Zack jerked his head, turned.

"Zack. Drop in later and let me know where you're staying. So I can tell Andy Manning—keep her from cutting my head off".

This lake was an odd one. There were no beaches as such. Hills came right down to the water. Gently rolling hills, wooded and calm. Settlements perched here and there around the mile-long body of water; scars on the forests indicated their whereabouts. Zack stood on the boardwalk, watched the dwindling crowd of bathers. It was almost seven and the thin strip of sand below the boardwalk was just about deserted. A thin youth with white hair and a very tanned swimmer's body went leisurely along the beach, picking up papers, smoothing sand castles. His eyes hit Zack several times.

Zack hadn't been to see Samson Coy. After the bar episode he'd decided that the first thing to do was take on natural coloration. So he'd found the Park barbershop, and had his thick hair cut to a half-inch black brush. A shave took another buck, but he had to have it. Then he bought three tee-shirts at the drugstore, a dollar blade-and-razor set and a cheap toothbrush. Soap he could steal.

The Park wasn't much. Hoopla, penny-pitch, fish-pond, a couple of cheesy rides, and a large Bingo emporium. The roller rink was tuning up, organ music pushing out into the humid evening. Everybody was half-dressed, or half-undressed. The girls were numerous and not all young, their dress running to peasant blouses pulled far down or shorts and halters with thonged sandals. Like a uniform.

The twenty had dwindled. If he did get a job, the chances were good he wouldn't be able to draw anything until he had worked several days. He'd have to take it easy. The suit coat, shirt, and tie he'd put in a public locker at the Pavilion. With his beard gone and a short haircut, the tee-shirted figure wasn't too much out of place. The slacks were wrong, though. But he couldn't have everything.

What he needed now was a job. A job and a place to blend into the atmosphere, to become a summer itinerant.

A check at Coy's office got him nothing. It was closed. A deck boy, pumping canoes at the adjoining pier, offered the intelligence that Mr. Coy had gone home for the evening, wouldn't be back. He said for Zack to see Bisto, the lifeguard.

The water was free of swimmers; only a few stubborn sun worshipers remained. The white-haired man stopped below Zack, stuffed a piece of paper into the sack he carried. Then he looked up.

"You want to see me?"

His face was unlined and deeply tanned. He wore a thin strip of red around his hips, a whistle at his neck on a braided cord, nothing else. There was a vagueness about his stare, a hint of a vacuous smile at his lips.

Zack said, "Yeah, I do. How'd you know?"

"You been watching me. People don't. Men anyway. What is it?"

"You coming up?"

"Pretty quick."

"I'll wait."

Bisto wasn't really young, seen close up. His body was wonderful, long-muscled and burnt almost black, with sloping shoulders and big hands. But the skin around his eyes was leathery; wrinkles showed at the neck. Zack revised his estimate upward a dozen years. He recognized Bisto, now. A beachboy. At Miami you stumble over them. He'd always wondered what they did in the off-season.

The two men walked toward the Pavilion, Bisto leading. Zack told him about the job, asked for Samson Coy's residence.

"Behind the hotel," the lifeguard said laconically. "No street. On the beach just at the end of the boardwalk. Second house. But he won't hire you."

"Why?"

Bisto stopped, smiled full and wet. "Too good-looking. Got a theory, Samson has. About most everything, but mostly about help. Keep 'em dumb, keep 'em ugly. No trouble."

"He hired you."

The smile slid, stopped at a thin-lipped quirk. "I'm strange. Anyone'll tell you."

He started off. Zack hurried to catch up with the easy-moving figure in the gathering summer gloom. Diagonally across the street, the Day-Night Café was getting a brisk play. It was on the corner of the beach street and the midway walk. Glass on both access sides; stark white neon tracing out the name above. Inside, it was all counter, functional tables. No frills. Food served quickly and antiseptically and expensively, because this was Vacation, Father, and why worry about pennies for just one time a year?

"Bisto." The man stopped. "If I should decide to see him anyway, what sort of a job is there? I mean, for a guy like me?"

The man shrugged. He jerked his chin at the Day-Night. "Be smarter to try that joint. Office upstairs. You're apt to catch Miz Kinchloe in any time." He burned the smile a few degrees warmer. "Ain't a damn bit o' doubt she'll hire you. Not a damn bit. I got to eat. See you …"

He stepped out into the asphalt street. At that moment a low-slung car roared around the bend past the Pavilion. Bisto jumped back, but the car stopped before it reached him. It was a Cad El Dorado, metallic grey with wire wheels and white walls. A very hefty guy stuck up over the low door at the driver's side; a blonde girl sat next to him.

"That's Mr. Malebar," Bisto said. "Runs the Ship on the other side. Bar, dancehall. Suppose to be a big racket guy from Pittsburgh. They call him Softy. But he ain't soft."

Malebar was dark and jowled, with grey streaks in his snarled black hair. He wore a beautiful lightweight silk suit and what looked like a pure wool turtleneck jersey of stark white. And Zack could see he wasn't soft. About fifty, he would go around two-ten. His suit bulged here and there—like concrete blocks stuffed into an expensive sack. He laughed loudly as the car stopped, said something to the woman. She laughed with him, a controlled contralto that set Zack's hair to rise.

He walked across the street. As he got to the Day-Night, the woman slid out of the car. Bisto stood beside him, smiling loosely.

"How about that."

She was lovely. Tall and supple, straight-shouldered and long of leg. She wore a black cocktail sheath, cinched tightly with a wide, cream leather belt; her hair was drawn back almost severely to a Grecian knot behind one ear. Zack was ten feet away, but he could feel the force of the woman, could see the hard glitter in her eyes. She swept away from the car, into a doorway next to the entrance of the café. The Cad purred off.

Bisto said, "There's your chance, fella. That hippy tornado is—"

"I know who she is," Zack said. He clapped a hand on the lifeguard's bare back. "See you. Thanks for the information."

He followed Marie Kinchloe up the narrow stairs.

CHAPTER THREE

The office was a lot larger than the narrow entrance had indicated. At the top of the stairs was a big, open room; there were desks and files, stacks of boxes and cartons. One half of the room, to the left of the stairs, was lit; the rest was quiet and dark. One girl worked at a battered desk next to the window overlooking the midway. Colored lights flashed from the rides, the shows. There was no sign of Marie Kinchloe. In the front corner of the room was a partitioned office. The door was closed.

Zack had made no noise on the stairs. Now he walked with his habitual stealth to within a foot of the lone girl. She was a young one—brown hair, neat dress, slight figure.

"Hello."

She jumped. "What—Oh, I didn't hear you."

Her eyes were dark and her skin pale. Probably the bookworm type, earning summer money.

Zack said, "I want to see Mrs. Kinchloe. She in there?"

He indicated the office.

"Yes, but—"

He raised a hand and she stopped. He nodded, made his way to the door. A neat sign said, Conaghton Enterprises, Inc. M. L. Kinchloe, Mgr. Well. He knocked.

"What is it, Gwen?" The voice. Like satin rubbing on a rough beard.

Zack pushed open the door, stepped in. The woman was working at a small desk in the corner; she didn't look up. The office was functional, no frills. And that was strange when you considered the woman's flamboyance. There were only the desk and some files, a few chairs, spilled cartons of plastic and plaster figures, paper cups and other miscellany.

Zack coughed, stood near the desk.

"Well, what—" Marie Kinchloe's eyes came up, widened slightly. She leaned back in the chair. "I don't know many things. But I do know you're not Gwen. How did you get in here?"

"Don't blame the kid," Zack said. "She tried to stop me, but I had to see you, Mrs. Kinchloe. I need a job."

"Badly?"

"Yes, badly. I've no specialty you can use. But I can do most anything if I have to."

Her eyes narrowed and a white line appeared next to the nose; very red, very soft-looking lips pursed.

"Your hands are monstrous," the woman said. Her own crept on the blotter, came together, gripped. "Why do you want to work here? You're obviously not a schoolboy. And you don't look like an itinerant. Are you in trouble?"

Zack's eyes left the woman's hands, worked slowly up over the good breasts, came to her face.

"If I wanted to give a pedigree I wouldn't be applying for a job in a summer resort. You got a job for me or not?"

He straightened, his chest swelling the cheap tee-shirt. He stuck his hands in his pockets, looked directly at the woman.

She said nothing. A lamp cast a yellow pool on the desk blotter, accentuated minute by minute as the outside light failed. Organ music drifted in, and a subdued roar that had to be hundreds of tiny wheels on wood came from the roller rink. Other music mingled; plus the midway sounds—yells and laughter, horns blowing and an occasional spate of snapping rifle shots from the nearby shooting gallery. Marie Kinchloe leaned back out of the light, turned her chair.

"Coy'll hire you if I don't," she said to the window. "But I don't think…"

"I've been told he won't. So it's you, or I take a hike. And I'm beginning to like it here."

She tilted the light with a sudden movement, bathed him in it. He didn't move. She said something under her breath, got up abruptly.

"Come with me," she said, sweeping past him to the door.

A wave of good perfume followed her. Zack inhaled, thought briefly of Washington and Fay and the hundred-odd little things he'd taken for granted that no longer existed for him. He followed the woman.

Gwen filled out employment forms. Zack answered correctly when he could, lied when he had to. Marie Kinchloe stood impatiently tapping a slippered foot, looking out the window. The woman was a dynamo. No wonder she was a business success.

"That's all," the mousy girl said, finally. "Where does he go, Mrs. Kinchloe?"

Marie turned, arms folded under her breasts. They didn't need accenting, but the pose did it. She frowned for a moment.

"These pants won't do. I suppose you haven't another pair? No, of course not. Gwen, get him two sets of whites, take him downstairs and tell George to break him in on the grill. Starting at midnight." She smiled, walked forward. "Can you cook a hamburger, Mr. Webster?"

There was a hot feeling in his belly, wanting to work upward, wanting to spread. He took a breath, said, "Anybody can cook a hamburger."

"We have a policy, Mr. Webster. No advances. I thought you should know that. You work seven nights. If you're late, you're docked. Three times, you're fired. The night fry cook is leaving Sunday. If you learn anything in three days, you'll get the job. Ninety plus tips, all your meals on shift. Okay?"

"Fine."

"And no advances."

The girl had opened a closet, stood there obviously waiting for him. He started toward her, then turned his head back to his boss.

"I don't want anything I haven't earned, Mrs. Kinchloe. Not anything."

He heard a door slam behind him.

It was eight-thirty. The Gableton Lounge wasn't much busier than it had been at five. Dale Normer, looking very natty in the lounge uniform of red-piped white jacket and gold tie' was behind the bar alone. Two young waiters worked the tables. A handful of the oval booths were in use; one was loaded with giggling girls, about six of them. Zack stood in the entrance, wondered about his clothes. He had the whites on, shirt and pants. They were starchy and coarse. A white hat stuck through his belt, army-fashion.

Dale saw him and waved. He grinned, tanned face splitting.

"Well, well—Aunt Jemima. What happened, Zack?"

Zack took the first stool by the wall, at the waiter's station. He motioned for a drink.

"Got a job. Twelve o'clock at the Day-Night." His lips quirked. "Smashing hamburgers."

Dale slid a double in front of him, burbled one quickly for himself. "Midnight? That's kind of rough, man. You better get some sleep."

Zack grunted. He picked up the drink, aimed at a light through the amber.

"Where? Can't afford a room. That Kinchloe woman told me quick there'd be no advances."

"Not monetary, maybe," Dale said, grinned, then stopped it quickly. "Johnny was in again, looking for clues. That guy is a mess. A woman like that just naturally needs more than one guy, that's all. He wants her 'cause he knows she'll push him, make him what he'll never be alone. But he can't stand her running around."

"Natural."

"Not the way he does it." The lanky bartender leaned close, waited until Zack had drained his drink. "You know what he does? He sniffs around, tries to find out who she's been with—all the details. You figure he's going to take her apart or shoot the guy, or something. But he doesn't. Nothing. I mean it. Nothing. He don't say a word to her. Afraid to."

Zack reached for his pocket and Dale stopped him with a gesture. "Nah. What for? Look, why don't you go into the lobby and—That's no good."

He straightened at a call, went to get an order for one of the waiters. While he did, a tall, pretty girl in a very tight black strapless gown came in, made for the station. She moved nicely, hips working, shoulders still. Her skin was coffee brown, her flesh firm, her hair glossy black.

Dale said, coming back: "Hi, Pam. Meet a pal, Zack Webster. Zack, this is the Gableton's answer to Eartha Kitt—Pam Jardin."

The girl nodded, her face unchanging. "Mr. Webster."

Zack nodded, hitched his legs aside so she could mount the stool next to him. She shook her head, smiled slightly.

"Have to slave," she said. Her voice was low, controlled and soft. "Music nightly in the lounge, you know. One quick one, Dale. Double."

Dale put red-knuckled hands on the bar. "Pam … Johnny told me to—"

She said a nasty word, very deliberately and distinctly. Zack saw her eyes then, the gold mirror filling the brown softness with highlight. Sad. She had moist eyes, suffering eyes—withdrawn and used to looking at dim lights, ugly sights.

"The drink, Dale. Johnny doesn't run the world."

"No, but he runs the Gableton. And you need the job as bad as I do, Pam. Don't make it tough on both of us. Go play piano. You been socking it away pretty good lately."

"Lectures I don't need, white man."

"Aw, Pam, for Christ's sake…"

The tall guy was embarrassed. He turned away to hide the sudden color in his face. The girl stood, waited. She was used to waiting, too.

Zack said, "Dale, give me two double bourbons, water behind. Then go take care of the bar."

Pam turned, looked at him. Her eyes went over the clothes, the bristling black hair, then moved to his hands, twisting the empty glass on the dark wood of the bar. She slid onto the stool, the motion graceful.

"There's nothing in it, big fella," she said.

"I like music," Zack said. "Dale tells me you play well."

She shrugged, lifted one corner of her mouth. Her shoulders were smooth and square; the dress pressed firmly against small breasts, emphasizing her hips.

"It's a living," she said. "Thanks for the rescue. The boss says I'm drinking too much and the boss thinks he's got the right to run my life."

Dale brought the drinks, slammed them down and took Zack's money. He came back with change, left again without saying a word. His lips were set.

Zack took one glass, pushed the other to Pam Jardin. She took it, knocked it back with a quick flip. No chaser. She blew out a breath, turned a smile on Zack.

"Thanks, big one. Needed that. Now I go make pretty noises for Johnny Kinchloe and the Gableton Hotel." She slid off the stool. "You could move closer … the piano's over there."

"No. Thanks. I was kidding about the music. I got to find a place to sleep until midnight. Then I go to work myself. Here, take this one, too. It's a long time till two o'clock."

She took the glass, looked at him over the rim. "One," she said. "I work till one. Where do you work?"

"Day-Night. Start tonight. If I don't go to sleep on my feet. Just got here today. Haven't got a place to stay yet."

The girl sipped at the drink, set it down. Then she looked at Zack for a long moment, eyes narrowed. Finally, she nodded. "Okay. Go around the back of the hotel, up the stairs. Can't miss 'em, they're the only ones. Inside, you turn right and walk till you find number twenty-two. That's me. The door's open, but you can lock it."

He turned. "Thanks. But I don't want to put you out."

"No hassle—what was the name—Zack? No hassle, Zack. I'm out till two, you go on at twelve." She shrugged, finished her drink. "Gotta go. It's nine."

Zack watched her walk to the piano. Several people spoke to her. She moved easily without seeming to walk at all. A small battery of pre-focused spots suddenly lit the stage and Pam Jardin sat down to a spattering of applause. She smiled professionally and began to play.

Dale came back. He leaned on the bar in front of Zack, looked toward the stage.

"Plays good. But she's too damn pushy for a dinge. Comes from sleeping with the—"

He was turning with these words, and they died on his lips when he saw Zack's face. He moved back, eyes wary.

"What's the matter? I do something wrong?"

Zack stood up, spilling the stool. "No," he said. "Nothing wrong. I'm going to sleep."

He walked outside quickly, not breathing until the warm dark covered him, till the hotel sounds had died behind. He stood on the lawn, kicked at the grass till the anger left him. This was no time to get messed up. Not now. What difference did it make to him if Normer was a bigot? But it wasn't that. Not entirely. It was the look of that girl, that Pam. The way she seemed just naturally to expect the worst, almost to welcome it.

What he had to worry about was Zack Webster. Not every underdog that came down the pike. That was Fay's phrase. She'd used it often enough when he insisted on doing cases for no money just because they interested him. For days she called him Ivanhoe when it happened, which was fairly often. Well, he couldn't afford it now. What he had to do was dig in, disappear until he could work out something ...

He found the girl's room without difficulty. It was small and without personality. Bare walls, thin rug, double bed; a bath adjoined. The girl's smell was there. But no evidence of her person. Everything was neat, clean. He rummaged quickly, investigated the window, finding a long drop to the paved back court, peering into closets and carefully ransacking drawers. It was habitual and thorough. In the past it had kept him alive.

The bureau held the usual collection of female junk. Zack ran his eyes over it, picked up a garish bottle of assembly-line perfume. "Torchy." There was a small leather case surrounded by the bottles of junk. He opened it, found a tiny vial wrapped in soft chamois. It was a split ounce of very good, very expensive perfume. He twisted the gold stopper, waved the thing in front of his face. The fragrance was elusive, dry—fresh sheets and a dying blossom. He put it away, making the same careful folds in the chamois. On the underside of the box's lid was a word scrawled with a lipstick brush: "Someday."

His eyes came up to the mirror, looked at the figure there. Suddenly he felt ashamed and he put the box back as he'd found it. There was a travel clock and he set the alarm, put the tiny timepiece on the bed table and stretched out on the made-up bed.

For a few moments his head whirled with new impressions, reviewed the events since he'd left Washington. Had it been just three days? From acceptance and status, financial comfort—to beggar for a bed in three days? He pushed the thoughts down firmly, sternly. He had to work. As it was he would get only two hours' sleep. He closed his eyes.

The lump irritated him and he moved his head several times before he was sure it was real. He slid a hand under the pillow, pulled out a gun. A real piece. He held it up so the moon slants from the window hit it squarely. Smith & Wesson .38 Banker's Special. He grunted, tapped the gun, snapping out the loads. Five lethal pellets lay in a moonpool on the coverlet. He got up on one elbow, loaded the gun expertly, flicked the safety off, then on again.

Pam Jardin. He lay down. His eyes looked into the dark. Pam Jardin. What need would she have for a gun? Strange things motivate people; he'd learned that early. You never knew—never.

Sleep came.

A sound woke him. His senses were still drugged by sleep, but he knew something had happened. Without thinking about it, he slid a hand to the gun under the pillow. Then a soft hand covered his mouth, a weight depressed the bed.

"Shh."

It was Pam. Her fragrance swam in his head, all mixed up with Torchy and no sleep and hours on a sun-seared road.

"Zack, wake up. Zack, please. You have to leave."

Zack shook his head once, sat up.

"What's wrong?"

The girl's face was drawn in the moonlight. There were streaks in the light powder on her cheeks.

"Johnny had a thing with Marie. Then he—"

The door crashed open, hit the wall. The overhead light flashed on and Johnny Kinchloe stood in the doorway. His yellow hair was mussed at the sides and he breathed raggedly.

"Well," he said, pushing it out. His mouth twisted nastily. "This is pretty. This is pretty. Yes, this is nice."

"Johnny, listen—"

"Shut up, you black bitch!" The hotel manager stepped into the room, closed the door behind him. "This is what I'd expect. After I give you a job, promise to make you a star if you listen to me. This is what I get. This!"

The man's eyes were wild. Zack couldn't move; Pam's weight leaned on him. He nudged her, wanting room to move.

"Dirty bitch," Johnny Kinchloe muttered, moving forward. "Dirty, dirty—laying, lying female, all alike ..."

The blue eyes shifted and flitted, the narrow head swiveled. Suddenly he broke and came forward with a loud cry, hands hooking. Zack shoved Pam, saw her hit the floor and roll free. Then he had his hands full as the little man lit on him, pummeling with both soft hands.

"Hold it, Kinchloe," Zack managed. A fist caught his eye. "For Christ's sake, take it easy!"

He rolled. Kinchloe clung, still trying to swing, to gouge, to maim. He couldn't hurt Zack. And Zack didn't want to hurt him. He tried to capture the flailing arms, to pin the sobbing, smaller man to the bed. He got hold of his coat, yanked. The material tore and Kinchloe pulled free, jumped him again.

"I'll kill you!"

"Take it easy, Kinchloe, you damn fool!"

Zack arched his body, threw the man off the bed, onto the floor. Then he rolled and fell on him, pinning him to the floor. Now ...

"Look out, Zack!"

The scream alerted him and he saw the gleam in Kinchloe's hand in time. The gun. He'd found it in the struggle. Zack's guts churned as the muzzle bore on him. He forgot where he was, who the man was—he was back again fighting to stay alive.

He rolled, stabbed with stiff fingers. One found an eye and Kinchloe screamed. Then Zack's leg lashed out, cracked a toe into the man's ribs. He jumped up, crouched. He swatted the gun across the room with his hand, wrapped the other around the man's neck and stood up.

"Zack! Stop! Stop!"

Pam shook his arm, pleaded with him. Slowly the red ebbed and he saw the weak face, the colorless eyebrows. Johnny

Kinchloe was almost out. Zack released his hold, let the man drop to the floor. He lay moaning.

Zack went into the bathroom, ran water on his hands, washed his face. When he got back, Kinchloe was sitting up in a chair.

"You're through," the man said, his voice husking. There were livid marks on his neck where Zack's fingers had gripped. "Get out. You can't work around here. If you're not gone by morning, I'll have the police on you."

The voice came from the door. "Why? Because you caught him with your chocolate whore?"

Marie Kinchloe pushed open the door, stepped inside. Her eyes found Zack, moved on to her husband. Her big lips curled.

"Hero," she said. "You, playing man. Now that's a real switch. Get up from there and act like a manager, for God's sake. It'll be hard, but try. Pretend."

The words hit at the little man. He sagged in the chair. Pam Jardin walked to him, put her hand on his neck and turned to Marie. Her chin lifted.

"That means I'm fired, I suppose?"

Marie looked at the girl. "Why? You play good piano. Go downstairs where you belong. Get your sex away from the hotel, that's all."

"Nothing happened," Zack said.

"I'll bet," Marie said.

"Miss Jardin let me grab a couple winks here so I could work all night. That's all."

Marie smiled, sharp teeth showing between the full lips. Johnny Kinchloe looked at Pam, hopefully, beseechingly.

"It's true," the girl said. "He was nice to me and he needed a bed. That's the bit, the whole bit."

Johnny said eagerly, "I believe it, Pam. I'm sorry for the way I acted. I—"

Marie laughed. She leaned against the doorjamb and laughed deep in her throat. Then, abruptly, she stopped.

"You," she said, pointing at Zack. "It's almost twelve. Get to work. John, get up out of there, and take care of business. We've still got a hotel to run. You, too, Delicia—back to your piano."

Zack stopped in front of Pam. "Thanks, Pam. I make a mess everywhere I go."

She shook her head; the soft eyes came up to his. "No, man. It's me. It's me…."

She straightened and walked past Marie, out of the room. For a moment nobody moved. Then Zack started out. Marie stepped in front of him. He stopped. She was tall; her head came almost to his nose. The eyes lifted and there was smoke there and heat—and swirls of shadow deep in the grey. She didn't say anything—just shook her head slightly.

"I'm late," he said, not avoiding either the gaze or the slight contact of their bodies. "You hear me?"

Her breasts touched him, burning through his thin shirt; the round of her thighs brushed, went away, brushed again. Zack felt the presence of Johnny Kinchloe behind him, heard a sharp breath. Marie's tongue came out, ran over the red lips slowly.

"You found the wrong room, big one. That's all."

CHAPTER FOUR

Seven days in a week. So many hours of daylight, so many of dark. A cycle. From Sunday to Saturday, or Saturday to Sunday; maybe from any day to the same day a week later. Just a week. Time. A week is long enough for governments to fall, short enough for love to retain its freshness. Relative and individual is a week. The first one Zack spent at Lake Conaghton was a lot of things, most of them odd, all of them puzzling to a man on the run.

First the police grabbed him.

It wasn't quite that bad, really. A private policeman, maintained by the various owners and business interests of the lake, came into the Day-Night not long after the scene in Pam Jardin's room. The man's name was Burris McCord, and when he pushed his starving-Indian belly through the plate-glass doors and looked around, Zack knew he was in for it.

It was late, after three. Most of the kids had run out of gas, gone to their cottages, tents, rooms and parked autos. That special quiet, reserved for deep summer and dark night, wrapped the antiseptic whiteness of the Day-Night Café. A swamper worked lazily with a long, dirty mop on the imitation-tile floor; a pair of drunk and surly musicians from the Beachcomber and a couple playing the pinball were the only customers. Zack had hot-scoured the huge, chrome-surrounded grill and set up cold-box supplies for the early rush. He stood sipping hot coffee gratefully, feeling the stimulant work in him, erasing the muscle-memory of the long day. George banged around farther down the long counter.

Burris McCord was back-country and looked it. His turkey neck stuck up out of a buttoned olive-drab uniform shirt on which hung a burnished badge. A three-hole leather belt swung from scrawny hips, dropped under the odd belly. He wore a tan police cap and tan trousers, badly pressed. Dull eyes swept the Day-Night. He shuffled a few steps inside the door, stopped. One hand rested on his pistol butt in what was obviously a habitual pose.

"Guy named Webster working here?"

Zack lowered his cup slowly, flicked his eyes toward the scullery. His mind, trained so long in professional deceit, quickly ran over what he knew of the building, the room, the ways out. Only the scullery.

"Any you guys got ears?" The man pushed the swamper with a forearm, advanced to the long counter. Nobody said anything. "What's the matter? I got B.O. or something? Come on, who's Webster?"

His eyes, flat as a pounded steak and dull brown, had found Zack. He knew who it was. It was there in his eyes—like a hunter following blood drops. But he looked away, jutted a thin chin arrogantly.

Zack pushed carefully away from the back counter, moved a step toward the scullery. The officer turned with his movement, walked toward him, grinning expectantly.

"You're him," he said. "Yep. Face like a rock, he said. Black hair cut short. Come out from behind that counter."

His hand was on the gun. Maybe it was just a pose. Maybe it wasn't.

Zack said, "What for?"

" 'Cause I said so, that's what for." The thin face cracked in a scraggle-toothed grin. "You picked on the wrong man tonight, fella. You better know that. This's a peaceful place, Conaghton Lake Park, by God—and we aim to keep 'er that way."

"Kinchloe?"

"We won't mention no names. You just come along with me."

Zack moved down the counter, stopped in front of the man. McCord backed a step, stood warily.

"No trouble, now. We just don't want your trashy kind around here."

"Look, officer," Zack said. "I've done nothing. I'm working, minding my own business. You have a warrant or a charge? No? Then I don't even want to talk to you. Unless you want something to eat."

McCord's face darkened. "Now, you look here, you tramp. You can't—"

"Trouble, Burris?"

The voice was a new one, and everybody turned to the midway door. A stocky man, neat and compact in a light business suit, stood there. He was short, about five eight, with thinning yellow hair and very sharp, dark eyes. He wore a tie.

Burris McCord said, "Little police business, Mr. Coy. Pickin' up, as they say." He laughed nervously.

Samson Coy didn't smile; he seemed like a man who seldom would permit himself that luxury. Zack tried to catalogue him, couldn't do it. The suit, the tie—a man who liked to be in possession of himself, obviously. And an important man, if what he'd heard this afternoon and since had any value. The stocky man moved to the counter, stood for a long moment looking at Zack. Then he turned to Burris McCord.

"What's the trouble, Burris?" His voice was cool, exact.

"Mr. Coy," McCord said. "What happened was, I came in here to float a drifter. Fella tore up the Gableton earlier."

"Kinchloe tell you to float this fellow?"

"Yessir. He claims this fellow, Webster, hit him, pushed him around when he caught him in one of the guest's rooms. He's lucky we don't put a charge on him. But Mr. Kinchloe, he just said run him out of the place."

Coy nodded. "That's fine, Burris. You go back and tell Mr. Kinchloe I said not to."

The officer blinked. "But this fellow, he—"

"That's all, McCord." The tone froze.

McCord glared at Zack, then at George, the fry cook, who'd been standing nervously in the background. The officer pulled at his belt, walked to the door with shambling speed.

"You're Webster," Coy said, when the man had gone. "I'm Samson Coy."

He stuck out his hand. Zack took it over the counter, watched the man warily. From all he'd heard, Coy wasn't exactly fraternal.

"Could I have some coffee? And would it be all right for you to join me?"

He straddled a stool, looked at Zack.

"Well…"

"Oh, yes, sir," George said, moving up. He pushed Zack. "Go ahead, Zack. Have a cup of coffee with Mr. Coy. Would you like anything else, sir? Pie? Eggs, maybe?"

Coy said no, and he and Zack took coffee to one of the linoleum-topped tables near the midway door. It was dark and dead out there. From his chair Zack could see a portion of the lake, moon-ribbon slicing liquid dark. He fiddled with his coffee, waited.

Coy said, "I've been hearing quite a bit about you, Webster. Pity you came to Marie for a job instead of to me. I run quite a few things around here, you know. Might have found you something a little better."

"Just got here today. Tried to see you," Zack said. He held the cup in front of his face, watched the other man over the thick rim. "Asked your lifeguard where you were and he said you probably wouldn't hire me."

The man's eyes came up quickly, narrowed. "Bisto? That fool! One of these days I'm going to forget he's harmless and—" He smiled suddenly, stopped in mid-sentence. "But you don't want to hear about that, do you? How does Conaghton strike you? Bustling little resort, don't you think?"

Zack shrugged. What was this? The man was going out of his way to be accommodating. For what? And what, for that matter, was a busy man like Samson Coy doing up at four in the morning, making small talk with an itinerant fry cook? The dark eyes told him nothing.

"No opinion yet, Mr. Webster? Well, I'm sure you'll see the potential of this area when you've looked around a little. Why, do you know in the month of June over twenty-two thousand people used Conaghton Beach? That may not seem many to you, but believe me—"

"Mr. Coy, what makes you think I'm interested in all this? I'm just a fellow working on a summer job. That's all. I don't care about anything else."

"Of course, Webster. If that's the way you want it. But if you feel it's necessary to work—why don't you let me give you something better to do? I know the money doesn't mean anything, but we could figure out something. I have the beach and the Beachcomber—plus the U-Drive-Em motor-boats and the Sport Club. And listen—" Coy leaned forward, coat sleeves held carefully away from the coffee-wet table-top. "What do you think of water-ski lessons? Eh? How about that for a source of revenue? I've been taking an audit survey and I find some very interesting facts."

"Mr. Coy, I'm sure I'll find out all about Conaghton just by being here. There's no necessity—"

"Of course, of course," the stocky man said. He rose quickly, stuck out his hand. It was tanned and square, like the rest of him. "I didn't mean to dictate to you. Marie is very capable. She runs her few little enterprises with a commendable lack of the usual female illogic." He smiled, showing very crooked, very white teeth. "A dish though, eh? Might influence a man."

Zack stood up, gathered up the dishes. "Thanks for the coffee, Mr. Coy. If I change my mind about the job, I'll let you know."

"Fine, fine. And I'd like you to meet the wife sometime soon. Can you make it?"

Zack mumbled something, got away. It was odd. And what was even odder, Samson Coy became a regular nightly visitor to the place. George said Coy hadn't been in twice all season before.

Burris McCord took an uncommon liking to the outside of the Day-Night during the hours of twelve to eight in the morning. But he never came in. Zack got to know the regulars. Tom Brulliard, the boatman—an independent operator, having nothing to do with either Conaghton Enterprises or Coy. He was a weathered, aging man with a son and daughter in college and a desire to hold onto his Conaghton lakefront until they had been provided for.

"Zack," he'd told him, "if that cold little weasel bothers me one more time about selling out to him I'll twist his neck."

"Why does he want your place, Tom? The location?"

The man didn't know or wouldn't say. Certainly the price Coy offered was fair. More than fair. But Brulliard was tough and opinionated, devoted to his surviving family—his wife was dead—and absolutely convinced that Samson Coy was a swindler.

He took immediate liking to Zack. He became, in fact, his landlord.

A quick interview got Zack a narrow cot in a room over the boatman's repair shop, right on the water. It was small, but he didn't have to pay until he drew wages and it was certainly out of the way. Good enough for a man on the run.

About one in the morning, Carol Normer came into the Day-Night with a young crowd. She stopped and chatted with Zack, promising to see him later. Frank Bonino was with her. Or seemed to be.

Zack was busy. The kids filled the place with noise and music. The long counter was crowded, as were all of the tables. The grill sizzled, covered with various orders. The fry cook, George, had told Zack to take it alone, since after Sunday he would have to. He worked grimly, good coordination and the coldly logical mind given him by fifteen years of tightly controlled existence standing him in good stead. The countermen nodded approval; George stood at the cash register and made change. It was hard, steady work.

"Zack! Zack, you wonderful man. Why didn't you tell me you were a cook? We could have got married yesterday and saved all this trouble."

There was no doubt who it was. Zack turned, a dripping spatula in one hand, his face sweat-slicked. Andy Manning leaned on the high, chromium pick-up station just opposite the grill. Her charcoal hair was piled high, pinned with a sliver of what looked like bone; the pulled-back eyes shone in the stark lighting, considered him soberly.

"You make a pretty good cook," she said.

"I thanked you for the ride," Zack said roughly.

"Oh, Zack. Don't be like that."

"Look, I'm busy, Miss Manning. Later, maybe."

She grinned, her smooth face breaking into amused curves. "You're a doll," she said. A man called to her from across the room and she waved. "See? Other people love me. You're a rude old man and your hair is grey. But you know what, Zack…"

"What? Look, Andy…"

"I'd make a wizard roommate should you ever want one." She smiled sweetly and left.

Zack stood there. He pushed the white cap back on his head, wiped his face with a wet wrist. Crazy, this girl. Absolutely crazy. She walked off, rounded hips working nicely as she made her way to the table where the summer theatre crowd grouped. Her dress was the simplest in the place, but somehow it looked better than all the others.

It slacked off about two-thirty. Zack found out real quick that no matter where else you might go at Conaghton, you always were obliged to end up at the Day-Night before going off to whatever bed currently attracted you. Everybody came in. He'd been too busy to catalogue people. Normer came in when the lounge closed, stopped to say hello. Johnny Kinchloe came in with Samson Coy and everybody made a little circle of silence around the two bland men, didn't invite them to join the festivities. Coy's wife, a wispy woman of thirty-odd with very sharp features and an appealingly submissive air, showed up briefly with Bisto, the lifeguard. The beachboy was dressed to the nines: cashmere coat, silk shirt—the works.

George said, "Well, I'll be damned. Look at that."

"What? You mean Bisto?"

"Yeah, Bisto. But that's Samson Coy's old lady he's got by the arm. Look at Coy—he's busting a gut to keep from strangling both of them."

Zack checked the order wheel, saw no slips. He walked to the register.

"What's the bit, George? It isn't smart for Bisto to bring his boss's wife into the same joint, is it?"

"I don't know. Funny. That Bisto, he does things Coy would can anyone else for. But this's the first time he ever got this far out of line. Everybody knows Karen hates Samson. He's in love with money, that guy. So Bisto cleans up around their place... you know." The fry cook's eyes narrowed. "Nobody knows anything for sure. But Bisto stays—and he spends most of his spare time working around the Coys' yard."

Zack grunted. The couple found stools and one of the countermen took their order. Bisto saw Zack and winked, deadpan. The woman was a little worn, but pretty. Right now her eyes were defiant and a bit scared—like a bookkeeper scooting with the company payroll.

The slack period came and so did Marie Kinchloe. Which could have meant anything except she came with Softy Malebar.

Zack sighed. Nobody around this crazy place went with the people they were assigned to. He snorted at his mental phraseology. Assigned. Well, he was assigned to the grill and he'd confine his interest to that. Let the jump-a-bed game go on—he had Zack Webster to take care of.

Samson Coy and Johnny Kinchloe had been gone about a half hour when Marie arrived with the big man from across the lake. Which was fortunate. Marie was loaded. And Malebar was surly. They took the corner table, blatantly set a full bottle of Scotch on the table and rapidly became popular with the remaining crowd. There was only the bunch from the Cow Shed Theatre and Bisto and Karen Coy, both getting quietly drunk from a bottle the lifeguard had brought.

Since there was no work, Zack carried a cup of coffee and a couple pastries around the counter and sat there. Andy Manning saw him. She slid onto the adjoining stool.

"Hello, corpse."

"Corpse?"

A shiver shook him—this bright girl had put in words the desolate feel of the place.

"Yeah. You're dead. Manning of the Royal Mounted is on your trail."

"Oh," he said. "I see. How am I ever going to tell my children their father consorted with a minor?"

"Minor, is it? I'll have you know, friend man, I'm twenty-two." She sobered, turned to him. "Don't you like me, Zack? I mean, here and there a girl gets told she has all the pieces. You know. And as hard as I've had to fight in back seats, I sort of figured mine were arranged pretty well."

"All right. You're pretty. Very attractive. That what you wanted to hear? Now go back to your friends."

"Zack…" Her voice dropped. "I'm not letting you make me angry. Swimming tomorrow? I'll wear a Bikini. I'm perfectly wizard in a Bikini."

"You're crazy," he muttered. "Look, I got no time for girls and no money. And besides, a guy likes to chase. You ever heard of that? You're supposed to be coy, wait for advances. Then flutter your lashes and succumb."

"Succumb," she said, grinning at him. "Now there's a word. And the hell with that coy stuff. If I did, would you chase me? Would you?"

He smiled. A very small smile. "No," he said.

"See?" She spun the stool, held her legs out straight and leaned back against the counter looking up at him. It was a very effective pose. "I'd be pretty silly to wait, then, wouldn't I? Huh? Admit it, come on. And you smiled just now. The first time. You look real nice when you unbend a little, Zack."

He took her hand from his arm, dunked his cigarette in the coffee dregs. His face was set again, the emotions contained. He looked at her.

She sucked a breath. "I goofed, huh? I said the wrong thing again?"

Marie Kinchloe appeared behind them. She stood there, weaving just slightly on spike heels, face loose and blurred by liquor. Her impossible body was draped in a white chemise that accentuated all the curves in spite of seeming not to follow them; her legs were bare—long and tanned, firm and bare.

"Webster," she said. "You work here?"

Andy Manning said, "Oh, oh. The wicked witch." And she said it loudly.

Zack turned.

Marie's eyes, cold blue chips, bore on the girl. "Customers don't mix with help, Miss Manning. We'd be obliged if you confined your hunting to summer visitors. Or better, stay on your side of the lake."

Zack started to say something; Andy stopped him. Her eyes swung to Softy Malebar advancing down the counter.

"That's some advice you might take yourself, Mrs. Kinchloe," the girl said sweetly.

Marie almost slapped her. Zack saw the thought cross her face, then it was gone, erased by a cold smile.

"Of course, dear. I'll trade you." Malebar had reached them and Marie took his thick arm, drew him forward. "This one for that one." She nodded at Zack. "Then we'll both be—"

"What's this?" Malebar's voice was marshmallow, laced with wire. He shook off the woman's arm, looked around. "How drunk you think I am, Marie?"

"Oh, shut up! Zack, get back to work. I'm bored with this whole scene."

"Shut up?" the big man said, grabbing her elbow roughly. "Shut up? I'll break your arm—"

Zack stood quickly and spun the man away from her, pushing him slightly, using his own weight to move him.

Andy stifled a scream; Marie stepped aside, the smile warming on her lips.

Malebar caught himself, started back. "Joker, you shouldn't have done that." His rocky face had lost color. Huge shoulders hunched.

"I don't want to fight," Zack said. He shifted, got his weight under him. "You hear, mister? I work here."

Marie stepped between them. She grabbed the big man, pressed her body to him.

"Don't Carl. I'm sorry, darling...."

She murmured, petting him, and Malebar relaxed. His eyes sent Zack a message, a dark message. But he walked back to the table with the woman, broad back tight and hard.

Andy touched Zack's arm. "Look. Over there at the side window."

Zack looked. A face peered in, white and strained in the distortion of the glass. It was Johnny Kinchloe.

Zack grunted. He looked down at Andy. She had his arm in both of hers, leaning her firm length against him. But she wasn't effervescing now. Her smooth face was solemn, the eyes hooded. She looked up.

"I don't like this place any more, Zack. It—it feels funny. I don't know. Just an odd atmosphere—too phony, too forced. Do you feel it?"

He nodded, didn't pull away from her.

"I feel it. I've felt it before. Someone's going to get hurt around here. Hurt bad…."

CHAPTER FIVE

H e did go swimming with Andy. The Sunday crowds jammed the beach, so instead they went to the grass pier not far from the hotel boardwalk. Andy was a sensation in a bathing suit. She hadn't carried out her threat to wear a Bikini. But what her tiny, perfectly proportioned firmness did to the black one-piece was almost illegal.

Zack said, "You don't look like a minor."

They walked down the steps from the boardwalk onto the spit of manufactured land. She looked up at him.

"Close there," she said. "Awful close. You better be careful, mister, or you'll be complimenting me. This good enough right here? The grass is pretty good."

"Fine," he said. "And I am complimenting you."

While she spread the blanket and arranged the portable radio and all the other junk that women think is necessary for lying in the sun, he walked to the end of the pier, looked out over the water.

Conaghton was beautiful. Wooded hills held it like a green palm full of purest blue. To the left the lake curved gently in an ever-increasing arc, widening to about a half-mile at the widest spot. To the right it narrowed and made a turn, extending for a mile or so to the town of Conaghton at the very tip. There were no other beaches. A few piers built out from the hill cottages; directly across, the big pier that was the landing for Malebar's place, the Ship. Which looked like a ship. It was pretty far, but Zack could see the clipper-type prow of a sailing ship sticking smack out of the hillside. It was bright and shining in the sun; flags flew from a stubby mast. Probably a nice place. Maybe when he got some money he would take the kid over there.

It was a nice spot, Conaghton. Very nice. Kind of middle-class and stodgy, cobwebbed; but not as commercial as some of the Catskill places he'd seen, and not at all like Coney Island. And it had charm. Behind him the weathered bulk of the Gableton loomed on its smoothed-off hill. On the lake, boats drifted and zoomed, spluttered and slid. Summer day, bright and warm.

Her hair had been braided into thick pigtails, then tied on top of her head. She tested the knot, lifting her arms, which lifted the front of her suit, which lifted Zack's eyes. He looked away from her tiny smile. What the hell was with this girl?

"Hey," he said. "What's that island out there? See it—almost around the corner toward town."

She looked. "Cone Island. Barren and rocky, not even a decent beach. Hills and woods and only one place where you can beach a boat. Sometimes they have weiner roasts out there. And everybody swims naked." Her eyes lifted to his slyly. "We could have one, you and me. All alone."

Zack grinned without letting it change his face. He'd caught the note that time. She was pulling his leg, probing him where she'd found him to be tender. He turned quickly, grabbed her in his arms.

"Zack! Zack, don't—"

But it was too late then. He ran lightly to the edge, carrying her slight weight without effort. Her body was firm and still yielding; one breast brushed his chest and her head bobbed on his shoulder.

"Please, Zack—"

He threw her far out into the water.

George left Sunday and Zack became night fry cook and man-ager. The countermen were kids; the scullery help changed from day to day. Marie was there when he went on shift. He went over the routine with her, wrote his name on the book.

"You'll be all right, Webster," she said.

Zack nodded, continued checking the register. Out of the corner of his eye, he watched her. She had her business look on. She wore a simple black thing with a slash of silver from shoulder to hip; her hair was Grecian-knotted again. A single strand of real pearls circled her throat. She was a beautiful woman.

"What's the total?"

"What?" Zack looked down at his hands, saw the money.

She moved close, pushed his arm away and took the money. She spoke without looking at him.

"On duty, pay attention to business. If you want to look at me, do it a better time."

"I wasn't—"

"You were. Don't add to the thing by being stupid. Check supplies."

Zack moved slowly to the cold box. His eyes came back to the woman in spite of a mental resolution to keep them away. She was cool and contained and utterly feminine. Yet when it came to business, she was an IBM with curves.

Zack knelt, worked automatically. Stacks of processed ham-burger pats, separated by waxed paper, had to be transferred to the higher shelf for easier access. Various condiments had to be placed on the grill-counter. For no reason he thought of Wilson Agnew and he laughed. Out loud. It was silly. There was no reason in the world for it. But here he was, Zack Webster, crack investi-gator, scourge of the politician on the take, stacking cold meat. And Wilson Agnew would look forty years before he found him.

Legs appeared at his side. He looked at them. Any man would have looked at them.

Marie Kinchloe said, "You about finished?"

"Yes, ma'am." He straightened, slammed the door. "What is it?"

"You went swimming with that kid from the Cow Shed Theatre today." Her eyes studied him. "All day. From the grass pier."

Zack lost his good humor. He felt the grooves in his cheeks deepening.

"I'm not prying, Webster … Zack," the woman said. "I just wonder about you. That's all. I wonder. You haven't looked over the operation. The park, the roller rink. You don't go anywhere, don't drink. I'm beginning to wonder if my first idea was correct or not."

Zack said, "If you're finished trying to pry into my private life, I'll get to work."

The woman said nothing. She looked at him, a line appearing between the lovely eyes. Finally she nodded.

"I'll talk to Coy," she said, half to herself. "Maybe both of us are mistaken."

"You are," Zack said. "And I'll swim with who I please. You better know that."

She laughed. "I don't give a damn who you swim with, Tarzan. Well, I have to check out the Bingo and close up the midway slum shops." She started out from behind the counter, looked back at him. "Like to come along sometime when I check out?"

"What for?"

She nodded as if she'd made up her mind to something. "Happy sunburn."

The rush came then and Zack didn't have time to think about it. Not that he could have come up with anything. The whole place was crazy, that's all. Worse than D.C. in election year. No more swimming. Not with Andy. That's the way it should be, he thought grimly. Andy Manning was no quick summer lay. And he could not afford to get mixed up deeply with anyone. Not even to erase the memory of Fay Temple.

"Zack."

One of the counter boys was beckoning to him.

"What is it, Chilly? I'm busy."

"Guy wants to see you. This guy here."

The man was short and dark; half bald, with a pleasant face and a deceptively rounded body. Zack saw the strength in the shoulders, the short arms. He wore suntans and no hat. His arms were brown and hairy, the hands short-fingered and broad. He smiled at Zack when they'd found a table, at the short man's insistence.

"Hi. I'm Jim Sick."

"Webster," Zack said. "Look, I don't know what you want, but that kid can't handle the grill at this hour."

"Sure, sure. Just take a minute. It's late for me, too."

He sipped at his coffee, watched Zack over the rim. His eyes were guileless. Zack lit a cigarette, waited. His face was carefully unfeeling, but his mind whizzed with possibilities. This boy defied description. He could be anyone—sent by anybody. Washington, Agnew, Malebar, Kinchloe—round went the clicking file of memory. Sick said nothing, and finally Zack relaxed. Whatever it was would come out. Then he would know what to do.

"You're very cool," the short man said. "This silence thing is a technique. One the latest books tell us is pretty effective when the suspect doesn't know what to expect. Don't seem to be working on you, though."

He grinned. Zack took a drag of his cigarette, blew the smoke out in a strong jet.

"Suspect?" he asked. "Of what?"

"Well, don't nobody seem to know, exactly. I don't either. Just thought I'd better take a look." He fished a worn, thick billfold from a front shirt pocket, threw it on the table. "You better look at that so's you don't punch me in the nose for being nebby. You're pretty big. What do you weigh?"

Zack picked up the wallet, twisting the cigarette in his lips to avoid the smoke.

"Right around two hundred," he said. He opened the wallet. "Sheriff… County of Plum—that's this county?"

Sick nodded, set his cup down. He put his stubby hands behind his head and leaned back.

Zack closed the wallet, slid it toward the other man.

"Pleased to meet you. What do you want?"

"Don't want nothing. Just thought I'd better take a look at you, see if maybe you matched any of the pictures I get from time to time. Don't seem to."

"Then I can go back to work," Zack said, standing.

"Wait, now," Sick said. "I like you Webster. You're direct, and I think you're probably all right. But I do get paid to uphold the law, and you're the first fella we've had around here in quite a while that got me four phone calls."

"Phone calls? What kind of phone calls?"

Sick shrugged. He stuffed the wallet back into his pocket, got up.

"I got to get to bed. This's awful late for me. I'm satisfied, Webster. Don't worry about it. But when people call and say they're taxpayers—well, I'm supposed to move around a little, I guess."

"Could I have an idea…"

The sheriff reached up, put a hand on Zack's shoulder. His smile seemed genuine. "Ah, the hell with it. Don't let it bother you. A man's as good as he behaves with me. You ain't done nothing yet that I can call bad. Not around here, anyway. Don't worry about it."

He started off, a short, broad figure in rumpled suntans.

That was Sunday and the week not yet full.

Monday was a bad day for sleeping. Tom Brulliard sent for him before he'd been in bed an hour.

The old man was out on the end of his long dock. The tall, spare-shouldered figure paced up and down, white hair blowing in the brisk morning wind. He saw Zack, waved.

The lake was choppy, wavelets slapping at the moored boats with a thocking sound. This early the lake still belonged to the fishermen, trolling in small boats, plugging along the shore with methodical patience.

Tom Brulliard greeted him with a sheepish glance, nodded, and then looked away, face set. They stood on the pier watching the lake.

"What are they doing?"

"Doing?" Brulliard asked. "Who? You mean the boats over there?"

Zack pointed. "Those. See? Casting back and forth close to the shore. Can't be fly-fishing. Can they?"

"No. You never fished freshwater? They're dropping plugs along the weed line. No deep. Smallmouth along there."

The boatman took a stubby pipe from his peacoat pocket, began stuffing it from a pouch. His eyes, dark under bristling brows of spiky white hair, avoided Zack's. He was agitated, all right.

Zack squinted against the glare, studiously watching the boats. It was a little chilly. All he'd taken time to put on was a tee-shirt and pants. He hunched his shoulders. The old man would talk when he felt like it.

"Sometimes there's muskies," Brulliard said, puffing on his briar. "But the motors drive 'em deep this time of year. You come up around September, November, boy—I'll show you some fishing. Fifty, sixty pounds. Fact. And get 'em on light line with a Redhead or maybe a Jointed Pikey Minnow. You fish?"

Zack nodded. Then he turned. "Tom, you're bothered about something. Anything I can do?"

The old man looked at him for a moment. Then he nodded, motioned to the bench at the dock's end.

"Let's sit, son. I got to talk to somebody or I'm apt to bust something. I'm bothered. I'm goddam bothered, and if I had a half a goddam gut I'd take a boathook and do something about it."

They sat, the old man perching on the wood seat, watching Zack. He spoke slowly.

"Maybe talking about it will help. And you're new—a stranger. Won't hurt so much that way. I gotta tell somebody."

"Tell me if you feel like it. Sometimes two heads really are better than one."

Brulliard slumped back, chin dropping. He stared at the water. "Nothing you can do, boy. Nothing anybody can do. I'll tell you about it. But it's hard, coming right out and saying you've been a fool. An old fool."

Words came out of the proud old man like chips off his soul. Slowly, bitterly, he talked, chewing on the stem of the worn briar, gazing out at the lake. Now and then, carried away, he gripped Zack's knee with a gnarled hand that still held amazing power.

It was a story that began with a simple man and his anything-but-simple love for his family. And ended with Marie Kinchloe.

CHAPTER SIX

Tom Brulliard had two children, a boy away at college and a girl. The girl was the mousy type Zack had met the first night in the offices of Conaghton Enterprises. The old Frenchman lived for the kids. He didn't say this, but the way his face lit when he spoke of them, the vehemence in his tones, told the story.

You'd have to say Tom Brulliard had done his work well with the kids. But he had a fixation—to amass enough wealth to leave them both provided for when he died. Self-denial was a friend to him; his work day was as long as his strength could make it. He had worked, bought property. Lately, Samson Coy's overtures to buy the land had made him certain he was near his goal.

Then he got mixed up with Marie Kinchloe. What happened was predictable. Marie waged a campaign of calculated sexuality on the old man. Years of thrusting aside his own considerable needs had left him susceptible.

They had an affair. Zack got no details. But it had been brief and clandestine—and to Tom Brulliard, more powerful, more moving than anything he had ever known. Marie was a beautiful woman, conscious of her sensual power. She was also a brilliant woman. For somehow, in the heat of the affair, she had talked the tough Frenchman into giving her an option on the lake property.

Customers came at this point, interrupting the monologue. Zack sat, sucking tasteless smoke from a cigarette, while Brulliard got the people set in a boat, came back. He walked old.

"I know what you're thinking, son," he said, taking his seat. "And you're right. An old fool. A horny old idiot who can't control his own body. You're right, you're right."

Zack murmured something, bent over to rub his bare ankles.

"You think I'm making too much of this, don't you? Making a lot of noise, feeling sorry for myself. But listen … that's just part of it. If it was just the option, I wouldn't mind. She put a good price on it. A fair one. I'd have done it for the money without—without the other. But here's the joker. The reason a young, pretty woman would fool with an old man like me. The property right now is worth money. But in one year—one year, mind you—it'll be worth a fortune. A fortune! This lakefront, the hill there. A goddam fortune, Zack, do you understand? Enough to set the boy up in business, send the girl to Europe like she's always dreaming and planning. And that dirty bitch stole it right out from under my nose!"

Zack gripped the man's arm. "Easy, Tom. That won't help. Tell me … what makes you think the value will increase so much? This place isn't exactly Lake Charles—or Banff."

"No. But it's gonna be. As good as either of 'em, maybe. Listen to this. A development company—" He patted his pockets. "I got the name here somewhere. Anyway, this big company's going to buy into the lake, get all the choice property it can. Swallow up everything that's for sale, pressure the rest. Then they're going to put millions into developing this into a class resort—modern hotels and such, publicity, new attractions. Can you see it? Another Lake Placid, or like those places in the Catskills. And, by God, it could be!"

Zack flipped his cigarette into the water, stared at the ripples it made. It was possible. The lake was beautifully situated, almost totally unexploited. Right now it was doing good business. But with the right backing and shrewd management …

Brulliard had a grimy slip of paper in his hand. Zack caught the letterhead—Gableton Hotel. The old man smoothed it on his knee. He bent forward, his white hair, still bushy and vigorous, falling over his forehead as he did so.

"Look here, see the name? Factors Limited. The man's name is Landworth—Johnson Landworth. That's the fella who'd pay a heap for my property if I hadn't been such a goddam fool."

He passed the slip to Zack, looked away.

"Johnson Landworth." Zack closed his eyes. He'd heard the name. "Johnson Landworth. Had some trouble with the FCC last year, I think. Same company. A Boston operator, real-estate shark. Good, I understand. Several times a millionaire."

"You know him? How would you know a man like that, Zack? A man with all that money? Why, come to think of it—"

"Wait, wait. I read a lot. Look—" Zack twisted on the bench, faced the old man. "You hold tight. Don't do anything rash. This is hot information. For damn sure Landworth won't want it getting out because then he'd have to pay six prices for the property. So chances are good not many people know about this."

"But my land is gone. That's the thing."

"Maybe not. It's just an option. Marie might not have the money to exercise it. Does she own the Conaghton company?"

"Don't think so. Don't know for sure. I was always thinking she worked for somebody—Pittsburgh firm, maybe."

"All right. I'll find out. Maybe she won't be able to exercise the option. Then—Look, you hold on and let me hot nose around a little. Don't say anything to anyone. Most of all to Marie. Promise? No matter how mad you get?"

Brulliard looked at him steadily. His flinty eyes bore on Zack's dark ones. Then he nodded, once, shortly. He stood up.

"All right. You talk like you know what you're doing. I sure don't. I been a fool once, but I'm not going to go on being one. Gwen and Roy got something coming and I'd do anything in the world to see they get it. Anything. You understand that?"

Zack nodded. They started down the dock toward shore.

"Tell me one thing," Zack said, walking beside the stern-faced old man. "How did you find out about … you know, about the development thing?"

Brulliard glanced at him, mouth lifting at the corners. "That's the oddest thing of the whole mess. You know who told me, laid the thing right out for me?"

"Who?"

"Johnny Kinchloe."

Zack went from Brulliard's dock to the offices over the Day-Night. His bare feet made no sound on the stairs. The place looked deserted at first. Then Zack saw Gwen bent over a ledger in the far corner of the room. She didn't look up.

The door to Marie's office was closed. A light burned inside. There was no sound. The midway hadn't wakened yet; the lake noises dissipated on the morning breeze before reaching this far. Zack walked quietly, headed for the office in the corner. He had no plan. He didn't even question why it was that he was interesting himself in something that was patently not his business. He just walked.

"Who is it? Who is that?"

The voice was high and childish. The girl, Gwen, rushed from her work desk, angled to intercept Zack.

"What is it you want? Don't go in there."

"I want to see Marie—Mrs. Kinchloe."

"No! You can't," the girl said. She stopped, thin face flushed. "I mean, she—Mrs. Kinchloe doesn't want to be disturbed."

He looked at her. One white hand held tightly to his arm. Gwen Brulliard. How much would she protect her boss, and obviously her idol, if she knew about old Tom and the option? He shrugged her off.

"Get back to your figures, kid. If there's a beef, I'll ride it."

"Mr. Webster—please!"

The girl pulled at him. Now he wanted very much to open that door. He brushed her off and strode to the door. He gripped the knob, listened. There was a rustling inside, a rumble of voices. He pushed, met resistance, pushed hard and the door tumbled a chair inside, flew back against the partition.

Marie was entertaining. At ten o'clock of a sunny Monday morning.

Dale Normer had gotten most of his clothes on. But just barely; his thin body twisted away from the open door as he fumbled with fastenings. Marie sat on the low couch, knees together, dress riding high on white thighs. She wore twisted nylons, no shoes; her fingers worked at the top of her dress.

She stared at Zack, no recognition in her eyes. They were flat and shiny; the pupils all but swallowed the iris.

"What...?" she said. "What..."

Zack looked at them. He felt the girl at his back and motioned her away without turning. This was a mess. The sort of mess he should have been used to, after Washington. But it was different here. Dirtier, more morally lacking, in this small place. He pushed his hands deep into trouser pockets, made fists of them.

"Pardon me," he said.

"It's a little late for that," Normer snapped. He turned. His lips trembled. "Don't you ever knock, fella?"

Marie had gotten control of herself now. She stopped fumbling, leaned back on the couch. Her hair was mussed and damp and she shook it, settling her head on the cushion. Her eyes were alive again. She smiled.

"Hello, Zack. Up early for a night fry cook. Can I help you?"

Zack's hands tightened in his pockets. Right now, at this moment, she looked so much like Fay Temple, sounded so much like her....

"Little early," he said. His voice was steady. "Hi, Dale. How's your wife?"

Marie's eyes narrowed; the smile stuck. The lanky guy held out his hands.

"Zack, listen. It's not like you think. Gimme a break, for Christ's sake. We were just—I mean, I got—"

"Oh, shut up, Dale," Marie said. She rose gracefully, moved to her desk. One button was still undone; her dress clung to her lush body, sticking here and there with moisture. "Obviously you want something, Zack. Or were you concerned with my chastity?"

"Yeah. That." He stepped into the room. "What I wanted—"

Gwen burst through the door, stood wringing her hands.

"Mrs. Kinchloe, I'm sorry. I tried to stop him. He just pushed in. I'm sorry, Marie…"

"It's all right, honey. Nobody's dead." She smiled at the girl. "Go back to work. It's all right."

The girl was almost in tears. "I tried—"

"Of course you did."

The girl left, head bowed. Marie sat down, tilted her head to look at Zack. Normer had his back to the room, stood rigidly at the window.

"What was it, Zack, that couldn't wait until a more—a more delicate time?"

He moved to the desk, leaned on it. He wondered if his thoughts showed in his eyes; his face felt hot and hard and set like concrete.

"I just want to know who I'm working for. You manage this operation, I know. But who owns it, who clips the coupons?"

The woman watched him for a moment without speaking. Then she leaned back. "I'm glad you asked that, Zack. It clears up a thing in my mind. Something that's been bothering me." She turned her head a trifle, said, "Get out of here, Dale."

The bartender jumped, turned. His face was drawn. The blond hair was darkened with sweat; beads stood out on the tanned forehead.

"Yeah, okay. Zack… could I see you later? I mean—"

Marie laughed. Loud and harsh, the sound riding around the small room, bouncing.

"We know what you mean, lover," she said. "Go. I must have been out of my head. But remember what I told you. And give my love to Carol."

She laughed again and the man ran. Zack stood, holding still, saying nothing, trying to feel nothing.

"You, now," the woman said. "I can't figure you at all, Webster. If that's your name. I thought I had you pegged, but now I don't know."

"You want to answer my question, Mrs. Kinchloe?"

She shrugged. "Why not? I work for Allegheny Rents, Clark Building, Pittsburgh. The salary is good. I've done the same job for three summers. There is no connection between Johnny's job and mine. He runs the hotel, I run the park—for the same company."

Zack nodded. "One more question. How long have you and Johnny been married?"

Marie smiled. "There's no way that could be any of your business. But—four years." The wet-lipped smile deepened. "Okay?"

"Okay."

He started out. The girl, Gwen Brulliard, brushed past him at the door.

"That singer's here, Mrs. Kinchloe," she said.

Zack saw Pam Jardin. She looked tired. And different in a simply-cut summer dress of cotton print. Her legs were bare and she wore no jewelry. A very pretty girl. She worked up a small smile for Zack, said nothing as she walked into the woman's office. Her eyes were sad and quiet. Zack watched her. She stopped in front of the desk, said something he couldn't hear. Her back was straight and her head was up. Marie began speaking. Before Gwen closed the door, Zack saw Pam's hand slide behind her, clasp tightly.

It was warming up outside. And getting busier. The Pavilion across the way held a few youngsters already. The beach, just visible to the right beyond the Beachcomber Club, was dotted with people. Mostly girls. Bisto was in his chair. Zack thought about going inside the Day-Night, getting coffee. He rejected the thought. He'd eaten just before coming off shift—less than three hours ago.

He heard his name and looked around. Dale Normer waved from the Pavilion. He motioned, waved again. Zack felt his pockets, found no cigarettes. He started toward the Pavilion.

"Zack, listen," the tall man said when they'd found a secluded spot in the big, covered dance place. "Don't say anything to Carol, will you? Will you please? That woman, she's—Zack, she's crazy. I mean it. She forced me."

His eyes searched Zack's face. He licked his lips.

"I know that sounds funny, but it's true. You don't know her. Listen, I love Carol. I never look at another woman—anybody will tell you that."

He gripped Zack's arm. Zack looked down at the tightening fingers; Dale pulled his hand away.

"Well, say something, for Christ's sake."

"Say what? I caught you laying up with another broad and now you want me to believe she twisted your arm." He turned away from the man, leaned on the bar, looked out over the gently moving lake. "You through talking?"

The thin man looked at him. His eyes narrowed and the tanned face got hard. He breathed deeply, controlled himself with an effort.

"You bastard," he whispered. "You dirty, rotten bastard..."

Zack smiled without humor. "Sure. Get away from me before I—" He stopped, pushed away from the rail.

Pam Jardin had stepped out of the doorway across the park street. Zack left the bartender standing, walked rapidly to catch up with the girl.

He spoke twice before she heard him, walking as she was with her head down, eyes straight ahead. She turned finally and he almost stepped away from the expression on the girl's face— anger and rebellion and outright hate.

"Hey, what's up?"

"Oh, it's you, big one." The girl slowed down, matched her steps to his. "Hi. How's the hamburgers?"

Zack took her arm. They were walking away from the hotel, toward the Brulliard dock.

"Fine. Where you heading?"

Pam shrugged. Her smooth face was again expressionless. She held her arm stiff in his gentle grip.

"Want company? Maybe it isn't so bad as you think. I'm a pretty good sponge and my shoulders are broad."

She glanced at him, lips compressed. Then she nodded.

They walked for a long time without speaking. Gradually Pam relaxed and soon was walking with her arm in his, thigh bumping thigh occasionally. The tension left her by degrees and once she jumped at a crooked stick on the wood trail they finally took, laughed at her fright. They ran together to the lake, and after a while, they swam together. It was good. No pressure, no pretense.

Afterwards, she lay back on the tiny beach, stared into the paling summer sky. Zack looked down at her, watching her face.

"You know about me and Johnny, I guess," she said, so low he had to bend forward to hear. "I won't make no excuses. I knew what I was doing, thought I knew what I wanted."

"What do you want, Pam? For real…"

She turned her head and looked up into his face. The eyes changed, took on life. "I want to be famous, Zack. Real famous. So big and rich and dripping with talent that nobody'll dare tell me the reservations are all gone or the seats are taken. With money—money that buys acceptance and respect. That's what I want, Zack. Is that so bad?"

"I don't see anything wrong with it. Everybody wants to stick up a little, tall enough to be seen. But I don't see where this place could help you. Why Conaghton? And—well, the thing with Johnny Kinchloe. What good is that?"

"Yeah, Johnny. All right, I'm sleeping with him. You know that. So does everybody else, I guess. That blonde bitch of his has told enough people." Pam turned her head, looked away. "Not because of Conaghton or the job in the lounge. That's nothing. I'm too good for that and it's easy to see. But Johnny made me come. Said I couldn't have the spot I care about, the real job at Miami Beach, unless I stayed with him. The poor idiot thinks he's in love with me." She twisted, came close to Zack. "Isn't that a laugh? In love with me."

Zack said, "I don't think it's funny. I think it makes sense. After Marie."

"Marie!" The girl sat up. "What a cold, calculating broad that one is. Do you know what she just did, man? You know how much she likes to twist people and watch them squirm? She fired me. Fired me! And I don't even work for her."

"Then how can she—"

"Huh, listen, she can. Johnny's scared to death of her. She's got the connections, the brains. He wants to be the youngest manager of a major hotel in Florida. And with her he's got a chance. Don't worry, he'll go along with her. Right along, like a good little dog. The dog!"

"What's this Miami Beach business?"

"Johnny is assistant manager of a small hotel in the winter season down there. The Golden Note, on Collins Avenue. Nice place. That's where he promised to spot me for the season. Feature me in the Note's main room. It would make me, Zack. It's all I need, just to have someone hear me, see me under the right circumstances. And now ..."

Zack sat up. The girl's back was a curved, rigid line. He couldn't see her face. He put one big hand on her shoulder.

"Pam, don't cry."

She whirled. Her face was twisted into the mask he'd seen in the street after the interview with Marie.

"Cry? Cry?" She laughed, high and nasty and full of the dirty little pieces of human suffering she'd found in her young life. "I ain't about to cry, man. Not about to. I'm going to work on Johnny. Oh, I can do it, don't worry. I can do anything I have to. I'll play on him, I'll caress him and make him feel big." She took a breath, strained erect in the sitting position; her face almost touched Zack's. "I'll do anything I have to do, and if that frigid bitch gets in my way I'll cut her heart out!"

CHAPTER SEVEN

Samson Coy was waiting at the boathouse when he got back. The blond man sat by the closed office, smoking and kicking his heels against the dock. A ring of cigarette butts lay about.

"Webster," he said, as Zack approached. "Been waiting for you. Wondered why you haven't been around to see me. My operations runs pretty smoothly; I can always take a few minutes off for a friend."

The stocky man was fully dressed; summer suit of silk and a white shirt complete with tie. Zack stopped by him. This guy defied description. He looked at Zack with obvious affability. Too obvious. Zack nodded at the man.

"Coy. Understand you've been expanding your operations, as you put it. That right?"

Coy's eyes changed; a hood, transparent, but palpable, dropped over them.

"Expanding? Well, if you mean trying to get the most out of the poor grossers, I have."

"I mean buying up land," Zack said. He reached into the man's pocket, pulled out a pack of cigarettes. "Land around the lake. You wouldn't know about that, I suppose?"

Coy licked his lips. "Now see here, Webster. A man does the best he can with what he's got. I'm a business man. I want to make money. Why should Land—why should you care if someone buys up a little? I've got only a little ready cash. How can I hurt you?"

"Doesn't take much for options. A little goes a long way."

"You know options are no good in this thing," Coy said. He offered a light to Zack, went on. "An option to buy must be supported by certificate of intent and the escrowed means thereby to consummate. Option …"

"Stop it," Zack said. "What's wrong with optioning for nuisance value? Waiting for—well, shall we say a sudden increase in property assessment? Then what? That's right, any investment company would underwrite the escrow."

Coy settled back. This was familiar ground. He looked genuinely happy. "You are from Landworth," he said. "I knew it. Believe me, Mr. Webster, I have no intention of optioning on that basis. Anyone would be a fool to try."

Zack sucked at his cigarette, watched Samson Coy over the coal.

"Why is that Sam?" He used the name deliberately, watched the reaction.

There was none. Coy was caught up, now. He reached out a hand, gripped Zack's wrist.

"Oh, come—we're adults. You know very well what would happen. A delay. A year, two. Then what happens to the options? So much paper without the promise of eventual development to lend them margin value." He pulled at Zack. His red lips, stark against the white of his skin, twisted. "About the job, Webster. Just a word. I won't tell a soul, I fervently promise. Who has the inside? Is that what you're here for? Tell me …"

"Get your hand off my arm."

"Webster, for God's sake—"

"Off!"

Coy drew back. His eyes, hooded again, looked away. He drew a breath, looked back with a weak smile.

"All right, Webster. Fine. You play your game and I'll play mine. But remember—Well, never mind that." He stood abruptly. "By the way. My wife and I are having a party Thursday night. I want you to come. A big affair; we do it every years. Everyone you know will be there."

"I work Thursday night."

Coy smiled. "Yes, I know. But we can fix that."

Zack started to speak and Coy raised a hand. "Okay," he said. "I'll fix it. All right? Will you come?"

Zack looked at the strange little man. The sun had gone now and the lights from the hovering Pavilion and the aura from the midway were beginning to have effect. It was quiet here, with only the waves slapping, the dock creaking.

"Okay, Sam. I'll be there."

He went up the narrow stairs slowly. It was about eight. He could sleep for a couple of hours. The loft was quiet and dark. He shucked the bathing suit, almost dry now, stood in the dark. His body felt good. Hard and hot and alive. He stretched.

"Put some light on."

The voice was a man's. Zack froze, then crouched swiftly, his eyes roving the small room. He saw no one.

"Wait, take it easy," the voice said. "Here I am."

A square of the floor raised and a head popped up. It was Bisto.

"I wanted to see you so I ducked into the shop down below." He pulled himself into the loft, dropped the trap. "Got locked in. Didn't you know about this thing? This used to be an icehouse. I stayed here for a while. Put some light on."

Zack straightened slowly, walked to the bed. "No lights," he said. "Just a kerosene lamp and I don't feel like lighting it. What do you want?"

The lifeguard prowled the room, looked out the small, grimed window. His pale hair glowed in the dark.

"Coy was there," he said, "when I got here. So I ducked inside. I knew about the trap."

"You said that." Zack fumbled around for his clothes, finally lit the lamp. He pulled on his slacks. "Well, what do you want?"

The man came over to the bed. He spread his legs and stood in front of Zack, looming over him. His strange eyes were shadowed.

"I don't want no advice from you, so keep it," he said. "I don't want no lectures. I'm gonna do something and I need help. If you want to help me, all right, but no lectures. You understand?"

"Sit down, Bisto."

Zack moved over on the cot. The slender man glared for a moment, then his eyes shifted; he sat.

"I'm not in the lecture business. Tell me why you want to see me bad enough to hide and sneak and crawl through trapdoors."

Bisto smoothed his hair. "It's Karen. Me and her want to take off, go away from here. We need some money."

"Coy's wife? You think that's smart?" The blond man started to get up and Zack stopped him. "Wait. All right, so you want to go away. I guess that's your business. But I haven't got any money. None. I drew two days Friday, don't get paid till next Friday. How can I help?"

Bisto's vague smile came on, the pale eyes flickered. Zack noticed that in the poor light he seemed to have no eyebrows at all.

"No sweat for you. Listen, I got money. Quite a bit—couple thousand. But Marie's got it. She keeps it for me, you see. I want to get it from her."

"Ask her for it."

"I can't, I—" He got up, prowled from one end of the loft to the other. "Look, you gotta understand. That Mrs. Kinchloe is a funny woman. And she's mean. Her and me—well, I worked for the Golden Note in the winter. Down Miami. Johnny, he manages that, too. Anyway, we had a plan, her and me. You won't tell none of this?"

He stopped by the cot. Zack had lain back; he looked up at the blond man. "No, Bisto. I won't tell. Go on."

"Well, we was gonna go in business. Her running it, me doing the work. A stand. On the beach down there. That was winter before last. So. I saved, and she was supposed to save, too. I don't spend much, living like I do. It mounted up pretty quick. But we haven't been—I mean, lately it's been different. She's getting to be a big shot. She don't see me anymore. That part's all right. But I want my money. I want my money so that bastard Coy can't catch us, bring us back. That bastard! That bastard …"

The lifeguard's face hardened; he slammed a fist into his other hand. Zack sat up.

"I still think you should ask her."

Bisto turned away. "No. I couldn't do that. I couldn't do that …"

"What are you afraid of? Has she got some hold on you, or something? Why can't you go to her, tell her the story? She'd probably be glad to help. She and Coy don't get along, you know. Just go and ask her."

"No," the man mumbled. "I can't do that. I can't. You want to help me or not? Do you or not?"

Bisto sat on the bed again. He dropped his head into both hands. His fingers trembled.

"You go to her, see? Tell her the whole thing. Tell her—tell her about Karen, everything. Tell her I need the money bad. That's all." He lifted his head. "Will you do it? Will you?"

Zack lit a cigarette, taking his time. Bisto's eyes never left him.

"One thing," Zack said through the smoke. "The money's yours—no strings?"

Bisto nodded.

"And she has no legal right to keep it. That right?"

The man nodded again. He moved forward on the bed. "Listen, Mr. Webster—Zack. You gotta know about Karen. He treats her bad. Not physical, you know—he'd never lay a hand on her. He don't hardly touch her at all. He's too busy trying to be a millionaire. She's a warm woman. And gentle." The vague eyes lit and the soft smile came to the man's almost lipless mouth. "And she likes me. You understand, Mr. Webster? You understand?"

Zack looked away from the open, defenseless expression on Bisto's face. It was like looking into the man's soul. He nodded, crushed his half-smoked cigarette into an old coffee carton.

"When do you want to go?"

Bisto sighed. "This weekend," he said. "I get paid Saturday. Karen, she wants to wait till after the party. Coy's throwing a party Thursday night. She figures she ought to help him with that. So, Saturday."

Zack nodded. "Okay. Sometime between now and then I'll see her. The fact that I know about the money should be enough to shake her loose from it. I'll do it."

Bisto bobbed his head. His lips moved, but he said nothing.

Zack dropped into the Gableton lounge that evening and ran into Carol Normer. Or rather, the girl had found him. She'd been looking. It seemed the lanky husband had told her that Zack Webster would probably tell her a story about him and it wasn't true. Normer had blamed the watch he'd bought from Zack as the bone of contention.

He listened for a while, then: "Listen, Carol. I'm not in-interested in your weak-kneed husband … or you, for that matter. So, leave me alone. I've got my own troubles—lots of them."

The girl shook her head wordlessly. She blew her nose, finally recovered her composure.

"I'm sorry, Zack. But Dale is my husband. I realize he's not the best, but he's mine." She leaned forward. "Zack, what happened to you? I thought you were such a nice guy. We all did. And then—Oh, I don't know. Everything started changing. Even Andy. She won't speak to Frank any more … I mention you and she almost hits me. I don't know what's going on. The whole place is crazy."

"It's the *Fahn*. Pennsylvania version." He drank quickly, smiled tightly for the girl. He didn't feel like smiling. "In Germany they have a superstition. About a hot wind that blows at a certain time of the year. While it blows, strange things happen. Meek little men go berserk, women of fidelity climb into bushes with strangers—all sorts of things. They blame it on the wind."

"What did you call it?"

"*Fahn*... like fawn, a young deer. It's all things to all people. In at least one recorded instance, it was the basis for a successful insanity plea in a murder trial."

Carol said, "*Fahn*..."

"Yes. That's what it feels like around here."

A pounding piano beat drew attention. Zack turned. Pam, sitting erect in her circle of light and smiling, looked toward his booth.

She said into the microphone, "For my swimming teacher, a torchy ballad I've had many requests for—'I've Got The World on a String'..."

CHAPTER EIGHT

ednesday was not particularly distinguished. It was the day Johnny Kinchloe apologized to Zack; and the day Burris McCord threatened him in the name of Dale Normer. But, other than that, not much as days go.

It was warm and very muggy. Even the sun freaks had sought the relief of shade and swift rides in open cars. The air was somnolent. Zack found himself thinking more and more of the *Fahn*. The hot wind. The bringer of madness. Strange place, Conaghton—strange people.

The encounter with Kinchloe had been brief and a little embarrassing to them both. Zack had climbed out of his cot, finding it impossible to sleep in the sticky heat. Noon. Hot, hot. And nothing to do, no direction. Stock-taking is no job for daylight in summer: walk, swim—don't worry about what's behind or might lie ahead. Just be.

The Sport Club was the coolest place around. It was a low building of log and stucco, set back from the main highway just at the Conaghton Park turn-off. A rectangular bar and a dance floor behind; a clutch of tables and old-style booths. And, of course, a jukebox.

Pinball machines clanged near the bar and a raft of giggling kids had the back corner stool where the closed part of the bar met the kitchen door.

Johnny Kinchloe came in. He took the stool next to Zack. Neat and smiling and wearing a beige silk suit that must have cost a couple of hundred, he sat and brushed at his corn-colored hair and turned to Zack.

"Mr. Webster," he said. His voice wasn't husky anymore; the fingermarks had disappeared from his white throat. "First time I've had a chance to see you. I wanted to apologize for my actions in the hotel that night."

Zack shrugged. The little man was keyed up about something. He sat calmly enough. But his hands moved in his lap, under the level of the bar, and his eyes kept sliding away to the darker reaches of the room as if he were expecting something to happen. Zack got a cigarette going.

"You don't hold any grudge, do you? I mean, when I found you in that room … You see, Mr. Webster—well, what I'm trying to say is, Marie is a busy woman in her own right. A business woman and a good one. You understand?"

"I understand, Kinchloe. Don't let it bother you. Forget it. I have. I don't know whether Pam can, but I have."

"Oh, yes. Pam."

Zack turned. "Oh, yes, Pam," he mimicked. "You haven't got any guts at all, have you, Kinchloe? You promise her something, then chicken because Marie badmouths her. What kind of a man are you? You think Marie is God?"

The man flushed. "Webster, listen …"

"I'm listening. Say it with something besides your mouth for once. You going to fire that girl?"

"Webster …"

"Are you?"

Johnny glanced up the bar, not answering.

"You want to see me for what?"

The pale eyes slid away. "About Marie," he said. His thin lips twisted. "I know you probably aren't supposed to say anything, but I've got to know if she's going to be picked to run the development project. I've got to know!"

The eyes came back to Zack and they were wild. "You understand, Webster?" He slid off the stool, left a bill for the drink he hadn't touched and turned to go. "I'll see you tomorrow, Mr. Webster—Zack."

Zack called after him. "Will Pam be there? At the party?"

The man paused at the door; sunlight, slashing through the opening, washed out his already pale features. He nodded.

The McCord incident was shorter and much funnier. To Zack, it was funny. The red-necked cop with the bulbous belly didn't think it was funny, maybe. He collared Zack on the way to the Day-Night just before midnight.

"Webster?" The belly came around the building, then the hand-on-the-pistol rest of him. "Want to talk to you."

Zack stopped. He'd just slept very badly, thinking of the whole mess—the Washington hassle, the meeting with Kinchloe, the sticky thing with Andy Manning. All he needed was an ignorant badge-toter leaning on him.

"You got a warrant?"

"Now don't start that again." The policeman blocked the walk, looked up at Zack. "I want to tell you to stay away from Dale Normer."

"Stay away—What the hell are you talking about? Dale Normer? What do I need with Dale Normer?"

"That's neither here nor there. You listen," McCord said. He pushed his belly close to Zack. "Leave him alone. That's an order."

Zack felt his muscles go slack; he closed his eyes for a moment, then opened them.

"The hell it is," he said softly.

"That's what it is," Burris McCord said, leaning on it, playing to the small audience that had gathered on either side of the walk. "An order and you listen. Don't bother that boy. He's a good boy. And—hey! What you—"

Zack gripped one thin shoulder, whipped the man around. He stuck his hand through the wide leather belt in the back and lifted McCord's feet off the ground. The officer dangled from the belt, scrambling for traction with hands and feet. He made noises, but the belt cut into him, smothering his best efforts.

The kids cheered. Zack pushed through the crowd, ran across the street, into the Pavilion. Dancers swirled and got out of the way as he pulled the struggling policeman across the floor. At the railing, Zack hoisted McCord, held him high and threw him far out and down into the lake.

The kids went crazy, cheering and laughing and pointing at the spluttering officer, thrashing in the oil-dark water. Burris McCord was not popular. Zack leaned on the rail until his rage was spent; he smiled finally. The hell with Burris McCord. The hell with letting everyone push you around, too.

"You can't stay out of trouble at all, can you?"

He turned. Andrea Manning stood there, very young and very lovely in a simple white thing that emphasized the black of her hair, the dark of her eyes. Her lips trembled.

"You just can't stay out of trouble at all."

Zack took a breath, feeling it swell his chest, tighten the muscles there. He wiped his hands slowly up and down the front of his uniform.

"No," he said. "I stay out of trouble about as good as you mind your own business."

Andy's face went white. Her eyes filled, then flashed. Her hand came up in a swift arc and exploded on his face. He stood, unflinching. She turned and ran.

Wednesday night—or rather Thursday morning—was something else again. After the encounter at the Pavilion, Zack went straight to work. The counter boys caught hell. The scullion caught hell. The grill caught hell. The usual rush came and went; the usual crowd—exclusive of Andy Manning—came in and carried the night far into morning. And about four in the morning, Marie Kinchloe came in.

She arrived with Jim Sick and both of them were pretty drunk. They took stools at the counter. Zack waited on them.

"Coffee, Zack. Black, Zack—old slick Zack," the woman said. She leaned back, smiled loosely at him. "Black Zack. That's good. Black Zack …"

Jim Sick nodded, grinned hugely, eyes moist and red from drinking. One arm encircled the slim waist of Kinchloe's wife. Zack brought the coffee. Marie was pushing at Sick half-laughing.

She said, "No, Jim. Not tonight. No, no. Oh, no, no …" making a song of it. "Drink the coffee and we'll go."

She was poured into a lime sheath dress that crossed only one shoulder, leaving the other cream and gold in the stark lighting. Her hair was up, held by a green cloth interwoven with the locks; a pair of jade earrings dangled from her ears. The crisscross effect of the gown separated her breasts, pushed them into prominence they didn't need, but certainly deserved. Zack saw the beauty, reviewed what he knew of the woman and felt sorry for Jim Sick. And vaguely disappointed. He didn't know why.

"Your coffee," he said.

"Thanks, Zack," Sick said. "You work all the time, fella? I been by here a dozen times, you been working."

Zack shrugged. "Anything else?"

Marie said, "That's all … right now." Her eyes, glittering and colorless, stared up at him. Her lips were wet and the color had smeared on them. She ran her tongue across them, smiled at him. "But I want to see you later."

He went back to the grill. Ten minutes later Marie and the sheriff had a loud argument. Sick left, chunky body hunched and seeming uncomfortable in the summer suit. Marie sulked at the counter.

"Webster! More coffee."

Zack moved to the urn, drew a cup. He moved deliberately. The place wasn't crowded, but a few late eaters remained. He took the cup to the counter, slid it in front of Marie, removing the other. He said nothing. She had sobered somewhat. Her gaze was sullen, accusing.

"You know what that was?" she asked. "All that noise? He wanted to sleep with me. Him, that little jerk."

She laughed shortly, buried her face in the coffee. Zack started to leave and she stopped him with an imperious gesture.

"Wait, you." Her eyes came up, focused, and the hard brilliance was back. She straightened. "I want to talk to you. Not here. Meet me in the morning before you go to that shack you live in. Meet me ... well, the Pavilion will be all right."

Zack looked down at her, didn't say anything. Her face changed under his gaze.

"What's the matter? My dress fall off?" She stood, spilling the coffee all over the counter. Her eyes narrowed; she leaned forward, her hands bracing in the coffee-wet. "You hear me, Webster? Meet me!"

Zack sighed. "This place is crazy. You're crazy. I quit work at eight, Marie. After that I do what I please."

She stood, held herself erect with an effort of will. "And you don't please to meet me? What's wrong with me, Zack? What's wrong with me? You a fairy? All the men in the place want to sleep with me. But not you. Not pure, sweet, ever-livin' Zack." She took a breath, leveled a finger at him. "You'll be there. And I think we'll make a day of it. Yes, we'll do that. You fix some food before you go off. I'll see you at eight-thirty on Brulliard's dock. You understand?"

"Go home, Marie. You're drunk."

"You be there, Webster." She turned, slim legs moving like perfectly trained things. Over her shoulder she said, "You be there and we'll talk about politics. Things every citizen should know ... like the investigation of Wilson Agnew."

She left. Zack stood without moving. There was a fragrance in the air, a subtle perfume mixed with whiskey fumes and food smells. His eyes watched the slim back, the regally held head until darkness swallowed the figure. He started wiping up the coffee. Marie Kinchloe was a brilliant woman—and somebody was going to kill her someday, just as sure as hell.

The day was bright, but not yet hot. That would come later when the golden ball lifted over the Alleghenies to the east, reflected in the smooth lake. The water was almost clear of boats; just a few fishermen were spotted here and there, rods flipping lazily. The racketing roar of the outboard seemed very loud in the stillness.

Marie shouted something from the center seat amidships. Zack shook his head, pointing to the motor. She smiled. Her face was clear, the eyes wide and ready for the day. And that was a minor miracle considering her condition just a few short hours before. Zack still wore his whites; he had opened the shirt. Marie Kinchloe was doeskin-clad, in slacks and thong-tied jacket. Her long hair, loose for the first time Zack had seen it, whipped with the boat's motion. Her fine legs were toward him, held together and drawn to the side, pulling tight the already molded slacks against the swelling thighs. She crossed her arms under her breasts and laughed—just for the hell of it.

Zack turned his attention to the engine. Whatever her motives, whatever her dark plans, she was a hell of an attractive woman. He felt heat in his face and jerked angrily at the engine handle, swerving the boat.

Marie shouted: "Stop, Zack!"

He cupped a hand behind his ear. She leaned forward, a line appearing distinctly between her eyes.

"You heard me—stop."

He cut the throttle. The quiet was loud for a moment as the boat lost way, floated gently in its own swell. Marie leaned back on her arms, looked at him from under lowered lids. Her lips were very red; her nostrils flared slightly. It was quiet.

"Zack," she said.

"What?" He stretched out his legs and leaned back.

"You're a beautiful man, Zack Webster," she said, very soft—almost breathing the words, pushing them gently through the warming morning air. "For a man, very beautiful. I'm sorry you're not smarter."

He tried to look away, but her eyes held his. Her glance didn't waver and the world narrowed down to this boat, this man and this woman. His throat thickened and he could not have answered even if he had had anything to say.

"I didn't mean it, Zack. About Washington—your past. I wouldn't tell anyone."

He laughed, short and harsh, the mood breaking. He sat up.

"The hell you wouldn't. You're a scheming bitch and everybody seems to know it, and they still get mixed up with you." He got a cigarette out, ripped at matches in a paper folder. "I'm no different. I'm no goddam different!"

She hadn't moved; the smile deepened. "Don't shout."

Her eyes moved over him, slowly, deliberately. The doeskin jacket rose more rapidly with her breathing. She sat up, suddenly, gripping her hands in front of her.

"Start the motor. See that island over there—Cone Island? Beach on the other side. And hurry."

He didn't move. "What for?"

Her eyes were almost closed. "Hurry," she said again. "I want you, Zack. Now. Right now. Oh, let's go, Zack, darling, Zack—please start the motor...."

Her hands twisted and she seemed to grind her knees together; her face was flushed.

Zack twisted on the seat, reached for the starting rope.

"You're holding all the cards," he said, trying for irony.

But his heart hammered and his big hands shook.

CHAPTER NINE

There would never be any danger of Cone Island being built upon. It humped from the water like a huge rock-dirt Stetson hat without a brim. Only on a couple of spots could any sort of landing be negotiated. The beach Marie directed Zack to find was not a beach at all, but a stretch of sandy loam angling sharply upward to the inevitable bushy hill. The island was covered with foliage, mostly scrub oak and birch; here and there clumps of wild haws colored the dull green. Through the center of the small island ran a cut, like the crease in a hat, timbered and steep and all but impassable.

"This is an island?"

Zack pulled the boat high, the sharp prow cutting blackly into loam. He felt the shifting earth pull at his bare feet. Marie held tight until he'd moored the boat, then leaped nimbly to dry land.

"It's my island, Zack. Nobody else has figured out a use for it. But I have. Come. Bring the basket."

She jumped a rotting log, started up the slight slope into the cut. Zack watched her. What a body she had—legs straight and rounded, shoulders wide, tapering to womanly hips. He snatched the heavy basket she'd brought, got the bag he'd prepared at the Day-Night.

He caught up with her. She walked fast, ducking limbs, skirting impassable brushy areas. She knew where she was going, all right.

Once she turned. "Hurry up. It's not far. Up a little farther."

They came out on the top of the highest knoll. Sun greeted them. A quiet you could hear descended on the island. There were no boats near. Zack looked for Brulliard's boathouse, but the Beachcomber and the Pavilion hid it. He saw the hotel, the boardwalk, the beach. And water all around. The bluest, cleanest water he'd seen in a long time.

"Isn't this fabulous?" Marie asked. "Isn't it just too much? I may buy this island someday, Zack. Just to have it for my own. Wouldn't that be wonderful? A whole island. Queen of the island."

She spun on the grassy knoll, whirled, her laugh echoing out over the water. Zack stood with the weight of the basket pulling at his arm. She danced around the clearing, shouting "Hi, hi, hi!" and laughing in sheer exuberance. Finally she stopped, whirled to face him from across the glade. Her hair was mussed and her face was full of color and the reflection of sun and grass and summer.

"Zack," she whispered. Then, "Zack…" in a long-drawn-out near scream.

She broke into a run, launched herself at him, arms reaching, knees drawn up and spread. He dropped his bundles, tried to catch her. The soft body bludgeoned him backward; they struck the hard earth together. She pinned him, pulled at his face, kissed him fiercely. Her teeth bruised him.

After the kiss, they got up slowly, holding close, eyes inches apart. Zack could see nothing but the sparks spiraling deep in her eyes, the spun gold of fallen hair, the red, red, red of her mouth. He pulled and she came against him.

Her lips caressed his eyes, his nose, went to his ear. "This is public, darling. From the lake. I don't care, darling, but they can see…"

He managed one word. "Where?"

They found the cave. It took just a few moments with Marie leading the way. It was just over a lip of ground that looked like a sheer drop. But the earth cut away beneath, scooped out to a tiny ledge. At one end of the ledge was the entrance; a six-foot, diagonal slash in rock.

It was strangely light inside. Zack found out later that the cave went back some twenty feet, then slanted upward to another opening directly on top of the peak. When they first got there, he could explore nothing but the wonder of this woman, this moment.

It wasn't public there.

Both were dressed. The day had all but fled and sun hit directly into the shadowy cavern from the high opening, speckling dust motes, warming the cold sand. Papers and bottles were stacked in one corner. Zack lounged at the cliff opening, looking out over the broad expanse of lake. He turned as the silence was broken.

She sat, fully dressed, smoking quietly. The excitement had left her, the need that had brought her here. Now she chafed to be on with it, with her dream. It was all there on the mobile face, the full lips. Willful and sulky again—imperious and aloof again.

His guess had been wrong about her background.

She was the only child of a very successful man. A contractor. She had never known her mother; only the driving, vital powerhouse of a father who had no time for children, no time for family. Money was his idol and he carved it lovingly. Marie worshiped him, naturally. And hated him a bit, too. All her childish blandishments availed her nothing by way of attention. He saw her when nothing else interfered; he packed her off to schools, camps, hired companions and governesses.

"The first war made him," she said, in the strange, dispassionate tone in which the whole story had been told. "And the next one broke him. He was always after more. Not money, exactly. It wasn't the money, Zack. It was the satisfaction of knowing he was running the show, cracking the whip. And knowing people would jump. People just like him, no different—except for the position they allowed themselves to keep.

"He was God to me. After the Korean War began, he tried to put together a monstrous corporation. It was his dream, his great accomplishment. Like everything else hadn't mattered. He raided companies, set up holding concerns. I don't know what all. He controlled a frightening number of industries. Oh, he reveled in it, Zack. The war would spread, he thought. Become global. Then they'd have to come to Steven Boyd. Then he would feel the positiveness of power, the vindication of what he'd given his life for. But … well, you know what happened. It was just a—what was it they called it?—police action. It ended suddenly, the economy broke. Not a very bad recession, really. Unless you were way out there on a margin and a promise like Steve Boyd was. It killed him. And broke him."

The rest came faster. The years of despondency after the shock of his death, the slow recovery. There had been enough for a trust fund for Marie, for school. And she'd gone to a good school for one year. The first summer she'd discovered Conaghton and Johnny Kinchloe. And the thrill of running things. That was the end of school for Marie.

Zack shoved away from the opening, rolled to her. She gave no sign. Her canvas shoes lay on the sand and he picked them up, shook them. He didn't look at her.

"Marie."

"What is it?"

"How old are you?"

"How—What difference does that make? I'm old enough, darling—if that's what you're worried about."

"No. I … just would like to know. You see, I don't like you very much. And I wish I had a better reason for it. Right now it's pretty—pretty nebulous. My feeling. You understand?"

"No," she said. I'm twenty-four. Sweet twenty-four and never been missed." She laughed and it was different from the other times; the steel was there, the sense of sneering at herself, the world—everybody and everything. "So don't like me. So what?

I don't like you either. But you were good to use. Let's talk about that silly party. Are you going?"

"Let's talk about something you said before. You said something about Landworth. And expected me to understand what you were talking about."

"I knew you'd understand. Coy's been hot nosing you for a week, hasn't he? I knew he'd spill his guts to you. Both of us though you might be from Landworth, looking over the local set-up. He still thinks so, I guess. I know better."

Zack sifted a handful of sand, caught it in the other hand. He watched the trickles.

"Yes, you do. I'm wondering how you know. I'm wondering how much you stirred the water in finding out."

She gripped his hands, stopped the sand play.

"And you're wondering if you should run?"

He looked at her, into the hard eyes. "I thought of that. I'm an investigator. You found that out, too. So forgive me if I play Sherlock Holmes. You came in last night with Jim Sick. He wanted to play house. You gave him reason to believe the door might be open. You are suddenly in possession of information that not just anyone could get. Conclusion?"

"Of course," she said. "I had Jim Sick send a wire to the FBI. They sent him the information. You're quite famous down there, darling. What did you do to that poor Senator?"

"Never mind the Senator. If you know, Jim Sick knows. Is he going to arrest me?"

"He says not. I think he reluctantly admires a man who would punch a Senator in the nose." She pulled a comb from the nearby basket and began running it through her silky hair. Sun shafts caught the stuff as she spun it 'round her fingers, picked out highlights and softened her face with reflection. "A local warrant, he called it. I don't think you need to worry."

He thought about it. Sick would gain nothing by arresting him. He seemed to be pretty relaxed about his job. And he liked Zack.

Maybe, just maybe, he'd wait to see what developed. In which case Zack Webster could make payday tomorrow, then slide quietly into the sunset with a couple of bucks rather than dead broke.

He felt better when he'd made up his mind. A course of action always made him feel better, more competent.

"Marie, about that party. I'll be there so I'd better arrange for someone to take the grill tonight. Everyone will be there, I understand. What's the occasion?"

She drew the comb slowly through a lock of hair, spreading it in front of her face. She looked up at him through it as through a gold silk veil, or the shadowed incarnation of desire.

"You," she said. "Samson's shooting for the moon. He'll do everything tonight but go to bed with you." She laughed. "And don't be surprised if he offers his wife for that little chore. He's a cold-storage apple, Samson is. Don't forget it."

"You didn't tell him I wasn't from Landworth?"

"Hell, no. Why should I? Any information I can use to my own advantage I'm going to use."

"Like optioning property to hold up the development company when they settle?"

She looked up sharply. Her hand pushed back the hair; she straightened, wrapping her arms around her drawn-up legs.

"You know about that, too, huh? Anything else you'd like to know, Mr. Investigator?"

"Yeah. There is. What makes you think Landworth won't buck, write the operation off when he discovers you're holding options to key land? Then what are you holding?"

She smiled. "You don't know much about business, do you? Big strong man. Smart man. Like all muscle heads. Of course he won't withdraw. He's committed. Financially committed. The frontage I control—or will control—means nothing to him. He's arranging to buy out Allegheny Rents, the whole outfit. Little bits he'll deal with when the time comes. And I'll be very easy to deal with, darling. Very easy, indeed."

"I see."

"Do you? Do you see the planning and the long nights of figuring? Do you see the frustration of being close to something like this, touching it—and only being able to scrape crumbs?"

She pulled back, consciously relaxing. The color climbed in her face.

"You don't know at all," she said. "Sure, I'll use the Brulliard land as an added inducement for Landworth to appoint Marie Kinchloe Managing Director. How do you like that? Managing Director." She turned toward the opening, looked out at the lake, but she wasn't seeing the afternoon sun, the curried blue of the water. "After that … what? Who knows?"

Zack said, "How are you going to exercise the option? It's no good as it is."

She leaned back, a wise smile pulling at her lips. "I'll exercise," she said. "You think I like Softy Malebar? Carl? The slob! The big, ugly know-nothing. Ugh! He makes me sick."

"But he's got money," Zack said softly.

"Yes. He's got it. And Johnny hasn't, and Johnny's done with little Marie. He doesn't know it yet. I don't think I'll tell him, either. And don't you."

He shrugged. "Nothing to me. Are you going to marry him?"

"Carl?" She twisted her hand in a ray of sun slanting down from the high opening. "Oh, we'll see. But I'm done with Joh—"

She stopped. Zack couldn't see for a moment what had startled her. Her body was stiff, unmoving.

"What's wrong?"

"Shhh!"

He lowered his voice. "What is it?"

"My hand. See? The sun stopped—just like that."

Zack rose silently, crawled rapidly to the back of the cave. He peered upward. The cavern narrowed as it went up; he could see nothing but the light sifting through. He waited. The shape of the opening changed. He turned, ran back.

"There's someone at the opening. I'll see who it is."

"Hurry," Marie said.

Zack slid out the front opening, scrambled up the soft face of the overhang. At the top, he stopped, looked all around. He could see the whole island But that didn't prove anything—not with all the trees and brush. He looked for the corresponding point of the high opening, found a clump of scraggy rocks thirty yards away. He trotted to them. After a short climb, he found the opening, peered in.

"Marie!" he called into the darkness. A rush of warm air hit his face. "Marie, it's Zack."

"Zack." The voice came small, hollow.

"Go to the boat. I'm going to try to run and catch our peeper."

He didn't wait for an answer.

He started for the beach. There was no sense in going any-where else on the island. He didn't know enough about it. If the beach where they'd landed was the only good one, then that's where the interloper would have to have moored a boat. And there was no getting there without one. Unless you were a swim-mer of Channel calibre.

He broke into the cut, ran along the few yards of cleared trail to the beach. There was only one boat. His eyes searched the loam for a point well back from the water's edge. No use messing up marks. And he found one. A prow mark. And fresh, only now filling with water.

He ran up a slight incline, clutched a sapling. There were all kinds of boats out there. They'd never pick the right one.

Marie arrived, hot and breathless.

"Did you see him? Who was it? Was it Johnny?"

Her eyes were anxious.

"I don't know. I saw a boat. Could have been anybody. Too far away."

Marie pulled her jacket together, tied the thong. She shook back her hair, smiled up at him.

"Okay, sport. Let's go. It's been a ball, but it's time to go."

Zack looked out over the water. The boat had disappeared. It could have been going anywhere. Marie's arms slid around him, brought his attention back. She hung on him, looked up without speaking.

"What's this?"

She shook her head. A pulse, a single blue line, beat at the corner of one eye. Her hands cupped his head, pulled it down. She kissed him slowly, thoroughly. At the end, he was helping.

Marie stepped back and smiled: "You're all right, Webster. You're all right. I think I'm going to enjoy having you around."

"Better than Malebar?"

Her eyes slitted; the smile tightened. "Oh, yes," she said, trying to make it blithe. "Much better. And better than Johnny and better than Dale and better than Bisto and better than Burris McCord and bet—"

"Burris McCord!" Somehow that shocked him more than anything else in the whole, crazy day. "Burris McCord—for Christ's sake. You're kidding?"

The smile was back, full bloom. "Why? Should I neglect poor old Burris? Oh, yes—I forgot Samson Coy."

Zack turned away. His face felt spongy, like a sagging flesh-tree. He tried to brush by her. She grabbed him, pulled herself tight to his chest.

"Tell me, Zack," she said. "Was it good for you? As good as your little colored girl? She gets all my leavings, you know. Was I—"

He slapped the words back into her mouth. She spun with the force of the blow, fell to the ground. For a moment she crouched there. Then she got up and moved slowly to the boat. One hand held a reddening cheek. At the boat, she turned.

"Take me home, Webster," she said. Her voice was dead, absolutely without feeling. "Take me quick and don't say a goddam word or I'll scream for police until they hear me in Washington."

CHAPTER TEN

No one really wanted to go to the party. It was like getting an invitation to an execution—you felt a morbid curiosity, but no real interest. Samson Coy wasn't a party-giver. And no one liked him, anyhow. You have to be liked to give a successful party.

Zack got ready automatically, not thinking about anything in particular. That was another thing about the lake—pretty soon you didn't care if you took care of your business or just drifted, soaking sun and lapping liquor. He walked slowly to the Coys' beachfront house, enjoying the warm night, the high, velvet sky. Why did he feel a chill? The lake was somber, dressed in ominous wisps of early fog. Zack walked faster, wishing this night were done.

Samson Coy had strung lanterns in his yard, which ran down to the lake. Zack walked off the end of the boardwalk, stone-hopped to the shore and headed in the direction of the lanterns. Figures moved around under them.

Samson Coy shouted as he walked up. "Zack! Good to see you, boy." He came toward him, arms outstretched. The party hadn't changed his clothing habits; he wore a blue suit, white shirt, neat tie. His stocky body moved very lightly on the grass. "Not everybody's here yet. But they will be, they will be."

Zack mumbled something, walked with Samson to the tables on the lanai. People greeted him. He saw Johnny Kinchloe and Marie; Kinchloe waved, Marie deadpanned him. Tom Brulliard was there, looking uncomfortable in a suit. Bisto sat back in the shadows of the porch, his pale hair gleaming in the dark. He watched Zack with eyes that didn't seem to blink.

A drink was thrust into his hand. A woman said, "Nice of you to come, Mr. Webster."

"Oh … Mrs. Coy." He took the woman's hand. "It's my pleasure. Very nice place you have. Very nice. Front lawn running to the lake, nice grass. Nice for parties."

The woman's pretty, rather expressionless face, did not alter. "We don't have parties," she said.

"I see," Zack said.

He didn't see at all. But the woman's direct gaze made him uncomfortable. He saw Dale Normer, nodded at the skinny guy. Normer turned away.

Zack said, "Look, Mrs. Coy. Is there something wrong with my make-up? Too much lipstick, maybe? You've been staring badly, you know."

Spots of red appeared in the woman's pale cheeks.

"Yes," she said. "I know. I wanted to see what sort of man Edwin had entrusted our secret to. I still want to know."

"Edwin? You mean Bisto?"

Zack drank, spilling the cold Martini down his suddenly parched throat.

"Yes," Karen Coy said. "Bisto. He told me about your interview. He shouldn't have done that. He thinks you're just an ordinary fellow. He doesn't know who you really are. Have you told Samson?"

"Who I—" He took her arm, led her into the shadows. "Listen, don't worry about that. Your business entirely. Bisto— Edwin—told me so that I could do something for him. That's all."

Karen's eyes held his levelly. "Did you? You were with her yesterday on the island. Did you get the money she stole from him?"

Zack blinked. Like a small town. Everybody knows everything, and damned near before you do it.

"I didn't—" he groped for an excuse, but there was none. He'd told Bisto he would ask and he hadn't. "I didn't do it, no, ma'am. I'm sorry."

Karen nodded. She crossed her arms, hugged herself.

"Of course. No one helps. But we don't need your help. Just don't say anything to Samson. Do you hear?"

"I won't."

Bisto materialized out of the shadows at the corner of the building. Both hands were in his pockets; his hair was mussed like he'd been running.

"He damn well hadn't better," he said, and his voice was dull, the vague, on-and-off smile hitting his lips, but not warming them at all. "He hadn't better …"

The party got better as the evening progressed. It was a fine night. Not too hot, a cool wind caressing dancers and gently moving the lanterns. There were many people there Zack didn't know. He had long since quit trying to remember them all. Pam Jardin came about nine-thirty, and that was a real surprise. Marie was getting loaded and she made a couple of remarks, but no trouble developed. There was an excellent buffet and Zack put a dent into it. It had been a busy day for him. He glanced at Marie. Real busy.

Marie walked away from Johnny in the middle of the dance floor. Her voiced floated back over her shoulder.

"You dance like a girl," she said. "A goddam girl."

Johnny stood there, a silly grin on his face. Someone tittered; it became a general laugh. But there was a strain.

Zack got hung up with a redhead named Sally, finally got to the porch where Pam was sitting alone at the piano, stroking the keys. A row of empty glasses sat on the music rack. She raised her eyes as he approached, winked without stopping the music.

Zack perched on the bench, watched the girl's fingers fly over the keys. There was a subdued murmur; voices reached them, but nobody came close.

"You're ruining your reputation, big one," the girl said. "Again, that is. I'm hired help."

"You weren't invited?"

She glanced at him. "You're kidding." She switched to a Latin rhythm, moved with it. Her face was sad and she seemed smaller. "I heard about your escapade today," she said, over the music. "Stepping up in class, huh, kid?"

"Pam, not you, too. Does anything happen in this goddam place that everyone doesn't know about?"

Pam smiled at him, her eyes lighting for a moment. "Not if it's sexy or dirty, kid. And that reminds me … what about that nice kid, that Manning?"

"Andy? What about her?"

She shrugged. "You talked about her enough that day swimming. I thought you had a little yen."

"Don't be funny. She's a kid."

"A kid, huh? Well, that's another theory shot to hell. This funny life. Nothing stays like you think it should."

"Pam, what the hell are you talking about?"

She finished the number, stopped. A few dancers applauded; Samson Coy shouted something to Zack. He waved, turned to the girl.

Pam said, "I thought you were a smart one. You know—a bright man? But you're not. Excuse me. Gotta powder."

He watched her go, fine body swaying in the professional gown, head down and eyes lowered. She was feeling low. All her plans shot to hell. He rose swiftly, angry suddenly at his concern for the girl. She'd made her bed. She chose Johnny Kinchloe as a coattail and it hadn't worked out. That's all.

He walked to the edge of the porch, looked out over the shimmering lake. Dreams die hard when you're young. Pam was more used to disappointment and adversity than most; but it's hard to watch your hopes go glimmering.

"Well, hello there."

It was Jim Sick, wide grin and all, in a suit and tie. His tanned, square face beamed at Zack. He'd had a couple of drinks; his eyes were watery, like the other night with Marie Kinchloe.

"Hi," Zack said. He nodded at the dumpy blonde woman on the sheriff's arm. "Hello. You must be Jim's wife." Sick's smile slid off; he glanced sharply at Zack. "Glad to meet you. Jim talks about you all the time."

She giggled. "Oh, that's nice. He didn't tell me about you. What's your name?"

"I'm Zack Webster, ma'am."

Sick looked at him. He tilted his head and looked and slowly the grin crept back. He put an arm around his wife's plump shoulders.

"Where you going, Zack?"

"It's almost ten," Zack said, starting across the grass. "I'm going across the lake, pick up Andrea Manning. After the play."

"Oh?" Sick called after him. "Bring everybody!"

His wife said, "Now, Jim ..."

The party had grown to a brawl when he arrived with Andy Manning. Everyone really was there, now. All loaded or getting that way. Frank Bonino ran up as they came through the house, stepped onto the lanai.

"Hey, Andy. Where'd you go?" The man's eyes found Zack. "This goon again?"

"Don't, Frank," Andy said.

"I thought we had a date for this rat race. Where does this come-lately figure?"

Zack squeezed the girl's arm, moved her aside.

"Be a gentleman, Frank," he said softly. The man's hot gaze didn't waver. "Look, Frank, I'm sorry, but I stole your date and

I'm going to keep her. Now, why don't you face that and go have fun? You're pretty enough to score almost anywhere."

Frank's face flushed. He took a rapid step toward Zack, and he might have hit him if it hadn't been for Softy Male-bar. The big man came off the porch, stuck out a beefy arm. Frank stopped like he'd hit a wall.

"Easy, kid," the gravelly voice said. "This guy'd scramble you. Take a hike and cool off."

Bonino moved off, got a drink at the portable bar set up below the porch rail. Malebar watched him all the way. He was dressed in the same odd costume in which Zack had first seen him: a lightweight suit of black Italian silk and a soft turtle-neck jersey of pure white. He wore no rings and his shoes were expensively plain. He turned to Zack.

"Let's walk, Webster. I want to talk."

Zack shook his head. "I like it here. In the light."

Malebar looked at him sharply. "Son," he said, more wire invading the marshmallow tones, "you breed lumps, you know that? I said talk, I meant talk. Let's go. Bring the little girl if you want to. Softy Malebar ain't nobody's enemy."

Zack looked down at Andy. She shrugged and nodded. They followed the blocky figure across the lawn, down to the boat landing. It was darker there. The lake chuckled softly against the shore, the pilings of the small dock. Malebar's wide figure made a blob in the gloom, the white jersey standing out.

"What's he want, Zack?" Andy whispered as they approached. "I'm afraid of him."

"I don't know. But don't be afraid. There's fifty people not very far away. There's no danger of him doing anything silly here. I hope. I don't know what business he'd have with me."

But he did know. Or thought he did. Malebar had heard about the excursion to Cone Island today. Zack really didn't think he'd try anything here, but he might threaten him, or use Andy's presence in some way. He slowed with the thought. That would be nice. Just get back in the girl's good graces and have some slob like Malebar put the kibosh on it. Too late now.

Softy Malebar said, "Webster, some funny things been going on around this lake. All of them since you came. Now, I don't say that means anything, but it's a big fat coincidence and I don't like coincidences."

Zack gently disengaged Andy's clutch from his arm. He moved a step to the right and upshore from Malebar. Now the lantern light was in the big man's face, at Zack's back.

He said, "Funny like how, Malebar? You mean funny ha-ha? Or funny peculiar?"

"Funny like you know damn well—and never mind the comedy." He fished a crumpled pack of cigarettes out of a coat pocket, shook some free and offered them around. "I mean all this jazz about development companies and the Las Vegas of the Alleghenies and all that. I mean everybody falling down to impress you because you come to look the place over."

Zack struck a match, held it for the big man. Malebar's rocky face was all angles and planes in the fluttering match light.

"Who told you that?"

"Nobody tells me anything," Malebar said. "I find out things."

"Marie didn't tell you?"

"Marie tells me nothing and that's the same thing I tell her. It works out real good that way. What I want to find out from you—"

"I thought you and Marie were—well, you know. Like the night in the cafe. Pretty chummy."

"Just leave that alone, Webster. Now what's with this development thing: is it going to happen? Wait—don't say nothing yet. Let me tell you why I want to know. That fair?"

His eyes, shadowed by the night and heavy brows jutting from a shelf of hard frontal bone, gleamed in the weak lantern light. A boat went by out on the lake aways, puttering softly. Pam Jardin's piano rode hot and lowdown, carrying on the warm air.

"Is it fair?"

"Fair," Zack said, "But useless. I can't help you. If you're going to be fair, then I better be. I don't know anything about anything."

Malebar grunted. "Sure. Just listen." He sucked a huge lungful of smoke, reddening the coal of his cigarette. "I don't care for developments. Who needs them? My place, the Ship over there—I run it for kicks and I run it at a breakeven level. Don't make a dime. Because I like the place, like the atmosphere. And I like to get out of Pittsburgh for a couple months a year. Make sense?"

Zack nodded. He reached for Andy's hand, found it in the dark. The small fingers squeezed his and her soft length came against him.

"So all right," Malebar said. "All this civic jazz does nothing for me. I stand to make no beans. But I do stand to lose. In a sense, that is. Take this party. Coy never threw a party in his life. I know him for years. Now, all of a sudden, he's Duncan Hines or somebody. This bit. He hates people. But he wants to manage the park. And so does Marie. That's where I stand to lose."

Andy said, "Zack, I think they're calling you at the house."

"Let them call," Malebar said. "Probably Coy wanting to make some points. Well, I got some to make first. As a matter of fact, I got a deal. I don't know what your connection is with this Landworth guy, but it can't be too much. So here's the bit—you make your recommendation and steer off of Marie. Understand? I don't want Marie to get the job. You do that and we'll make a settlement, you and me. Cash like, a settlement."

Zack held his shortening cigarette in thumb and forefinger, coaxed a last drag out of it. He flipped it into the water.

"Malebar, that's a married woman you're talking about. Maybe I better tell her husband what you've said."

Malebar snorted. "Kinchloe? Go ahead. But how about the deal? I can make it very attractive."

"How about if I tell Marie?"

An arm shot out like a striking snake; a hand clamped on Zack's throat, cut off his wind. Andy stifled a scream. The move had been so swift and so expert that Zack was completely at a loss. His knees bent and his mind scrambled for a way out; the pressure on his throat was terrible. He clawed at the man's fingers.

The Malebar seemed to get hold of himself. He dropped his hand suddenly, wiped both of them on the front of the silk coat.

"Sorry," he husked. "Lost my head."

Zack stepped back warily, cleared his throat. His neck felt like he'd swallowed carpet tacks. Andy gripped his arm.

"Are you all right, Zack? Zack, are you hurt?" She whirled on the big man. "You goddam racketeer! Keep your hands to yourself. What do you think this is—your smelly saloon?"

"Lady, I'm sorry—"

"Sorry!" Andy's little figure vibrated with anger. She shook a finger in Malebar's face. "You touch him again and I'll—"

"All right, Andy." Zack said. He pulled her aside. "That's one for you, Softy. Next time you try, don't let go."

CHAPTER ELEVEN

"What time is it?"

Zack pulled up, bumping against another couple as he did so. He twisted his arm, then remembered he had no watch. He started dancing again, holding Andy close.

"I don't know," he said.

"Zack..."

"What?" He stopped. They were near the porch. A noisy table held Marie Kinchloe and about eight others. "Step on your toe?"

"No," she said. "You move good, boy. I'm tired, is all. I don't want to wear out my mystery in one outing. What time is it?"

Zack caught Dale Normer's eye at the table.

"Got the time, Dale?"

The blond bartender glanced at his wrist, said something. Zack didn't catch it. He walked to the table.

"Twenty after two," Dale said. "You think you did something smart, throwing McCord in the lake, Webster? You think so? You better remember—" He glanced around; the table's attention had centered on him. He looked at Zack, back to Marie at the end of the table. "Nothing. I'll talk to you tomorrow."

Zack turned. Marie said, "Zack, darling—where are you going? You've been avoiding me all night."

Carol Normer was watching her husband with narrowed eyes. Dale's face was dull red under his tan; he avoided her eyes.

Samson Coy said, "You've been hiding, Zack. That isn't nice. We're all friends here."

The stocky man smiled, his agate eyes not getting into the act at all. Tom Brulliard came up behind Zack, said something. Zack started to turn and Coy caught his sleeve.

"Will you join us, Zack? This is the core of the party. This is—"

There was a high, silly burst of laughter and Marie Kinchloe collapsed against Softy Malebar sitting next to her. Johnny was nowhere in sight.

Zack said, "Look, Samson, I'm neglecting a very delectable female. Suppose—"

Marie spilled a drink. It was the funniest thing since the Keystone Kops. She thought. Even Malebar was a little disconcerted at the woman's actions.

Zack thought of Bisto, of his promise. He looked for Andy. She was talking to Tom Brulliard. Frank Bonino was with them. He went down the table to Marie's place.

"Marie…"

"Ah…the beautiful Zachariah Webster." She tilted her head way back, looked at him upside down. "What is it, darling? All you gotta do is ask."

She giggled. Zack bent near her, perfume washing up into his nostrils. He said in her ear, "I'd like to see you a minute. Alone. Just take a minute."

Samson Coy shouted down the table: "No secrets, now, people. No secrets. Marie—let him up."

The woman twisted and smiled upward at Zack. Her face was flushed from alcohol. Her lipline was smudged and the hard eyes were shifting and watery.

"Darling, you know what's eating lovely old Sam, don't you? He thinks we're talking about business. He doesn't know about sex, our Samson. He doesn't know about anything, really. He's a creep."

"Look—"

"Darling, listen," she said. Her hands wrapped around his arm, held strongly. She turned to Coy. "Forget the job, Samson.

You won't get it. You're out of the race, old kid, so save your phony smiles."

The table quieted. Coy's face went a little whiter in the swaying lantern light. He tried a smile. A weak one.

"No, I'm not kidding and I'm not drunk," Marie said, very clearly, enunciating over the piano sound. "You're dead, Jocky. D-e-a-d!" She laughed.

"Marie, straighten up, for chrissake," Malebar muttered.

She brushed off his hand. Suddenly she was sober. Her eyes hardened. And all the imperiousness returned. One hand swept glasses off the table.

"Shut up! Shut up, all of you." Malebar looked at Zack. Coy had risen. Some of the other guests were drawn to the scene. "And you, Softy. Dear Softy... you think you run me, don't you? Don't you?"

"Will you just be sane, for chri—"

She said a real nasty word. Even for three-thirty at a drunken party it was a shocker. Malebar jumped up.

"Oh, don't get moral," Marie said. "Do you run me? You think you do? Zack, tell him about today—about our island. Go ahead, don't be afraid. He's only a racketeer to women and children. He's only—"

Malebar's face had gone dead. His eyes jumped to Zack, held while the woman rambled. He stepped forward, right hand flashing toward her throat.

Zack pulled the chair out from under Marie; she fell away, Malebar's hand meeting open air. Zack grabbed the hand, jerked the heavy man off balance. Malebar was powerful. Zack knew if he gave the man half a chance, there would be hell to pay. As the stocky body came toward him, he stuck out his right hand, rammed stiff fingers into Malebar's throat. Softy gasped, grabbed his neck with both hands. Zack doubled huge fists, sent a left hand from his hip pocket to the unprotected side of the big man's head, a sledging right to the ear. He sagged, teetered, finally fell.

Everyone was talking. Zack caught a whirl of faces, heard questions and demands. Marie was still at his feet. Her dress was torn at the bottom. One breast was all but exposed.

"Zack," she said. "Zack, help me …"

He took her arm, drew her upright. She fell against him. He pushed through the crowd. Andy waved at him over heads.

"Be right back," he called. "See if you can find Johnny. I'll take her inside and let her lie down."

Karen Coy materialized beside him. "Put her in here," the small woman said, opening a door. "I'll find her husband."

For once Marie wasn't saying anything. She slumped on the cot in the downstairs room, dropped her hands between her legs. Her face was blank, shocked.

Zack studied her. "You see what happens when you push people—move them around like you want to?" He stood in front of her, not trying to soothe or comfort her. "You almost got hurt. Maybe killed. That's what he had in mind."

"His face …"

"Sure. You kicked him in the guts, Marie. What do you expect? Well, that's your business. But you treat people pretty badly. You better quit it. Like Brulliard. You see him look over when you got dumped? He laughed, the old man. He liked it. And Coy—after the way you harpooned him?"

"Leave me alone. Just leave me alone."

"I will. One thing first. Bisto tells me you have some money of his. He wants it. How about it?"

She shook her head.

"What do you mean? It's his and he wants it. You'd better start thinking a little clearer, Marie. If you want to torture some-body, use your husband. He's got a license. You get that poor guy's money and you get it fast. You hear?"

She looked up. Her eyes were shifting, vague. "I can't, Zack. I used it. For the Brulliard option."

Johnny Kinchloe came in, corn-colored hair awry. He breathed heavily.

"What is it? I came from the hotel ..."

Marie fell back on the cot, covered her eyes with her hand. "Get out," she whispered. "Both of you get the hell out."

He got Andy away, finally. Bisto tried several times to corner him, but they never were alone and that was fine with Zack. He didn't want to tell the man what Marie had said about the money. The man's eyes followed Zack accusingly as they left.

Samson Coy said his goodbyes, tight-lipped and cold-eyed. No pretension now. He moved around, supervising the exodus. When he and Zack met face to face, he turned away.

They got away, walked up the dark back path toward the hotel. Neither spoke. At the hotel they turned, by silent consent, and walked toward the lake. They met Pam Jardin on the end of the boardwalk.

She was leaning on the railing, staring out into the quiet, dark, deserted lake. It had grown cooler. A slight wind came out of the Conaghtons to the west. Pam still wore only the topless black evening gown; she had on neither coat nor sweater. She turned as their heels sounded on the boards.

"Zack? That you?"

"Me," Zack said. "And Andy. What are you doing here? The fun's over."

The girl smiled tiredly. "I know. I saw the main event. Why didn't you let him choke her?"

"You know better than that." He pulled Andy around to face the other girl. Moonlight struck her face. The make-up, the heavy stage stuff she hadn't had time to remove, killed glare, gave her face a flat appearance. "You two know each other?"

"I've listened to Miss Jardin," Andy said. Her tone was stiff. Pam's smile slid, stuck at half-mast. "She plays very well."

There was an awkward silence. Zack got out his cigarettes, passed them around. Pam took one, lit it, got it going. All the time, her eyes remained on the small girl. Andy refused a smoke, stood quietly.

"Look," Pam Jardin said. "This is silly. This girl looks at me like I was day-old gravy. I'll go."

She started. Zack grabbed her arm.

"Hold it. What's wrong with you, Andy? Are you tired?"

She looked at him, then turned her eyes to the Negro girl. She shrugged, moved to the rail.

Zack lowered his voice. "She's all right, Pam. A good kid. She's just—"

"I know what she's just. You took me swimming." She dropped her cigarette through a hole between the boards. "Well, I won't be around to embarrass you long, big fella. I'm finished Saturday. And maybe this thing tonight will make it quicker."

"Why should it?"

Pam shrugged. Her sad eyes were clear. "She hates me, that woman. Don't know why. She doesn't care about Johnny. Maybe it's like with this one, the little one. Maybe it's you, Zack."

He looked at Andy. She was standing hipshot against the railing, facing away from them, looking toward the beach. She looked very small in the deep dark.

"Pam, I'll see you tomorrow, all right? I want to—well, I have to take Andy home, and …"

Pam nodded. She moved back and Zack could not tell if she were smiling. But her voice wasn't—still deep and measured, warm without being sexy or obvious.

"Okay, champ. See you. Tonight I need the sleep."

The boardwalk ended here, one pair of steps leading downward to the grass pier, one pair leading to the walk from the hotel above them. The end of the walk was raised ten or fifteen feet from the shore, dipping away to where Coy's house was. Lights still burned on the lawn over there, visible from where they stood. Pam walked to the steps, started down to the grass pier.

Zack said, "Where are you going? Hotel's that way, kid."

"I know. I go around this way, up the back. It's just as short and the scenery's better." Her voice came up. "And I still wish you'd have let him strangle her."

Zack watched her until he couldn't see her along the shoreline. The night was very dark; the moon had a scum on it and sliding clouds from time to time obliterated it completely.

"Zack…"

He felt the girl come up behind him. He didn't turn. He didn't like the way she'd acted with Pam. He didn't like the way she just accepted the gossip without question, without doubt.

"I'm sorry, Zack." Her voice was small, almost lost in the bigness, darkness of the night. "I really am. That was a sloppy way to act to that girl." She paused a moment. "You can beat me."

Zack turned. She looked down, an expression of mock humility on her face. Her eyes slanted with the effort of hiding a smile.

He held his own smile back, the trained features not moving. After a moment she became uncertain. The eyes lifted, doubt crept in. Then Zack let his lips relax, turn slightly at the corners.

"Oh, Zack…" She fell against him, hands flying around his neck. "Zack, please don't push me away. Please don't—"

His lips stopped the words. Her firm, perfect body came against him, pressed. It was a frenzied sort of kiss—like high-school kids at a tea-dance intermission. All slippery lips and reaching and seeking.

Zack held her tightly. His hands pulled and he knew the pressure was great, but he couldn't relax. It was hot and sweet and wild—and it scared him to death.

"No," he said, breaking away. She held tight. "Andy, don't. It's no good."

He thrust her away, walked to the end of the walk. His eyes burned. Lack of sleep. Lack of conscience. Lack of lack. She came up quietly.

"That's not the answer, Zack. It was good." Her arm slid inside his, gripped his bicep. Her head touched his shoulder lightly. "You know it was. Why won't you let yourself go with me? Why, Zack? Is it me?"

"Let it go, Andy."

"I won't. That's not any good either. Both of us hurting. What good is that?"

"Stop, I said. I mean stop."

He pulled his arm loose.

"Zack, don't do this."

"Listen," he said. "You're a nice girl. A young, pretty, healthy, bright girl. You expect a lot from life. And you should. All the good things, the regular things. Well, I can't give them to you, so forget it. You hear? Just forget it and don't let it get messy again."

Her eyes searched his face. Her black hair blew in the breeze, whipping tendrils across her face.

"All right, Zack. No mess. I promise."

Zack turned to the rail, gripped it. His muscles cracked with strain, but none of it showed. He stood, head back, feeling the wind on his heated face. Andy moved beside him. Both stood quietly.

And it was quiet. The lanterns in the Coys' backyard blinked out as they watched. The house lights were still lit. The hotel was dark above them. No activity there, either. It was very late.

"Now can I have a cigarette?"

Her voice sounded very loud. He got cigarettes out, lit for both of them. Andy slumped against the rail, back turned to it. He watched the water where nothing at all was happening, and she watched his face where nothing at all was happening.

"Don't be mad, Zack. I don't want that. It was such a wizard evening. So exciting and everything. And then I have to goof again. I'm sorry, and I'll apologize to—that girl. I will. I promise."

"Okay, Andy. Okay. Now let it go."

She nodded. The coal of her cigarette glowed. She blew on it, waved it in the air, drawing squiggles and circles and red zig-zag lines. Like time exposures of a freeway at night. Zack smoked in silence.

"Why did she say that, Zack? Pam Jardin. Doesn't she like Marie?"

"Does anyone?"

"No. I guess not. Unless—no, I guess not."

He turned, leaned beside her. His collar had begun to chafe, so he tugged it open, spread the tie. Andy was still in costume, bare-armed and without stockings. Zack realized that she must be chilly in the lake breeze. He took off his coat.

"Here. Put this on. Put it on."

She did, allowing him to drape it over her shoulders. Then she took the heavy bundle of her hair and flipped it out over the collar in a gesture so feminine Zack almost grabbed her, crushed her to him. He didn't. Instead, he smoothed the coat across her shoulders, stepped back. She looked at him obliquely.

"Okay," she said. "So I ain't neat. But what about Pam? Why did she say that about Marie? Marie hasn't done anything to her. And from what I hear, she has reason."

"She has reason? How about Johnny? Does he have reason?"

Andy shrugged. "Sure. I guess. Anyway, this Pam should know better. Johnny wouldn't leave Marie for a movie star. She pushes him. He's a big nothing and he knows it. Marie is his engine and I wouldn't be surprised but what he loves her, too. So what's Pam got to gain by playing house with Johnny?"

"A future," Zack said. "A future with some recognition and a little simple dignity."

He told Andy about Pam. About the dream of success, the deal with Johnny for the Miami spot. He tried to tell her about the girl's eyes, how they looked—like those of a slaughterhouse steer about to be butchered, and yet compassionate. In order to tell it all, he had to include the incident in Pam Jardin's room his first night at Conaghton. Andy listened without comment.

"So you see what Marie's edict did to Pam. She's fired and she loses the big chance at the Miami hotel. At least, she thinks it's the big chance."

"She's terrible," Andy said. "That Marie. Just terrible. I wish—"

"What?"

She smiled, looked down. "Nothing. I heard the story about— I mean, Frank told me that ..."

She trailed off, eyes lifting to his. The grooves at her eye corners were shadowed; the shifting blue, accentuated by stage make-up, was wet and shiny.

Zack took a breath. "About the island today. About me and Marie. All right, so he told you. What's it to you?"

She didn't move. Then her eyelids dropped and she turned away slowly.

"Nothing," she said. "Nothing. You're right. Why don't—" She stopped, lifted her head, looking out into the dark beyond the boardwalk. "What's that?"

"What?" He looked with her.

"There. See? By the Coys' dock. Looks like a—"

He grunted. "Just a blotch of white."

"Looks like a dress. Someone's down there."

"Well, what's wrong with that? We're up here."

It was very dark and the figure was very hard to see. Whoever it was seemed to be alone. Zack slitted his eyes remembering the lessons taught by war. The image was no clearer. There just wasn't light enough down there. He started to turn when they heard a cry—like the squawk of a crow, suddenly stilled.

"Zack ..."

"Shh—I heard it."

He leaned forward, eyes straining. A shot rang out, snapping in the night air. A blob of orange gleamed where the figure had been. Zack tensed. Three more shots sounded, the flashes making an almost continuous red flare.

Then silence.

He pushed the girl's hand off his arm, stood high on tiptoes. It looked like—yes, a figure running down the beach, in their direction. So damned dark! Zack tried to see, to pick out a distinguishing characteristic, but he couldn't tell if it were man, woman or beast. There was a gleam, like moonlight on skin, or blonde hair, or a shirt front—moving, bobbing.

He cursed, whirled away from the railing and ran down the steps to the grass pier. Andy called after him. He ignored her, ran around the end of the boardwalk, ducked under the last stanchion, and hit the rocky beach that wound tortuously to the Coys' dock, about a hundred yards from the end of the walk. A hundred yards. All of it abutting hilly, bushy shoreline. Plenty of cover.

"Zack, wait ..."

He looked back. The girl was right behind him; she must have followed his path, there was no other way to the beach save around the hotel grounds.

He moved swiftly, knees flexing, toes turned in to lessen sound. His eyes covered the terrain as he approached the Coy dock. But he saw no one. Nothing moved. There was no sound save his own ragged breathing and the scrape of his shoes on shale. Then he saw the looming shape of the Coy house on his right. One light was lit, upstairs. He could see no one. He ran to the dock, looked around. One of the boats—an inboard runabout—was drifting, its painter trailing in the water. Someone had untied it, let it go.

Andy came up breathless. "Zack, what is it?"

He shook his head, motioned for her to be quiet. He stepped to the dock, walked out. Then he kneeled and reached out for the trailing rope. His body stretched and he finally got reaching fingers on the slippery thing. He gripped it, pulled; the boat slid toward the dock-bumpers.

Andy screamed.

Zack dropped the rope, scrambled down the dock. The girl was standing on the shore, staring at the shadowed ground. Her face was white and one hand covered her mouth.

"Andy, what is it? What is it?"

She pointed, eyes staring. He followed the direction of her point, saw the body.

Half under the dock, half in the water.

It was Marie Kinchloe. Her white dress was muddy and torn; one hand had dug splinters out of the side of the dock. Her head and shoulders were in water, the blonde hair swirling against the black.

"My God!"

He moved quickly to Andy, shook her hard.

"Andy. Snap out of it. Turn your head. Now listen to me. We have—"

"Zack, see if she's—" She shuddered. "Look at her, don't stand there! I'm all right."

She turned away. Zack moved carefully, avoiding the soft mud near the water's edge. He stepped up on the dock, knelt there. He put his hand down, touched the hand that had torn at the dock. The nails were broken, the flesh torn and bloody. He felt for pulse; there was none. He leaned closer and just then the moon slid out from behind clouds, pale light spilling over the body.

There were three black holes in the woman's back.

He dropped the limp hand, looked around. No alarm yet. Andy hadn't moved. He looked at the Coy house; they should have heard the shots. Nothing stirred there, either. He went to Andy, put his arms around her.

"Is she ..."

He nodded. "Yes. She's dead. Someone shot her. Now, listen, Andy. Listen careful. We have to get out of here. Right now. We have to run and get far enough away so someone else will find the body. I can't—"

"Zack! You've got to call the police. You've got to."

"Andy, I can't." He stopped, lifted her chin. His heart was hammering and he knew it wouldn't be long until someone came. "Listen, I can't. I'm in trouble, Andy. Remember when I first came? When you saw the blood on my handkerchief? And you said that day on the pier—remember? Andy, listen, we have to go."

She fell against him, burrowing her face in his chest. His coat had slipped off her shoulders and he pulled it up, soothed her. She began to cry and he tried to pull her into motion. She shook her head against him.

"No, Zack. We can't run from it."

"Andy. Will you listen to reason? I'm in trouble. I can't stand a lot of questioning and that's what'll happen if we—"

A light hit them, a bright, glaring beam. Zack froze. The light pinned them from the hill.

A voice said, "Hold it down there! Don't move. Don't move at all."

Zack recognized the voice.

It was Sheriff Jim Sick.

CHAPTER TWELVE

It was pretty confused. Burris McCord and Jim Sick tied up the area like an atomic testing ground. McCord came moments after Sick had pinned Andy and Zack in his hand spot. Everybody talked at once. Except Zack. He was feeling much too deeply to talk. Now the whole thing would come out. The mess in Washington, the lie about his service record—probably jail at the end. Not for long, perhaps. But to a man like Zack Webster, always his own man, the thought of being locked up for whatever length of time was abhorrent.

Andy took the burden. She explained the latter part of the evening to Jim Sick, told about the meeting with Pam, the talk on the boardwalk, hearing the shots.

By eight in the morning all the people who'd been at the party the night before were gathered in the Coy living room. All except Softy Malebar. He couldn't be found.

Johnny Kinchloe, hollow-eyed and wilted, in a dressing gown and pajamas. He couldn't realize his wife was dead, kept saying, "It can't be, it can't be ..."

It was. Marie had been packed into the usual wicker basket, carried to the black coroner's panel truck for the trip to the laboratory in Plumton, forty miles distant.

Pam Jardin, hair mussed and wearing no make-up, smoking quietly by herself in the corner of the big living room. Zack caught her eye and she smiled wearily, shrugged with fatalistic acceptance.

Dale and Carol Normer, the guy pallid beneath his tan, fully dressed; his wife tousled and sulky, blonde hair hanging loose over a blue quilted housecoat. She kept shooting burning glances at Zack. He didn't know what for.

Tom Brulliard came, made enough noise to quell a riot in talking the sheriff out of bringing in his daughter, Gwen.

Samson and Karen were there, both dressed and chafing at the invasion, the crowd trampling the grass outside trying to get a glimpse of the roped-off area where the body had been.

Bisto, in jeans and sneakers and a wool sweater, smiling vaguely, hands smoothing, smoothing at his hair. His eyes stayed on Karen, drifted now and then to Zack.

Andy had gone to sleep against Zack's shoulder, the emotional spending finally wearing down the tiny frame, the courageous spirit. Zack looked down. Her face, now almost clean of the make-up, twisted in troubled sleep. He remembered the way she'd flown at big Malebar for grabbing him. Too bad he was in no position to …

He brought his attention back to the room. Jim Sick was talking to a technician at the front door. A thin deputy in a whipcord uniform, shotgun cradled in his arms, stood by the kitchen doorway. Morning sun pushed at the line of front windows facing the lake.

It would be a pretty day.

Sick turned, raised his hands. The murmur in the room ceased.

"Listen, now," the sheriff said. His square body was still draped in the ill-fitting suit he'd worn to the party. But now a gun bulged, one side of the coat. "We don't want to keep you here all day. But you know we got to find out what happened. That's our job. We aim to try, anyway, and if you'll help we'll get it over soon."

Samson Coy said, "Soon isn't good enough, Jim. Not near good enough." He got up from the kitchen chair next to his wife, walked to the sheriff. "I have a business to run, you know that. All of us have things to do. You can't keep us tied up all day."

"Now simmer down, Samson," Jim Sick said. "We can arrest all of you and we will if we have to. By God, this is the first murder in Plum County since 1936. And that was just a neighbor shooting the fella next door. We have to wrap this up and do it quick, and we'll do anything we have to, to do it."

Coy's face hardened for an instant. Then he nodded shortly.

Sick and Burris McCord pulled a table into the hall, interrogated each of them in turn. They spent a long time on Johnny Kinchloe; he was the first and the natural suspect. That is, Sick spent a long time on him. Zack could hear the stocky man's voice, Kinchloe's high-pitched answers.

The remaining suspects were quiet, trying to hear and trying not to appear to be trying. Zack woke Andy, gave her a cigarette. They waited, huddled together. It would be his turn soon. When it came, he was as good as in jail.

"Zack … did they find out anything? Did I miss anything?"

"No," he said, scaling his voice down. "They're talking to Johnny Kinchloe."

"Do you think he'd—Zack, he wouldn't. He was crazy about that woman."

"Sure. And sometimes that's plenty of reason for murder. Especially when it's a woman like Marie. She gave him motive enough."

Andy's young brow furrowed. "No," she said, speaking slowly. "Not even with all her—her philandering. Johnny needed her too badly. Not as a wife—in the business. He knew how much her drive did for him. He wouldn't do it."

"Maybe not. But in a murder investigation the first thing you look for is the means. How it was done. Then you try to fit that to motive and then to opportunity. Johnny's got motive."

"Have they found the gun?"

He shrugged, took the half-smoked cigarette from her and stuck it in his own lips. There was no lipstick on it, but somehow it still tasted faintly sweet.

Sick's voice raised. "All right, Johnny. That's all. You go on to work. If we need you, we'll call."

Johnny said something. Sick said, "Don't worry about it. If we have any luck at all, someone's gonna get arrested right soon." He raised his voice, this time on purpose. "Right soon."

"Zack, what will this mean to you?" Andy asked, whispering the words. "Are you—I mean, will it hurt you bad?"

"Bad enough. If they drag the investigation out, dig around in everybody's life, then I'm in trouble. Not real bad trouble—but trouble. Forget it, Andy. What you don't know can't hurt you. And they'll be talking to you soon."

"Maybe they'll find out who did it quickly. They know you didn't. I can prove that. Why should they investigate you?"

"They will. This is a hot potato to Jim Sick. This isn't murder country; nobody knows what to do. So they'll touch all the bases, pull out all the stops. I've seen it a dozen times. And they'll be looking real hard for someone to hang it on, someone to put the cuffs on to take the heat off them."

"But they wouldn't arrest you," the girl said. She turned on the small couch, gripped his arm. "They have to believe me. You were with me when we heard the shots."

"Yes, Andy. But I'm a stranger. Alone. Everyone else here his friends, business acquaintances—I'm automatically suspect. And if they're really stuck for someone to pinch ..." He shrugged.

"Why, that's monstrous," Andy said. "I don't believe it." She was quiet a moment, then said. "Anyway, maybe they'll find out who did it."

"Maybe."

But Zack had no confidence in Jim Sick's detective ability. And Burris McCord was a joke. Thinking of the special officer narrowed Zack's eyes as an uncomfortable thought struck him. He'd thrown the man into the lake. McCord would not be likely to forget that. Whether or not Jim Sick would expose Zack Webster as a warrant-dodger, McCord would make it uncomfortable for him.

Samson Coy caught Zack's eye. "Webster," the blond man said, pitching his voice low. "What did she—Marie—what did she mean I didn't have a chance for the job? Is it already set? This changes things, doesn't it? I mean, if she was the choice..."

Zack looked at the man. A repugnance he couldn't keep down twisted his lips. This man was sick. A beautiful woman dead, cooling flesh that just hours before had been desired and wanted—and this fish of a man concerned himself with what he could make out of the situation.

Coy's cold eyes stayed on Zack. He waited, hands rubbing, feet jittering. Zack regretted at that moment that he was not a Landworth representative, as Coy believed. What pleasure it would be to destroy this man's eagerness, deflate his hope. Instead, Zack leaned forward, spoke in a voice calculated to be heard throughout the room.

"I'd go a little slow on that tack, Sam," he said. "If that's the case, then you have pretty damned good reason for wanting Marie Kinchloe out of the way. And in case you've forgotten, what they're investigating here is a murder."

Coy sat back. "Why, don't be silly. I'm simply—"

His wife got up abruptly, walked to the window. Bisto started to follow, thought better of it. Coy's eyes followed his wife. Tom Brulliard cursed in a low tone.

"What's the matter with you people?" Coy asked. "She's dead, isn't she? Are we expected to tear our shirts and heap dirt on our heads? Not me. I'm worried about Samson Coy and if I can take advantage of her death I'm going to."

Jim Sick said from the doorway, "Is that right, Samson? Are you going to take advantage of Marie Kinchloe's death?"

Coy stared at the officer for a moment. His face lost color and he licked his thin lips. He shook his head, looked down.

Karen Coy said, "Jim, I can't stand this. I'm going upstairs and lie down. You can arrest me if you like."

She walked past the deputy into the hall. Burris McCord's voice came through the doorway.

"Just a minute, there, Mrs. Coy. You can't go noplace without permission. You get back in there."

Sick turned. "Shut up, Burris. Let her go." One square hand rubbed the top of his head. His bulky shoulders twisted the wrinkled suit coat. "Go ahead, Karen. Don't go out and don't make any phone calls—please."

McCord murmured something and Sick shouted at him to shut up. He turned, slouched against the doorway. His eyes, which ordinarily held a shallow smile ready to blossom out if given the slightest opportunity, were secretive now. The brows jutted and the lids half-concealed expression.

"Well," he said. "That's one down, folks. And we're no farther along. All we know for sure is Marie is dead. I let Johnny go home because he needs to work right now, keep busy. I might as well tell you Johnny didn't kill her. I know some of you been thinking that. He had reason, God knows. But he didn't do it. We—the law is satisfied to that. Somebody, though … somebody knows who did."

His hooded eyes moved around the room. Dale and Carol Normer; Tom Brulliard, slumped and motionless; Coy, head hanging, shoulders sagging; Bisto, smiling, smiling; Zack, hard-faced and erect; Andy, drawn and theatrical in the costume and traces of make-up; Frank Bonino, handsome and sulking in his corner.

Sick looked them over deliberately, eyes lingering on each face. It got very quiet. Outside, there was no sound except the occasional harshness of a voice from down by the water. A radio played very softly in the kitchen, the sound drifting in snatches to the taut living room. Sick nodded suddenly, turned away.

"Coy," he said over his shoulder.

Samson Coy got up slowly, eyes down. He smoothed his pale hair, fussed with the knot in his tie. He straightened, stalked to the door.

Andy said, "Zack, who did it? Do you think they know?"

"I don't know, kid. I don't have any idea. Almost anyone could have, I guess. She wasn't particularly lovable. Anyone could have—except you and me."

"Don't joke about it," Andy said sharply. "It's not funny. She was young and beautiful—everything to live for. So she wasn't nice, so what? She had a right to live and nobody can talk around that. It's not right and it never will be for one person to take a life."

Zack took the girl's chin in his hand, tilted her head. Her eyes were smoky, the grooves deep in the morning light. A very good-looking kid, Andrea Manning.

She put a hand over his. "Zack..."

"I wasn't kidding, Andy," he said softly. "We heard the shots, practically saw the thing being done. I wouldn't joke about anybody's death. I've seen too much of it. Too much blood and waste—sickness and suffering. Half my life has been spent with dead and dying—Italy, Germany, Korea. I respect the human right to live more than you could know."

"I'm sorry, Zack. But I don't know anything about you. You won't let me..."

"I will," he said. "You wait, I will. But I meant it about who killed Marie. I don't know. I only know it wasn't you or me. And it couldn't have been Pam Jardin. Anyone else could have. Anyone at all."

"Not Pam? Why, Zack? She had reason—"

He put a finger over her lips, frowned at her. "Never mind. It wasn't Pam. Couldn't have been. When they ask you what happened, tell them everything, just like it happened. Don't try to slant the story. And don't sign anything unless you're absolutely sure it represents what you have to say."

"All right, Zack. Whatever you say."

A hand touched Zack's shoulder, pulling him roughly. Burris McCord said, "Your turn, slicker. Get up out o' there and let's go talk. This one I'm gonna enjoy. Yessir ..."

The paunchy officer stepped back, one hand on his gun. His odd face was twisted with obvious relish. His belly, swelling over the pistol belt, bobbed with repressed mirth.

"Come on, hotshot ..."

Andy felt the tightening in Zack, the drawing up. She held him, whispered, "Zack, be careful. Don't let him get you angry. Please ..."

Zack nodded. He got up slowly, stretching to full height, looking down at the officer. His mouth felt dry and the burn in his eyes was from more than lack of sleep. He had to be careful; Andy was right. The last time he'd felt like this his fists had torn up a planned existence, erased ten years of hard work. Wilson Agnew and Burris McCord were the same type—both insensitive, both without scruples, incapable of feeling for anyone except themselves. Agnew was a little smarter, a little deadlier, perhaps. But Zack would have to be careful. Careful, not of Burris McCord, but of Zack Webster.

Sick greeted him from behind the hall table he'd converted to a desk. "Sit down, Zack. Be with you in a minute."

There was a deputy outside the door, visible through the screen. Another sat on the steps leading upstairs, drinking coffee from a carton. There was none of the paraphernalia usually associated with a murder investigation. No recording secretary, no tape machine, no bespectacled police scientist measuring shoes and playing with plaster of Paris. Just a stocky man in a wrinkled suit—and the grim certainty hovering in the room that someone would pay for disturbing the tranquility of the Plum County Sheriff's Office.

Zack sat, fished a cigarette from his mashed pack. Last one. He crumpled the package, looked for a place to put it.

"Here," Sick said, shoving forward an ashtray. "Light?"

McCord stationed himself at Zack's right shoulder. Sick's eyes flicked to the special officer, back to Zack. He leaned back.

"Tell me what happened. Right from the mess with Male-bar."

"I told you already."

"Tell me again."

Zack told him. Just the way it happened. Except for the part about seeing the murderer. That could only get sticky. After all, what had he seen? Just a flash of white in the darkness, a moving blob of paleness, nothing more. He told about the shots, seeing the flame of the pistol, running to the dock.

"Where were you when Andy saw the body?"

"I was out on the stringer, about ten yards—fifteen. Looking the other way, opposite the side the body was on. I hadn't seen it until Andy pointed it out to me."

"What were you doing on the dock?"

"Well, I was trying to capture the boat. The line—"

Sick leaned forward. "Boat? What boat? What's this about a goddam boat?"

"I guess I forgot to tell you. A boat was loose. Coy's runabout, I guess. Small Ventnor, or something like that. It was loose. I tried to tie it up. I fished out the line, pulled it in, and that's when Andy screamed."

Sick looked at McCord. "Go down and tell Carny about the boat. When we went over that dock there wasn't any runabout there. Tell him that. Tell him I said to find it."

McCord said, "Jim, you better not take this feller too serious. I think him and that actress girl know more than they told us, anyway. I like this feller for the murder. I like him real goddam good!"

Zack sat without turning. He could feel the man's animosity even with his back turned. He smoked in silence. Sick watched his face as McCord ranted. Then he cut the paunchy man off with a wave.

"Do like I say, Burris. Now."

The man left, muttering.

"Don't like you much."

Zack expelled smoke, crushed his cigarette in the ashtray. "Don't like him much. Tell me something."

"If I can, Zack." His voice lowered. "I know you're much more experienced in this type of thing than I am. I'm counting on that. You hear?"

Zack nodded. "Yeah. You know about me, my background. But there's no need to bring it up, is there? I'm not important to the investigation."

Sick shrugged, settled back with an enigmatic expression on his face. He smiled a little.

"Well, never mind that," Zack said. "I want to know about Kinchloe. You said he was clean. "Why?"

"Alibi. Pretty good one. He took the Brulliard girl home, met Burris on the way back, walking. They walked to the hotel together, stood on the veranda for a while. They saw you and Andy on the boardwalk. And they were still talking when the shots sounded. That's how I got there so quick. My wife and I were having a bite in the café. Burris came, white as a ghost, said there was a gunfight at the Coys'." Sick grinned. "He thought it was Malebar come back to wipe you out. I think he kinda liked the idea."

"I wondered about that. How you got there so quick. How about Malebar? Wouldn't he fit this thing?"

"We'll get him. Right now we can't run him down. But we will. Right now what I'm interested in is finding someone who fits all the pieces. Someone..."

He trailed off, busied himself with a cigarette.

"I know," Zack said softly. "Someone to put in jail to take the heat off."

Sick's head came up. "You better hope so. Especially you. The longer it drags on, the worse it is for you. I'm not worried about no assault warrant from as far away as Washington. But in a murder investigation everything comes out. You know that. Unless—"

"Unless you find a real hot suspect right quick." Zack nodded. "Yeah. I know that. I'll help all I can. I got no choice."

McCord came back. He pushed his belly through the screen door, came into the room like Columbus must have stepped ashore on the New World. There was a malicious look of triumph in the watery eyes. He grinned a yellow-toothed grin at Zack, held up a canvas sack.

"Got something here, Jim. Got something they'd call a hot clue in the big city."

He grinned all over his pinched, flushed face.

"Well, don't stand there like an idiot. What is it?"

McCord's eyes stayed on Zack. He minced forward, laid the sack on the table.

"Gun," he said. "Four empties. Smells like it's just been fired. It's the murder weapon, all right." He pronounced it "weepon".

Sick opened the sack, spread the mouth of the canvas thing and peered in. McCord chortled behind him, still looking at Zack.

"The murder weapon, huh?" Sick used. "Well, that's what we need. Now we can do something. Where'd they find it, Burris. Who came up with it?"

"Bob Carny. He found it."

"Where?" The tone was sharp.

"In the boat. They found it drifting down around the south bend. They was just bringing it up when I went out to tell 'em about it. They found that there gun in the bottom of it."

Sick's eyes came up.

McCord laughed out loud. "The boat this slick son-of-a-bitch says he was trying to tie up."

CHAPTER THIRTEEN

McCord's happiness didn't last long. Zack pointed out that if they tried to make a case against him, the first thing they must do is impeach the positive testimony of Andrea Manning. Not an easy thing to do since she was a person of good character and reputation. Sick accepted it immediately; McCord groused a bit, but finally admitted that it would be difficult to get around.

"Plus which," Zack said, "I really have no solid motive, Jim. And that's always a prime stone in the structure of any capital crime. Also—" He turned to Burris McCord— "Jim says you and Johnny Kinchloe were on the veranda when the shots were fired. If you were, then you know damned well it couldn't have been me. Because there is no way you could miss seeing Miss Manning and me on the end of the boardwalk."

Sick looked at McCord. The special officer scowled, pushed his belly to the kitchen door.

"I need some coffee," he said.

"He knows it," Sick said. "Look, Zack, this gun changes things. You know that. Because if we put it in someone's possession, or get lucky enough to find some prints on it ..."

"How long will that goon take?"

"Hardy? Oh, about ten minutes. He's pretty good. That mobile laboratory is equipped to handle everything from ballistics to reaction tests for blood. He'll be back right quick."

"Good. Jim, I'll tell you what this looks like to me. I've been in several murder investigations, in one capacity or another. You get to recognize patterns. This one—well, it's not the usual murder for profit or murder for revenge. This looks to me like the spur-of-the-moment thing. You know, an overflowing of resentment, an argument. Blooey—somebody gets dead."

"How come? I mean, what makes you thank that?"

"Look at the physical facts. First, the weapon. A gun. Guns make noise, anyway you look at it. If you plan a crime that'll get you fried if you're caught, chances are you're going to try very hard to get away with it. You might think of poison, or drowning or—well, anything before a gun. Because the reports are going to be loud. Your time is necessarily short. Nobody would plan a murder that gave him seconds to get away."

"He might if there was no other way to do it. Maybe getting the person in the right place at the right time was impossible."

Zack shrugged. "That could be. Anything is possible. But to me it looks like a sudden flare-up, no planning, no premeditation."

Sick grinned. "Don't let the District Attorney hear you say that."

Zack settled back in the chair. His eyes burned. It had been quite a while since he'd slept. Jim Sick sat across from him, humming unconsciously, tapping a ballpoint pen on the table top.

"You know, Zack," he said softly. "I got an idea about this thing. A pretty good idea. I wouldn't be surprised if I wrapped it up today. You'd like that, wouldn't you? No hassle, no digging around in everybody's life."

"I'd like it. What's your idea?"

Sick shook his head. "Not now. We'll wait awhile. Something Kinchloe said …"

The ballpoint stopped. There was a commotion on the porch and Oswald Hardy came in carrying wet photo negatives.

"Got 'em, Jim."

Hardy was a tall redhead with very fair skin and a prominent Adam's-apple. He didn't look like a cop, thick glasses giving his pale blue eyes a very washed-out look, print shirt flopping over skinny-shouldered, thin arms. He looked at Zack, put the negatives behind him.

"How about this guy?"

"It's all right, Ozzie. What did you get? Don't tell me we got prints, I couldn't stand it."

"No prints," the redhead said. He pulled the dripping paper up where the deputy could see the front side. Zack caught a glimpse; a fingerprint in enlargement. "Smudges all over. Like over-grip on previously registered prints."

Sick's face fell. "Well, what the hell did you come in here spouting about we got 'em for? Goddam you, Ozzie—"

"Now, Jim. You wait. I said no clear prints. But we got one that's classifiable." He grinned, his milk-white face splitting away from yellow teeth. "Small one, like the rest of the smudges. A woman's, Jim ..."

Jim Sick leaned back in the chair. He swiveled, looked at Zack. "You're home free, Zack. Everybody goes home in ten minutes."

Zack said nothing.

Ozzie said, "You trace the gun, yet?"

"Don't have to. We—"

The screen door banged and Burris McCord bustled in followed by Johnny Kinchloe. The hotel manager looked weary, worn out—like a pale negative of a bad carbon copy. He'd changed his clothes, wore the light suit, white shirt and tie. His corn-colored hair was precisely combed. But the eyes were red-rimmed and dark underneath. His face sagged.

"Jim Sick, you listen to me," Burris McCord said importantly. "We got something for you." He pulled Kinchloe forward. "Go on, Johnny. Tell him."

The officer's eyes glittered with lethal malice and he shot a smug look at Zack.

"Well," Kinchloe said. "It's about the gun, Jim. I recognized the description Burris gave me. It sounds like mine."

"Yours?" Sick pushed the negative aside, motioned for Hardy to wait. "What do you mean, John? If you're playing games with me, so help me Christ..."

"No, no," Burris McCord said. "No games, Jim. None at all. This here gun is John's, all right. I seen it before, you see. So I thought I'd go see him about it, find out what he did with it. He told me he give it to that colored girl 'cause she was afraid walkin' around at night alone. And nobody'd go with her." His little eyes fastened on Zack, beady and malevolent. "That is, almost nobody."

"Go to hell, McCord," Zack said. "I saw the gun myself, Jim. You heard about the tussle Johnny and I had."

"I heard."

"Well, John boy pulled it on me that night. In the girl's room. I guess it was his, all right. But that doesn't prove the girl pulled the trigger. Why would she?"

Sick laughed. "Why? She was playing house with Kinchloe, wasn't she? And Marie made Johnny fire her. That's plenty of motive for a dinge. You know how they are—just any little thing sets them off."

"Oh, come on, Jim. You're too smart for that. What makes you think—"

"Who's running this here investigation, Sick?" Burris McCord asked. "You or this city slicker? Why you askin' him, anyway?"

Sick stood abruptly. "Shut up, Burris. I'm running things here. Long as I am, you keep your place or I'll break your jaw."

McCord's face drained and he backed to the wall. Hardy grinned. Johnny Kinchloe stood miserable and alone in the center of the room, fussed with his hair.

Hardy said, "About this print, Jim. Should we get all the women in and specimen the right index?"

Sick turned from the window. A thoughtful expression held the beefy features. "No," he said. "No need for that. Burris, bring in Pamela Jardin."

Zack stood up. His shirt felt too small. He put a hand on the table for balance.

"Jim, if you're through with me, I'd like to get out of here."

"Sit down. You said you'd help."

"But I have work to do tonight. Look, you don't need me. I'd just be in the way..."

Sick looked at him, began to smile deep in the clear, grey eyes. The smile got as far as the lower lip and stopped right there, making it clear that it wouldn't take much to turn it into a scowl. Zack nodded, pulled the chair away from the table. He straddled it, looked out the window. He heard the girl come in, felt her presence in the room.

Sick said, "Sit down, miss. We have a few questions. Routine. Just answer honestly and it won't take long."

The unction in his voice, the purring, gloating quality—Zack almost threw up. He stared out the window at a flowering bush, watched the morning breeze push it around. The buzz in the air wasn't in the air at all, it was in his head. He turned on the chair, faced the room.

"...and everyone is asked questions, you see?" Sick was saying. "Now, first—what's your name?"

Pam looked at Zack. She looked very young without the make-up, the professional slickness. He hair was drawn back severely, clipped at the nape of her neck. She was very simply dressed, no jewelry. She was very pretty. She smiled. Zack nodded at her, then had trouble stopping his head from bobbing. Her smile stiffened, slid off.

Sick said sharply, "Name?"

"Pamela Jenkins."

"Jenkins?"

"You asked my name. That's my name." The voice was low-pitched, crawling up out of the fear in her. Zack watched her eyes, saw the darting thing there, the slowly awakening knowledge that she was being fitted for a familiar role.

"Pamela Jenkins," she said again. "And I did not kill Marie Kinchloe."

"Answer when you're asked, dammit," Burris McCord said. Then to Hardy. "Got to keep these people straight. Walk all over you if you don't."

Sick said, "Shut up, Burris. Now, Pamela ... Would you mind going over your movements last night? Just from the time you left Mr. Webster and Miss Manning on the boardwalk."

The girl sat back in the chair. Her square shoulders slumped a little and her eyes flitted about the room. She turned to Zack.

"Zack ... they're trying to say I killed her, Zack. They're going to try."

Zack jumped up, spilling the chair. He stood there, not knowing what he wanted to do, knowing the only thing he could do was go along with Jim Sick. Or go back to Washington—back to jail; back to Fay Temple laughing in her elegant sleeve and peering down her elegant nose. He turned away.

Sick's voice went on, punctuated with the soft murmurs of answer from the girl. She told it straight. The meeting on the walk, the decision to walk around the shoreline instead of going around the hill to the backstairs and her room. She had stopped nowhere, met no one. She had been in bed when the deputy awakened her, brought her here.

Zack stood throughout the recital. He stood before the window, but he could not have told if someone had staged a war outside of it. His eyes were open, but he wasn't seeing.

"Now, Miss Jardin. Jenkins, excuse me." Sick's voice had taken on the creamy quality of a slick lawyer who knows he has a fool on the stand. "I have a gun here. A .38. Have you ever seen this gun before? Speak up, Miss Jenkins—have you ever seen this gun before?"

There was a silence. Then a commotion, the sound of running feet. Zack whirled and saw Johnny Kinchloe break past Burris McCord, stiff-arm Hardy and slam out the door.

Burris yelled, "Hey, stop him!"

"Let him go," Jim Sick said. He motioned to Hardy, turned back to the girl. "Answer the question, Pamela."

The girl had slumped in the chair now. Her face was shadowed. She bobbed her head.

"That's no answer. Say it in English. Did you or did you not see this gun before this morning?"

"Yes, yes, I saw the goddam gun!" Her head snapped up with the words, her eyes came alive. "I saw it, I had it—Johnny gave it to me, the gutless bastard! But I didn't kill Marie. I didn't kill Marie ..."

Zack stuck his hands into his pockets. His lids were burning again. He really needed sleep. That was it. Some sleep. That would do it. Then everything would be clearer. He fumbled for cigarettes, discovered he had none.

Sick said, "Now, Pamela ... isn't it true that you and Johnny Kinchloe were—well, didn't he visit your room on occasion?"

He settled back, satisfied with himself over the wording. The girl said nothing.

"Well, is it true or isn't it?"

"You know it's true," she said, barely getting the words out. "Everybody knows. Nothing new about that. I didn't kill Marie, whatever you say."

"I'm not saying you did, Pamela." Sick leaned forward, fiddled innocently with the ballpoint. "You know that print we took when you came in?" He looked up at Hardy; the redhead nodded. "What would you say if I told you it matched a clear print on the gun?"

Pamela sat without moving. Her long-fingered hands lay quietly in her lap. Her ankles twined under the chair, seemed to massage each other in the only manifestation of unrest the girl showed.

"What would you say?" Sick thundered, half-rising from the chair.

Pamela looked up. "I want to call a lawyer."

Sick sat slowly. "Now, wait, Miss Jar—Jenkins. We're just trying to get things straightened out here. That's all."

"You're just trying to railroad me," Pam said. She sat up a little. "Be nice to hang it on the spade broad, wouldn't it? No mess, nobody hurt that matters. Yeah, man. Be real nice." Her voice slurred and thickened the words. "You better get me a lawyer. You better let me call somebody because I'm not letting you railroad me. I'm—"

She broke. The strain ate at her courage, tore away the strength she'd husbanded through years of prejudice and indignity. She started crying soundlessly, not bowing her head. The great, brown eyes filled and overflowed, the good breasts rose and fell with sobs that should have been racking, but didn't make a sound.

Zack spoke, voice harsh in the loaded quiet. "Hardy. Was that print a grip position impression?"

That stopped everybody. Burris McCord stopped smiling at the sobbing girl; Sick looked up sharply. Hardy turned from the comparison cards he was examining in the light.

"What?"

"You heard me, Hardy." He stepped into the room, wiped his hands on the front of his trousers. "Was it a grip position impression?"

Sick turned to Hardy, his stocky figure tight and bunchy. His big jaw bulged. "What's he mean by that, Ozzie? Webster, what are you trying to pull?"

"Not pull, Jim. You asked for my help. Well, I want to know about that print."

Hardy looked at Sick, turned his thick glasses on Zack. He shook his head, mouth gaping. "No," he said. "It ain't. But how'd you know—"

"What the hell's going on?" Burris McCord asked.

"Wait, now," Jim Sick said. "Wait, here, now. Let's not let this thing get away. What the hell does that mean, Zack? Grip position—whatever it was? And it better be good."

His dark eyes held Zack's. There was no mistaking his immediate animosity. He had his mind made up. Pamela would do, and he would pin a quick conviction on his own chest, clean up the first murder case in Plum County in years. Zack knew he'd have to tread easy.

"Grip position," Zack said. "What it says. You grip a gun ready to fire. There's only a certain number of places you can leave prints. For instance, you wouldn't expect the thumbprint to be on the right side of the piece. It would be alongside the safety or against the shell housing. The forefinger imprint would ordinarily be on the trigger or trigger guard. What hand do you write with, Pam? Pam ..."

She looked at him, the wet eyes confused. The soft, susceptible look was back. Her lips trembled as she spoke. "Right hand, Zack," she whispered. "Oh, Zack ..."

Her eyes thanked him. He turned away. "All right. The grip position would be clear. Just as I've outlined. Middle, ring and little fingers could only be on the left of the grip, having wrapped around in shooting position. This print is a—what is it, Hardy?"

"Right ring," the redhead said reluctantly. He looked at Jim Sick, who had slumped in his chair, was watching Zack without movement.

"Okay," Zack said. "Right ring. Have to be lower half, left pistol grip-position impression. Right? Is that right, Hardy?"

Hardy nodded, turned away from Sick.

"Where did you lift this grease, Hardy? From where?"

The police scientist squirmed. His eyes, magnified by the thick glasses, shuttled. He said, "From the underside of the barrel."

It got real quiet. There was the sound of the radio, the murmur of far-away summer activity. Birds made a morning racket outside.

Sick said, "It doesn't figure." He looked at Zack. His eyes were dead. He turned to Pamela. "Don't let this stuff fool you, Miss Movie Star. You're hooked and hooked good. I'm going to prove you killed Marie Kinchloe. How do you like that?"

The girl didn't move. Her eyes flicked to Zack, back to her hands. Sick pushed the pen out where her eyes had to see it, flicked it slowly back and forth.

"You hear, missy? We burn 'em in this state. Two thousand volts. But you can stop all that if you cooperate. We'll make a good recommendation. You'll get off with life. Maybe second degree. What do you say?"

She said the same bad word she'd said to Dale Normer that night in the Lounge. Sick's head snapped back. Burris McCord slapped the girl from behind.

"Don't!" It was a roar and it came from Zack.

Everyone froze. The deputy on the door lifted his shotgun, peered through the mesh. Zack wet his lips. His fingernails dug into his palms.

"I mean ... that's no way to conduct an investigation. That's— that's no good, Jim."

Sick looked at him.

"I mean it. Don't hit her. She'll have grounds for claiming coercion. A smart lawyer will tear your case apart. Don't touch her."

McCord started cursing. "This here nigger-lover is worried about this woman so much, why don't we let him defend her?" The officer's belly shook and he fumbled with his holstered pistol. "Why don't you take her away, slicker? Why don't you? I'd like to shoot you, slicker, I swear to God I would."

Sick said, "Burris."

Zack didn't move. Hardy stood by the window, looking out. The kitchen radio got loud again.

Sick looked at Zack. He slumped in the chair, his cheeks pushed up, his lips moving in and out. Finally he sat up, breathed deeply, expelling a long breath.

"Carny," he barked.

The outside deputy came in, shotgun poised.

"Yeah, Jim?"

Sick's eyes stayed on Zack. He spoke quietly. "Take this girl to Plumton. Lock her up. Incommunicado. No visitors, no phone calls. Book her for investigation of first-degree murder."

"No!"

Pam stood, clutched her hands in front of her.

Zack stood taller.

"No visitors, no calls. Understand that, Carny?"

"Got it, Jim. Anything to tell Paul?"

"I'll see him. When I get some statements here. Leave the lab truck, the one patrol car and two men. Take everybody else. Go ahead."

The young deputy motioned to Pam, stood waiting by the door. She moved slowly, circling the long way around. She stopped in front of Zack. Her eyes came up to his and for a minute the life came back to them, the soft awareness.

She said, "Thanks, Zack. You tried."

"Let's go, lady," Carny said.

"Zack, don't hurt yourself," she said hurriedly, too low for the others to hear. "I'm all right, I'm used to it. Don't get yourself hurt, big man ..."

Burris McCord wrapped a hand around the girl's arm, jerked her roughly. Zack tensed. Sick's eyes were on him, dark and brooding. Burris laughed.

The quiet descended again when the girl had gone. Zack waited. He knew something was coming. He'd been too long in danger situations not to recognize the imminence. He waited; that was all he could do.

Sick straightened up finally. The deputy looked ill. His face had gone grey and the white of his eyes was almost eaten up by red streaks, flecks of orange. His lips were stiff and awkward.

"Burris, get out of here. You're done. You, too, Hardy. We'll talk to the others in a while. Get some coffee, take a smoke—but get out of here."

They left. Sick toyed with his pen, looked at Zack. Finally he motioned for him to take the seat across from him. Zack sat, kept his feet flat on the floor. He rested his hands on the table lightly, ready to use them for leverage or to tip the table if it was to be that bad.

"Webster, I made a mistake. I made a bad mistake. You see, I figured I had a case against that girl. And I figured you'd help because of the little squeeze I got on you. He's smart, I said. He'll go along, he'll show me how to tighten it, make it stick." His eyes got hard and dark, full of some fierce purpose. "That girl did it, Webster. She did it and I'm going to prove it."

Zack said, "Jim, you got no motive…"

He said it without much hope. He'd encountered this look before. The eager and almost passionate intensity of a man who sees the opening ahead, the big break.

Sick's voice was dull, without vigor—but deadly serious and exact. "I got motive. Marie fired her, ruined her chance at the Miami hotel job. Johnny spilled his guts, what did you expect? But the hell with that. I'll make the case. I'll make it and it'll stick, you hear, Webster? It'll stick!"

"Jim…"

"Shut up! I'm tired of being a two-bit sheriff in a two-bit town. This is big. How many big ones do we get? A whistle stop like this. I'm gonna take advantage of it, Webster. My advantage."

He sat back, tapped the pen against his teeth, the lips pulling away like two slabs of burnt leather. His eyes were wide open, but

all Zack could see were twin points of hard, diamond-like brilliance, far back in the dark.

"You stumble around in it, Webster, mess up my chance—I'll
send you back to Senator Wilson Agnew in shreds."

He waited, expression unchanging.

After a long moment, Zack nodded, dropped his head.

CHAPTER FOURTEEN

Now the week was full. Everything had happened that could be expected of one puny week, seven days. A husband grieved; one lump of clay was cold, no vibrance, no mystery—no breath of that which separates the quick from the dead.

Zack had watched them take Pam away in the black car with the huge, obscene sheriff's star on the side. Now he walked the back road, behind the hotel, away from the park; shady and sun-spattered through leaves, cool-smelling and just a little forest-moldy in the green tunnel. Once again walking. In shirt sleeves and beginning beard, face hard as polished oak. A little more tan, perhaps.

One week.

Jim Sick would question the rest of the people perfunctorily. He would let them go. Tom Brulliard, back to his boats, his mousy daughter—long of face, maybe, but happy that the option he'd been gulled out of would not be used now. Samson Coy, on a dead run for his books, his ledgers and expense sheets; annoyance at the business delay his main consideration. Cold fish, was Samson coy. Karen wasn't cold. She wasn't much of anything, accepting a half-man like Bisto in order to get out of a bed she'd made.

Dale Normer, skinny weakling, clinging to a woman much better than he deserved—Carol, wondering at the strange quirks brought out in people by violence and greed. Frank Bonino, handsome nothing—he would console Andy when she discovered that Zack would not be back. He thought about that. Never again to see the tilted eyes, the swirling mass of black hair, the stubborn jaw that grew so soft…

"No coat," Zack said. He kicked at a rut, moved slowly along. His eyes burned very badly now. Long time no sleep, kid. "No coat, no goddam cigarettes!"

He thought about the arrest of Pam Jardin and the way Sick had made it clear he meant to stick the girl. He could do it, too. She had everything against her. Hell, maybe she'd killed Marie. Maybe she had crept around in the dark after leaving the boardwalk, seen Marie by the dock, shot her.

And where did she get the gun? Shut up. What would Marie be doing at the dock, pray tell? Shut up, shut up!

Anybody could have done it. Anybody in the whole goddamned silly world—but not Pam Jardin. Not Pam of the chocolate skin, the dark hair, the black dress. Not her.

Because, Zack—you know why, Zack. Face it, Zack. You saw the killer, Zack. Killer and diller and all roads lead to Washington. First in peace, first in war and last in the American League.

It couldn't have been Pam.

A car horn blasted and Zack snapped erect. He'd been stumbling, half bent over, and he had almost walked out onto the Conaghton Highway. The car roared by, blaring horn sound diminishing. He looked around. He'd made it to the main road without thinking about direction. To the right he could see the park sign. The other way was the town of Conaghton, from where he'd started more than a week ago.

Full circle. He shook himself awake, took stock. Brooding would get him nothing. He had to leave, go on as he'd planned to do a week ago. But first he needed money. The check he had coming. He could go get it; Sick wouldn't bother him so long as he had Pam Jardin. But if he went to the office he might run into someone. Someone, hell—Andy. And he didn't want to see Andy.

He stood there in the strengthening sunlight, squinted down the highway. That way was the Sport Club.

He started walking. At least it was something to do.

It wasn't open yet. The neon sign was dead; the solid door closed, the screen door locked. No lights, no sign of life. Zack stood in the gravel, red-rimmed eyes searching the weathered roadhouse. No cars in the lot, either. He sighed. Weariness was a blanket, sneaking up on him. One time he had been able to go days without sleep, without food, sustained by the excitement of whatever chase he was involved in. But this wasn't Italy or France. This was Conaghton and he was tired.

He walked around the building, treading softly. More parking space, no doors. At the back he found an entrance. It was locked. There was a small shed jutting out of the building's rear. Store room—loaded with cases of beer, boxes of this and that, pieces of tables. He tested the door, found that the spring lock was an old type. He got a card from his wallet, slid it through the crack and had the door open in no time. Inside, he stumbled around a stack of cases, cleared a space against the wall and lay down. The ground was cold, but he was asleep before that fact registered.

He woke slowly, numbed by cold and stiff from contact with hard ground. At first he had no idea where he was. Then it came back to him. He lay unmoving, eyes opening slowly, accustoming themselves to the gloom in the shed. He remembered now. Pam Jardin and Marie and the whole stinking mess. He started to turn, caught a movement out of the corner of his eyes. He froze, crouched on the cold earth.

"Hi."

He looked up. Andy Manning sat on a beer case against the back wall. Her eyes were shadowed. His coat lay across her lap. She'd been home; her clothes were different.

Zack sat up, rubbed at his face. It felt stiff. His beard scratched. He looked down at himself. A real mess. The white shirt was dirt-streaked; his trousers looked like they'd never seen a press. The shoes were all messed up again. He leaned back against the stack of beer cases, closed his eyes.

"Cigarette," he said, croaking it.

He heard a soft rustle, smelled the clean linen-and-soap odor, felt Andy bending over him. He kept his eyes tight shut.

"Here," she said, stuck a cigarette into his lips.

The smoke made him giddy. He puffed in silence for a while. Andy went back to her seat, sat quietly.

"How'd you find me?"

"Bartender called me about noon. He came out for beer, found you."

"What time is it now?"

Pause. Color scrambled on closed lids.

"After three," Andy said. "What are you doing, Zack? Why are you running?"

His eyes opened slowly; he turned his head. "What did you say?"

"Why are you running, I said. You heard me."

He snapped the cigarette against the wall of the shed, showering sparks. He rose, tall and lithe, no longer stiff from floor-sleeping. He flexed his fingers.

"How long you been here?" he asked, not facing her.

"Since twelve-thirty."

"You sleep?"

"I tried. I'm all right."

"What are you doing here? Why don't you stay where you belong?"

Silence ... stretching.

He whirled on her, face twisted, chest full of breath and the hot, hot feeling inside. She sat. Her chin came up. He swallowed the words he'd had ready, the blasting words that he could take care of himself, didn't need a nurse, didn't want anyone running after him. Her eyes were wide, strangely bright, fixed on him with unblinking concentration.

"Why don't you—Andy, why don't you—"

He stopped, not sure what he wanted to say. Not sure of anything anymore. Where was the strong Zack Webster who fearlessly followed leads, jousted with Senators, vied with the top political minds of the country? Where was he?

She said, "I just brought your coat, Zack."

He snatched the offered garment, rushed out of the shed.

The sunlight clawed at his senses, battered him. He was breathing hard. There was a weight in his chest and the sleep hadn't helped the burn in his eyes. The highway stretched and Zack pushed along it. He pumped his legs, thinking about the act of walking, feeling the sweat start and liking it, the feel of hot wind on his face. He came to the park sign, turned down the blacktop toward the beach. He walked. The sweat streamed down. Head wasn't working right. Something he had to do. What was it?

The convertible glided up alongside of him, kept pace. Andy sat at the wheel, eyes straight ahead. He glanced at her, increased his speed. The car came up even with him, stayed there. He stopped. The car stopped.

Andy said, "It's too hot to walk. We're going the same way."

Zack walked to the car, leaned his forearms on the door.

"How do you know we are?" he asked, the words coming out like unused things, rough and without texture. "How the hell do you know?"

She turned away. "Get in if you want a ride."

"If I don't you'll tag me, eh? Drive alongside, make it look real nice? Why don't you leave me alone?"

She bit her lip. For a minute he thought she would drive away. But she didn't. The firm little chin came up, the fine eyes squinted a bit. She sat.

He tore open the door, flopped on the seat, slammed the heavy door behind him. She eased the car in gear, started off.

The air felt good. He leaned back on the leather, closed his eyes. He could smell her even with the motion and the sun and the scent of trees and water. It was clean and sharp—and just Andy.

"Zack, what's—"

Her hand touched his arm, went away quickly. He opened his eyes.

"I'm sorry," she said. "Where do you want to go?"

He sat up, pulled his coat up off the floor. He watched her as she drove. Her face was expressionless, jaw set. She wore a sand-colored dress that hugged her petite figure. Her hair hung down her back, a black mass, curling and tendriling.

"How did you get Frank Bonino's car? Borrow it?"

She turned down the beach road, slowed approaching the Pavilion.

"It's not Frank's car," she said. "It's mine."

"Yours?"

She looked at him. "Why should you be surprised? You don't know anything about me. You don't know anything about anybody."

They came to Brulliard's and she pulled into the parking area near the stairs leading down to the dock. Zack got out of the car, slung his coat over his shoulder.

"Thanks for the lift," he said.

She didn't bother to answer; just turned off the ignition, slumped down in the seat.

And that's where she was when he came back up the steps. He went right by the car, face set. He'd taken off the soiled shirt, washed, donned a clean tee shirt. He carried his coat, pockets stuffed with toilet articles.

The park was packed. Sweating parents and squealing kids, fat ladies in pastel-colored slacks and sunburned men looking uncomfortable in bright shirts. Zack pushed into the Day-Night, went behind the counter and got a hamburger the day man was grilling for one of the milling customers, made his way back outside.

It was hot out here, too. He rubbed his chin on his shoulder, catching sweat, looked for the red convertible. It was still there, but Andy was gone. He ate the hamburger, realizing how long he'd denied himself food. He rejected fighting the crowd for another, got a drink at the public fountain and went upstairs to the offices of Conaghton Enterprises—M.L. Kinchloe, Mgr.

M.L. Kinchloe had gone from Mgr. to D.O.A. He felt a quick catch at his stomach, seeing the office in the corner, the familiar desk, empty now. Gwen Brulliard was there alone. Zack was thankful for that. He didn't feel up to Samson Coy.

"Gwen."

The girl looked up, quick fright leaping into her liquid eyes at the sound of his voice. What a mouse she was. He smiled a little.

"Hi, there. Can a guy get paid around here? I'm the brokest man in Pennsylvania."

The girl came to the long counter, looked into a drawer, extracted an envelope. Her eyes, when she looked at him, were reproachful. He felt awkward, ill at ease—as if he had done something to this girl that he should apologize for.

"Terrible about Marie," he said.

"Sign the slip," she said. "You don't care about Marie. You never did. You're like all the rest."

"You liked her, didn't you, Gwen? Marie? You thought she was something."

The pinched face was suddenly pained. "She was good. Good and pretty and smart. She didn't need someone doling out nickels to her, telling her how to spend her time." She turned back. "Sign the slip."

Zack signed. The girl stood without moving as he took the cash from the envelope, counted it. Ninety-two dollars. One week. Quite a week.

"They arrested that colored girl," Gwen said suddenly. Her eyes took on life. "I hope they hang her. Hang her high and let her dangle so people can spit on her. Decent people. She's lucky she's not down south."

Zack turned. "Is she?"

"Yes," the girl said, raising her voice. "And you're lucky, too. You're lucky Johnny Kinchloe doesn't take you and—"

She stopped abruptly. Zack turned and the girl had one hand over her mouth, eyes wide.

"Go on, Gwen. Lucky Johnny Kinchloe doesn't do what to me?"

She shook her head, hair bun bobbing. Zack went back, looked at the girl until she turned away. Her shoulders shook.

"Gwen..." Zack went around the counter, took the girl's shoulders. "Gwen, listen. Your hair is long, isn't it? When you don't have that silly bun? Long and dark, isn't it?"

She began to sob.

"Was that you in the boat, Gwen? Did you follow us to Cone Island, listen at the hole? You did, Gwen, didn't you?" He shook her. "Didn't you?"

She turned against him, crying heavily. "Yes," she sobbed. "I did, I did! She was so beautiful. So pretty and everybody wanted her. All the men panting—all the..." She gulped, rubbed her face on his chest. "I just wanted to see what it was like. Just to see ... that's all."

Zack held her clumsily. She cried on his chest, thin arms clutching his neck. He waited until she quieted a little.

Then he said, "You heard us talking, didn't you?"

She nodded, sniffled.

"You heard Marie say she was going to leave Johnny, go with Malebar?"

"I heard. But I didn't care about the—about my father's land. He's an old fool! For years he didn't care about us. Now he wants to be a father. I didn't care!"

"But you heard. And you told Tom, your father..."

She shook her head, held him more tightly. Her face lifted and the sun glare from the lake through the window caught tear streaks, slicked them. Her thin lips trembled.

"Mr. Webster, I'm afraid. I'm afraid..."

"Why should you be afraid? The girl, Pam, killed Marie. You said so. The police think so. What's to be afraid of?"

"I don't know. But I didn't tell my father—I told Burris McCord. I wanted him to hurt you. I wanted—"

Zack dropped his hands. Burris McCord. He pulled away from the girl, got a cigarette out of his pants pocket. The package was crushed.

"Look, don't tell me about it, it's none of my business. You understand?" He scratched a match, missing the sand-strip repeatedly. "Tell the police, not me. Tell Jim Sick."

Her shoulders slumped and she sat in a chair, rested her head on one hand.

Zack twisted away, picked up his coat and started for the stairs. The girl called after him. He went down two steps at a time, running from the high-pitched voice.

There was another voice, the one in his head.

He'd have to do something about that one.. . .

CHAPTER FIFTEEN

One little, two little, three little whiskies … four little, some little, many little whiskies. The tune went on. Nobody heard it but Zack and he wasn't sharing it. He looked around the Gableton Lounge, a crafty gleam in his eye. Nobody heard it; they heard the jukebox. Rock with me, Murgatroyd. He snickered, covered it with his hand. Rube, the bartender, stood in front of him.

"Whatta you want?"

"Mr. Webster," the bald man said hesitantly. "You're getting pretty rocky, you know."

"Whose business is that? Yours? Naah … gimme a drink."

The bartender pulled down on his pretty jacket, his chins came up, all of them. "No, sir," he said.

It was funny. Rube the Samaritan. He snickered again, drained his drink. All wet there on the bar. He picked money carefully out of the moisture.

"Y' oughta wipe the bar," he said.

He stood, waited for his legs to know he was using them. He blinked; the gold light softened everything too much. Fella couldn't see, hardly. There was something he was forgetting—what was it? Andy? Yeah. Right there, in the front booth. Still hanging around, still looking smug. What's she got to be smug about? What? Huh, what?

He walked to the booth, bent down to the girl. His breath drove her back a little. He steadied himself on the booth.

"What makes you such a smug? Huh? What makes a such …" He lost it, straightened suddenly. "Aah, hell with it."

He stopped in the lobby. He wanted to see Johnny Kinchloe. Where was little Johnny? Here, Johnny … He looked around, but no Kinchloe. Why did he want to see him? What for? The hell with that, too.

He went outside into the warm Pennsylvania night.

The alcohol really had him. With just a mild bun on, or even pretty drunk but in control of himself, Zack would never have let the men walk right up on him. When they got out of the car—a shining, black car—an alarm began deep in his mind. But the whiskey had too good a hold. He knew there was something he should do, but he couldn't snap, couldn't function. One walked up to him; the other circled a little on the wide veranda.

"Mr. Webster?"

Zack started to turn and the other man caught his arm, moved him gently but positively down the steps, across the drive and into the car. His mind struggled to shake the fog.

"What's this? What's going on?"

They put him in the front seat; one got in back, the other drove. The one in back sat directly behind Zack. He could see no gun. There had been no threat. But he knew a ride when he took one—and this was expert and professional. He knew where he was going, even though neither of the dapper men would say a word all the way around the lake.

Zack opened the wind wing, stuck his face into the rush of air. The fog receded some. He gulped night air, mind racing again. He made a gurgling noise, felt the car slacken speed.

He mumbled, " 'M sick …" He pushed his head out the side window, lolling it on the metal sill. The wind whipped sweat off his brow, brought tears to his eyes. He turned his head on the sill, looked back.

His pulse jumped. There it was. A hundred yards behind, out of sight now around a curve. But she was back there, pushing the little Ford for all it was worth to keep up with the Lincoln.

He pulled in his head, sat quietly. He closed his eyes—because the wind had brought tears, of course. He set his teeth, willing himself to sober up. And all he could think of was the gutty little girl in the red Ford who wouldn't ever give up on anything she believed in. Not ever.

They didn't go to the Ship. That was a surprise. Zack had been expecting to see Malebar in his native habitat for the first time. They went to a golf course. Near the Ship, because they had passed a big sign on the highway pointing off to the right that said the Ship was the only place to eat and drink and make Mary.

The Lincoln bumped along a potholed blacktop, came out on a rounded hill near a small cluster of buildings. No lights. It was obviously a golf club. Zack saw a flag waving on a nearby green. Eighteenth, or maybe the ninth. It was a ratty joint. And quieter than a Harlem cemetery.

Zack was prodded out of the Lincoln, pushed to a side door in the neo-pseudo-California style building. He stumbled at the door, caught himself. The two silent young men stepped back warily, waited for him to right himself. They were pros, all right He held onto the door casing, looked back the way they'd come. Nothing. Trees waving in dark silhouette, tunnel of road winding down to the main highway. No cars.

"Come on," one said.

They went into a smelly locker room, through a couple of dark corridors and finally came to an office with a light in it. The door was open. Softy Malebar was there with a bottle and a siphon and a sulky look on his rocky face.

"It's about time," he greeted them. "Where'd you find him?"

The shorter of the two men said, "We found him long time ago. But he wouldn't leave the joint, that lounge in the Gableton. When he did, we got him."

Malebar looked Zack over from shoes to close-cropped hair. His face said nothing. He was seated on a low couch behind a marble-topped coffee table loaded with bottles and ice and other junk. He wore a silk dressing gown that emphasized the chunky-muscled hardness of shoulders and chest. His grey hair was mussed. There was a blue streak along the right side of his head and ugly bruises around his throat. He would be unfriendly, Zack thought, remembering how hard he'd hit the man.

"Sit down," Malebar said finally. He jerked the slab chin at the other end of the couch. "Let's talk. It's about time you and me had a talk."

Zack walked to the couch, eased himself down. The fog in his head was gone, but he was a long way from normal. He'd taken about twice his limit in alcohol.

"So talk," he said, settling back.

Malebar looked at him, mixed a drink. The two dapper men stayed in the room. They were unobtrusive, but they were there.

"Here," the club owner said, the wire-and-marshmallow husking. "Drink this and let's talk about a murder."

Zack took the drink. He balanced it on his knee, did not touch it.

"What about a murder? You left before it happened. I got an alibi. What's to talk about?"

"Plenty. I found out about you, Webster. I should have known from the first. The name—Zack Webster. The guy who built the government's case in the Bulla thing. The bright young investigator who made a thousand union men pull in their expense accounts. I must be slipping."

"You know quite a bit, Mr. Malebar."

"Yeah, I know." Softy picked up his drink, swished it in one big hand. "I know about the trouble you had with Agnew and why you left Washington. I wish I'd known sooner, that's all. Just sooner." His piercing eyes came up. "You know about my family?"

"Your family?"

"Yeah, my family. You think I hatched on a rock? Look, Webster, get the straight of this. I had you brought here, remember? And I still feel that belt on the ear so don't for chrissake get loud, and don't get smart or you'll wind up counting the buttons on a pair of hospital pajamas."

"Okay," Zack said. "What about your family?"

Malebar stared at him for a moment, then grunted softly. "You're smart. I guess you'd have to be with that pedigree. But what'd you run for? All you had to do was twist that thieving Agnew's tail a little and he'd have got off you. You had the goods—or at least all the insiders thought you did."

"I had it," Zack said. "Never mind me. What about this Chicago interview? Picking me up like a bad movie. What's the bit? The girl is dead. There's nothing you can do about that. If you want to chip me up because I nudged you at the party, get on with it and let me go."

Softy smiled. "Nudged, huh? Okay, Webster—here's the scam. I got a family in Pittsburgh. A nice family, three kids. One's just starting high school. Now, everybody knows there was a thing with Marie and me. That's all right. That's life. But I don't want the mess to get stirred, the papers to get excited and make something out of it now that she's dead. And they'd like that in Pittsburgh, believe that. We've had a swarm of those slimy reporters down at the Ship all day. That's why I'm here and that's why I'm staying here."

"But the police made an arrest—"

"What the hell difference does that make to the press? I'm Softy Malebar—a big name. They'd like to mix me in just any way they could. And besides—" Malebar leaned back, pulled his brows forward, shadowing the eyes— "they tell me you're not satisfied with the arrest. That's bad, Webster. That's real bad. Let the little spade broad ride the beef—what's it to you? That way there's no trouble, no hassle—and the newspapers get off my back."

Zack sucked a mouthful of smoke, held it before expelling it. His eyes narrowed thoughtfully.

"Well," Malebar said. "What do you say? Just let it alone, that's all. The Jardin broad will scream prejudice, get a flock of lawyers from the colored association and everyone'll be happy. Especially Softy—and his happiness concerns me, Webster."

"I can see." Zack set his drink down untouched. "Who told you I didn't like the way things came out? How'd you find out?"

"What's the difference?" He looked at Zack a moment, shrugged. "Okay. McCord told me. He's supposed to. I pay him a little to tell me things. I told you that once. I find out things. Burris called me early, told me you gave Sick a fit when they arrested the girl."

Zack thought rapidly. It might have looked that way to Burris McCord; he'd left before Sick had delivered his ultimatum. Before Zack had capitulated and decided that life wasn't really earnest and whiskey made the mare go.

"So you want me to let it alone, that it?"

"You catch on quick. And I'm not asking you, Webster—I'm telling you." He leaned forward; the broad face got lumpy and dark. "Make no mistake about that. Mess in this thing, and you're paid for."

Zack nodded. He rested both hands lightly on his knees, tried to get his weight under him without moving too much.

"I understand," he said. "Pressure and money—get the right things for the right people. Justice with a price tag. What if that girl isn't guilty, Softy? What if she's just a nice kid caught up in a situation she couldn't get away from? Should she die, Softy—so that your kid can go to school without embarrassment?"

"Never mind all that jazz. She's nothing, don't worry about it."

"She's nothing. She's nothing." Zack shook his head. "I owe you something, Malebar. I owe you quite a bit. I'll tell you about it someday. Can I go?"

He stood. Malebar slumped in the corner of the couch, eyes puzzled. "I don't think so. No. I don't think so. You missed the point, maybe, Webster. And I don't like that. I want very bad you don't mess in this thing. You're too smart, too hip. You'll pull too many chestnuts out where the air can ruin them. You better stay here awhile. Yes, I think you better …"

There was a sound outside; a funny sound considering the circumstances. High heels tapping on concrete. The pocka-pock rapped in the suddenly quiet room like pistol shots in a church. Malebar twisted on the couch, looked toward the French doors. One of the men started that way.

The glass of the window-door was opaque because of the inside light. But they all knew someone was there. The heeltaps stopped, the handle on the door turned and Andrea Manning stepped into the room, blinking in the sudden light.

"Zack …"

Malebar looked at the girl, the back of his neck red. He jerked his head at the hood and the man melted back into the shadows. Andy stood there, looking at Zack. She was working desperately to be calm, to look unimpressed with the situation.

But she was scared to death.

"Well, Miss Manning," Malebar said. "Don't you think it was clever, Zack?"

Zack got his feet unglued, moved to the girl. "Andy, what's wrong with you? Do you want to get hurt? I ought to—"

"You ought to thank me for doing what you said." She gripped his arm, moved beside him. Her brilliant smile broke out suddenly at Softy Malebar. "Wasn't I the good girl, Mr. Malebar? I stopped at your place, the Ship, to phone Sheriff Sick."

Softy leaned his head back, closed his eyes. The short young man came forward.

"What should we do, boss? Hold them both?"

Malebar didn't move. The room's soft light accented the angled features. His lips moved.

"You figure maybe she's kidding, Henry? Maybe. And maybe she ain't and what the hell difference does it make?" He came up, smacked one hand against the other. "Get out of here—both of you. Get out and don't get in my hair."

Zack put his arm around Andy, pulled her slight roundness against him. She held tight to his waist. He could feel the tremors in her, like light shock waves. She was scared. Still scared—but her eyes were clear and her lips were firm.

"We're on our way, Softy," Zack said. "Thanks for the drink."

"You remember what I said, Webster. You'd be smart if you did."

"I'll remember. Don't mess in the Kinchloe murder. Don't stir up the water so Softy won't be embarrassed. I'll remember, Softy. I won't ever forget."

They moved to the door in a deep silence. It was still warm and the humid night air cooled somewhat the perspiration on Zack's body. His jaw clenched. Malebar might believe Andy had called Jim Sick—but Zack knew better. He walked rapidly, pulling the girl along to the car.

In it, roaring down the drive from the golf club, the girl relaxed. She sat back, face drained while reaction shook her. At least she was smart enough to know she had brushed violence. Zack spared a glance from the road. Her face was turned toward him, the eyes open and watching him. She pulled her legs up on the seat, held them with one hand. She hugged herself with the other.

"Are you ready, Zack? Have you fooled around enough?"

She slid over on the seat, close to him.

"Don't run, Zack." Her hair streamed in the wind, hit his cheek, wrapped around his neck. "Don't run any more...."

Zack slowed, held the wheel steady. Her eyes were on him, a glow in them like whatever the hell was wrong would be all right; like the war could begin tomorrow and Zack was here; like foreclose the mortgage, like take the car, like beat me and misuse me—my man is here and nothing can happen now. All of this was there in her eyes; chips of stormy sky where clouds part and stars peek through.

"Andy..."

He reached for her, his feet finding the brake pedal, pushing. The car slewed, slackened speed and stopped, inches from a ditch, but nobody cared. Not Zack and Andy. She came into his arms, against his hard chest as if that was her home, the place where she belonged.

The kiss was too hurried to be expert; too much wanting and noses in the way and the heat, heat, heat of perfect rapport. Zack felt the girl, crushed her slightness to him. Against her cool lips his own softened, grew warm, worked with knowledge and passion and a deep, frightening thing happened inside him. There was a loosening, a soft giving and a warmth that spread and dissipated the tight control, the contained and strictured emotions finally breaking through.

"Zack," she said, breathing it when her lips were free. "Oh, darling, why are you so stubborn?"

Zack pulled back her head, looked at the oval face starkly lit with pale moonshine. Her lips were open and dark-rimmed; they looked bruised and her cheeks were flushed.

"Christi" he said, pushing it out, feeling the unaccustomed looseness of his lips, the slack in his cheeks. "I'm dead."

She twisted suddenly to face him. Her breasts swelled against him as their eyes hovered inches apart.

"I told you that a week ago."

Her arms clamped and she kissed him hard.

Zack pulled his head up. His breath came ragged, whistling out of his chest. The Ford was cross-parked on the road, light beams slanting off into the woods. The moon rode low and full in a dark sky full of smudged clouds. There were wood sounds and the chirp of crickets; wind made a song in the leaves.

"I told you a week ago. You're dead, dead, dead…."

"Wizard," he said, and kissed her deeply.

CHAPTER SIXTEEN

"You have the most ridiculous hands, Zack. They make a girl feel all fluttery and—and feminine."

Andy stroked his hand in both of hers. She sat away from him a little, legs drawn up.

"And susceptible?"

She stuck out her tongue. "You'll marry me, my fine bucko. I'll see to that. You'll never get out of this world unwed."

Zack's smile dropped off and he straightened in the seat. He put both hands on the wheel. The Ford sat as he'd stopped it during that first, fierce kiss. No traffic had come. He had switched to parking lights instead of high beams. The road was dark.

She put her head back, closed her eyes. She sat that way a moment while he got the Ford started. Then she turned her head, opened her eyes and watched him. He started the car, pulled away. There was a deep unrest in him, nagging.

He drove very fast, pouring the protesting Ford around the curves in reckless swoops. He felt her eyes. But he could not speak. A lifetime of keeping his own counsel, of husbanding his emotions, was too much to overcome in an hour. He drove fast and neither spoke.

It was early yet and the park was in full swing. The midway eddied with humanity; lines of kids marked the rides, like grounded kites with moving tails. The thousands of lights made an umbrella, pushing up against a sky grown dark. It growled up there. A storm was close. From time to time fat, curly clouds obscured the low-riding moon.

Zack stopped the Ford near the Day-Night. The street was busy. Music blared from the Pavilion and Beachcomber. The lights were blazing on Brulliard's dock. Zack lit a cigarette.

"A man has got to protect himself, Andy," he said, not looking at her. "That's the way the world is. But sometimes you have to do something for a stranger—just to prove your wires are hooked up right."

He watched a skinny kid in jeans and rougue-shirt angle toward a pair of fresh-faced girls newly arrived at the Pavilion across the way. The kid would score. The girls ignored him too positively.

Andy stirred. Zack turned to her.

"You're nice, Andrea Manning. Awful nice."

He got out of the Ford, slammed the door.

Burris McCord came busting out of the tiny Park Security office, situated in the parking lot behind the Day-Night. His belly bounced and for once he was moving too fast to keep his hand on the swinging pistol. He stopped, looked around. He spotted the Ford, bustled importantly toward them.

"You there," he said, his twangy voice climbing. "Need your car. Emergency."

Zack said, "Get another car, McCord. Miss Manning is tired. She—"

"You just get in and drive, mister. Never mind being so all-fired smart." He opened the door, slid in beside Andy. "Let's go. Maybe now they'll get me a car, like a real policeman ought to have. Well, come on there."

"I'll drive," Andy said, looking at him, then at Zack.

"Wait," Zack said. "What's the rush, McCord? You playing G-man?"

The officer sneered, yellow teeth showing. "Lot you know, big shot. Big-shot investigator. I heard about you. You don't know nothing."

"If you want a ride, tell me what happened."

McCord's eyes narrowed. He settled back, one thin arm thrown behind Andy on the seat back.

"Sure," he said. "Got to get to Plumton. That burrhead that killed Miz Kinchloe just tried it on herself. Chopped herself all up with a razor blade."

Plumton was forty miles and Zack got the convertible there in under that many minutes. Nobody spoke. They couldn't with the wind increasing and the sky growing more sullen and the roar of the speeding car drowning everything.

The county seat was a pleasant town with trees and wide streets and bad lighting. Zack slowed inside the city limits, looked over at McCord. The officer had both hands gripped on the door-sill, his face reflecting weirdly the light of passing neons.

"Where's the hospital?" Zack shouted.

McCord shook his head. "County jail," he said. "That's where the sheriff called from."

They went to the jail and learned that Pam Jardin had been taken to the hospital. The hack on the desk said she'd lost a lot of blood. McCord stayed at the jail, Zack and Andy drove to the hospital, neither speaking.

Walking down the white corridor toward the room the receptionist had indicated, Andy said, "Why, Zack? Why would she do that?"

He shrugged, pulled the girl along. He was wet with sweat, the white shirt soaked, the coat damp across the back. His eyes were scratchy again and the whiskey no longer sang in him—it lay like sludge in his veins, dulling him. There was a strange urgency in him. An impatience to do, to take hold, to strike out.

They reached the door at the hall's end. A deputy lounged outside in a tilted-back chair. He had the McCord belly; maybe it was a regulation.

"Whaddaya want?"

"Pam Jardin," Andy said, when Zack stopped but did not speak. "Is this her room? We're friends."

"She's a prisoner, Miss. Can't see nobody. She killed a woman over at Conaghton last night."

The man stood up. He was big, husky except for the bulging belly. He wore suntans and a green cap with a badge on it.

Zack said, "We're going in."

"Now, you wait there, fellow—"

He said the rest from the floor by the wall where Zack's powerful straight-arm put him. The door was unlocked.

It was a semi-private room, two beds and one window between them. Right now the window was shaded, the light coming from a single bedlamp. A white-coated man was bent over a table arrangement between the two beds fiddling with blood apparatus. Pam Jardin lay on the nearest bed, arm outstretched. A tube ran from her arm to the apparatus, then to the arm of a man in the other bed. Jim Sick was there, and a young doctor. They turned at the intrusion.

"What is this?" Sick said. "You, Webster. What do you want here?"

Zack pushed to the bed, looked down at Pam Jardin. She looked bloodless—like a plaster doll dipped in coffee. Vaguely he heard the outside deputy come in, leave again at Sick's command. The girl on the bed was very still. Except for a slight rising and falling of the sheet over her breasts, there was no sign of life. She lay absolutely still. Both wrists were bandaged; one white covering was spattered with dark spots.

"Pam," he said. "Pam … can you hear me?"

There was no movement. The doctor looked up, met Zack's eyes across the still form. He shook his head.

Sick said, "She's about done. She don't want to live, that's for sure. She fought us all the way, even after we found her bleeding to death in the cell."

"In the cell," Zack repeated. He turned away, looked at Andy, then at the wall. His teeth scraped together. "She'll never go back to a cell. What happened, Sick?"

The man looked up at the power, the insistence of the question.

"Well, now, I don't think that's any of your business, Webster. This is a police affair. You—"

"Don't give me that crap. You got your headlines. You got your patsy. There she is. You like it?" His voice rose. "Do you?"

Sick's eyes dropped. He'd lost some of his hard purpose of that morning. He turned away.

Andy said, "Zack, take it easy. She'll be all right. The blood will keep her going and then we'll talk to her."

The doctor straightened from the bed, stethoscope hanging. "I hope the blood will be enough," he said. He was young and he looked tired. He nodded at the girl on the bed. "She seems healthy. But she's lost an awful lot of blood."

There was a noise at the door and the outside deputy stuck his head through.

"Guy out here, Jim. Says his name's Kinchloe. He's with Burris."

Sick nodded. Kinchloe came into the room as if it might explode at any moment. His pale eyes drifted all over, avoiding the figure on the bed. His blond hair was mussed, but his suit and tie were neat and unruffled.

"What are you doing here, Johnny?" Zack leaned on the question. "This girl killed your wife, haven't you heard?"

Kinchloe flushed. "I don't know about that. Burris called me. I thought—"

"Never mind, John," McCord said, pushing in. "This feller ain't nothing. Don't worry about him. And why shouldn't he be here?"

The last was directed at Zack. He nodded, turned away. "Why not?" he muttered. Andy gripped his arm.

McCord whispered to Sick and the sheriff's voice rode over the special officer's, finally silencing him. Zack stood and waited, not knowing what for, only sure that he was where he ought to be and feeling whole and competent again. Andy stood very close to him. He caught the doctor's eye.

"Doc, is she going to make it?"

"She has a chance. I wish she'd come out of it, though. The shock shouldn't be that deep, that hard-holding. The physical trauma is considerable when you've nerved yourself up to die, you know. We're built with a natural reluctance to hurt ourselves and it takes quite a determined person to do it. Especially this way, with a razor blade."

"Is she … cut bad?" Andy asked. Her face was white, the dark hair emphasizing the pallor.

"Yes. She went to the bone on the left wrist. She must be righthanded. The other, probably done after the first cut was made, is more shallow. Both got the vein, however."

His eyes turned to the bed. The sheet had moved. He bent forward. The sheet stirred and Pam Jardin moved her head on the pillow. The eyelids fluttered, then opened wide. The doctor gripped the arm with the tube, removed the thing. The girl stirred, moaning very softly.

The doctor put a vial under her nose, took it away. The eyes came open. They were unfocused, strange—like no living eyes ought to be. There was horror there, and dull recognition; but no life.

Everyone began talking at once. The doctor tried to keep them quiet, but Sick pushed to the bed, leaned over the awakening girl.

"Miss Jardin. Pamela … listen, you're gonna be all right. Can you hear me?"

The room got very quiet. Burris McCord crowded up next to Zack; Johnny Kinchloe hovered over the end of the bed, hands fussing with his tie, his coat, his hair. Pam licked her lips, looked straight up at the deputy. Her eyes closed.

"You better leave her alone," the doctor said.

"In a minute, Doc. Pam, listen…" Sick straightened. "McCord, do you have that statement? Get it on something hard, bring it here." He turned back to the girl and began speaking.

Zack tensed all over. Andy shot him a warning glance, pressed his arm.

"No," she said.

On the bed, the girl had come out of it again. She croaked for water and the doctor gave her some through a glass tube, wiped her face. She was very pale, the dark skin showing pallid underneath. Even against the hospital white, she appeared bloodless.

"Pam, this is Jim Sick. Pam, there's no use going out with a thing like that on your conscience. We know you had reason to kill her. Pam, what do you say? Will you sign a statement?"

It got quiet again. The girl moved her eyes slowly, focused for one bright instant on the beefy face hanging inverted above her.

She said that unprintable word again.

Zack laughed. Andy looked up at him and her lips were curved. "She's wonderful," she whispered.

"Zack…" The voice was weak, thready and querulous. "Zack, is that you?"

Zack pushed Sick aside, stood by the bed. The girl's eyes lifted, found his face and she smiled. It was weak and the effort to hold it was too great—but she smiled.

"It's me, Pam. I'm here."

She moved her hand and he took it, telling himself he mustn't squeeze hard, mustn't shake her.

"I'm a mess, huh, guy? Can't do nothing right."

"You're fine. Just fine."

The eyes were alive now, and the sad awareness was back. She looked at Zack, shook her head a little.

Zack heard Burris McCord whining about something in the background. The doctor moved to the other side, felt the girl's forehead.

"Make it quick," he said. "I'm giving this girl a sedative and when it takes effect nobody sees her until we've built her up again." He smiled down at Pam. "This kid's lost a lot of blood. We gave her almost a gallon."

"Should have saved it, Doctor Kildare. I don't need it."

"Pam, look here." Zack bent over her, spoke hurriedly. "Get better. You'll be out of jail. I promise you that. Just get well. I'll take care of the rest. I'll turn over so much dirt this county won't ever recover—until I find out who killed Marie. I promise you..."

"They won't let you," she whispered. "But thanks, big one, for wanting to."

He straightened and his voice deepened, echoed in the room. "Who the hell's going to stop me?"

Burris McCord grabbed at Zack, his pinched face livid. Sick said, "Wait, now..."

Zack spun with the officer's grip, slashed the back of his hand into the bulging belly. McCord stepped back, fright and pain replacing the anger on his rat face. He bent forward, holding himself.

"Keep your hands off me, McNasty," Zack said. He turned to Sick. "You heard what I told the girl, Jim? I mean that. I know she didn't kill Marie. I saw the killer."

"Listen—"

"No. I've been listening too long. We were too far away to see any characteristics. But I saw something. I saw the gleam of white—like hair, or a white shirt, or something. The only person in the whole mess it couldn't have been was this girl here."

The room was still. Burris McCord had forgotten his hurt, and was standing close again. His belly quivered.

"Webster, you just put yourself in jail," Jim Sick said. "You just got yourself arrested. Burris..."

"Touch me, McCord, I'll scramble your face," Zack said, tone level.

McCord hesitated, hand on pistol.

"Arrest him, Burris. You remember what I told you, Webster? I don't make phony promises."

He turned away. Jim Sick was agitated. Jim Sick was nervous. Jim Sick was a lot of things and all of them had to do with the rosy vision he'd conjured up about breaking a major case, acquiring a pogo stick to bounce clear out of obscurity. His half-bald head gleamed in the lamplight; dots of moisture beaded there.

Zack spoke quietly, with sure force.

"You arrest me, Sick, you're cooked. You don't know who killed Marie. You don't know how to find out. I can find out. And I will. But I can't do it from jail. You'd better think about that. Think good."

McCord said, "Jim, don't listen to this feller. He's a slick talker, but he don't know nothing. Nothing, I say."

Sick waved him quiet. He turned; his fleshy face was tired. The pace was getting to him.

"No, You're pinched, Webster."

"On what charge?"

Sick looked up blankly. "On what charge? On the thing in Washington. You think I don't know about it?"

"Sure you know. Let me see the warrant. Washington is in the District of Columbia. This is Pennsylvania. Show me your warrant."

"Well, now, look here—"

"Look here, my—" Zack stepped close. "Jim, think a little. You put me in jail, Andy goes fast to a lawyer. I'm out in twenty minutes. You got no charge. There is no Unlawful Flight warrant or you'd know about it. So you better let me go. You better bet on my knowing enough to crack this case and lay it in your lap."

He paused, looked around the room. Kinchloe was in the corner, fidgeting. Burris McCord had his pistol half-drawn. The doctor looked harried, sitting on the other bed with the blood doner, who just looked bewildered. Andy and Pam were holding hands, watching Zack.

"Because," he said, deep and sure, "this girl isn't guilty of a thing. And I can prove it."

An excited babble broke out. The doctor rose, alarmed. He got a needle from a tray, went to the girl. Sick pulled at his lip, watched Zack. Burris McCord made noises like a cow in deep water. Andy whispered sibilantly to Pam, whose eyes had come alive.

"Wait, wait," Jim Sick said. He spoke heavily. "What's your notion, Webster? If it figures maybe we can work something out."

"No," Zack said. "I need a little time—a day or two. Do some checking, ask some questions. And I can start right here."

He looked at Burris McCord. The officer backed a step. He looked at Sick, then Johnny Kinchloe.

"You, Burris. I want a couple of answers from you first."

"Not me," McCord said. "Not me, you don't talk to. Maybe you got these fools blinded, but not me. Not Burris McCord, oh, no." He fumbled at his shirtfront, pulled off the star. "Take your tin. I ain't working with no fools who won't do what they think is right." His pinched face swung from one to the other; the badge glinted in his hand. "You fool, Jim!" he shouted, flinging the star. "The girl is guilty, the dinge is guilty, you damned fool!"

Sick said, "Just a question, he said, Burris."

"No," McCord said, backing to the door. "No questions, no nothing. Bury your own dead!" He opened the door, slammed it in deep silence.

Zack spoke finally.

"What do you think, Jim? Something fishy or not?"

Sick looked at the door, pulled at his lip. He sighed.

"You better be right, Zack. You better be right or I'll arrest you for nothing and beat you to death with a wet towel, let the chips fall where they may." He turned, pushed at Zack's chest with a finger like a small sausage. "You understand?"

Zack nodded.

Pam Jardin began to cry softly.

CHAPTER SEVENTEEN

Pennsylvania summer rain, like buckets of water sluiced by giant arms, jagged lightning streaking across a sky so low and so black the world seemed narrowed, confined, packed in cork and cotton. It came in sheets. Big drops hitting the car like pebbles. The air was blue and charged, and headlights gleamed like yellow eyes with hazy nimbuses of gold.

Zack drove. The rain brought no relief from the sapping heat. The night was breathless. He peered through the streams of water the wiper could not control, kept his speed reasonable.

Andy sat against the far door. She seemed to sense that this was not the time to be intimate. Zack knew his face was hard and set, the square jaw jutted. He felt a sense of urgency. As if he'd left something behind and could not remember what it might be or how important it was. A thought, a twinge—like trying to recall a well-remembered name that wouldn't come.

"What did you say to Kinchloe?" Andy asked.

"Asked him a couple of questions. Light me a cigarette."

She complied, using the dash lighter. The convertible had a good top. Rain struck it, thundered. But none came through. Andy puffed the cigarette to life, stuck it in his lips.

"What kind of questions? Tell me, Zack. Maybe I can tell you something. Or maybe you can order your thoughts better if you speak them to someone."

He glanced at her, back to the road. "Maybe," he said. "What time is it?"

"Eleven-thirty. Early yet." She moved closer on the seat. "Who do you think did it, Zack? I know you have an idea."

"I have an idea. But it's a bad one. There's not a hell of a lot to go on. Sick gave me all they had. Just the cause of death, the weapon. And Pam's fingerprint, which doesn't mean a thing. There's something here we have to get around. Something I just can't put my finger on."

"You said once that anyone could have done it."

He nodded. "Motive-wise, I meant. Opportunity is something else. Why the Coy dock? And how would the murderer get Marie to go there? That's assuming it was a planned thing, and I don't think it was, frankly." He banged a palm on the steering wheel. "One little thing, one pointing fact, and I'd have somewhere to start."

"How about Burris McCord? You said you—"

"McCord," he said. "Yes, ol' Burris. I wanted to ask that potbelly a question or two. I wanted to find out why he didn't tell Jim Sick about Gwen Brulliard's story. You heard me ask Sick about it. He didn't know what I was talking about. But the girl told me she talked to Burris, told him about Marie and me on the island."

Andy said nothing, very pointedly. Zack felt a touch of heat in his cheeks. He fiddled with the wind wing, flipped the cigarette out and it bounced along the window, disappeared.

He looked at Andy, saw the weariness in her smooth face. He reached out, touched her cheek.

"It won't be long, kid. There's no time now for subtlety. I'll have to wade around like a mad bull until someone makes a bad move. Then we'll have an idea where to look."

"Everybody had a motive," Andy said. "Sounds like a book title."

"True, though. Brulliard profits from Marie's death. Indirectly, so does his daughter, Gwen. And Samson Coy for sure."

"You said blonde."

"What?"

"You said you'd made up your mind whoever killed Marie had blonde—or white hair. You said so to Sick. Remember?"

"Yes. So what? Brulliard's hair is dead white. Coy's is blond …"

"But not Gwen."

"Okay, not Gwen." He thought a minute, unconsciously allowing the Ford's speed to diminish. "There's Dale Normer. He's real blond, almost bleached. And Bisto. Yeah, Bisto. Motive, too. I wonder …"

"There's the park road."

He turned the Ford into the park road, stopped it.

"What are you stopping for?"

"No use moving until you know where you're going. Right now, I don't."

"There's not much time, you said." She put a hand on his shoulder. "Zack, you need sleep. Two days and not two hours good sleep. You'll conk out pretty soon."

"I'm fine. Right now I'm thinking about Pam. About what this is doing to her spirit. When she's ready to come out of that hospital, I want to make sure she isn't taken to a cell."

"Sick believes you, doesn't he? He seemed to. About Pam's innocence?"

"It doesn't matter what he believes. The best case right now is the one against Pam. Motive, means—the works. And that finger-print might just be enough to get a conviction from an all-white jury. And you can bet that's what the prosecutor would have." He fumbled for a cigarette, stuck one in his lips without lighting it. "No, we have to come up with something. Otherwise, Sick is going to stick with his pat hand. And he'll win the pot with it."

Andy leaned forward, put her forehead on his shoulder.

"Not now, Andy." He was irritable suddenly. He shrugged her off, squinted into the wet night. "That damned dock. Why the dock? She was on the far side, half under the thing. Sick said the first shot hit her in the chest; she fell. Then the three in the back…"

He stared out past the steadily swishing wiper. The Ford vibrated gently. Why the four shots? And why the dock? And why the boat? And why the party dress and ridiculous shoes for a boat ride? When he found the answer to one of those questions, he would be making time.

The rain beat down. Andy had retreated to the far door, waiting.

He snapped his fingers. "Burris McCord. He crops up in this more than somewhat, as Damon Runyon would say. Burris McCord, indeed…"

He got into driving position, threw in the gear lever on reverse, howled backwards onto the streaming highway. There was no traffic. The world seemed dead—wet and hot and dead.

"Where we going?"

He looked at the girl. "Find Burris McCord…"

"Burris McCord?"

He nodded, got the Ford moving.

"Burris. After I talk to Dale Normer…and find out why McCord protected him. Or tried to."

"Then try the Ship," Andy said. "That's where they'll be. Dale's off tonight."

The Ship was not popular this rainy night. Seven cars sat in the drenched parking lot. The halyards and signal flags whipped in the darkness; fixed spotlights did nothing to the slanting rain. The Ship was stormbound.

Zack sent Andy into the place while he stayed in the car. She came back with Carol and the skinny bartender. Both had been drinking.

Dale started to climb into the Ford, saw Zack in the driver's seat. He backed out.

"What is this, Andy? What the hell you trying to pull?"

"Get in, Normer," Zack said. "You'll be all right. Nobody's going to hurt you."

"It's wet," Carol Normer said. Rain blew in the open door.

"Drive, Andy," Zack directed. "Carol, get in front with Andy. Take us to their place."

Dale Normer retreated as far on the seat as he could get. His eyes flashed white in the car-gloom, rain-gloom.

"What are you going to do, Webster?"

"I'm going to beat your brains out," Zack said matter-of-factly.

Carol cried out. Andy shushed her, murmured in the front seat. The car was moving, now.

"Webster, listen, for God's sake…"

"I'm going to listen, Dale. I'm going to listen while you open your lily guts and say something for a change. And I'm going to slap you silly every time you lie."

"You got no right—" Normer began and Zack whipped a hard palm across the man's face.

Zack twisted, got a handful of the man's coat. He pulled him close. He spoke rapidly, the words running together.

"Listen, weak sister. There's a girl in the hospital damned near dead because of you and people like you. Too concerned with your own petty little worries to care whether another human is treated right. Well, I'm concerned and I'm going to see that you get that way. So talk to me, Dale boy. Talk, and you better say something, because I've been pushed around and beat up, cursed at and spit on and I'm sick and goddamned tired of it." He shook the man like a rag doll. "You hear what I say?"

"Yes, yes," the man said.

Carol was bent over in the front seat, head down on her knees, crying softly. Andy had one hand on the girl's back, soothing her, talking to her.

It was a nasty thing he was doing, Zack knew. Maybe a bad thing. But Pam was human, too. He thought of Pam, and of his own professional competence, and he shook the man again for effect. Dale pulled away to the corner, hands covering his face.

"All right, all right," he said. His voice was weary and without timbre.

"Okay," Zack said. "First, about Marie. You had an affair with her. Don't worry about Carol. She's twice the woman you give her credit for being. Level with her for one time and see what happens."

Dale nodded.

"Don't mention—say it," Zack insisted. "You had an affair. You and Marie. And this is odd. It's one of the oddest facts in this odd, goddam mess. Why? I want to know why and you're going to tell it. Now."

Dale sat up a little. His voice gained volume as he spoke, as if he had reached bottom and could only go upward. His lips had stopped shaking.

"I'll tell it," he said. "Carol, darling—please believe that I love you. I've always loved only you. It'll be hard to do, maybe, believe it. But it's true. I didn't want you to know about—" He stopped, unable to continue.

"Come on," Zack said. "It's no good in the dark. Say it. Whatever the hell it is as long as you hide it, you fear it. Why don't you give your wife a chance to be a wife?"

Carol turned, leaned over the back of the front seat. Her emotions were in order again. She smiled wetly for her husband. "Go ahead, Dale. I've been wanting ever so long to find out what's bothering you. The thing that's lain between us. I've felt it, you know that."

Normer nodded, dropped his head.

"You've got to know about Marie. She's a witch. Was, I mean. A real weird one. She was sensual. She liked men, and yet she didn't. I don't know how to explain it. The thing was, she had to have men that she could force to make love to her." His head swiveled to Zack. "You know what I mean? She could have any man. But she didn't want any man. She wanted the man who didn't want her and then she had to force him to sleep with her. It was like a drive, a sickness. She tried it on me. And I didn't fall because—well, because Carol's all the woman I need, or want. Marie kept coming back. And then one day she called me, threatened to tell Carol about my—" The voice stopped, then went on again in a rushing monotone— "my record, my police record. I was arrested for transporting a stolen automobile three years ago. I did fourteen months in the Federal Reformatory in Chilicothe, Ohio. That's what I didn't want Carol to know, what I've been hiding and living with."

Carol said, "Oh, Dale, you damned fool. Why didn't you tell me?"

He shook his head. "I don't know, I don't know. I just didn't want you to know. Anyway, Marie found out about it. She thought it was a great joke. The unassailable Mr. Normer, she called me. And she laughed like an idiot. Then she made me—"

"We know the rest," Zack said. He felt a bubbling excitement. There was something here—he was close to something, and his instinct held him alert. "But how did she find out? That's the thing. How?"

The lanky guy sighed, turned his tortured eyes on Zack. "Burris McCord told her."

The rain sound came up in the car; the motor purred and the rumbling thunder and the kish-kish of the wiper. Zack leaned back. He rubbed his eyes. Something was here. What was it?

"Burris knew," Dale went on, seemingly needful now to talk it out, get it all where the light could hit it. "How he found out I don't know. Maybe at the sheriff's office. But he knew. For months I've been paying him off, keeping him quiet. Not much, but more than I could afford."

Zack sat up. "That's it. That's the bit. You had to pay him off to keep quiet. Then when I threatened your safety by walking in that day, you had Burris McCord lean on me. I wondered about that. I wondered about that a long time."

They came to the little house and Andy stopped the car. Zack gripped Dale Normer's arm.

"You didn't kill her, did you, Dale?"

The man's face was lit by the flooding light from the dash. The rain beat on the canvas, a continuous rataplan. He shook his head.

"No. I haven't got that kind of guts."

"Stop feeling sorry for yourself," Zack said. He nudged the man. "Go on, get out. Talk it out with the girl, there. She's a good one. Better maybe than you deserve. She loves you. God knows why. Give her a break, will you?"

Normer nodded, got out of the car. He grabbed his wife and they embraced in the rain, Carol crying against him. He held her, leaned down. Zack had taken the driver's seat again.

"What can I do, Zack? Just tell me."

"I will, don't worry." He started the engine, nursed it with a nervous toe. "If your testimony is needed I'm going to ask for it."

Normer seemed to straighten, though he didn't move.

"You'll get it," he said, and stepped back.

Zack grinned at Andy when they were humming along the highway headed back to the park. "What do you think?"

She smiled, sat just a little closer so their bodies touched. She nodded.

The car came roaring up from behind, the lights cutting through the Ford, falling off to the right. And then the black shade was racing alongside, windows obscured by pouring rain. There was no other traffic. The heavy car bore over on them.

"What the hell!" Zack said.

Andy grabbed the dashboard with one hand, his arm with the other.

That did it. The Ford was traveling about fifty-five and the slight correction on the wheel sent the little car slewing into the Lincoln. The black sedan had the weight and it turned in, touching fenders with a grinding sound. Zack cursed and fought the wheel, stamping full on the accelerator. The tires whined, sliding on wet asphalt. The Lincoln's horn was blowing and Zack twisted frantically to stay on the highway. It was a losing fight.

"Get down!" he shouted to Andy and, at the same time, whipped the wheel hard right.

The Ford arced, tires screaming, hit the Lincoln behind the front door and spun it like a top. The big car went completely around at least twice and then canted backwards into the ditch on the far side of the road. But Zack didn't see it stop. He was too busy looking for a soft spot for the Ford.

All he could do was miss a telephone pole, banging against it, and pile into the side of the cutbank, tearing brush and uprooting trees until it seemed a whole jungle was piling around the car, scratching and ripping and slapping.

It finally stopped. And they were both alive. The Ford had carried up the cutbank twenty yards into the close-grown brush. The car settled, groaning. The motor stopped.

Zack said, "Andy, are you all right?"

She came up off the seat, eyes wide. "Yes, yes. I'm all right, I think. What happened to the other car?"

"We'll see. But if it was who I think it was, our troubles are just beginning."

It was Malebar, but the trouble was over. Softy was sitting in the rain by his wrecked car nursing a broken nose and a wrenched shoulder. He had no desire to continue the contest. He started cursing Zack in a gravelly monotone when they had maneuvered the Ford down off the cutbank, backed to the scene of the skid.

The window on Zack's side was shattered. He rolled it down, leaned out.

"Softy? Anybody with you?"

"You dirty bastard," Malebar said. His beautiful shirt was wet and dirty, his suit a mess. "You lousy shamus. Had to stick your nose in. Had to play hero."

His rocky face twisted with a spasm of pain. His nose was bent oddly and a rivulet of blood ran from it.

"I asked if you're alone," Zack said. "You're through pushing me around."

Malebar just glared. Zack shrugged.

"Okay," he said, and stepped on the gas.

"Wait!"

It was a shout and when he got the Ford stopped again, Malebar staggered up on the far side, scratched at the window.

"I'm hurting," he said. "Take me to the doctor. I'll forget about you breaking our deal."

"Get in," Zack said. "But your logic gets away from me, Softy. I made no deal. You put a shotgun to my head and told me what to do. That's the wrong way to operate. You and your stooge, Burris McCord—"

He stopped, got the Ford started toward the park again with Malebar in the seat with Andy and himself. He thought for a moment.

"McCord," he said. "I want to see that fella. That's where I was headed, Softy. I'm glad you came along. Now I can find out if maybe you weren't buying more for your money than just information. McCord's even more disturbed about my messing in the case than you are, Softy. Now why is that? And why does he take anybody's money that offers it? Yes, sir, I want to see that fellow real bad."

Malebar was huddled against the door, one hand holding the bad shoulder. His slabbed face was all angles and planes in the bad light. The Ford's fender was touching a tire and the rubbing sound blended with the rain and the laboring engine—and Malebar's laugh.

He laughed like he'd just heard the greatest joke since who did what to who. Zack looked at him angrily.

"What the hell you got to laugh about, Malebar? You fit this thing pretty good yourself. That white sweater you always wear—why didn't I think of that sooner?"

Malebar stopped laughing, wiped his eyes with the sleeve of his coat. "Yeah—why didn't you?" he husked. "You want to see Burris, do you? Well, you will, Jocko, you damn sure will."

"What's that supposed to mean?"

"I was headed for the park when you rammed me. That's what I wanted to stop you for—to tell you I just got a call from Sick. He ordered me to come to Brulliard's dock right away. They got another body." Malebar laughed, a barking cough. "This one ain't as pretty as the last one.

"Burris McCord, hard guy. Burris McCord is dead."

CHAPTER EIGHTEEN

Tom Bruilliard found the body floating off the end of his dock, dead flesh caught on a protruding nail. He'd heard a boat banging free, gotten up to investigate.

Three o'clock—dead dark. The park buttoned up tight. Police cars parked above the Frenchman's docks, lights shooting out into the slacking rain. Cops on the pier; Zack and Andy, Sheriff Sick, Softy Malebar. A lump under a tarpaulin on the end of the dock. Why the Tarpaulin? Burris wouldn't feel the rain...

Zack felt a vague pity for the dead officer. The talk washed it quickly away. Sick wanted to know where everyone had been, the same inconsequential questions, the same nothing answers. He kept asking, pencil hovering but not writing. He didn't know what else to do. He was weary of the mess, too.

"Everybody had a motive," he said doggedly. "It could be anybody."

"A reason, Jim," Zack said softly. "There has to be a reason. For everything. For the boat, the gun—for Burris. It'll fit, all of it. When you get it right."

Sick made a whooshing sound through his lips, said nothing. The rain fell. The sky was gone and the black rain talked on the water.

Sick cursed without spirit and walked to the end of the dock, slicker gleaming. Zack looked out at the pitching lake but there was no answer there. The answers were locked up inside people.

"Too many odd things," he said. To nobody, but he said it aloud. "Odd. The place, the gun—Marie's scratching at the dock. Four shots. Crazy, all of it."

Sick came back, stood listening, not interrupting him.

"Could have been Coy. Really a driver, a climber. Enough reason there. Or Brulliard. His land and his ... well, it could have been him but I know it wasn't. Bisto ..." He chewed that for a minute, found no juice. "Something I'm forgetting."

Nobody knew and nobody answered. Sick broke the silence.

"You people go. Go on, get out of here."

They started, a strange threesome. Softy Malebar hugging his pain to him; Andy drinking from Zack and he lost in the controlled whirl of his mind. They left.

Nothing to say. They started for the Day-Night and coffee. The Pavilion was rain-whipped, a shadow in the dark. Feeble light from the café was a beacon. Zack walked in thought and Andy guided him.

A shot broke the night in half.

Zack slammed Andy to the ground, rolled beside her. Softy stood, bewildered, and the gun rapped out again. The big man cursed, scrambled to the ground.

"Freeze!" Zack said.

He raised on tensed arms. Beside the Beachcomber. A shadow there in the lighter shadow. He turned his head away, shouted into the rain. "Over there, men! The Beachcomber. Hurry!"

For a moment, no sound. Then three quick shots streaked from beside the dark building, flame burning through the steady rain. Zack had his eyes narrowed against the flash, watching the corner.

A figure darted out, scrambled away down the wooden boardwalk fronting the public beach. Zack leaped up.

"Take care of her, Softy."

"Zack! Wait—"

But he was already running, feet seeming to feel the slippery ground. The boardwalk was empty when he got there. He pounded along it, heedless of the noise. At the end, near the grass pier, he stopped. The gun barked again and pain burned along Zack's arm. He crouched, searched with his eyes. There, on the end of the pier.

"Stop!" he shouted, and knew it was useless. He had no gun. The killer must know that, having had no return fire.

A motor roared into life below and the lake sound muffled it quickly. Zack flew down the steps, to the pier's end. A boat. He looked, feverish and trembling. He couldn't let him get away. One skiff had an outboard attached, covered by a patented tarp. Zack spun it into life, shoved out into the tossing lake after the disappearing sound of the killer's engine.

Cone Island. Zack knew it the moment the engine sound ahead of him sputtered out. Only thing around. Marie's island. Queen of the Island, Marie. A fitting place for her killer to come to bay.

Zack beached his boat, crawled up the slick hump that gave the island its name. The wind was sharper up there. The rain cut more. But there was nobody on top; no crouching figure with a killer's gun.

"The cave," Zack said.

He slid the last few feet, clinging precariously to the slippery ledge. There was no light except when lightning streaked. The cave opening was hard to see. Zack felt his way. He was wet. And muddy. But no longer tired. The instinct of the hunter who has himself been hunted awakened in him. All of his senses were acute, attuned to the night, the danger, the crackling electric tension. A killer was in the cave. Zack's skin tingled and his lips pulled back.

He reached the dark angle that was the opening, flattened himself against the outside. He waited, quieting his ragged breathing, listening. Soon he could hear the sibilant rush of air that was emotional breathing; an animal at bay. He grinned there in the dark. This was what he was trained for. He breathed slowly, mouth open, ears tuning out all sound save the muffled hiss from within the cave. His hand moved slowly, found a rock, lifted it. He pushed his head cautiously around the edge of the opening.

Dark. Dark and blown with cold wind from the upper opening. The breathing sound stopped. No sound. Just the patter of rain and the pitching of the angry lake far below. Zack pitched the rock into the cave and a shot boomed.

Before it did, Zack heard a startled exclamation. Then he knew who the killer was.

Without waiting for anything, Zack dove into the dark cave, rolled on the floor. Another wild shot blasted the cavern, shattering, reverberating. Zack crouched, tight-hugged against the wall. Silence came down.

"Webster?" The voice was high, unnatural.

Zack sat up, making no sound. It was torture to control his breathing.

"You bastard," the voice crooned. "I know it's you and I'll kill you, you bastard."

Zack peered into the darkness. He saw a blob back there. White and just visible. He'd seen it once before. Once before when shots had rung out in the night and a woman had died. He took off his soaked shoes. The tee shirt would be visible from the back so he folded the lapels of his coat across the chest, held it there. He moved a little, putting an angle of rock between himself and where the killer had to be.

"I heard you, Zack," Johnny Kinchloe said. "I'm coming for you, Zack."

It had to be. Zack cursed himself silently for not knowing it sooner. Johnny Kinchloe. The sissified hotel keeper, the gutless cuckold.

"Hear me, Webster? I'm going to kill you."

Zack hugged the wall, pulled himself a few feet along the roughness.

"It's all over for you, Johnny," he said. And waited.

Kinchloe laughed. "All over? Hah. It's all over for all of us. All of us!"

Zack flopped suddenly, warned by something. A shot echoed and the slug whistled close, buried itself in the sand. There was a scurrying, a sound of rapid movement and Zack froze, belly tightening. His senses screamed. He'd made a mistake. A bad one. Johnny Kinchloe had run past him in the dark, gotten between him and the cave opening.

Kinchloe laughed, high and wild. Zack saw the outline of the man visible against the outside glow.

"Now, Zack ... right now."

"Wait, Kinchloe!"

Instead of a shot, a light blossomed, blinding Zack. He held his eyes, jumped erect, slamming his head. He stood, head buzzing. When his eyes had adjusted, he saw Johnny Kinchloe. He held a Coleman lantern. His eyes were wild and he looked like a man overdue for the whips and jingles.

"Johnny—"

"Shut up!" the man hissed. He lifted a hand, waggled an efficient-looking gun. "I should have shot you long ago. Long ago. You were the one. The only one she ever cared about. She told me that, Webster. Does that make you feel better? Does it?"

The last was a scream. The man was gone, his control a wire-tight thing of screaming nerves.

And he had a gun.

Zack searched for a way out. There was none. Johnny was at the opening. The aperture at the top wasn't big enough to get through Zack knew that from the first trip with Marie when Gwen Brulliard had used it for a spyhole.

"Kinchloe, use your head. What good is this? You know—"

"Don't say anything, Webster. There's nothing you can say. Nothing anyone can say. Marie's gone and that's all there is."

The little man, blond hair hanging, thin lips loose and wet, moved forward. The gun led the way. He grinned at Zack. "You should have brought help." He stopped with the thought, placed the lantern down on the cave floor. "Maybe you did, Webster. Maybe you did, at that …"

He spun, ran to the side of the opening, flattened himself there. His thin face moved from side to side, like an animal scenting an enemy. He listened, gun poised.

"No help," Zack croaked. He cleared his throat, said louder, "No. help. What do I need with help Johnny?"

Kinchloe laughed. "What, indeed? It would do you no good. You're a dead man no matter what. If the army was outside, they couldn't save you." The man's eyes glittered. He licked thin lips. "Nothing can save you, Webster. Like nothing could save her."

"Marie," Zack said, making it almost a whisper. "She was alive, John. Firm and alive and soft and full of fire. Why did you kill her? Why?"

"You tell me," Kinchloe said. He crouched against the wall, held the gun in firing position, aimed directly at Zack. "Go ahead, big and strong. Handsome Harry. Go ahead, you tell me."

"Because she was going to leave you, Johnny. She said so and you believed it because you've always thought she was too good for you. At the dock. What did you do that for, Johnny? Bring her to the dock? I don't understand that."

Kinchloe started laughing. A few short barks, then a full-throated shrilling, sharp and high, filling the cavern. Zack gritted his teeth against the insane sound.

"You fool," Kinchloe said, when his mirth had run its course. "You egocentric idiot. I had no intention of killing Marie. I loved Marie and I needed her. Why would I kill her? No. You were wrong, Webster. I had the gun that night and I was on the dock. But not to kill Marie. To go across the lake, to the Ship. That animal, that Malebar—he offered her what I didn't have to give. The money to buy control of the park and the lake. I was heading for him that night. Him, not Marie." He laughed, caught it before it got away again. "Not Marie, you see. Not ever Marie."

Zack's legs were beginning to cramp. He had not moved since the light pinned him. And now he could not, with the gun's blue mouth centering him implacably.

He wet his lips. "And she tried to stop you. On the dock, when you tried to go, to get the man who threatened to take her from you—she stopped you."

Kinchloe rubbed his free hand quickly across his eyes. "Don't talk about it, Webster. It doesn't matter."

"Oh, but it does, Johnny. It matters to me because I thought you were a snake and now I know it. You let Pam Jardin go to jail for what you did."

The gun jerked. "Stop it, Webster—"

"Why? Why should I? You'll kill me anyway. You let that poor girl go to jail, think she would pay for a crime she didn't commit. She tried to take her own life, Johnny. You caused that."

Kinchloe's face went dead. All feeling left the pale features and the eyes became dull.

"Stand up, Webster. Stand up straight."

"About Marie, Johnny. Did she follow you that night? Try to stop you from going? Or did she taunt you, Johnny? She was good at that. You had the boat untied, ready to go. Then she came to the dock, stood there. Why did you shoot her. Why?"

Kinchloe spoke like a robot, lips scarcely moving, voice shrilling higher and higher, nasal and penetrating.

"Because she said I wasn't man enough to kill anyone. She said Malebar would eat me alive. Alive, she said. Johnny, you haven't got guts enough to kill a flea, you poor queer bastard you, she called me. Poor queer bastard you—"

He stopped abruptly, clicked something on the gun. It made a liquid sound, chilling and definite.

Zack said hurriedly, "McCord saw it, didn't he? Then he made a deal with you, right after it happened. And tonight, in the hospital, you realized how it would be. Ever after, McCord around your neck like a weight."

"Yes," Kinchloe said. "I knew he couldn't swim and I got him out on Brulliard's dock. To get a boat, I told him. To go to Malebar for money, I told him. He was puny, too, Burris was. I hit him with this gun."

Saying the word brought it to him. His eyes took on spark and he pushed away from the wall.

"This gun," he said, and lifted it until the muzzle held strong on Zack's face.

The time had all gone, then. The sands had run down and Zack Webster would die here in a sandy cave on a rainy night with the world shut away and uncaring. He tried desperately to think of something, but the ten feet of sand that separated him from the man with the gun was no-man's land. He'd never make it before the finger, even now tightening, pulled the trigger, cut off the life beating inside Zack Webster, stopped the surging heart that had only lately learned to love. Kinchloe's hand steadied.

A scream shuddered through the cavern, shattering the silence like a brick through a giant window. The screech of a woman in mortal agony, the cry came—tearing out of a quivering throat, treble and terrible.

It glued both men, froze them. That saved Zack. He recovered first from the sound and leaped, pushing off from the wall with a powerful shove of his legs. Two long strides and a headlong plunge—and Johnny Kinchloe came alive, turning the pistol, firing.

Shots rang out and Zack felt the hollow boom in his head, his ears, his mind. He didn't know if he was hit. He didn't care. The boom kept echoing in the cavern or in his mind and he struck the slender figure with his body, closed reaching arms, and reality faded away as he beat the twisted face, slammed the blond head on the hard floor of the cave again and again....

CHAPTER NINETEEN

Jim Sick and Softy Malebar got through the opening in time to keep Zack from killing Johnny. The whole thing was confused and emotional—the exhausted reaction to violence. Andy crying and holding Zack, both sprawled on the sandy floor of the cave. Both weary of the mess and clinging to each other. Johnny Kinchloe was unconscious, but alive. He would pay for his weakness. He lay on the floor, crumpled like a Kewpie doll, broken and forgotten. Sick stood over the hotel manager, the Coleman lantern throwing his stocky shadow in huge detail on the wall of the cave.

"Crazy," he said, to nobody in particular. "Absolutely nuts."

Malebar grunted. "So the little bastard was after me that night. Well, I wish she'd have let him go. She'd be alive anyway."

His rocky face was shadowed; Zack pulled Andy's head to one side on his shoulder, looked up at the big man. Malebar saw the look, nodded emphatically.

"That's right, wise guy. Slice it anyway you like, I mean it. I wish she'd have let him go."

Zack said wearily, "Stop it, Softy. She dealt this little guy a fit. And anybody else that was foolish enough to get mixed up with her. She was sicker than he was. They deserved each other."

Andy held him, moving her head against him.

"Darling, you're all right," she said. "I was so frightened. But you're all right...."

Zack got up, pulling her with him. He watched Sick put handcuffs on Kinchloe, dab a little at the man's torn face with a soggy handkerchief.

He said, "Who made that noise?"

"I did," Andy said. "And it was easy. Jim was near the hole and I couldn't hear what was going on. When the gun thing came out, when the light flashed on, Jim gave Softy his pistol and told him to come in this way." She indicated the front opening. "But then we realized Johnny would shoot you anyway before Softy could get in. So..."

Sick laughed. "I told her we had to do something to distract him, give you a chance to help yourself. That was a hell of a position, Webster. There I was, listening in on a murder. And I couldn't do a thing."

"I'd given up when I heard that—what the hell did you do, Andy?"

She laughed nervously. "I just screamed," she said. "I thought, he's killing Zack, my Zack, and I'll have to go through life without him—" She stopped and her eyes came up to his, soft and possessive and strong with love. "So I screamed a little."

Zack pulled her close, put his hard cheek in her hair, and closed his eyes.

"A little, she says."

It took them about an hour, everybody moving like puppets on stiff strings, to get Kinchloe out of the cave, into the boats and back to the Brulliard dock.

The rain stopped. It was almost morning. The freshest, cleanest smell Zack had ever experienced came to them there, when the police had gone, the crowd had dispersed. There were only three of them, then.

Three tired people. Zack and Andy and Softy Malebar. They stood and watched the taillights dwindle into the greying morning. The lake had quit pitching. It was quiet, as only the country can be before the dawn.

"God, I'm tired."

"I'll carry you, darling," Andy said. She had rolled up the sleeves of the slicker, opened it. She looked neat and trim and cute. "I'm not tired, I'm just beginning to live."

"Give the guy a break, Andy," Softy said, and his voice was more marshmallow than wire, now. His face broke up into an angled smile. "Quite a fella you got there."

"I know."

"I agree, I agree," Zack said. "But I'm so beat that I couldn't lift a finger to break Wilson Agnew's jaw."

"About Agnew," Malebar said, as they walked toward the steps. "You going back?"

Zack looked at Andy, felt her arm around him.

"Yep," he said. "And the good Senator is in trouble. One Webster gave him a little hassle. But two…"

Andy stopped him, kissed him. Zack looked at Softy over her shining head. "See you, huh, Softy?"

Malebar grinned. "Sure, sucker."

"One thing," Zack said. "You got juice in Pittsburgh. I know that. Big juice. Can you get a singer a job? In a real good club, I mean?"

"A real good singer?"

Andy turned. "A dandy," she said. "Top flight. Could you, Softy? It would be so nice to tell her tomorrow—"

The big man waved his good arm, turned abruptly. "It's done. Forget about it. Take that guy home and put him to bed."

Zack grinned.

Andy colored. "Put him to bed?"

Malebar's bull laugh echoed in the morning air. He stopped halfway up the steps.

"Put him, take him—what's the difference?"

Zack spun her, looked down at the lovely, weary, expressive face. His chest was taut and he felt shaky down to his shoes. It was sharp, this particular awareness—and new.

"Yeah," he said. "What the hell is the difference?"

THE END

BEYOND DESIRE

RICHARD HIMMEL

CUTTING EDGE

ISBN-13: 978-1-952138-60-7

Published by
Cutting Edge Books
PO Box 8212
Calabasas, CA 91372
www.cuttingedgebooks.com

This book is for Stud

CHAPTER ONE

It Begins Here at This Cocktail Party

T HE SOUNDS of the party were coming from the third floor. I stood at the foot of the stairs, motionless, undecided. My eyes traced the crooked pattern of the staircase. I looked up through the well of the stairs to the broken skylight at the top. The building was on the verge of becoming a tenement. It had been built too long ago, too quickly and not well enough. The building was one of many once gaudy apartment houses built on the south side of Chicago before the World's Fair in 1893. Gingerbread had been substituted for substance. Like the Fair itself, these buildings had been built for short but flam-buoyant lives. Its age was showing, and the flaws in its design and con-struction were glaring in this dim light. I was seeing the hallway of this building and analyzing its decadence, waiting for some invisible force to decide whether I would go on up to the party or go back to the street to walk again, endlessly, in the rain and in the darkness.

I hadn't intended to come here. I was in no frame of mind for a cocktail party. I had even forgotten I was invited until twenty minutes ago. I had been walking. Walking and walking without direction, without purpose; hardly aware that I was walking or of the constant, slow drizzle of cold rain. I went for a walk to get fresh air to clear my head of confusions and to clear my lungs of the stale air of my own being. But it was the same as everything else I had tried; the walking was futile. I was still who I was and faced with what I was, and the people pressing into my life were the same, pressing with the same, maddening impact.

For three days I had locked myself in my apartment, didn't answer the door, let the telephone ring. Three days. Those three days were for me to think things out, to come to decisions, to make up my mind as to what I was going to do. Three futile days. Then this walk, this bursting out of suffocating, self-inflicted solitary confinement and into air, the air of the city streets. But the decisions would not be made. As strong as my will was to make them, some other force was equally powerful, keeping me undecided, suspended in confusion.

When I had stopped in the shelter of a store to light a cigarette, I remembered this cocktail party, that it would be going on now. Maybe, after all, I had thought, a beautiful bender is what I need; to tie one on, to become paralyzed with liquor, to dissolve my own identity until the morning. And in the morning, I knew my head would be heavy, hung over, but as it cleared, I thought maybe the answers would be there. Under the mist of the hang-over would be big, beautiful decisions. And I would see them and know them as surely as I would see the sun when the clouds finally cleared.

Now I wasn't sure any more. With one foot on the first step, I wasn't sure that the cocktail party was the answer. I listened to the hum of talking, an even hum broken by shocks of laughter. It was a good party, at least it had the sound of a good party. I started up the stairs, still not certain that I would get as far as the third floor.

The girls who were giving this party seemed to be always giving a party. They were good parties. As I kept walking up, I thought about some of the parties I had been to in this last year and a half. Wonderful times. Wonderful people. The excitement of being with wonderful people; people who were different, strange sometimes, and fabulous. Yes, I decided, what I needed was to go to the party. And in the morning, when the clouds cleared, there would be the sun.

Maybe.

They called themselves Jackie and Jill, these girls. Those weren't their names, of course. Their real names were not important. Jackie and Jill suited them very well. Both girls were about the same size, both blonde, uneven and careless bleach jobs. They were neither pretty nor homely. They were attractive enough and well built enough. Their ages were somewhere between twenty and thirty but that didn't matter very much, either. They had the kind of personality which was at home with any one of any age. They had that wonderful genius of being good listeners.

Jill had acquired a small son who seemed to live permanently in the kitchen. He was always there when a party was going on, sitting in his high chair until ten or ten-thirty, then being transferred to his play pen where he either played or slept, depending on his mood. Noise never bothered him. When all this happened, the boy was about four. He seemed happy living as he did and was very well behaved. His name was Andy, and he had got to know me and we were good friends.

Besides the kitchen, the apartment had a living room, a dining room, a bedroom, and a bathroom, which was off the entrance hall. The bathroom did not have a door. I remember someone asking Jill once what had happened to the bathroom door. "Charlie Schmid got drunk one night," she said, "and walked off with it." No one had ever heard of Charlie Schmid and very likely there was no one named Charlie Schmid. It was Jill's way of dismissing something very unimportant. It was a little rattling at first, this bathroom without a door, but either you became used to it or you waited until you went someplace else.

The basic furniture of the apartment was box-springs and mattresses variously covered with shawls and spreads and loaded with odd pillows. Someone was always asking why they had nothing but mattresses. If she were asked, Jackie would say, "Jill used to know the nicest boy in the mattress business." If Jill were asked, she would say, "There was a mattress king once who was simply crazy about Jackie."

Music played constantly, good music, some classical and some jazz. There was an immense Capehart in the dining room, which Al Terwilliger contributed when he and his wife split up, and there was a marvelous collection of records. Somehow, no one ever came to these parties empty handed. People brought food and liquor and records. A few of us kept Andy well supplied with toys. I doubt if the girls had much income other than what their friends brought them. Yet there was always plenty to eat and drink, the rent was paid, doctor bills were taken care of, and any emergency met.

Many kinds of people came to these parties. Some of them were wealthy and their pictures were on the society pages of the newspapers from time to time. These were old friends of Jill's from when she had been a debutante. These people left early because it was a long drive to the suburbs where most of them lived. Others were famous in their own way. Not famous, really, but special or well known in a limited area. There was a top flight atomic scientist whom I had known in college. A drama critic from one of the big newspapers was almost always there. This particular night, a girl who had made a dazzling hit in the road company of a mediocre play was there with her husband, who was bewildered both by the party and by his wife's success. The gossip columnists ran in and out. There were enough celebrities there to make the trip worth while. There was an all night disc jockey who had to leave at eleven-twenty to make his twelve o'clock show. There was a woman who did quite well at abstract poetry and a man who did very well drawing very definite covers for two-bit novels. There was a girl who was somebody on one of the morning soap operas. There was a terrible-looking redhead who entranced children on a Sunday television show. There were other special ones. I can't remember all of them.

Then there were the rest, not special in any way but interesting or interested in one way or another. No matter what you wanted to talk about, there seemed to be someone around who was well informed on the subject or at least opinionated enough to be provocative. There were talented people who sometimes entertained. There were several men who were fine amateur chefs and spent the whole evening in the kitchen. There were usually a number of unattached women around who could be talked to and, sometimes, into something. Like at any other cocktail party.

That night the crowd was bigger than I had seen there for some time. There was no room in the front-hall closet so I put my hat and coat on the floor. George and Eve Janerton were just leaving and we mumbled a few words to each other. There was a girl in the bathroom whom I didn't know. The door to the bedroom was closed. Jackie was in the middle of the living room telling a story about an Irish cop on St. Patrick's Day. I had heard it before but I stopped to listen anyway, she told it so well. When she had finished and everyone was laughing, she edged over to me. "Petey, darling."

"Hi."

"I was hoping you wouldn't come."

"Wouldn't come? That's a hell of a greeting."

"But, darling, we did something dreadful. We forgot and invited Monty, too. He's here now."

I hadn't planned on that, on Ralph Montgomery being here. I smiled. "So what? So he's here."

"It's not my fault, Petey. Jill did it. You know how she is sometimes, not a brain cell working. She completely forgot about you two."

"Don't worry about it. It was bound to happen sooner or later. We can't go on forever without running into each other."

"Well, at least you didn't bring Clarissa. Oh, Petey, think how dreadful it would have been if you had brought Clarissa. By the way, darling, how is she? Everyone says she looks like hell."

"She's fine. Just tired. It's been a strain."

"Yes, I suppose it has. You look rather like hell yourself."

"I need a drink, that's all. I'll see you later."

Jill didn't seem to be around anywhere. I didn't see Monty either. I nodded to a few people as I went back to the kitchen.

In the kitchen, Harry Triss was trying out a new recipe for a Spanish omelet which smelled very good. Young Andy was asleep in his play pen, hugging a very dirty stuffed giraffe. A man I had never seen before was fixing two drinks on the sink. As soon as he was through, I poured a Scotch, drank half of it down, and refilled the glass. I wandered back through the dining room and into the living room. I saw Monty, but his back was to me and he didn't turn around. At the far end of the living room there was an angular bay. The big chair there was empty. I sat down, started drinking slowly, watching the others and wondering what I would say to Ralph Montgomery when we finally came face to face. Or what he would say to me.

There was no escape anywhere. I knew that now. I had come to this party to lose myself, to become dissolved and disintegrated until the next morning. Now here was Monty, across the room and in the center of my confusion. No escape. Anywhere. One thing, I decided, I would have to watch my drinking. If I got drunk I couldn't depend upon keeping myself in check and under control. To have a run-in with Montgomery at that point would be disastrous. I knew it and wanted desperately to avoid it. I would have one drink, I figured, maybe two, and then I'd leave. If getting loaded was the means to the end, I would have to find another place, other company.

I saw Mitchell Swaine for the first time over the fat, bare shoulder of a woman who played at being an interior decorator. She was talking rapidly to Swaine and making broad, sweeping gestures with her hands. Swaine was looking beyond her, at me, studying me carefully through narrowed eyes. I knew at once, in some way, that there was an impact to his looking at me, an importance. This was not a casual curiosity. This was a deliberate sizing up, a measuring of what I was.

The first thing I noticed about Swaine was that he looked rich. His being sunburned in the dead of winter was part of it, but there was more to it. He wasn't the flashy, monogrammed, solid-gold looking kind of rich. You could tell at once that he'd been born rich, wealth inbred, not applied. He looked as though he had been to the best schools, had done all the right things, belonged to the right clubs, knew the right people. It is an indefinable quality which some men have. They can be shabby-looking and still have it. They carry it with them into the shower. It is a look which is impossible to imitate or acquire. You have it or you haven't it. Mitchell had it.

At first I classified him as being another old friend of Jill's, in from Lake Forest for a bit of slumming. Yet as we kept staring at each other, I saw another dimension in him which went beyond suburban living and horse shows. There was a quality of mystery, or perhaps it was sadness. I couldn't tell at the time. I only knew that he was rich and that there was something about him which set him apart from other people of his class, made him look alone in this crowded room. He would be a killer with women. That I knew instantly, instinctively.

He weaved slightly. I realized he was drunk or he wouldn't be gaping so openly. I tried to look away from him, break off the stare, but my eyes seemed to be magnetized to his. Each time I turned my head away, my eyes came right back to watch him, to watch his eyes watch me. I forced myself to stand up, started to walk away. Mitchell Swaine pushed past the fat interior decorator, leaving her in the middle of a sentence about something chartreuse.

"Don't go," he said. "We ought to talk. We have a lot to talk about."

"Look," I began.

"Sit down," he said. Then he smiled. "Please."

7

I sat down in the chair, and he sat cross-leggedly on the floor in front of me. He was in no hurry to say anything. He kept looking at me, taking small sips of his drink without moving his eyes. From a distance he had looked younger, under twenty-five. Now, up close, I could see the web of lines around his eyes and at the corners of his mouth. His hair was cropped close to his head and there were shocks of gray in it. Yet there was a boyishness about him, in his face and in the way his body moved. It was difficult to determine exactly how old he was. He wore a blue flannel jacket with leather patches at the elbows, gray flannel slacks, and black loafers. His collar was open and his tie pulled down. He was taller than I, much thinner, tighter nerved and tighter muscled.

"My name is Mitchell Swaine."

I nodded, said nothing.

"You know," he said, "it's astonishing, really astonishing." His voice was clipped, a Midwestern sound coated by Eastern schools and a British manner. He swallowed some more of his drink. "I couldn't have believed it possible at all. But it is true, isn't it? It's true, and here you are."

I thought that perhaps I ought to go to Bermuda for a week, make up my mind there what to do. The sun would feel good, and I would feel better and look better if I were as tanned as Swaine.

"You *are* here, you know," he said.

"I'm here, all right, but I don't know what the hell you're talking about."

"But it is. It's absolutely astonishing."

"Look, you've got the wrong guy."

"Of course I haven't. I can see, can't I?"

"But I'm not who you think I am. You have me mixed up with someone else."

"But that's it, old man. I do have you mixed up with someone else. That's the whole point. I know you aren't he, but you could be. Don't you see that? You look enough like him to be him."

"Who?"

"Jerry, of course." He drank again, emptying his glass. I finished my drink in one swallow.

"Look, if you expect me to keep up with this conversation I'd better catch up on the drinking." I started to get up again.

He grabbed my glass. "You stay there. Right where you are. I'll get a drink for you." He jumped up and started off.

I called after him. "That's Scotch and soda."

Swaine stopped, turned around to me. "Of course it is. I know that." Then he was gone.

Jackie was close by. I went over to her. "Who is that guy?"

"What guy, darling? There are thousands of men here. Of course, you're the most attractive, Petey. Which one do you mean?"

"That one." I pointed toward the dining room. "The man in the blue flannel jacket. With a crew cut. Slightly loaded."

"Discreetly, darling, point him out discreetly. Wait until I put on my glasses. Now, which one?"

"He's gone into the kitchen. Very tall and sunburned. Crew cut. He's slightly loaded. Strange-looking, in a way. I don't think I've ever seen him here before."

"Oh, that one. I know who you mean. That's Mitchell Swaine. Stinking rich, darling. Steel on his father's side and flour mills on his mother's side. You knew him before, didn't you, Petey? They had a place up at Lake Geneva."

"You forget, I'm new around here."

"They had that big place, the rather rambling white house with green shutters. You remember. Perhaps they weren't green. They may have been blue. No, they were green. I remember it very well. They were definitely green." She looked up at me. "Why the hell are we talking about shutters?"

"We aren't. We were talking about Mitchell Swaine."

"Certainly we were. God, but he's attractive."

"You think so? He kind of gives me the creeps."

"You must have heard of him, Petey. He's the one who killed his brother."

"Killed his brother?"

"Yes, he's the one. In that hunting accident. They were hunting in one of the Dakotas. It was either North Dakota or South Dakota. It's so damn confusing having two Dakotas. You'd think people could be more original than that. Or just have one big Dakota. Except that that would rather louse up the flag, wouldn't it? Of course they could make Hawaii a state and then everything would be lovely again."

"I think I remember reading about it. It must have been ten years ago. Or more. Something happened after that, didn't it? I think I read about it in a Sunday supplement. His mother died and there was a fire."

"It was dreadful. Everything happened at once. It was like those strings of firecrackers. Things just exploded one right after the other. Of course, I was quite young at the time, but everybody knows about it. It was awful. I feel so sorry for him, and he's so damn attractive and so stinking rich."

"How did he get here?"

"Monty brought him, as a matter of fact."

"Monty? How did that happen?"

"I don't know, really. I suppose Monty has adopted him for some project or other. You know how Monty is, always adopting attractive young men for something or other." She looked up at me, took off her glasses. "Sorry, darling. I forgot."

It was Monty who had brought me up to the flat for the first time. "Skip it," I said.

"Mitch has just come back from Africa. Now, isn't that horrid? I can't remember whether it was North or South Africa, except that it seems to me it must be North because he went away to forget, and you wouldn't go to South Africa to forget a hunting accident, would you? I mean South Africa is so Frank Buck, big-game hunting, and all that kind of thing."

"Yes," I said, "Africa does seem like a funny place to go."

"He was other places before that but he finally stayed in Africa. I should like to go to Africa and ride an elephant. Don't you think it would be hysterical to ride an elephant?"

"Yes, hysterical. Jackie, do you remember his brother's name?"

"It was Swaine, too."

"I mean his first name, jerk."

"I don't remember, Petey." She thought for a moment. "Wait a minute." She paused. "No. I thought it was John but John is somebody else's brother. I don't remember. I could ask someone. I could ask Monty. You know, he always knows everything. I could ask him discreetly so that he'd never guess you're the one who wants to know."

"Never mind. It's not that important. Here he comes back. Forget the whole thing, will you?"

"You *are* being mysterious."

"I'll tell you about it later."

I went back to the chair and sat down. I was intrigued now. I wanted to hear the rest of it. Swaine handed me my drink, sat on the floor again, and began talking as though the conversation had never been interrupted. "You do see, don't you, that this is the whole point? I haven't mistaken you, at all. I know very well you couldn't be who you look like because you look like Jerry and Jerry is dead."

I drank this drink more quickly, still saying nothing.

"How old are you, old man?"

"Thirty-two," I said.

"Of course, you'd have to be, wouldn't you? And your birthday is in July, isn't it?"

"No, it's in May."

"Well, the month isn't terribly important."

"I guess not. I still don't know what this is all about."

Then he looked at me straight, his eyes wide open. Something in his face changed. "You think I'm half crocked, don't you?" He lowered his eyes and shook his head. "I'm not. No more than usual. No less than usual. Did you know your body can reach a stage where you can drink as much as I do and not be drunk? You drink just to the point where you get a clarity of vision. You can see things a sober man cannot see."

"And you see that I look like someone named Jerry."

"I could see that drunk or sober or with my eyes closed. I've met men before who I thought looked like Jerry. It was always from a distance, but when I got up close they didn't look like Jerry any more. You do. I didn't think you would, but you do. That's what is so astonishing. You do. Jerry was my brother, did I tell you that?"

"No," I said, "you didn't."

"We were quite different, Jerry and I. He was the better of the two. There was more to him. You're like that. There's a lot to you, too. You look sad, the way he always looked sad. Not unhappy. I don't mean that. He laughed all the time and smiled. But even then you could see the sadness, as though he knew that about himself. Do you know that about yourself, that you're going to die?"

I laughed. "Sure. Some day. We all do, don't we?"

"But I don't mean like that. I mean before you're supposed to. Die horribly. Before your time."

I finished the drink but instead of it warming me, I was chilled. "I don't feel that way," I said. "I feel as though I'll grow old and bounce grandchildren on my knee."

"I hope you do, old man. I really hope you do." He saw that my glass was empty. "Here, let me fill it for you again."

"No, thanks. I'll get it myself. I'd better say hello to a couple of people." Enough, I thought, was enough. Swaine had made me edgy, nervous. I decided to tie one on in spite of Monty's being there; if I got out of hand, so what? Monty had it coming to him.

"Don't go. Please, don't go. Can't you see that this has meaning? Nothing happens accidentally, really. Everything has a design, a master plan. It's not just an accident that you look like Jerry and that you're here tonight and that I'm here too. I've been all over the world, running away from home. I was never coming home again and then suddenly I wanted to. For no reason. Have you ever wanted to do anything like that, suddenly and for no reason? But, of course, there was a reason. I know that now."

I stood up. "You're letting this get away from you. Maybe you're just a little past that period of drunkenness when you see everything clearly. Tomorrow you'll have forgotten the whole thing. Maybe you'll pass me on the street and won't even know who I am. Tomorrow, I won't look like your brother at all."

His voice was low, carefully aimed at me. "You'll look like Jerry tomorrow. You know that as well as I do. You'll look like Jerry until the day you die." He fumbled in his wallet. "Here. Look at this." He had pulled out a small snapshot, discolored with age and frayed at the corners. The photograph was of two boys in swimming suits, standing at the edge of a pier. The faces were so small it was almost impossible to distinguish them. I assumed the taller one was Swaine and the other was Jerry. I handed it back to him. "You can see now, can't you," he said, "that you do look like him?"

"I can't tell from a snapshot very well." Swaine looked disappointed, so I said, "I can see a little resemblance, though."

"This was taken at a house we had at Lake Geneva. It was a wonderful house. We used to have wonderful times there. It burned down exactly one year from the day my brother died. No one ever found out how or why. No one was living there. It just burned down." He put the wallet back in his pocket. "I'm going to get another drink. Let me get you one, too." He took my glass.

"Do you know," he asked, "how my brother died?"

I shook my head. Not because I didn't know but because I didn't want to hear it. I didn't want to hear him tell it. All around me the sounds of the party were getting louder and gayer. I wanted to be there, with the others, not here where I was.

"I shot him," Swaine said. "We were hunting. It was an accident. The safety wasn't on. He'd told me a thousand times about the safety. But I forgot, and then I stumbled over some brush and the gun went off. It didn't sound very loud. It just went *pop*. It was just a little sound but Jerry was dead. Do you hunt? We used to hunt all the time, Jerry and I. I used to love it. I haven't since, of course. I won't even touch a gun. I miss it, sometimes, walking through the fields with my gun. And the dog. Our dog was with us that day, Jerry's and mine. When she saw that Jerry was dead, she put her tail between her legs and took for the woods and never came back. No one ever saw her again. Isn't that funny? She was a nice dog. We had just got her broken in. I'd better get the drinks."

"Go ahead.

"You'll wait here, won't you? I won't be a minute."

"I'll be around," I said.

The crowd was heavy in front of us. Swaine held the empty glasses over his head and pushed his way through. I watched him until he disappeared into the kitchen. When he was out of sight, I moved, too, threading my way through the people and moving toward the front door.

A girl stopped me. "Petey, how are you?"

I had no idea who she was. "Fine," I said. "I'm fine. You're looking fine, too."

"Isn't it funny, Justin and I were just talking about you. We're going to build at last. We've bought a lot and we're going to build. I told Justin it was going to be just like 'Mr. Blandings Builds a Dream House.' We've been fighting like cat and dog about what kind of house we're going to build. That's why we were talking about you. Justin has his heart set on a real modern thing, you know all flat and glass and that horrid stone everyone is using so much. I couldn't bear living in it. I want a house with charm, something traditional. You know, like those houses in that Williamsburg Village you designed. Only larger, of course, and lots finer. But Jus won't hear of it. He gets stubborn about the oddest things. Of course I told him that if we did build some-thing Williamsburgy I wouldn't hear of anyone but you for the architect. I don't think anyone builds that kind of house as well as you. You have a real feeling for it. But Jus is stubborn. We're still fighting it out. If I win you're certainly going to hear from us. That is, unless you're too terribly expensive since you're doing so well."

"I build modern houses too, you know."

"Do you? I had no idea?"

"It's what I do best. The Williamsburg Village was a project for mass housing. It was designed to sell. It was designed to hit a low common denominator. It wasn't what I like to do or what I do best. Tell Jus I can build his horrid, flat modern thing and do it damn well."

"Yes, I will, Petey. Of course, I will. Excuse me, Petey, there's someone I haven't seen in a long time."

I walked closer to the front door. The bedroom door was opened now and Jill was at the dresser, looking into the mirror and brushing her hair. I went in. Her glass was set on the top of the dresser. I picked it up. "Scotch?"

"Water, not soda."

"I don't care. Do you mind?"

"No. Go ahead."

I took a long swallow. "How are you, Jill?"

"Fine, Petey. I'm always fine. You look beat out. Is everything all right?"

"Sure. Everything is swell."

"Even with Clarissa?"

I didn't answer. I drank some more.

"I suppose you know that Jackie made a horrible mistake and invited Monty. She forgot. She's on such a merry-go-round, that girl, she doesn't remember anything."

I laughed. "Jackie blamed it on you. It's wonderful that you have each other to pass the buck."

The rhythm of her brushing continued without an offbeat as she spoke. "Would it surprise you if I told you I invited Monty purposely, deliberately, because you would be here?"

I sat down on the edge of the bed and started to drink again. I don't like water with Scotch but I drank it anyway. I remembered then that Mitchell Swaine would probably be looking for me. I got up and closed the bedroom door, and sat on the bed again.

Jill put down the brush and leaned toward the mirror, examining an area of her cheek. "What was that for? Why did you close the door? Are we going to have a scene?"

"No," I said. "There's a guy I don't want to see."

"Monty?"

"No, not Monty. Someone else."

"You are exasperating sometimes, Petey. Aren't you going to say anything about my inviting Monty deliberately?"

"Sure. Sure, I am. What do you want me to say?"

"Ask me why I did it."

"O.K. Why did you?"

"I don't know, really. I suppose it's because I expected something to happen."

"Do you want me to slug him?"

"It seems to me it should be the other way around. But then he's not the type, is he? He's smaller and rather older than you are. He has other weapons, though. More deadly, perhaps, than yours."

"Stop it, Jill. What's the matter, anyway? Why the mad on?"

"Do I sound mad? I don't mean to. I'm not mad, really." She banged the brush down against the dresser top. "I guess I'm hurt, Petey. Terribly, terribly hurt."

I didn't say anything. I couldn't look at her.

"I sound awful, don't I, Petey? Like something out of an old movie on television. You think dialogue on soap operas is so very corny until something happens to you and then you find yourself saying the same words in the same way. But that's what I am, terribly, terribly hurt."

"You have no right, Jill. You know that. You made the terms, I didn't. I could have loved you, maybe. I don't know. I never even thought about it. You said that what we had together was for the moment and that it didn't mean anything. You said there were to be no feelings involved. You used the words, physical necessity. Do you remember?"

"Yes, I remember. My mouth can be so damn hard-boiled, say such hard-boiled things. But I'm not that way, really. I try my damnedest. Sometimes I wish I were as tough as I sound."

"I'm sorry," I said, and then I knew I shouldn't have said it.

"You sound like a soap opera, too. Don't be sorry for me. I'm just in a mood, that's all. It'll be over in a minute."

The door opened suddenly. Swaine stuck his head in the door. "There you are," he said.

"Get the hell out of here!" I shouted. "Can't you leave me alone for a minute?"

"Don't get angry, old man. I have your drink."

I got up and took it from him. "Now beat it." I slammed the door and locked it.

Jill said, "Is that who you're trying to avoid?"

"Yes. You know him, don't you?"

"For a long time. Poor man."

"Did you know his brother?"

"Jerry? Yes, of course I did."

"Do I look like him?"

She turned to me then and faced me. "You do—in a way. It's been so long. As a matter of fact, you look very much the way he did."

"I was afraid of that." I finished Jill's drink and began on the one Swaine had brought me.

Jill walked up to me and roughed my hair with her hand. "You were such a nice boy, Petey, and you've got yourself all fouled up. You began by being so wonderful and then ..."

"I know. And then Clarissa."

"Not only Clarissa. She's only a symptom of everything. You were so much nicer, Petey, when you had your eye on where you were going. Now that you've got there you don't seem so nice any more. You've lost something in the process. Your boyishness, I guess." She leaned forward and kissed the top of my head. "I'm saying all these terrible things to you and I don't mean them. It's just that I'm so damn fond of you. You aren't taking me seriously, are you?"

"I guess I've got it coming."

"No, you haven't. Everyone thinks you're more charming than ever and you've done so well. You're so damn successful. It's only I who can see what's happened to you."

"About Clarissa," I began.

Jill moved away from me. "Yes, Petey. What about her?"

"It's only that I couldn't help myself. It began almost a year ago, even while we were still ... Well, you know what I mean. It didn't mean anything at first. I didn't think I was being unfair or unfaithful to you because of the way things were with us. Then I got in so deep, I couldn't get out any more."

"Do you want to get out, Petey? Do you want to now?"

"I don't know. God, I don't know. It's all I've been thinking about. I honest to God don't know." I became aware then that I was gripping the glass with all the strength of my fist. I put it to my mouth and finished it. "I need a refill. Come on, I'll buy you a drink."

"Do you love her?"

"I don't know."

"Or do you just feel responsible for her now that she's left Monty?"

"I said I didn't know."

"She would have left him anyway, even if you hadn't been in the picture. You know that, don't you?"

"For God's sake, stop the questions. I'm not on any damn witness stand."

"All right, Petey, let's get that drink." She unlocked the door and started out.

"I'm sorry, Jill."

She held out her hand to me and smiled. "I know you are. Come on, we both need a drink."

On the way to the kitchen I brushed by Swaine. "Helen has just come," he said. "I want you to meet her." I kept walking.

Monty was on his way out as I was on my way in. We came face to face midway in the kitchen. He always looked so damn neat, so carefully groomed. And he was smiling, that half-grin of his which was so patronizing. Jill's pressure on my hand increased. I pulled away from her. "Fix me a double, will you, baby?" I didn't look at Jill as I spoke. I kept looking square at Monty.

"Well, Petey, it looks like the next club you'll make is Alcoholics Anonymous." He had a way of talking so that his mouth hardly seemed to move.

"Hello, Monty. Long time no see."

"Yes, Petey. Long time no see."

"What's new?"

"Very little. And with you?"

"Not much that you don't know," I said. "You keep pretty well posted, I'm sure."

Monty's grin narrowed and his lips were thin and white. "Aren't we being terribly civilized," he said. "We're just chatting here as though we don't hate each other."

Without turning my eyes, I knew that everyone in the kitchen was watching us, waiting to see what was going to happen. We were being the third act of a very bad play. I could smell the remnants of Harry Triss's Spanish omelet. It didn't smell so good any more.

"I don't hate you, Monty," I said.

He smiled again, brightly. "That's too bad, Petey, because I hate you very much."

"Let's try to keep it civilized, huh?"

"All right. Let's talk about something." He paused for a moment. "You ought to come to the gallery sometimes, Petey. I have a new exhibit. Paul Lautrobes. Do you know his stuff?"

I nodded.

"Like it?"

I shook my head.

"I didn't think you would. He paints so that you can tell what he's painting. The exhibit has been successful. He sells very well. Almost as well as you're selling houses in the Williamsburg Village."

"Above the belt, Monty. Keep it above the belt."

"You'd be making a big mistake to pull out of it now. It's a big thing, the Williamsburg Village. It wouldn't look well if you chucked it."

"Who told you I was thinking of chucking it?"

"That would be telling. You know I have ways of finding things out. You used to find it very useful."

I felt Jill slip a drink into my hand. I whispered, "Thanks, honey."

"Be good, Petey," she said.

Monty turned to her. "Are you afraid he's going to hit me, Jill?"

Jill walked away without saying anything.

"Don't think that's so funny, Monty. I consider it from time to time, taking a healthy poke at your smug face."

"Yes, Petey, I'm sure you do. I've thought about it, too. I've wondered what I would do if you did. I shouldn't hit you back, certainly. I'm not the type, I'm not built for it. I'm afraid people would be sympathetic with me rather than with you. After all, it was my wife you ran away with, and it isn't considered good form to hit someone smaller and older."

"I may anyway," I said.

"I suppose you might."

"Why don't you give her the divorce and get it over with, Monty? Clarissa will never come back to you. Even if I weren't in the picture, she'd never come back to you. You know that."

"Yes, of course I do."

"Then why won't you let her divorce you? It's driving her crazy the way you've got her tied up. She's a wreck from it."

"In my own way, I love Clarissa quite as much as you do. Even more than you do. If I let her go she would marry you and that wouldn't be good for her. As a matter of fact, it wouldn't be good for any woman to be married to you. Face it, Petey, you're a stinker."

I didn't say anything, I just held tight. It took all my power to keep one hand on the glass and the other at my side. Everything I had inside me wanted to burst out at him and smash him. But I was still able to keep myself controlled.

"I love it when you get angry," Monty said. "There's a muscle in your cheek that tightens and your left eyebrow twitches. I used to try to get you angry purposely so that I might watch your face. It really is very interesting."

I knew then that I wasn't going to hit him. Hitting him would not be enough. I wanted to kill him, I hated him so. I hated him for knowing me so well, for knowing what happened to my face when I got angry, how my eyebrow twitched and how a muscle in my cheek tightened. I wanted to kill him because everything I was and everything I had, I owed to him. My money, my job, being at this party, and even Clarissa. All these things I owed to Monty. My debt to him was enormous. I hated him for that, for all the things which he had done for me.

Ralph Montgomery was a dilettante. I should have known it that first time I saw him and I should have stayed away from him. But I was from Dubuque, Iowa, and there aren't many dilettantes in Dubuque and I didn't know one when I saw one.

Monty had a lot of money and a great deal of artistic taste. He did not need to work but he ran an art gallery as a hobby. He painted, too, but he didn't show his work to many people. As far as I know, the only painting that he didn't still own was the portrait he'd done of me. When I was made a partner in Murdick, Howell and Maguire, he gave it to me to hang in my fancy new office.

Murdick, Howell, and Maguire were a good firm of architects. They did solid things, big things. I was lucky to get a job there. It wasn't a very good job, really. I began as nothing more than a draftsman. After a year they began giving me a little designing to do, small jobs, pieces of big buildings. Some of what I did was good and some was not. I wasn't impatient. With a big firm, it's a long, hard pull to the top, and I was prepared to sweat it out.

Then one day Mr. Murdick called me into his office. Funny, I still think of him as Mr. Murdick and he keeps telling me to call him Bill. "Watkins, some of the things you have done for us show promise. We are pleased with you."

"Thank you."

"A man I know wants a new front on his store. He's a friend of my wife's, really. He runs an art gallery near North. Store fronts are not in our line, but I can't very well refuse to do it. I want you to run up there and talk to him, see what he wants, and then do some sketches for him. He'll have pretty definite ideas. I wouldn't try to talk him out of them. Do what he wants as well as you can do it. I suppose it will be good training for you."

To Mr. Murdick it was an obligation to get rid of, remodeling a store front for his wife's friend. To me it was a great big world opening up outside the confines of the office. Riding the bus from downtown to the gallery, I saw countless store fronts in my mind's eye, magnificent ones, more magnificent than an eighty-story building could be.

The gallery only fronted about eighteen feet but those eighteen feet were a mile to me. And it was on Michigan Boulevard and when my family came from Dubuque they could ride the bus and I would be able to say, "I did that store."

Ralph Montgomery looked amused the minute he saw me. "You must be exceptionally bright," he said.

"Why do you say that?"

"They're so stuffy, Mr. Murdick and Mr. Howell and Mr. Maguire. I didn't think they ever gave anyone a job until he was over fifty and prematurely senile. I don't know whether to be flattered because they have sent a boy to do the job for me or to feel insulted."

"Don't worry," I said, "they won't let me do anything wrong. They'll check over everything I submit."

"Yes, I know they will and I kind of wish they wouldn't. They have no imagination, you know. I'll tell you a secret.... What's your name?"

"Watkins," I said.

"I know that. They told me a Watkins was coming. What's your first name?"

"Peter."

"Well, I'll tell you a secret, Petey, if you promise not to tell Mr. Murdick or Mr. Howell or Mr. Maguire."

No one ever called me Petey. My mother called me Peter and everyone else called me Pete. But to Monty I was Petey. That should have been a clue, but I thought it sounded good being called Petey by this man of the world.

"I won't tell," I said.

"The only reason I called them was because Mrs. Murdick is a very good client of mine. She buys thousands of dollars worth of paintings every year and she would consider it a personal affront if I hadn't called her husband's firm to do this job. But now I'm glad I did for they have sent me young blood."

I listened to Monty talk about the new front he wanted on his store and his conversation branched off into generalized discussions about art and architecture. It was only a few years ago but I was different then, I was malleable. In school, I learned economy of design; the clean, broad strokes of modern architecture. I had come to hate anything that was not modern, which featured functionless detail and architectural froufrou. I thought myself a bold artist, not afraid to break architectural conventions. I came to the city a missionary for straight line, areas of glass, rough stone, and woods in their natural states.

But no one at Murdick, Howell, and Maguire talked about art and architecture. There was a contract and the owners wanted the building a certain way, and the style was determined by what the owners wanted and by the cost of building. There was no room for the consideration of basic concepts and artistic approaches.

Now there was Monty, with his soft, persuasive voice telling me about the history of architecture, the beauty of things which I had come to believe were no longer beautiful. There was Monty, smiling at me, poking gentle fun at what I believed in and what I stood for as an artist.

My idea for the store front had been to open it up, let the light and sights of the city come in, as well as the paintings inside come out to the street. Monty's idea was just the opposite. He wanted the front stoned in, with small openings only big enough to show one painting on either side of the door. He wanted some detailing on the outside which was functionless but which he said would indicate the good taste and the sense of the artistry inside. Mr. Murdick had said to do as Monty wanted. So I went back to the office and worked straight through dinner and late into the night, sketching designs for the eighteen-foot front of the gallery.

The next afternoon I showed up at the gallery, portfolio in hand.

"You are conscientious, Petey. I'll say that."

"I hope you'll like what I've done." I started to take the sketches out of the envelope.

"It isn't smart business to give too good service, Petey." He was smiling, and somehow when he smiled it made everything he said all right. "Murdick, Howell, and Maguire can't very well send me a whopping bill for your time on the sketches when here you are only twenty-four hours later with a trunkful of them. You should have waited a week, made me think that it was a lot of work. You have a lot to learn, Petey. You have to learn business guile. Everyone thinks that I am the artistic type. I'm not really. I know business better than anyone suspects. It's part of my success."

"As a matter of fact, I worked all last night on this. I did put in a lot of time."

"Never let anyone know you've worked overtime or on your own time for them. It puts you in a class with domestics. You should have said that you dashed off a few quick sketches this morning to see if you are on the right track."

"But that isn't true."

"No, of course it isn't, Petey. It isn't true at all. You've worked very hard on what you've done. But you mustn't let me know it."

I scratched my head and laughed. "I guess, after all, I'm just a country boy in the big city."

"You're a little more than that, Petey. I saw that right away. You'll take working on, but I think you have the raw material." He put his hand on my shoulder and directed me forward. "Come on back in my office and we'll have a drink and chat for a while."

"What about the sketches?"

"Maybe we'll get around to looking at those, too."

We didn't get around to looking at them that day. We talked instead. Rather, Monty talked and I listened. Even now I am aware that he has a vast kind of wisdom. I learned a lot that day, not in the way one learns the meaning of a word or learns the distance between the sun and the moon. It was no particular thing I learned, but many things, evasive things, bits of things. He took me back into a small room he used as a studio and showed me some of his paintings. I liked them. I liked them because I liked Monty.

"Do you think they're good, really?"

"Sure, I do. I don't know anything about painting, but they look good to me. I think you've got a good feeling for people."

He looked at me, cocking his head to one side. "Do you, really? I'm glad to hear you say that."

"I think that one is beautiful. It kind of makes me think of ... Well, Titian, I guess."

"That's a portrait of my wife, Clarissa," he said. "I'm afraid she makes everyone think of Titian. I think it's one of my best things. I never show any of these things publicly, you know. I do it as a hobby, for relaxation."

"Gee, that's great."

"It might be fun to do a portrait of you sometime. You have the typical American face. It might be fun."

I didn't say anything.

"Sit down on that stool a minute, will you, Petey? Do you mind?"

"I guess I don't mind." I sat down on the stool. "I feel like a goof, though."

His easel was set up with a clean piece of paper, and there were several sharpened sketching pencils in a trough, waiting and ready for use. It was as though he had expected me here and expected me to sit for him. "Don't try to pose, Petey. Talk to me."

"I don't know why you want to paint me. If I have the typical American face, it seems as though it wouldn't make a very interesting painting."

"Perhaps it won't. But it might be fun to do. Turn your head a little to the right."

"Is this going to take long? I'd better call my office."

"Don't worry about your office. If you have trouble with Mr. Murdick or Mr. Howell or Mr. Maguire, I'll take care of it."

I relaxed a little and laughed. "This beats the hell out of working, I'll say that for it."

"Petey, did you ever build model airplanes when you were young?"

"Yes. How did you know?"

"I didn't know. I asked. Most boys do, don't they?"

"I suppose. It was a special thing with me. I won a prize three years running at the state fair. Why did you ask?"

"I just wondered if you were good at that sort of thing. I have an idea for something. You might be a good man to fool around with it."

"What is it?"

"We'll talk about it later, at dinner."

At first I didn't say anything, then I said, "I've got kind of a date for dinner."

"A girl?"

"Yeah."

"Is she pretty?"

"Pretty enough."

"Will she wait?"

"I guess so."

"Well, then," he said, "you can call her later and tell her you can't make it. I'll call my wife and tell her I shan't be home. Now, don't talk for a moment and hold your head still. Tip your chin up a little. That's good. Now hold it."

At dinner that night, Monty told me about a plan to build a huge village of low-cost housing, each house patterned after Williamsburg buildings. Everything was to be colonial and terribly authentic. I wasn't very keen on the idea. "It's a big deal," I told him. "Who would undertake a project like that?"

"There are people who would be interested."

"It doesn't make any sense to do that kind of thing Williamsburg. A project like that should be modern, clean lined, easy to take care of."

"There are lots of projects like that, Petey. Rows and rows of modern monsters. There is nothing that has captured the charm of a whole village. It will sell. It will appeal to a great number of people."

"You know more about this kind of thing than I do, but somehow it doesn't make any sense to me."

"When we go back to the gallery, I'll give you some books about Williamsburg. You'll get the feel of that kind of architecture. Just for the fun of it, do some sketches of houses you think can be built at not too great a cost. Make a plan for a five-room house, a six-room house, and some six-room duplexes. I can't promise you any money for it, but it might be rather fun for you to do."

It began that way, with what sounded like a casual idea. In my spare time, I did some layouts and sketches based on drawings and photographs in the books Monty loaned to me. I cleaned up as much of the gingerbread as I could, but each time I showed Monty a drawing, he sketched all the fanciness back in. When the layouts and sketches looked good to Monty, I began building models. I built a model of each unit and they were good models. As far as I could tell, Monty still had nothing definite in mind. It was fun in a way but it made my work at the office more boring than it had been before. Also, it took up more and more of my leisure time and I found myself losing touch with my friends and being with Monty almost every night. I wondered about his wife, what kind of marriage they had. He never talked about her and I never saw her in all the time I was working on the Williamsburg Village. Evidently she didn't care that Monty never came home.

When the models were complete, we laid out the whole village on paper; streets and parks and playgrounds and shopping areas, all very colonial, all very authentic. Monty was pleased with it but I wasn't. I still thought it should be modern. All the quaint gimmicks made me feel unclean. I wanted to go over everything, blue pencil out all the unnecessary trappings and decorations. But Monty said no.

One night after dinner, we went back to the gallery and Monty took me into what had been a big storeroom. It wasn't a storeroom any more.

"What are you going to do in here now, Monty?"

"We're going to build the village," he said. "The whole thing in exact scale, even to the swings and teeter-totters in the playground."

"What for?"

"I told you I had an idea, Petey. I have hired six people to work on it. I estimate that it will take six months to complete."

"Then what?"

"Then I'm going to have a showing of it here in the gallery. The Williamsburg Village designed by Peter Watkins. And for the occasion I'm going to hang my portrait of you right in front."

"Now, wait a minute, Monty. I'm not sure about this. First of all there's the office. I'm not sure how they're going to like the idea of my doing this for you while I'm working for them."

"I told you, Petey, let me handle Murdick, Howell, and Maguire."

"I don't know, Monty. I don't know."

"Of course you don't. But I do. I know very well what I'm doing. Just wait and see."

Monty knew how to draw people into that gallery when he wanted to do so. The exhibit opened with a cocktail party. Monty made me buy a new suit for the occasion, he even took me to his tailor and picked out the material and told the man how it should be made.

It was a hell of a good party. Plenty to drink and plenty to eat. The village had been set up in the center of the gallery and was flooded with light. There was always a big crowd around it. They were saying wonderful things but that could have been because the food and the liquor were free. No one knew me or paid any attention to me. One of my bosses was there, Mr. Howell, but he passed me by without even recognizing me. Monty was too busy being charming that night to pay much attention to me.

The painting of me was hung on the main wall. There was no identification on it as to who had painted it or whose portrait it was. It didn't look very much like me, so no one recognized me from that.

Finally, I got guts enough to stand up and look at the village which we had created. I edged my way through the crowd and tried to see it as other people were seeing it. Even in this flood of light, this dramatic presentation, I didn't like it. It was still unclean looking, unnecessarily fancy. The woman next to me said, very quietly, "Messy little beasts, aren't they?"

I looked over at her. She did look like a Titian portrait. Monty's painting had not done her justice. "Yes," I said, "they are messy." And now I knew about their marriage, too. She didn't like the houses and she didn't like Monty. She thought he was a messy little beast, too. I wanted to talk more to her, but she walked away.

The whole project was sold two weeks later, to be built by a big insurance company. Monty coached me carefully and I approached Murdick, Howell, and Maguire with the contract for the job, contingent upon my becoming a partner in the firm. It was one of the fattest jobs any firm had been offered in many years. They opened their arms to me, Murdick, Howell, and Maguire, and told me to call them Bill, Charlie, and Harry. Monty had played his cards just right. I was exactly where he had designed to put me. I had sky rocketed to success. I was the boy wonder of the architects. And all the time I kept remembering what Clarissa had said. *Messy little beasts, aren't they?*

I owed it all to Monty. Everything I was and everything I had. It's not decent for one man to be so much in debt to another man. No man can feel that much gratitude for another man. I wished many times that I was back in the drafting department working my own way up, the hard way. Then in the next breath I would kick myself for thinking that. I told myself how lucky I was, that this only happens to one man in a million and I should be grateful that it had happened to me.

It may have been all right if I hadn't fallen in love with Clarissa and if she hadn't fallen in love with me. Maybe I could have come to believe in the Williamsburg Village if I hadn't fallen in love with Clarissa.

I don't know if every man harbors the power to kill. I know that I do. I learned it that night in the kitchen of that apartment, with the smell of the omelet in my nose and the feel of the liquor in my stomach. I knew that night I had the power to kill.

But Mitchell Swaine broke back into the picture. No one else would have dared. They all knew about Monty and me, knew enough to keep out of our way. But Swaine didn't.

"Helen has come," he said. "She's got to see you. She'll know you look like him."

"Get lost, will you?"

Monty spoke to Swaine. "I'd like to meet Helen, Mitch, even if Petey doesn't. Come and take me to her. You'll excuse us, won't you?"

"Sure," I said. "Go meet Helen."

I let out a breath of relief. Nothing had happened.

After they left, I looked around me. Jill was still in the room, standing in the corner near Andy's play pen. I went over to her. "Who the hell is Helen?"

"I don't know, Petey. I suppose she's the girl Mitch brought back from Africa."

"A Ubangi?"

"I doubt it. I hear she's very attractive."

I nodded toward Andy, who was still fast asleep. "That's the way to be," I said.

"Yes. It would be lovely." Jill moved close to me and kissed me on the chin. "I'm proud of you. You did very well. There was a minute there when I thought you were going to hit him."

I laughed. "There was a minute when I thought I was going to hit him, too. How does a guy get himself so fouled up, do you suppose?"

"Who are you talking about, you or Monty?"

"Me, I guess."

"I don't know. You have a certain appeal, Petey. People want to take care of you."

"Do you?"

"No." She shook her head. "I have Andy. He's ever so much more faithful."

"I'm going to the john," I said. "I'll see you."

I had to wait a minute until Joe Regan came out, then I went in. I had drunk an awful lot.

While I was standing at the sink washing my hands, Swaine caught up with me again. "Here he is, Helen. Come and see him. Do you see what I mean?"

Through the mirror over the medicine chest, I saw Helen appear behind Swaine. She was not a Ubangi at all. She was rather tall, very thin, and had red hair cut short, worn close to her head. Her lips were very full and painted to match the orange-red color of her hair. You saw her eyes only after you saw her hair and her mouth, and then you wondered why you hadn't seen her eyes first. They were green and they were cat's eyes and they told you a lot about her very quickly.

"Well, what do you think, Helen?" Swaine asked.

"I can't very well tell from his rear view," she said.

"Turn around, will you, old man?"

"In a minute, Swaine. In a minute." She could see my face now reflected in the mirror, and I was watching her face. It wore no expression, nothing.

"Isn't the resemblance amazing, Helen? He even talks like him. His whole attitude. Do you remember the man in Algiers? I was so sure about him until I talked to him and then I knew he wasn't like Jerry. But this one is."

I turned then. "O.K., so I am. So what?"

Helen was dressed very simply, almost mannish. She wore a plain, tight-fitting skirt and a shirt tailored like a man's shirt but ruffled up a little. "You're right, Mitch. He does look like your brother."

"You see it, too. I knew you'd think so."

"But don't shoot this one, Mitch. He's attractive."

Swaine's face turned red. He started to say something, changed his mind, pushed Helen out of the way, and walked out of the bathroom.

"That was pretty rough, wasn't it?"

Helen smiled for the first time. "I'm a pretty rough girl."

"Do you really think I look like his brother?"

"How should I know? I never saw his brother. I've only known Mitch for six months."

"But he said ..."

"I know what he said. When he gets drunk he gets mixed up, he loses his sense of chronology. He thinks I was around when it happened. It doesn't do any good to argue with him when he's this way, and he's this way most of the time. He's got a real thing about finding a double for his brother. Tonight you're it. If you're lucky, tomorrow he won't remember anything."

"And if he does?"

"Who knows?" She shrugged her shoulders. "Like I said, maybe he'll shoot you, too."

"You've got a lousy attitude, Helen."

"You're cute," she said. "I think you're cute."

"Come on, I'll buy you a drink."

"I don't drink."

"O.K., you can watch me."

"You've had enough."

"What are you, a watch dog? Watch out for your boy friend. I can take care of myself."

"I suspect you can take care of more than that," she said.

I looked her up and down. "Yes," I said, and then I didn't say any more.

"I'm glad I decided to come," she said. "I wasn't going to. I loathe crowds. I told Mitch to come alone, that I'd come later. I didn't intend to, really. But I was bored being alone so I came to get him. I'm glad now that I did."

"I almost didn't come either. I'm not sure I'm glad I came. It's not you, particularly, or your friend. It's a lot of things."

"Point of information. Mitch is not my boy friend. He's my husband."

"I'm sorry. I didn't know."

She smiled again. "He doesn't know most of the time, either. It was something he did when he was drunk and forgot it the next morning. He forgets periodically."

"I've got enough troubles. I don't want to hear the story of your life."

"It's interesting. If I get to know you better, I might tell it to you."

"Excuse me, I want a drink."

The crowd had thinned out but those who were left were going strong. Maylou and Tom Foss were singing their parody of "Some Enchanted Evening" in a corner of the living room. Bob Quage and Hal Blum, who had been on the same gym team in college, were performing a trick which people usually save for the beach in summer. Grant Bendix was necking with Stan Harris' wife in the dining room.

Surprisingly, no one was in the kitchen. At least I didn't think anyone was there. There was a tremendous stack of dirty pots, pans, and dishes on the sink. They made a racket when my elbow hit a pot handle as I was reaching for the Scotch bottle. Then I heard someone say, "Shhhh!"

It was Mitchell Swaine. He was inside the play pen with little Andy. The boy had his finger in his mouth and seemed to be sleeping against Swaine's shoulder. But as Swaine tried to move away from the boy, Andy opened his eyes. "Tell it to me again," his sleepy voice said. "Tell it to me again about

Cinderella." Then Andy saw me and smiled. "Hello, Petey. He tells stories good."

"Does he, chum? You'd better go back to sleep."

"I want to hear it again about Cinderella. Tell it to me again."

"Well," Swaine began, "once upon a time there was a little girl named Cinderella." Funny thing was that Swaine didn't seem loaded as he told the story. His voice was calm and steady. He seemed to have lost his affected way of speaking. His voice was soothing and soft, and I watched little Andy getting groggier and groggier until his head fell against Swaine's shoulder and he was asleep. Still the story went on until Swaine was certain Andy was fast asleep. Then he laid the boy down on the floor of the play pen and covered him with a ragged piece of blanket. Andy opened his eyes once more and said, "Kiss me good night." Swaine leaned over and kissed Andy's head. "I like you," Andy said and then put his finger back in his mouth and was asleep.

I liked Swaine then, too. For the first time that evening I liked him. He was different with Andy than he had been with any of the rest of us. I had caught him off guard with the kid. He was better off guard, and I realized that underneath all his confusion he might have been a really nice guy.

He came over to me and said quietly, "I'm sorry about Helen."

"It's all right," I said.

"She's a nice girl. If it weren't for Helen I don't know where I'd be now. She's a nurse, you know. She takes awfully good care of me. I need a lot of care sometimes. Isn't that strange, I don't feel drunk any more."

"You reach that point sometimes." I poured the rest of my drink down the sink. "Helen said that you were married to her."

"Did she? She tells me that sometimes, too. She never shows the document to prove it. She says she has it tucked away in a safety-deposit vault in New York. We may be married. I have long periods when I don't remember what I do. I'll be damned if I know why she married me. I'm not good for anything, no good at all." He lowered his head. "The time I shot my brother finished me. I'm impotent."

"It could have been your dough," I said. "Maybe she wanted the security of your dough."

"I suppose so. She didn't have to marry me for that. She could have anything she wants, any time she wants. Money doesn't mean very much to me. It's never brought me any happiness. I'd be glad if it brought her some. She's had a rough time. She was a nurse during the last war, stationed in Africa. She fell for a doctor there, half French and half Negro. After the war she went back and married him. He died of something or other and left her stranded. She was having a rough go of it when I found her. I'm not sure it's been much easier since. It's no fun being married to a blank cartridge, you know. I've told her she was free to go out and get what she wants but I don't think she does."

"It looks like we all have our little problems."

"Maybe it was a mistake to get sober."

"Maybe it was."

"Sure. Let's drink up."

The minute the drink was in my stomach I realized I hadn't been sober at all. It was the period in drunkenness when you think you're sober that comes just before you get roaring drunk.

"It really is astonishing," Swaine said, "how much you look like Jerry."

"Now, look, we're not going to go through that again, are we?"

"He was worth twenty of me. Jerry was the apple of my mother's eye. It killed her, too, you know. She had a heart attack when they phoned her about the accident and she never came out of it. You see, I killed her, too. I did a thorough job."

"If you killed her, too, why don't you go looking for someone who looks like your mother and leave me the hell alone." It was a mean thing to say. O.K., I knew it was, directly after I said it. But I was loaded and not responsible. Tears came into Swaine's eyes and he cried, his face screwed up like a kid's. "Stop blubbering, for God's sake. It looks lousy for a grown man to cry."

"I can't help it. I can't help it."

"I'm sorry. I didn't mean to say it. I was sore." I handed him a handkerchief. "Stop it. It looks lousy."

Monty's timing was perfect. He walked right into the middle of the scene and stood between us, looking first at me and then at Swaine, then back to me again. I hit him before he had a chance to open his mouth and say anything. He fell to the floor quietly and lay motionless. Swaine cried louder and Andy woke up and he began to cry, too. The kitchen filled up quickly with people and they all talked at once. I didn't listen to anything. I walked out through the dining room and living room to the front hall. The fat interior decorator caught up with me in the hall.

"Petey, I've been looking for you. I wanted to ask you a question, a professional question. And I want you to answer me and not send me a bill." She was pretty drunk and her dress was mussed up and her hat was on the back of her head and her bleached-blonde hair was mangled over her face. I pushed her away and kept walking. I found my hat and coat and started out the front door.

"Hey, there!"

It was Helen, looking very calm and very neat. "What the hell do you want?"

"Which one did you hit?" she asked.

"Monty," I said.

"That's good. I was afraid you had hit Mitch."

"I almost hit him, too."

I started down the stairs and she followed me into the hall, hanging over the banister and watching me go down. "When do you want to hear the story of my life?"

"Never."

"It has some high spots. I think *you* particularly would like it."

"Listen, Helen," I said. I had stopped on the first-floor landing and was looking up at her. "Listen to me carefully. I don't want anything to do with you and I don't want anything to do with your boy friend, either. Keep him away from me, do you understand?"

"What are you afraid of, big one?"

"I'm not afraid of anything. I just don't want complications. Do you understand that? I don't want to get any more fouled up than I am."

"You may be sorry." She smiled at me. "You may be passing up a good thing."

"Sure. You look like a good thing, all right. But I don't want the best part of you. Or him. Is that clear?"

"Perfectly, big one. I'll be seeing you." She blew me a kiss. I ran outside into the night. It had become much colder. I put on my coat, turned up the collar, and walked until I found a cab. I climbed in and gave the driver my home address. My key ring was in my overcoat pocket. I took it out and jangled the keys. There was one new key on the ring, shining new, the edges of it rough from being recently cut, not yet worn smooth from use.

"Driver. Take me to 120 East Cedar instead, will you?"

I didn't know why, but I knew I needed Clarissa.

CHAPTER TWO

Then There Is This Night with Clarissa

"Peter, is that you?"

I could see a dim light from the bedroom. "Yes," I called back. "I thought you'd be sleeping."

"No, I've been waiting for you."

I dropped my hat on a bench, took off my coat, and let it fall on the floor. "How did you know I'd come?"

"I just had a feeling, that's all. You know, a woman's intuition."

"Intuition, baloney!"

"Are you drunk?"

"Yes."

"Come in here, darling, and let me look at you."

Always when I saw her for the first time in a long time, I thought of Titian and the way he would have painted her, and Monty, the way he had painted her. Clarissa was very lovely as she lay in her bed, all soft and glowing with wonderful pink highlights in her hair and on her skin.

"You look awful," she said. "Where have you been?"

"At a party."

"It must have been quite a party." She sat up in bed, adjusted her nightgown, and moved to her right, patting a space she cleared for me. "Come and sit here and let me look at you." I sat on the edge of the bed. "Peter, I can't look at you if you keep your back to me." I turned around to face her. She put her hand to my cheek; it felt soft and cooling against the heat inside me. "You are such a baby, Peter. You need someone to look after you."

"I hit Monty," I said. "He was going to say something terrible so I slugged him."

Clarissa laughed a little. "Did you really? How marvelous. But I imagine it was rather disappointing, wasn't it? Hitting Monty must be rather like sleeping with him, very disappointing."

"You're not sore?"

"For heaven's sake, why should I be sore? Of course I'm not sore. I think it's cute. You've been naughty and now you've come to Clarissa to tell her about it." She put both hands on my face. "But you see, Clarissa isn't going to punish you at all."

"For God's sake, don't mother me. I can't stand being mothered."

There was an age difference between Clarissa and me. She was ten years older, and sometimes it caused tension between us.

"I'm not mothering you, Peter. I'm not mothering you at all. If I were mothering you, I'd take down your pants and slap your backside."

I smiled. "I'd like to see you try."

"The party sounds like fun. Whose party was it, Jackie's and Jill's?"

I nodded. I kicked off my shoes, loosened my tie, undid my collar, and stretched out on the bed so that my head was in Clarissa's lap. She massaged my head at the temples. The pressure felt good.

"Who was there?"

"The usual," I said. "I didn't know Monty was going to be there. It was an accident. I didn't mean to hit him. I almost hit him once and I didn't, but the next time I couldn't help myself."

"Who else was there?"

"Just the usual. No one special."

"Mitch Swaine was there, wasn't he?"

"How did you know?"

"He phoned here a few minutes before you came. He was looking for you. I have a number where you can reach him."

"He can drop dead. How do you suppose he knew enough to call here?"

"Monty told him, I suppose."

"Well, I'm not going to call him."

"Darling, why don't you get comfortable?"

"I'm not going to stay. I didn't even intend to come. Why don't you ask me where I've been for three days?"

She laughed again, just a little. "Peter, you really are a baby. You'll tell me when you're ready."

"Weren't you even curious? Or worried. For all you know some monster might have swallowed me up."

"I don't worry about you. You're a big man and can take care of yourself. I did phone your office once or twice. They said you were out of town on business."

"Well, I wasn't. I was home. I was locked in those four damn walls trying to make head or tail out of my life."

"Don't talk about it now, darling. Get out of your clothes and get comfortable. I'll fix a hot bath for you. It'll do you a world of good to sit in a hot tub."

"I don't want to sit in a hot tub. I want to talk."

"You're in no condition to talk until you've soaked in a hot tub." She got out of the bed on the other side and went into the bathroom, and I heard the water begin to run. I must have dozed for a minute. When I opened my eyes, Clarissa had taken off my socks, unbuckled my belt, and was pulling off my pants.

"You going to whack my backside, lady?"

"I shall have to get used to handling you. You are so much bigger than what I'm accustomed to."

I started to say something, then changed my mind and relaxed while Clarissa struggled to undress me. When she had finally got off all my clothes, I was face down on the bed, smelling the fragrance of Clarissa which still clung to the sheets. She whacked me, then, on the backside. "Now, off to the tub with you," she commanded.

I turned around, jumped up, and caught her in my arms, kissing her hard. Her mouth yielded to mine without a protest. When the kiss was over, she said, "Now get in the tub before you catch cold."

"Look, Clar, I'm sorry about Monty. Not because I hit him but because I made a scene. I'm sorry on account of you and what people are going to say."

"You know me well enough to know that I don't give a damn what people say. If I did, I should never have left Monty and I shouldn't want to live with you."

"About that, Clar, about living together, maybe we ought to wait a little while. Maybe Monty will come around and give you a divorce."

"Darling, will you get in the bathroom? You're all goose pimples. Now off with you." She put her hands on the small of my back and pushed me gently into the bathroom.

"I hate bathtubs. They never fit. Let me take a shower, Clar."

"No, sitting in a hot tub will do you good."

"It's too hot."

"You haven't even tried it." She waved her hand back and forth in the water. "It isn't too hot, at all. Now, get in."

I put one foot in, tentatively. "It's hot."

"Don't be a sissy. It's not going to hurt you."

The blood rushed to my head when I stood in the hot water and I was dizzy and groggy for a minute. I gripped the side of the tub. Clarissa sat on the bathroom floor at the side of the tub. "Are you all right?"

I nodded. "In a minute." My head cleared, my body adjusted to the heat of the water. "I've got a feeling I'm going to have a hell of a hang-over tomorrow."

"Hand me the soap." I reached for it and gave it to her. She began soaping my back, massaging the soap in gently.

"I love you, Clar," I said.

"You have a lovely back, Peter."

I looked over at her. "You've got a hell of a front."

"Hand me the washcloth. I'm going to get behind your ears."

"Clar?"

"What, dear?"

"Don't let me get away from you, will you? I'm ashamed now about all the things I've been thinking."

"What were you thinking about, getting rid of me?"

I swallowed hard, looked down at the soapy water in the tub. "You knew, didn't you?"

"That you've been thinking of getting rid of me? Yes, darling, I knew. I think it's only normal. I think sometimes of getting rid of you, but I know how ridiculous it is because I love you so much and want you so hard."

"Clar, I'm ashamed of myself. You don't know half of what has been going through my mind. When I'm with you everything is all right but when I'm alone it's so mixed up about you and me. When I look at us with a clear eye and a logical head, we don't make sense together."

"Sense has nothing to do with this. This has to do with love, Peter." She hesitated pointedly. "It does have to do with love, doesn't it, darling?"

This has been part of my torture, perhaps the core of the torture. Did I love Clarissa? That was a question I had asked myself countless times these past few days. Did I love Clarissa? It wasn't in the cards for people like us to be happy together. We were from foreign areas of background and experience. There was the difference in our ages. There were many things. But the question was, did I love Clarissa? I still didn't know the answer. I knew the physical need I had for her but I knew, too, that there is more than that to love.

"Answer me, darling," she said.

"Yes, Clar, it has to do with love."

"And you've been cooped up in that old apartment thinking to yourself that you've stopped loving Clarissa, haven't you?"

"Like I said, Clar, when I'm with you everything is fine. I know I love you. But when I'm alone all kinds of crazy things go through my head. We have so many strikes on us before we start. Maybe if you were divorced now it wouldn't seem so mixed up, I'd be surer of us, of our ... Well, loving each other."

"Monty will give in sooner or later. Eventually he'll consent to the divorce."

"But in the meantime I don't think it's right that we should live together as though we were married. I think we ought to wait. It isn't right to live together until you're divorced."

"You are a peasant at heart, Peter. Turn around so I can wash your other ear. What difference would it make that we're not married? Who could it make any diffference to as long as it's all right with us?"

"But the firm. What do you suppose is going to happen at Murdick, Howell, Maguire, and Watkins when Mr. Watkins suddenly takes up residence with Mrs. Montgomery. I don't think it's going to do business any good."

"We've discussed this. You promised me you'd get out of there. It's not your cup of tea, darling, being a member of a firm like that and wasting yourself on those messy little houses Monty got you involved in." She pushed the washcloth into my hand. "Here, I've gone as far as it's decent. You take over."

"I think sometimes, too, that I'd be a sap to chuck that. Gee, Clar, some guys would give their left arm to get the break I got. It doesn't seem right to just chuck it."

"But you didn't earn it, Peter. You didn't get it honestly. You coasted into it on Monty's coattails. We can't expect to build our happiness on something Monty is responsible for. And besides, you know that there you'll never do the kind of work you really want to do. It's a prostitution of what you believe in, Peter.

You're prostituting yourself for the Manchester Life Insurance Company's money."

"We've got to have money, Clar. We can't live without money. If I pull out of the firm now, it's not going to be so easy to hook up with someone else. There's going to be plenty of talk. Everyone is going to know why I left. There are going to be some dirty things said."

"Then we'll go away and start somewhere else. We'll go to Mexico. You'll be divine in Mexico, darling. You can lie out in the sun and turn a beautiful golden brown. You tan so wonderfully."

"Mitchell Swaine is just back from North Africa. He's plenty suntanned. I was thinking maybe I'd go to Bermuda for a while, just to think things out."

"Of course, if you want to, we can go to Bermuda for a while. But we can leave permanently if you want, start fresh somewhere else. There are plenty of opportunities in Mexico once you've established residence there."

"Money, Clar. I wouldn't have very much money. We're used to living high, you and me. What would we use for money?"

"I've got plenty of money," she said. "We certainly don't have to worry about money."

I stood up. "Get me a towel, will you?"

"You have such great potentialities, Peter. I want you to be absolutely free to express yourself in any way you want." She handed me a new towel. "Here you are, darling."

I stepped out of the tub, opening the towel. My monogram was on it. "Hey, what's this?"

"It was to be a surprise. I've had some linens made up for you."

"That's very nice. You kind of anticipated a lot."

"I know you, Peter. I know what's good for you."

I felt better now, clearer in the head. "I don't want to be kept, Clar, and that's what it would be if we lived together. I'd be kept."

"You don't want to be bound by silly conventions in your profession, darling. Why must you impose them on your personal life, too? Kept is such an obsolete word for people like us."

"Tell me something, Clar."

"What?"

"Why did you marry Monty?"

"It was so long ago, darling. Why talk about it now?"

"I was just curious. Did you love him when you married him?"

"No, of course not. We married because it was convenient to marry. We had the same backgrounds, the same friends, and we had many mutual interests."

"Like us?"

"Yes, dear, like us. But we have more. We love each other."

"Yes," I said.

"I must get you a terrycloth robe," she said. "Stay in here a minute until I fix up the bed."

"I don't want to sleep here tonight, Clar. I'm still mixed up about things. I promised myself I'd stay away from you until I was certain in my own mind what I wanted to do. I got loaded and weak-livered. I shouldn't have come. It wasn't fair to come here."

"Where else would you come, Peter, except to me? You belong here." She came up to me, put her arms around my neck, pressing her body close to mine. "You'll always belong here, belong with me."

"No, Clar, please. Not tonight. Let me just have this one more night to think this through. I've just got to have it."

"Don't argue with me, Peter. Now get into bed. I'm going into the kitchen and fix you something to stave off a hang-over. We'll talk about it again in the morning." She went to the kitchen without giving me a chance to answer. I went into the bedroom, pulled back the other side of the bed and lay down. It was Monty's side of the bed and this was Monty's pillow my head was against and this was Monty's room and Monty's apartment and it would always be this way and I knew it. I knew it that night very well; I got up and began to dress again.

"Peter, you're still drunk. You wouldn't dare go out into this weather after a hot bath and in your condition. Don't be a fool. Now, drink this quickly. Hold your nose and you won't taste a thing."

I held my nose and drank the concoction down. "I'm not going to stay, Clar. Don't make a scene over it. I'll wait a minute and then I'm going home."

She gave up momentarily, shifting to a neutral subject, but I was aware that she had not given up. "Are you going to call Mitchell Swaine? He said for you to call at any time you showed up here."

"No, I'm not going to call him. He's a terrible pest."

"What does he want?"

"I don't know what he wants. He keeps telling me that I look like his brother. O.K., so I look like his brother. So what does he want me to do?"

Clarissa sat at her dressing table and began to brush her hair. The electricity from it made a crackling sound in the still room. Jill had done that, brushed her hair while she talked to me. How different they were, Clarissa and Jill. Even their hair was different. Jill's was short, bleached dry and lusterless. Clarissa's hair was long and full and radiant with its own natural color. "I've heard that Mitch's wife is most attractive," she said.

"Is that news around already? I didn't even think anyone knew they were married. Who told you?"

"Monty. He said if I wanted to hold on to you I should keep you away from her. Is she that attractive?"

"Did you talk to Monty tonight?"

"Yes, darling, as a matter of fact, I did."

"When? After I left the party? Did he call you after I left the party?"

"Yes."

"Why didn't you tell me? You knew all about it, then. You knew that I had hit him and you knew about Swaine and everything else. Why didn't you tell me?"

"You were upset. I didn't want to upset you further."

"That son-of-a-bitch must have got up from the floor and on to the telephone. Just like a kid tattling on another kid. I feel like going back and letting him have it again only this time I'd put enough heft behind it so that he wouldn't get up for a while."

"They were going to take him to the hospital. You may have broken his nose."

"Good," I said. "That makes me feel better."

"It worried me about what Monty said about Mitch's wife. I may hate Monty but I lived with him long enough to know he has a sixth sense about people, how they react to each other."

"Well, his crystal ball is a little cloudy this time. She's not my type at all." I was putting on my suit coat.

"Peter, you're not going through with this ridiculous idea of going back to your apartment. It's unheard of."

"Look, I'm a big boy. I can take good care of myself. I said I wanted to go home and I'm going home. Good night."

She kept brushing her hair. "All right, Peter, if you insist on being ridiculous. Please come and kiss me good night."

I hesitated. "I'd better not."

"Are you afraid?"

"You know damn well I'm afraid. Once I kiss you, I'll get all fouled-up again. I'll see you tomorrow."

"All right, Peter. Good night."

At the door, I stopped. "You know I love you, Clar."

"Do you, Peter?"

"I've got to be able to think this out myself. You said yourself that I'm nothing now because everything I am Monty has made me. I'm not really myself. Well, if I let you make up my mind about things now, I won't be myself either, I'll be what you make me. Can you see that?"

"Good night, Peter."

"Damn it, Clar, I wish you'd see that this is hard for me. I want more than anything to hit that sack and put my head right in the hollow of your shoulder and sleep till next month. But it's no good. It's no solution."

"I'm tired, Peter. If you're going to leave, leave."

"Smile at me like you understand."

She turned and smiled at me perfunctorily. I went to her, kissed her hard and long, and then bolted out of the room, picking up my coat from the hall floor on the run, forgetting my hat which lay on the bench.

Outside in the night which was becoming morning, I felt safe for a moment. And strong. The strength had come from being able to resist Clarissa, the soft, absorbing warmth of her. I had exerted my strength in being able to resist her, to go back to my own apartment and think things out in my own way.

But was it strength? Was it strength or the beginning of the end of love? There was that to be thinking about, too, as I walked the long way home.

CHAPTER THREE

And the Night Goes On until There Is Morning

MITCHELL SWAINE seemed very sober. He was sitting on the floor outside the door to my apartment very relaxed and smiling.

"Where have you been?" he asked. "I've been waiting."

"Look, Swaine. I've had enough. I'm tired. I'm beginning to get a hang-over. I don't want to talk and I don't want to listen."

He laughed. "You get more like him the longer I know you."

"And another thing, it's enough with this business about your brother. I'm getting bored with it. I'm getting bored with you. I'm getting bored with listening to people."

"You know what your trouble is, old man?"

I put the key in the lock, hesitating before I turned it. "I told you I didn't want to talk. Go home. Please, go home."

"The trouble with you, old man, is that you need a change of scenery. You ought to get away from it all."

"Maybe." I unlocked the door and edged it slightly open. Swaine jumped up ready to come in with me.

"Helen and I have been talking about going to Mexico. Good fishing in Mexico. Why don't you come along?"

"What's with Mexico tonight? Everybody wants me to go to Mexico. I don't want to go anywhere but to bed."

Swaine reached over my shoulder, pushed the door open and walked into the apartment. I didn't have strength enough to argue with him. I let him go in. The apartment was in bad shape.

I had been thrashing around in there for three days not paying any attention to how the place looked. I hadn't let the maid come in and I hadn't bothered to straighten it up or to empty ash trays.

"Nice place," Swaine said. "Do you have a drink for a fellow?"

"If you want something it's in the cabinet. I'm going to bed. I told you I'm tired. I don't feel like talking. Drink all you want only don't make any noise."

"Don't worry about me. I'll find my way around just fine." He pointed to the swinging door. "Kitchen in there?" I nodded.

"Good night, Swaine."

"Good night," he said. He was cheerful and very much at home in my apartment.

"Look, I just can't hold my head up any more. I don't know why you're here. You must have a reason. You must want something besides a drink. I'd like to help you but I'm too tired. It'll have to wait."

"Don't worry about it. It'll keep until morning. It's safe here. I like it. Good night."

I didn't even turn on the lights in my room. I peeled off my clothes, let them lay on the floor and piled into bed. Just as soon as I had fallen asleep I heard Swaine calling to me in the darkness. There was the sound of his voice as though it were a sound in a dream. There was also the sound of ice cubes being swirled around in a glass.

"Old man," he called.

I felt the pressure of his body as he sat at the edge of the bed. Quietly, holding myself tense and motionless, I said, "You want to get your face pushed in, Swaine?"

"She's going to kill me," he said. "That's why she wants to take me to Mexico. She wants to kill me."

"Who wants to kill you?"

"Helen."

"You're nuts. Why should she want to kill you? Where could she find a better meal ticket than you?"

"She has a plan to kill me. I don't know what it is or how she's going to do it but I know. I know Helen."

It was silent in the room for a moment, just the sound of his breathing and my breathing. Then, gradually his breathing began to be gasps of breathing. "I told you before," I said, "it looks lousy for a grown man to cry."

"You can't see me," he said. "I can't help it. It's not that I want to live, it's that I'm afraid to die."

"Look, fella, tomorrow. We'll talk tomorrow. Go out and sleep on the couch. And lay off the booze. Tomorrow. We'll talk about it tomorrow."

"Good night, old man. I'm sorry."

"Good night, Swaine. I'll see you tomorrow."

He closed the door on his way out. I tried to fall back to sleep but sleep wouldn't come so easily this time. I lighted a cigarette and walked to the window. The street below was deserted. Somewhere, behind the night, daylight was beginning. I was thinking about Swaine and thinking that I was a damn fool to be thinking about him. He was psychotic. He was suffering from everything in the psychiatric book. Yet there was a quality to him that got me, that attached me to him in some way. I could have slammed the door on anyone else but somehow he was like a puppy out in a cold rain. I couldn't do that to a dog and I wasn't able to do it to Swaine.

This delusion he had of Helen's wanting to kill him was a delusion, I decided, and nothing more. There would be no reason for her to want him out of the way. O.K., so he was impotent. He gave her license to go out with whom she pleased and do as she pleased. And there was all that dough. She could have anything she wanted even with Swaine alive. And in a way he was really an appealing guy. It came through all the phobias and the alcohol and psychotic fog. He was warm inside. There was the way he had been at the party, with the kid in the play pen. Kids have a sixth sense about people and Andy had liked Swaine all right.

I opened the window a little wider and flicked out the cigarette, watching the progress of the pin head of light until it landed on the street.

You have enough trouble without his troubles, I told myself. There is what you're going to do about Clarissa. Tempting, isn't she? She's got enough dough to keep you so that you can do what you want and when you want to do it. There is also that office downtown with your name on the door. Are you going to chuck all that, say the hell with it because you like flat roofs and straight lines? It doesn't make sense. It's dough in your pocket, more dough than you ever thought you'd have. But Clarissa says you owe all of that to Monty, because Monty helped you.

Damn Clarissa.

Yes, there is another thing, too. Clarissa. This isn't a punk kid or a girl with her eye on your bankroll. This is a full-blown woman who knows how a woman should be and how a man wants a woman. You can't just throw that out the window.

There was a scream from the other room. A scream screamed with fright and screamed from the depths of a man. More horrible than you can imagine a scream sounding. For a moment I didn't move. Then I ran into the other room.

I fumbled for the switch on a lamp, knocked the lamp to the floor, finally got it lighted, leaving the shattered base where it had fallen.

Swaine lay on the couch, fully clothed. His face was streaked with perspiration and his mouth was twisted. His eyes were closed. I leaned over him, he was breathing and the sound of his breathing was heavy but coming in regular rhythm. I pulled down his tie and loosened his collar. He didn't move. His shirt was wet with sweat and his face was white. I shook him. And again. He jumped up suddenly and all the fright which there had been in the scream was there now in his eyes.

"You all right?"

It took him a minute to realize where he was and who I was. "What's wrong?" he asked.

"You screamed. I thought something happened."

"It was in my sleep. I should have warned you. I do that sometimes. I'm sorry." He smiled. "You told me no noise, didn't you?"

"Can I get you something?"

He shook his head. "Nothing, thanks." He lay back again, closing his eyes. "It's too bad you're such a gentleman, old man. Otherwise you could have slammed the door in my face and you wouldn't have to put up with this."

"You're sure you'll be all right?"

He nodded. "I'll be all right."

"Good night, Swaine."

"Good night, old man."

I went back into my room and lighted another cigarette. I pulled a blanket off my bed and took it in to Swaine, who had fallen asleep again. I put it over him and tucked it in so that it wouldn't fall off. As I looked down at him I thought I saw a shadow of a smile on his face. I couldn't tell. The room was dark and it was very late and I was very tired. Very tired. I fell asleep quickly, but it was a light sleep, harassed by dreaming.

The telephone was ringing. I opened my eyes. Outside the window there was the bright light of the day. I checked the clock next to my bed. It was almost noon. Surprisingly enough my head was clear, no weight hanging over it. I took the phone.

"Yes."

"That you, old man?"

"Swaine! Where are you? Aren't you ... I mean, did you leave?"

"Sorry about last night. I'm afraid I was a terrible nuisance. Drinking, you know. I lose all sense of good behavior. I'm very sorry I put you to all that trouble. You should have thrown me out or called Helen to come fetch me. I'm afraid she's rather used to it."

"You didn't seem drunk. I thought you had sobered up."

"Don't feel bad. I've fooled the best of them. Seem very sober and then, wham. Drunk as hell really, all the time. I called you up to thank you and to ask a question."

"What is it?"

"Don't want to intrude, really, or stick my nose in where I don't belong, but you look like a man who has a lot on his mind. Then there's a bit of gossip around about you. Can't help but hear it. I have a wonderful solution to all your problems. Helen wants to go fishing in Mexico. Good weather in Mexico this time of year. Think it would be a great idea if you came along. Do you good."

"Don't you remember what you said last night?"

He laughed. "I guess I said a lot of things."

"You talked about Mexico. About fishing there. You wanted me to come along."

"Did I? Well, you see then I really mean it. Drunk or sober I think it's a great idea."

Slowly, not sure myself what was real and what was a dream, I said, "Do you remember anything you said about Mexico and Helen?"

"I tell you what, Petey, let's all meet for cocktails at five. We'll meet at the bar in the Drake. We're staying here. You know the bar downstairs."

I didn't want to press him about what he had said about Helen, about the fears he had, because I wasn't sure whether he had really said it. I realized that I must have been still drunk or slightly drunk when he had been in my apartment. Yet he avoided my questions now so completely that perhaps he really had said it, remembered saying it and was trying to cover up.

"O.K.," I said. "I'll meet you at five. Will Helen be along?"

"Of course. She never leaves me out of her sight if she can help it, do you, baby? She's right here, Petey. You want to talk to her?"

"No, I'll see you at five."

I took a cold, hard shower not thinking about anything, remembering anything, or analyzing anything. When I came out the phone was ringing again. It was Jill.

"Hi, baby."

"You all right, Petey?"

"Certainly."

"You were so drunk last night. I didn't see you go. We were all taking care of Monty. I called your apartment until late, but there was no answer. I was worried. Where were you?"

"I don't remember exactly. I think maybe I walked about ten miles trying to sober up."

"Monty was sure you went to Clarissa's to show off and brag about what you had done to him. He was frightful the way he talked about you."

"I'll bet he was. Is he all right?"

She giggled. "His nose is broken."

"I'm sorry. I really am."

"It's terrible to laugh, I know, but it is funny."

I laughed too. I wasn't really sorry. If I had had it to do over again I would have done it the same way.

Jill's voice changed pitch then, became lower and almost plaintive. "Petey, I want to see you."

"Anything wrong?"

"Not wrong, really. It's just that…I can't begin it on the phone. I want to see you. As soon as possible."

"O.K. You want me to run up there?"

"No, I want to get out of here. I can't stand looking at this place one more minute. I've never felt this way before. It looks as though it belongs to someone else, another girl lives here. I can't believe that I live here. It's like I'm seeing myself for the … Stay there, Petey. I'll be right down. Please wait for me."

"Sure, Jill. I'll be here."

I held the phone in my hand for a moment. There were so many things and they were all coming at once. Yesterday I had thought that my life held all the confusion any life could hold. But that was before the cocktail party. Now there was Jill on her way over. And there was Mitchell Swaine at five. And Helen. Yes, there was Helen. And there was Monty with his nose broken, and Clarissa angry because I had left her last night, not satisfied, not content that she had mothered me completely.

The dial tone came on. I dialed my office.

"Superior nine, nine thousand," a cool voice said.

"This is Mr. Watkins. Connect me with my office, please."

"Pete, it's Ethel. Mr. Murdick said if you phoned in he wanted to talk to you right away."

"O.K. Connect me, will you."

Ethel had been at the switchboard for many years. She had never bridged the gap I had made from the drafting department to a partnership. I was still Pete to her.

"Pete?"

"Yes, Mr. Murdick."

"Where the hell have you been?"

"I . . . I had to go away for a few days. I may have to go back. Family business."

"What the hell did you get into last night? Between my wife and Ralph Montgomery this phone has been going like crazy."

I didn't say anything.

"Well, Pete, what about it?"

"What difference does it make? It doesn't have anything to do with business."

"You wouldn't think so to hear my wife or Montgomery talk. I can't say I blame you for hitting Montgomery. The way he swindles my wife with those lousy oil paintings, I've had the notion once or twice to take a poke at him myself. But he's an influential man. Don't forget if it weren't for him this whole Williamsburg Village project would be nothing."

"I know that."

"My wife was telling me a long story about you and Montgomery's wife. Is there anything to that?"

"I don't see what difference it makes."

"It makes a lot of difference, my boy. This is an old firm and there's never been any scandal connected with it. Or us. We've all behaved pretty well here because we know how important a solid reputation is. You know how these things get around. One man's wife tells another man's wife, and pretty soon you lose a big commission because somebody's wife thinks the firm is full of … Well, you know what I mean."

"Sure, I know. I'm sorry this had to flare up like this. How are things on the Village? Are there any pressing problems that the office can't handle? Anything I should check up on?"

"No, it's all right. We can handle it just fine. Maybe you ought to take a vacation or something, Pete. Get away for a while, rest up. Maybe you worked too hard on this project. You've been going like hell on it for almost two years. Maybe you ought to get away and rest. Go fishing or play golf. Do you play golf? Wonderful thing for the nerves, playing golf."

"What you're saying is that I ought to leave town until this quiets down."

Murdick cleared his throat, coughed, and cleared his throat again. "You're a young fellow, Pete. Hell, I can understand. You're an artist, too. But you got to take it a little easy. I guess Charlie Howell got wind of some of this, too. He says it was a mistake shooting you up so fast, that in spite of the Williamsburg Village, maybe it wasn't worth it. I can take care of Charlie, all right, but I think it would be a good idea if you left town for a while. It makes sense all the way around. For your own health, too."

"All right. I'll clear out for a while. I'll let you know where I am."

"You're not mad, are you, Pete? I want you to understand that I don't like meddling into this, but seeing as my name is the first on the door, I'm kind of responsible for all of us."

"I understand. I'll let you know where I am as soon as I can."

"Good luck, Pete. Get a good rest."

"Thanks."

And there it was. Monty had begun his campaign to take me down from where he put me, to destroy the monster that he had created. I knew Monty very well; I knew the ways in which he worked and I knew how effective he could be. If I wanted to hold what I had, I knew I would have to fight for it. But did I want it? That was the question which had been circling my consciousness for these last days. And not as simple as that because Clarissa was tied up with it, the heart and the intellect hopelessly linked together. Hopelessly. I knew that now. I knew that the decision I wanted to be made would not be made, that what I would finally do I would drift into doing, pushed into doing by external forces. There was no use thinking or plotting. There was only the doing of what I was feeling compelled to do.

I telephoned Clarissa.

"Are you still mad, Clar?"

"Peter, you are a child. Of course I was never angry. I was only concerned about your health. I didn't want you to catch cold."

"I just spoke to the office, to Bill Murdick. Monty has got to him. I guess there's going to be a stink."

"Did Monty actually call Bill to tell him about last night?"

"That's it, Clar. Did you know Monty's nose is broken?"

She laughed too. "How dreadful," she said. "Tell me what Murdick said."

"A lot of guff about how it was bad for the firm's reputation for one of the partners to be mixed up in a scandal. And Charlie Howell is on the warpath, too. He didn't want to take me in in the first place, you know. Murdick wants me to blow town for a while until this has died down."

"This doesn't sound like Monty. Monty usually isn't as direct as this. His campaigns are always elaborate. You certainly must have roughed him up."

"Oh, he used the indirect approach, too. Through Murdick's wife. They're buddies, you know. Monty sells her a load of paintings. I guess he gave her an earful, and she turned it back on Murdick."

"I'll call Monty right away, darling. Don't worry about it. I'll handle Monty."

"You stay out of this, Clar. Stay away from Monty. I can take care of myself. I can handle myself with Monty, all right. I don't need you."

She was silent for a moment and when she spoke I could see how her face would be looking, how her lower lip was pushed forward in a suggestion of a pout. "Is that quite fair, Peter, to say you don't need me?"

"Well, sure, I need you, Clar. But not for this. I ought to handle this myself."

"But you're overwrought, Peter. You can't possibly be objective with Monty. I can be because I don't even hate him any more. I can be perfectly calm with him and not get upset in the least so that I would say anything wrong. I know Monty much better than you do. If I ask him to stop behaving like a child, I'm sure he will. He's still very fond of me, you know."

"But I don't think you should do it, Clar. It's not that you can't do it. I'm sure you can handle Monty. It's only that I thought I ought to talk to him myself. I mean I think from my own standpoint.... It sounds kind of corny, but for my own self-respect, I ought to."

"Peter, darling, you are such a child. Self-respect has nothing to do with this. It doesn't make any difference what Monty tries to do to you, really, because it won't matter. I've thought it over very carefully and I'm more certain than ever that we should go away, to Mexico or perhaps Italy. So it really doesn't make any difference if Monty does try to ruin you with Murdick and Howell. It's just that I think it's awfully bad taste on his part and I think he should be shut up on general principles. You leave Monty to me. I'll take care of him."

"You sure you think it's the right thing to do?"

"Of course it is. I'll phone him right now."

"Call me back and let me know what he says."

"All right, darling. Are you sure you feel all right? No ill effects from last night?"

"No. I'm all right. I guess I was kind of a slob last night. I'm sorry."

"Forget it, darling. You were overwrought. Did Mitch Swaine get hold of you?"

I hesitated a minute. "Yes," I said. "He called me this morning."

"What did he want?"

"I don't know. I think he's slightly off his nut."

"Are you going to see him?"

"No. What for?"

"Did you know his wife was married to a Negro?"

"He was half Negro, and besides, what's the difference?"

"Nothing, darling. I only thought it was curious."

"Look, Clar, you'd better not call Monty."

"Don't be ridiculous, Peter. Of course I'm going to call him."

"No, don't."

"Peter, what's got into you all of a sudden?"

I could hear the sound of my own voice becoming louder and tighter. I listened to myself as though I were one man hearing another man's words. "It's a bad idea. You stay out of this. If there's any handling of Monty to be done, I'll do it."

"I know what's best, Peter. You must trust me."

"This is a man's business. I'm telling you to stay out of it. I'll fight my own battles. I forbid you to call Monty. Is that clear?"

"What makes you think you have the right to talk to me this way? You can't forbid me or command me to do or not to do anything."

"Nevertheless, I'm telling you, Clar, stay out of this. Don't call Monty. This is my affair and I'll take care of it."

"Peter?"

"What?"

"Are you still drunk?"

"Of course I'm not drunk. I'm cold sober. I'm not sure I'm going to stay this way, but right now I'm cold sober."

"Do you feel warm or feverish? I told you not to go out last night."

"For God's sake, what do you think I'm made out of, sugar or something? I'm perfectly healthy and I'm perfectly sober and I know damn well what I'm doing. You are not to contact Monty under any circumstances."

She cried suddenly and without warning. But I was used to that, not hardened to it yet but not surprised by it. "We're having our first fight," she blubbered.

"Now, who's acting childish?"

"But, Peter, I don't know how you can talk to me like this."

"This is silly, Clar. Stop crying. I'll call you later."

"I'm coming over there," she said.

"No, don't. I don't want to see anyone."

The tears and the crying stopped almost as suddenly as they had started. "There's someone with you, isn't there?"

"No. There's no one here."

"Then why don't you want me to come over."

"Because I feel like being alone."

"But you've been alone for three days?"

"And if I want to be alone for another three days, that's my business, too. Don't come over."

"Maybe we just better forget everything, Peter. About you and me, I mean."

It was time to stop. I could assert myself only so far and then I knew that I did need her, that no matter what I said I would be coming back to her. I wasn't sure in what way I needed her. But this much I knew, my body would go to her and find satisfaction in her and it was this way with her and it was with no one else.

Softly, I said, "Look, Clar, we're both worked up. I'll call you later, baby. Maybe we'll have dinner or something."

"All right, darling. Be sure and call me. You didn't mean what you said, did you?"

"I didn't mean to talk to you the way I did, Clar, but I meant what I said about not calling Monty."

"But, Peter ..."

"Later, baby. We'll talk about it later."

"Blow me a kiss."

"Oh, Clar."

"Blow me a kiss."

Although I knew I was alone I looked around anyway to see if anyone was watching, and then I made the sound with my lips and listened while the sound was returned to me.

"Good-by, darling," she said.

And I said, "Good-by, darling."

Then I took another shower.

After that I lay on the bed, looking out the window, at the grayness of the day which had come to blank out the sun. It would rain again today. It had rained every day for the last week. In Mexico the sun would be out and there would be warmth to the sun and the sun would give strength. I had always wanted to go to Mexico. When there had been time there had been no money, and when there was the money there was no time. Now there was time and there was money. But also there was Clarissa. Or there was Mitchell and Helen Swaine.

I lay there and my mind went far away. To Mexico. I was in Mexico and I was doing the things that I had always dreamed of doing, seeing places I had dreamed of seeing. And always these pictures began in the brightness of the sun, but each time there came to be a veil over the sun, a shadow. Clarissa. Or the Swaines. I lay there, daydreaming, until there was the sound of the doorbell ringing. I got up, wrapped the towel around my waist, and opened the door for Jill.

In the daylight, she was hard-looking. The crass color of her hair was even crasser, the tight, hard lines of her body gave her a gauntness in the daylight.

"Hi, Petey."

"Come on in."

She walked into the room, sat on the edge of the couch and crossed her legs. She lighted a cigarette, and her hand shook as she held the match to it.

"Are you all right, Jill?"

"Yes, of course I am. Why shouldn't I be?"

"You seem kind of nervous."

"Well, I'm not nervous. I'm not nervous at all."

I walked closer to her. "Is Andy all right?"

"Yes, he's fine. Everything is fine. Really." She looked up at me. "Petey, go and put on some clothes, will you?"

I laughed. "You're getting kind of moral, aren't you? You've seen me reduced to less than a towel."

She threw her purse on the couch and ran her hand through her hair. "Maybe I'm not in the mood today. Or maybe I'm too much in the mood. Go put something on."

"O.K. Make yourself comfortable. Want a drink?"

"God, no. Go ahead. Hurry."

I pulled on a pair of blue jeans and a T-shirt and went back into the living room. "What's the matter, Jill? You don't seem like yourself."

"That's it, Petey. I don't know what I am, really. I don't know what myself is." She looked straight at me for a long time. I didn't move. She was trying to say something without words. There was a strangeness in her, projecting out of her and getting into me, into my bones. Then, abruptly, she looked away. "I can't look at you and say what I want to say. Petey, I didn't have anyone else to come to. You were the only one I thought would understand." Then she whispered the words, more to herself than to me. "I'm not sure you'll understand, either. It doesn't matter. I've got to say it, and once I've said it maybe I won't feel this way any more. Maybe I'll be the girl I was yesterday. I want desperately to be the girl who woke up yesterday morning. I want to be that girl and I don't want last night to ever happen."

"I'm sorry about last night. I didn't mean to start anything."

"I'm not talking about that. That was only one little thing. Yesterday morning I was Jill and we were having another party and all those smart, fascinating people were coming and Jackie and I were going to be as fascinating as anyone. As unconventional as anyone. It really takes quite a lot of effort to be unconventional when it isn't natural to you, do you know that?"

I didn't say anything.

"You really know very little about me, Peter. I'm afraid I was brought up very well. I've tried to ignore it, forget it, even overcome it. I lived in a lovely house filled with lovely Chippendale furniture. I hated it. I hated the horrible Chippendale furniture with its lovely coverings and beautiful wood. That's why I thought our apartment was so marvelous. All those beds and those funny, crazy throws we've got on them. All those meant so much to me because they weren't lovely Chippendale. Is all this a horrible muddle to you, Petey? Can you understand what I'm trying to say? It was all so wonderful until suddenly last night, when every one had cleared out. I looked at it and it was more horrible than the Chippendale had ever been. And I picked up Andy out of that dirty play pen in that dirty kitchen smelling of liquor and the dregs of that Spanish omelet and I felt wicked and depraved, as though I had committed an outrage on Andy. Suddenly I wanted him to be brought up with Chippendale furniture. To have what I had as a child, a well-scrubbed, protected life. Only I want him to love it and want it and want to keep it. I want him to be able to be happy in that kind of life. I hated everything last night, all those people with their smart talk and their veneers of depth and knowledge. I wished I had been a guest at the party, out slumming at the apartment of a girl who had gone to the dogs. If I had been a guest, I could have gone home to my house in the country and looked in on my little boy fast asleep in a spotless nursery. I wanted that suddenly, what my old friends have, the things I used to laugh at them for treasuring so much."

She was on the edge of tears. Jill wasn't like Clarissa. I had never seen Jill cry. I knew that when she cried it would cost her a great deal. "How about a drink, baby. Huh?"

"No, Petey. Really. Let me finish. Don't stop me. I've got to get rid of it." She turned to me. "I guess I can look at you now. All the way down here I wasn't sure I would be able to tell you all this. I wasn't sure that it would come out."

"Go ahead."

"About Andy, Petey. What do you know about Andy?"

"He's a good kid, Jill. Even if he doesn't have a spotless nursery, he's a good kid."

"Of course he is. But I don't mean that. I mean how do you think I got him?"

"I don't know. I guess I never thought about it."

"I've always made fun of it. I've always said I wasn't quite sure who his father was. I've deliberately tried to make people believe that he was illegitimate. I thought it made me sound like such a free person to be able to have an illegitimate child. I thought it made me sound free of all the pettiness that I detested in other people. It all seems so childish today. I can't quite believe that it is I." She walked to the fireplace and looked into the blank expanse of mirror over it. "Not even when I look in the mirror can I believe that I'm the same person I used to be." She touched her hair. "It used to be quite lovely," she said. "It's very dark in its natural state. Very dark and very soft." She turned again to face me. "Andy is not illegitimate. His father was a fine, wonderful man. Rather like you, Petey. He rather looked like you. He was finer than you, really, stronger inside. More sure of himself."

She stopped talking. I waited a minute, then I said, "Where is he?"

"He's quite dead, Petey. More than dead. He's disintegrated. There wasn't even anything left of him to bury."

"How?"

"An airplane. While I watched. It was such a beautiful, beautiful day. It was in Florida. He was in the Navy. I was waiting for his plane to land. We had bought a car. Not much of a car, really. Second hand, but it was bright blue and it was a convertible. I was sitting up on the back of the seat watching all the planes, thinking how beautiful they were and how wonderful they were and how wonderful he was. There were other wives waiting for their husbands to land, too. All of us there as conventional as Chippendale. And happy. Then one plane exploded, suddenly and without warning or anything touching it. They all screamed, these other wives. But I didn't scream because I already knew it was he. I knew it, I knew it."

I tried to find some words, but no words would come out.

"There was nothing to do, Petey, but to watch the pieces of the plane and the pieces of him fall to the ground. I didn't move and I didn't cry. I just sat there and there were sirens sounding and screaming and talking. And I just sat there not moving. I don't know what was going through my mind. I just knew that it was his plane and that he was gone."

"That's tough, Jill."

"Yes, it is tough. Very tough. Because, you see, it took a long time for me to meet him. I was one of those girls who had had the golden spoon and somehow was never happy with it. I was indulged at home and loved and yet I was never happy there. I had to prove something to my parents and to my friends. Maybe I was trying to prove that I was better than they. Or maybe I knew that I wasn't really as good as they so I proved instead that I was different. I was one of those girls who left home to live a free and independent life in the big city. I was going to have a career. I went to New York the summer after I graduated from college. I wasn't like this, Petey, I wasn't the way I am now. There were lots of girls like me in New York then. We were all rebelling against home, but we were well bred and we damn well showed it. We lived in the Village, but it was rather the smart part of the Village. We were variations of the girls we had been at home, variations of the same theme. Not like I am now." She shouted, "Not like I am now! Not a different person completely, like I am now."

"Easy, Jill."

"Yes, easy," she said. "I did rather well in the city. Better than most. I worked for the International Ladies Garment Workers Union and I handled personal problems. You know, 'Should I have an abortion, Miss Bainbridge?' Or 'My husband drinks and takes all my pay. What should I do, Miss Bainbridge?' I was rather good at it and I was made head of the department. It was rather smart, coming from the background I had, to be work-ing for a labor union. I fussed a good deal about politics, too. I thought Henry Wallace was rather wonderful. I can see now that I was typical. Do you know what eventually happens to those typical college girls?"

"What happens?"

"They get married. The less successful in their careers they are, the sooner they get married. I was successful and the novelty lasted longer. But almost all of them get married, and they try to keep it up, being interested in music, modern art, labor move-ments, and all of that. They vow to themselves that marriage won't change them, that they won't fall into the rut of being like other people. It would be such a lovely rut, Petey, being like other people. But in spite of themselves, they become like other people. Their politics are a little less liberal, and they have less time to listen to music and they begin to play bridge because it relaxes them. Children are so wearing. Gradually they are other people. They are in that lovely, lovely rut."

I had been standing all this time, almost in the same posi-tion, not being aware that I was standing or aware even of myself.

The room was filled with Jill. Jill as she had been and Jill as she was and Jill as she might have been. But I felt tired now, weary. I stretched out on the couch. My hand touched something hard and cold. I picked it up. It was a foreign coin. It must have fallen out of Mitchell Swaine's pocket.

"It was waiting for me, Petey, that lovely rut. Even I was headed for it. I met him one night at a friend's apartment. There was a Navy officer in town, a girl's husband's roommate in college. She said wouldn't I please date him, and I did. He was very handsome. Like you, Petey. The same kind of boyishness in his face. He laughed at me a lot because I was so serious and so concerned with labor unions and politics. I knew the numbers of the bills up in Congress and knew which ones benefited labor and which ones didn't. He laughed at me and I was very angry. I thought he was horrid and middle class, but he was damned attractive and I had my human side even then.

"He had six days left of his leave, and I saw him every day and every night. Sometime during those six days we knew about each other, that we loved each other and that each of us was what the other had been waiting for. It had taken a long time, but I was ready now, ready to slip into that lovely rut that I had been born into and fought to get out of. I thought how pleased my parents would be and what a model Navy wife I would make. You probably think none of this is true, Petey. It's all so different from the way you know me. But it is true, all of it. This is exactly the way it was."

"No, Jill, I can believe you. I think, maybe, I always saw more of you than you thought I saw. You're not like Jackie, really. Jackie, I guess, was never any different from the way she is now. You are. I could always see you were different. I see it now very clearly. I believe you, Jill."

"Thank you, Petey."

"What happened then?" I threw Swaine's coin into the air, missed catching it. I groped on the floor, found it, and held it in my hand again.

"We were married," she said, "on the last day of his leave. He suspected he would be shipped out of Florida after a few weeks so I took a leave of absence from my job and we went to Florida. We behaved dreadfully, I guess, except that it was lovely. We took a room in the hotel and I never left it. I just waited for him to come there so that I could love him. He came home at noon but we never ate lunch. He came home at four and we didn't eat dinner until nine. For five days we were like that, completely out of touch with everything and everyone. No one knew we were married. Then on the sixth day he said, 'It's time I showed off my bride.' He threw some car keys to me. 'It's a wedding present. It's bright blue and it's parked across the street. It's second hand but it runs. Pick me up at the field at three-thirty. And mind you don't be late. We're flying this afternoon. Look your prettiest. The boys are very critical and their wives are worse.' " Jill snorted a laugh. "That's all. I looked my prettiest and I drove to the field and watched him explode into nothing. That's all there was. I watched the excitement die down and one by one the other men left the field and got into the other cars with the other wives but there was no man for me. He was gone. As completely gone as a human being can be."

"No one ever knew? You never told your folks?"

"No. There wasn't time and when there was time it was too late. No one ever knew. I was all right for a while. I guess the full blast of it didn't hit me. I packed my clothes and drove that car back to New York and went to work and tried to forget that it had never happened to me. It was quick and ended so finally. There was only the blue car and the wedding ring to remind me. One day I sold the car and threw the wedding ring into the Hudson River. Then there was nothing left. I thought in that way I could forget completely and go back to being the young woman at the International Ladies Garment Workers Union. Except that I found I was pregnant, and then I knew I could never forget for there would always be Andy to remind me."

"It was a rotten break, Jill."

"Yes, wasn't it. It sounds like such a little thing, getting a rotten break. But it was such a damn big rotten break. It changed me so thoroughly. I went to extremes in everything trying to forget, trying to get that picture of the exploding airplane out of my mind. To this extreme, Petey, to this person I am now. I thought I had it licked. It was such fun rooming with Jackie and living from one party to the next, becoming rather a legend around town, embarrassing my family so terribly and amusing all my old friends. It was so smart, so exciting, so consuming. Until last night when I hated it all and hated myself and hated what I was doing to Andy."

She came to me now, kneeling at the couch, her hand over mine. "I think I know why I changed, Petey. I think I know what happened that made me see everything so differently. Do you know what it was?"

I didn't answer.

"It was you, Petey. It was seeing you in that brawl with Monty last night and seeing you getting mixed up with Mitch Swaine and knowing you were thinking of pulling out of what you've made for yourself. I guess I saw myself in you. I saw myself ruining myself the way you're going to ruin yourself. And there was one other thing, Petey, one other thing."

Still I said nothing.

"Ask me what it was, Petey. For God's sake, please ask me what it was."

Slowly, knowing the answer, I asked, "What was the other thing?"

"I knew last night that I was in love with you."

She cried then. She sat on the floor and cried. There was nothing to do but let her cry. She cried almost gratefully, glad that at last she could cry. I listened to the sound of her crying and I didn't move, and after a while the sound was still there but I was not hearing it. I was thinking that if I had met Jill three years ago … If the girls husband's college roommate had been a young architect … If it had been I who had laughed at her seriousness about politics and labor movements … If it had been I three years ago, we might have been very happy, Jill and I. There wouldn't be this, this apartment and the money I had come to make, or my name on the door of the office downtown. I would probably still be in the drafting department, the young man showing promise but not yet having fulfilled that promise. Not at the top yet, but on the way up. If three years ago …

"Jill," I said. "Stop crying a minute."

She tried to stifle the sobs. After a minute she was quieter.

"Have you ever thought," I said, "that people who mess up their lives can sometimes tear up the past and start over again?"

Her voice was faint, still almost the same sound as crying. "Can they, Petey?"

"Have you ever thought about going to Mexico?"

CHAPTER FOUR

Again There Are Cocktails

THE SWAINES were late. I was sitting at a table across from the bar drinking slowly, enjoying the calm in the room. I was thinking about Jill, haunted by her. She had always seemed so strong before, so impervious to other people, to conventions, and to ups and downs which other people are subjected to. Now I had seen her stripped of her defenses, naked and shivering in a world which she no longer wanted. And I was the way out for her. There was that to think about. Jill had told me that I was the way out for her.

Any man is flattered when any woman is in love with him or says she is. Yet this frightened me, too. I was frightened that I could become so important to anyone who was not important to me. Jill could have been important once. But not now. There was too much in my life now to make room again for Jill. I had asked her if she had ever thought about going to Mexico, and she had asked why, and I had stopped, unable to go on, to lead her on any more.

And it had ended without anything happening. She had offered herself and I didn't pick up the lead or follow through. It hadn't ended, really. It had tapered off into nothing. No decisions, no plans, no establishing of any contact between us. In a way, it had been rough on her, not being able to say to her, I love you, I want you, too. Now I could rationalize it, explain it away, by thinking it would have been worse if I had asked her to go to

Mexico with me, if I had let her think that I loved her or wanted her. In the long run, this was the better way. What I had done was the better thing. It was the stronger thing to do.

That made the second time that day I had been strong and unyielding. You've established a record for yourself, old man, I was thinking. Then I smiled out loud for having thought to myself in Mitchell Swaine's words, almost hearing Mitchell Swaine's voice. My conscience in Mitchell Swaine's voice. It was the second time that day; first with Clarissa, not letting her fight my battle with Monty, and the second with Jill.

So I was feeling pleased with myself when Helen Swaine walked into the bar. I was pleased with myself and felt more secure than I had been feeling and I was determined to be friendlier to her, try to understand her. She looked around for me. I stood up and she walked slowly over to the table.

"Hi, big one," she said.

"Hi, Helen." She was dressed very much as she had been the night before, the same kind of fluffed-up man's shirt except it was pink this time and she was wearing a tight, straight gray flannel skirt which hugged her body so tight her bone structure showed through.

Wonderful eyes. I had seen them the night before and had thought they were wonderful. They were even more exciting now with my vision unclouded by alcohol. Wonderful cat-green eyes with tiny flecks of brown. Set off by the orange-red hair and the orange-red lips. She was too flat in front for my taste but, what the hell, I thought, I was here for drinking.

Helen sat down next to me. "Where's Swaine?" I asked. Before she could answer, the waiter came over. "What do you want to drink?"

"Seven-Up," she said, smiling at the waiter. "Straight."

"Funny, you don't drink."

"Mitch drinks enough for the two of us."

"I know but it's still funny you don't. You look like the kind of woman who drinks it straight and fast, like a man."

She seemed amused. "Do I? It shows you, big one, that things aren't always what they seem. Or people." Her cat eyes came right up to stare for a long moment into my eyes. "Are you?"

"Am I what?"

"What you seem to be."

"Shucks," I said, "it depends on what you think I look like."

Helen laughed loudly, so loud that the sound of her laughter filled the room, making the waiters and the two men at the bar turn around.

"What's so funny?"

"You have a corn-fed quality about you, big one. Every once in a while through that smooth interior, a corn-fed streak shoots out."

"It's not so surprising. I'm from Dubuque, Iowa."

"You're not, really?"

I was rather pleased that she seemed so surprised. "Sure."

"That's marvelous, absolutely marvelous."

"You wouldn't think so if you were from Dubuque."

"No, I don't suppose I would. You've overcome it very well," she said. "You shouldn't tell anyone. No one would ever guess."

"I don't usually. People always expect such a hick when they know you're from Dubuque. Where did you come from?"

She smiled. "From a little bit of everywhere."

"You haven't told me yet what you think I seem to be."

"Let's save that, shall we, for some nice, little intimate time."

"This is plenty intimate," I said, moving away from her a little. "Where's your husband?"

"Didn't I tell you? He can't come. He's rather … Well, under the weather. He said for me to take charge of you." She licked her lips. "He's so sweet, Mitch is. He gives me the most beguiling jobs to do."

The waiter brought the Seven-Up. I waited until he had poured it. Then I ordered another Scotch. "Why didn't you call me? We could have skipped it today. You didn't have to knock yourself out to get here."

"But it was nothing. No trouble. I wanted to. Now let's talk about something."

"O.K. What?"

"The party last night. Wasn't it fun? I adored it when you slugged that poor little old man. He bled so beautifully. He was such a mess. His nose was mangled so marvelously."

"Stop it.

"Are you sensitive about having hit him? I wouldn't be if I were you. You have to practice on little ones before you take on ones your own size."

"I don't think I like you, Helen. I don't like your attitude."

"You said that last night, do you remember? You said I had a lousy attitude and you didn't like it." She laughed again, throwing her head back. I liked that all right. I liked the stretched line of her neck and the way her small breasts thrust forward to be prominent suddenly, the tight, hard shape outlined through the thin shirt. Mitchell Swaine, I decided, was a poor unfortunate man to be owning this piece of machinery and to be unable to set it in operation. "Attitudes are not important, big one. The only important thing is physical being. I learned that and I learned it the hard way."

"O.K., so you had a rotten break somewhere along the line. Other people have had rotten breaks too. They make the best of them. They don't just turn completely sour like you have."

"I'm not sour. I thought I was being very sugary with you. You bring out the sugary side of people. I only exist for what I can get physically, for my physical appetitie and well being. Attitudes are part of a mental world, a part of thinking about things. I don't do that anymore, I don't think about things."

"How," I asked, "can you tell when you're happy or unhappy?"

"There's no question of that in my life. The only question is if I'm satisfied or not."

"You know what I think, Helen? I think you talk tough but you're not so tough."

She leaned closer to me and whispered in my ear. "You're wrong, big one. You're very, very wrong."

I pulled my ear away. "And another thing, don't keep calling me 'big one.' It sounds nuts. Call me by my name. I do have one."

"I was thinking about that. I was thinking what I should call you. I don't like your name. I loathe it when they call a grown man Petey. And Petey sounds inadequate and unsatisfactory. The name Peter is rather like the name Fanny, outmoded as a proper name. I wondered what I would call you when we became better friends."

"If you called me Mr. Watkins it would be all right, too."

"I couldn't call you Mr. Watkins. If we're going on this trip to Mexico together, it would sound odd for me to keep calling you Mr. Watkins. Perhaps I should just call you Watkins. Watkins," she said testing the sound of it. "How does that sound, does that please you, Watkins?"

"You make it sound like I was a butler."

"There's no other way. Unless I call you darling. But people wouldn't understand if I called you darling."

"There's going to be no reason to call me anything. About that fishing trip, I don't think I can make it."

"That's too bad. I was looking forward to it. I thought it might get terribly involved and entertaining. Mitch will feel terrible. He's much more anxious for you to go along than I."

"He'll have to struggle along without me."

"Don't worry about it. If you don't go, Mitch won't go either. Perhaps I'll go alone."

"No, you don't. You know what will happen. If you go without him, he'll stay here, and I'll wind up playing nursemaid to him."

"That would be sweet. You could hold his head when he vomits. He always insists someone hold his head then."

"I've got news for you. He's got the wrong boy."

"Has he? I don't think so. I think that's just your speed, holding someone's head while—"

"No, that's your line. Someone told me you used to be a nurse. Is that true?"

"Yes," she said but then she didn't say any more.

"Sorry," I said, "if I brought up something which is better left … Well, better left not brought up."

"Do you have things like that, big one, things better left not brought up?"

"Some things, I guess. Not very much. I haven't done many things I'm awfully ashamed of."

"Stealing another man's wife is part of your everyday life?" Helen was smiling.

"That's another story. A long story. I'd rather not talk about it." Then I smiled, too. "I guess there are things better left not brought up."

"Yes, we all have them. Except the lucky ones. The lovely, lovely lucky ones. We aren't that kind, you and me. I'm not, anyway." Her eyes were half closed as she looked down into her Seven-Up and a million miles away.

"Careful, Helen, you may begin to sound human."

"Don't be deceived, big one, I'm not. I may sound human now, this minute, here with you like this. But I'm not. I'm as cold and calculating as if I had been manufactured by International Business Machines, Inc. It took time to get this way. It wasn't easy. Every once in a while I slip back and become human, feel human, feel like a woman. But not often. The times are becoming fewer and they last for shorter and shorter periods. The way I am now may pass any minute and I'll be the machine again. It takes practice but very soon I shall be perfect, the perfect calculator."

She was pretty just then. Not only handsome and startling and exciting looking but pretty, the way the girls back home are pretty. "I don't believe you," I said. "Underneath that man's shirt beats a woman's heart."

Helen shook her head. "No, you're wrong. Don't believe it. Believe what I say I am. Believe that I'm cold and calculating. Men who haven't believed it have been sorry."

"I won't be sorry," I said.

Softly, almost timidly, she whispered my name. "Petey."

"What?"

"Watch out for Mitch. Watch what he does to you."

"You're kidding, aren't you? What have I got to be afraid of him for?"

"This is one of those times I feel human. Take advantage of it, listen to what I say. Watch out for Mitch."

I laughed, forcing the laughter. "Do you think he'll try to shoot me?"

"Maybe. He killed his brother."

"But that was an accident."

"Maybe."

"But why would he want to kill me?"

"You look like his brother. It's his obsession, to find the reincarnation of his brother, his brother's double so that he can have a brother again. I've seen him before when there has been a man who looked like Jerry. I know how he's acted. You're the closest resemblance yet. Watch out for yourself."

"You're talking nuts, Helen."

"You have never seen Mitch when he sees a gun or knows that a gun is close to him. He goes crazy, gets frantic. He loses all control. He hasn't held a gun in his hand since he killed his brother. I'd hate to think what he would do if the time ever came."

"Why did you marry him, Helen? Why did you marry Mitch?"

She drank her drink, sat up straighter, then smoothed the back of her hair with the flat of her hand. The prettiness was gone, and she was back to the state she had made normal for herself. "I had many reasons for marrying him," she said. "Money is one."

"In his case that's a big reason." I smiled trying to coax back the human Helen. "He's got lots of money."

"There are many men with lots of money," she said.

"What else was there?"

"He's damn attractive, don't you think?"

"I suppose so, but it doesn't amount to anything. It seems to be no secret that he's impotent and has been since the accident. That can't be any fun for you."

"Sex didn't enter into it."

"Then what were the other reasons?"

"There were several. Rather personal."

"Feeling sorry for him didn't have anything to do with it, did it?"

I watched her face, watched for the prettiness to be coming back. I waited for the short, non-calculating minute to come again. But it didn't come. "When I married Mitchell Swaine," she said, "the only person I felt sorry for was myself."

"You can't make me believe that."

"Believe what you wish. I know facts."

"What were you like when you were … not younger, really, because you're still so damn young, but before whatever happened to you happened. What were you like then?"

"It doesn't matter now. I'm not that way any more."

"You said last night that you would tell me the story of your life."

"Did I?" She smoothed her hair again, petting her own hair as though it were the fur of a cat. "It was only a line to intrigue you. I never tell the story of my life. What is over is over and there is only now, this minute, you and me. Don't try to make me out something that I'm not. I am exactly what I seem."

"I still don't believe that." This time it was I who moved closer to her. "You know what I think? I think this attitude of yours, this mystery you've spun around yourself, is a lure, a decoy. It's a bait. It makes you a challenge to a man. All men like a challenge. Me for example. I'd like to crack the steel shell of that calculating machine and see what's underneath."

She made that quick movement of her tongue over her lips. "You must have heard," she said, "that because of my husband's unfortunate condition. I have license to show what's underneath. Mitch even encourages it. He's rather a pimp for me."

"I'm not talking about sex. I'm not talking about your body."

"That's too bad."

"I'm talking about getting to the woman part of you."

"You see," she said, smiling, "were back to talking about my body again."

"O.K., Helen. I give up."

"So easily?"

"Yeah. Easily and gladly. I just don't care."

"You've given me an idea, though," she said. "I've never thought about it before, about my being the way I am as a challenge to men. It's a nice idea to entice men. It may come in handy sometime. Perhaps soon."

"You have the personality of a spider," I said.

She laughed, pleased with what I had said. "I only have two legs, however."

"Do you want a drink?"

"Don't sound so disgusted, big one."

"I am disgusted. If I had eaten anything today I could vomit now, easily. Well do you or don't you want another drink?"

"No, but why don't you? You're just beginning to get interesting."

I looked at my watch without seeing the time. "I've got to get going."

"Oh, do have another drink. Then we can talk some more. Perhaps you'll get to dislike me even more intensely. Maybe you'll even grow to hate me. Hate is such a wonderful emotion, it can lead to such interesting complications."

"I have a life full of complications without you. Thanks all the same."

"Have one more drink with me. Please." She put her hand over mine. "Stay with me a little while longer. It's important. Please."

"You just turn it on and off like a radio set, don't you? You don't give a damn about other people. Just about yourself." I signaled for the waiter and held up my empty glass.

"Don't look so surprised, big one. That's exactly what I've been telling you about myself. I do nothing that I don't calculate to do."

"I guess the person I feel sorriest for in the world is Mitchell Swaine," I said. "A couple of hours ago, it was I. I was the guy I felt sorriest for. But I've got a cinch compared to Swaine. At least the women complicating my life are good ones, well-meaning women. Not like you. Not like you at all."

I knew even as I spoke that what I was saying was food for a woman like Helen. She thrived on torture the way some women thrive on flattery. She calculated to make men hate her. She wanted it. She demanded it. She craved it as a drug. I wanted to be able to stop, not to satisfy her by playing into her hands like this. But I guess I was enjoying the letting loose of this venom almost as much as she enjoyed being on the other end of it. You could build a house for a woman like this, I was thinking, and it could be stark and bare and clean and straight lined. Yet it would have a cobweby, Charles Addams quality because she would live there.

"Tell me," she said, "about the women in your life."

I didn't answer, I kept thinking about the house I would build for her, a prison and a cage of glass, stone, and steel.

A bellhop came through the cocktail lounge, calling my name. I didn't believe it was my name at first because no one knew where I was. Finally, as he was about to leave, I ran after him. "I'm Peter Watkins," I said. "What do you want?"

The bellhop was a young kid with bulging eyes and skin still blemished. "There's a guy upstairs," he said. "I don't know if he's fractured or nuts. He wants you."

"What are you talking about?"

"Upstairs." He pointed. "Room 713. This guy is nuts or something. Maybe he's just loaded. He says for me to find you in the bar and bring you back up."

"Come on."

In the elevator, the bellhop explained that the switchboard had had a flash from Room 713, the phone was off the hook but no one answered. This boy was sent up to investigate. "He's laying there," the bellhop was telling me, "like he's paralyzed or something. He's got the phone in his hand only he don't seem to be able to move it. You see a lot in a hotel like this. Usually there are broads or something mixed up with it. But this guy just lays there like he's paralyzed. Finally he gives me your name and says something about the bar downstairs." The elevator stopped on the seventh floor and we started down the corridor. "I figured it was a blind alley, that the guy was fractured and there wasn't nobody name Peter Watkins. I was going to call the house dick. I should of, you know. This is against regulations. But maybe when you call the house dick there's a lot of scandal and I figured maybe it's worth something to this guy there shouldn't be no scandal."

"You'll be taken care of," I said.

Room 713 was not a room but a suite of rooms overlooking the lake. There was a large entrance hall, an immense living room, and an open door which was the bedroom. "He's in there," the bellhop said.

Mitchell Swaine lay on the bed, frozen motionless, the phone in his hand. He still lay as the bellhop had described. There was no doubt as to whether this was drunkenness or insanity for the odor of gin was heavy in the room, and I spotted the neck of a bottle underneath the mangled bed clothing.

The expression in Mitchell Swaine's eyes was fear. Clear, pure, undiluted fear. It was in his eyes and it was taut in every muscle of his body. It was fear, but more powerful than the fear that had come in his sleep the night before. I don't know, medically, if a man can be actually scared to death. Mitchell Swaine was close to that point.

I pulled a five-dollar bill out of my pocket and shoved it into the bellhop's hand. "Get out," I said, "and forget what you saw."

"What's the matter with him? He ain't sick or nothing? It'll be my job if this guy croaks or something."

"Get out and close the front door."

I didn't move until I heard the front door close, then I went to Swaine. "What's the matter? What frightened you?"

He opened his mouth but no words could come out. He tried to move his hand to point at something, but he had no control over his locked muscles. I looked around, trying to find the object that was frightening him. I saw the gun on a table five feet away from the bed. I grabbed it and turned around, not realizing that I was pointing it at Swaine. His mouth opened to scream, his face twisted with the motion of a scream coming, but all that came from his throat was a dry, voiceless croaking sound.

I threw the gun in a drawer in the big dresser, slammed the drawer shut and turned back to Swaine. Slowly, while I watched, the fear subsided, and I could see the tightness in his body beginning to soften, his grip on the phone relaxing, and a great sweat breaking out over his entire body. When the phone fell, finally, I picked it up and flashed the operator.

"Yes?"

"This is Mr. Swaine," I said. "I must have knocked the phone off the hook before I went into the shower. I'm sorry." Then I hung up. I looked around the room for a robe to cover him. I found one in the bathroom and threw it over his shoulders. He was still propped up on one elbow, not yet fully relaxed. He tried to smile at me, but the smile wouldn't come. He tried to speak but he was still voiceless. I waited and watched for him to come out of the shock.

Suddenly, the network of his muscles collapsed completely and he fell flat on the bed, a soft blob of flesh sobbing silently. I reached over and touched him tentatively on the shoulder. He seemed to feel nothing, not knowing that my hand was touching him. I grabbed him hard, then, by the shoulders and shook him. His head bobbed back and forth like a balloon on the end of a stick. "Snap out of it," I commanded. "Snap out of it."

The first words he said were, "Does Helen know?"

"Does Helen know what?"

"That you're here."

"No," I said. "She doesn't know where I went."

He seemed relieved. "I need a drink."

"You've had enough."

He pulled the robe around him as though he were cold. I maneuvered him so that he was sitting up at the head of the bed and I pulled the covers over him. "Glad you came," he said. "Sorry I had to make a pest of myself. Didn't know what else to do."

"It's O.K. You feel better now?"

"It was the gun, you know. Go to pieces when I see a gun. Afraid to ask the bellhop because of the gun. Thought it might make trouble. Get like this when I see a gun."

"It's all right, it's all over now."

"Yes. All over. Until the next time."

"What do you mean until the next time?"

"I would have used it, you know. She knows that. She expected me to use it. Guess she gives me credit for more guts than I have. I would have used it though. I was close to using the gun when you came in. Would have been better. It's what she wanted."

He wasn't making sense and I was too rattled to try to put together the jigsaw of his words. And he was beginning to get the shakes. It was time to do something. I reached for the phone.

"Don't." He almost screamed the word.

"Don't what?"

He shook his head. "Helen. Don't call Helen."

The operator answered, I asked for room service and ordered a pot of coffee to be sent up.

Swaine looked sheepish and muttered, "Sorry. Thought you were going to send for Helen. She mustn't know how this turned out."

"Are you trying to tell me Helen put the gun there purposely?"

He turned his head away to avoid answering me.

"Did she, Swaine?"

"Forget it, Petey. Stay out of it. Sorry I had to drag you into it at all."

"You can't get me mixed up in a mess and then tell me to forget it. What happened?"

"Forget it."

"I won't forget it. I want to know what happened."

"She..." He stopped.

"Why didn't you come down with her and meet me as we planned?"

"Started drinking. Helen's idea. Said it would pick me up. I meant to come. Wanted to. Wanted to talk about Mexico, you know. But I drank too much and passed out. Then this. The gun was there. Waiting for me. There is always the gun waiting."

"That bitch," I said.

"You don't understand, Petey."

"What the hell is there to understand? It's black and white. What she did is black and white."

"Petey, about Mexico... About why I wanted you to come with us..."

"Forget Mexico. I've got enough troubles without Mexico. And without you. Big, live, real troubles of my own." It was not true at that minute about my problems. They seemed nothing compared to this nightmare Swaine was caught in and living in. Yet I wanted out. While there was still time I wanted to get out,

out of the Swaines' reach and go back and indulge myself in my own wonderings and in the juice of my own living.

"I know," he said. "When I'm sober I don't want to get you mixed up with me. Rotten. Me and everything close to me is rotten. You're a good guy. You oughtn't to get involved. I keep trying to let you alone but ... Well, if Jerry were alive I could turn to him, but with Jerry dead I ..."

I cut in. "If Jerry were alive you wouldn't be the way you are. Nobody can be your brother, Swaine. Face it. Everybody is like me, too caught up in himself to be a brother to anyone."

"Yes," he said, "that is the way it is."

"I don't want to be rough on you. I mean I know you're sick, but ..."

"Go on back to Helen," he said. "She'll be wondering about you. Don't say anything about this to her, will you?"

"No, not if you don't want me to. I don't think you should be alone just now but I guess Helen wouldn't be much help." I got up and started for the door. At the door I hesitated. "Would it help if you explained this whole thing to me? About the gun, I mean, and what Helen is trying to do. Why is she trying to do it? Any guy is bound to get curious," I explained, "and maybe you'd feel a lot better if you told someone about it."

"I'm all right."

"Last night you said some funny things. You had a nightmare too. Maybe if you could talk to someone, get it off your chest."

Swaine shook his head. "You said you didn't want to get mixed up with me. You're smart. Stay smart. Stick to your word. For your own sake, stay out of this."

"Look, Swaine, I'd like to help if I could. I don't know the details of the mess you're in. It doesn't make sense what anybody is trying to do. If it were any other time, I'd try to help you out of this. You're a nice guy and I'd like to help you but right now it's kind of rocky in my own life and I just don't have the time or the mind for it. If I weren't all involved myself I'd stick by and try to help you out. But the way it is, I can't. You understand, don't you?"

He nodded. "I understand and you're smart. I'll try to leave you alone. If I don't, you know it's because I couldn't control myself. Kick me away if I bother you again. It's all right. I'll feel bad but I'll understand."

I smiled now to show him that we were friends. "Hey, you know what?"

"What?" he asked.

"You haven't called me 'old man' once today."

He managed the smile this time and it was good to see a smile where before there had been so much fear. "Tomorrow," he said, "when I feel more like myself."

"O.K., Swaine. Take it easy and watch yourself."

"Thanks," he said and just as I closed the bedroom door I heard him add, "old man."

Helen Swaine was very much as I had left her except that she had a fresh bottle of Seven-Up. I thought I could spot a shadow of concern underneath the veneer of self-assurance on her face but maybe I was looking for it too hard. "Long phone call," she said. "I was beginning to think I had been ditched." She lowered her eyelashes. "I feel rather relieved."

I slid onto the leather seat next to her. "What happens when you do get ditched? Ten demerits from the union?"

"What union?"

"I don't know. Any union. Women like you must have a union. You're all alike."

"Are we? I thought I was rather unique."

"This drink is warm. I need a new one." I signaled to the waiter.

"Did she give you proper hell?"

I was tired suddenly. Tired and weary and sick of playing cat and mouse with the world. "Who? Did who give me hell?"

"The woman on the phone. Someone told me her name. Clarissa, isn't it?"

"It wasn't Clarissa on the phone and I don't want to talk about Clarissa. I don't want to talk about anything." The waiter brought the drink and I gulped half of it down in one swallow. "That feels good."

"One of those girls, was it Jackie, or Jill?" She hesitated. "I don't remember, they're so much alike. One of them told me you were hopelessly tangled up with a frightful female named Clarissa."

"I told you I didn't want to talk about Clarissa." I finished the drink.

"She's older than you. No one had to tell me that. I could guess that from the way you are. And she probably has a very large bosom, very soft and very comforting."

"Shut up."

"You see, I know all about you already. I know all your needs."

"I don't need you," I said, and I didn't care how it sounded.

"Nobody needs me," she said, "until they've had me, and then they need me very badly."

I reached into my pocket, pulled out another five dollars and laid it on the table. "I don't like you, Helen. I don't like you at all."

"We're rather alike, big one, you and me. We appear quite different and we're rather the same. You said before that I was a challenge. You're a challenge, too, to make you like me."

"Is that all?"

"Not quite. To make you like me and to make you know that a big, comforting bosom isn't the best part of a woman. You have a lot to learn, and I think I'd rather like to teach you."

I stood up and pointed down at the money I had left. "The five bucks," I said, "is for the waiter.

Then I left.

CHAPTER FIVE

Clarissa before Dinner

"DO YOU feel better?"

"Yes," I said, "but it doesn't solve anything."

Clarissa laughed into the half-darkness of the room. Clarissa seldom laughed. She smiled easily and laughed seldom but when she laughed it was wonderful sounding laughter. "No, it really doesn't solve anything," she said and stretched her arms above her head so that her hands hit the headboard of the bed. "But it is a lot of fun anyway, isn't it?"

"No argument."

"It was frightfully dull with Monty."

"Is there a cigarette on your side, Clar?"

I heard the clinking of the cigarette container against the ash tray as she reached for a cigarette, saw the sudden flare of the lighter. Then out, the half-darkness of the room again and then the feel of the lighted cigarette being placed between my lips.

"Monty," she said, "has no imagination. He always treated me as though I would break. And I don't break very easily do I, darling?"

"No." I let out a mouthful of smoke and watched it disintegrate into the air of the room. Then I said, "Clar, is it always going to be like this?"

"I hope so, Peter. Being with you makes me feel years younger. I haven't had a backache since I've known you." She laughed again. "Well, since I've known you intimately. I used to have dreadful backaches all the time. You are a tonic, darling, a lovely, delicious tonic."

"I'm not talking about that, Clar. I mean you're always comparing me to Monty. Are you always going to be doing that? I mean about everything."

"Peter, you're getting serious and I feel much too wonderful to be serious. I'm tingling all over. It's been four nights, do you realize that?"

"Yes."

"Were you faithful to me for four nights?"

"Yes."

"Please, don't sound so serious about it, Peter. I'm only teasing. Of course, I know you've been faithful."

"You do it all the time, comparing me to Monty. Last week you did it in front of your brother."

She took the cigarette from my hand and started to smoke it. "The comparison is always favorable. I don't see why you object."

"A man doesn't like to be compared with his predecessor."

"Please, don't get serious, Peter. Don't spoil the way I feel. I feel so wonderful, so alive and gay. Where shall we go for dinner? I feel like drinking pink champagne."

"Love," I said, "doesn't solve anything. When we fought this afternoon about Monty ..."

"We didn't fight about Monty."

"Well, he was part of it. Tell me the truth. Did you call him?"

She hesitated a minute. "Why do you insist on spoiling this wonderful time?" Clarissa made her voice sound gay. "This is the quiet, wonderful afterglow of love."

"You did call him, then. After I told you definitely not to, you called him." I grabbed the cigarette away from her, mouthed it purposely so that the end of it would be wet if she took it back to smoke it. "What the hell kind of a basis is that for love?"

"Peter," she said softly, "I didn't call Monty."

"You didn't?"

"No, I didn't."

"Oh."

"You sound disappointed. I think you rather wanted me to call him."

"I forbade you to call him."

"I observed your commandment."

"Well, you needn't sound so condescending about it."

"I don't know," she said, "quite how you do want me to sound. You seem determined to pick a quarrel." She moved closer to me, put her head on my chest. "Let's not quarrel, Peter. Please. Please. Please. Let's laugh and be young and be gay."

"I want it clearly understood," I said, "that there is to be no more of this comparison between Monty and me. We are two different people."

Clarissa sat up, moved back to her side of the bed. She took the cigarette from me, noticed the end of it was wet, and squashed it out in the ash tray. "Since you're determined to have a battle, Peter, I must get in a few licks. As a matter of fact, I do compare you to Monty. I only voice the favorable comparisons. The others I keep to myself. But I make them nonetheless. I think it's only natural in my position."

"It means we're going to have a hell of a life together. I'll be afraid to do anything, wondering if Monty did it or didn't do it. Or something."

"But, darling, don't you realize how new this is. Of course it will stop, my comparing you to Monty. It will stop very quickly. I'm only too ready to forget that Monty even exists."

I didn't say anything. I guess I was sulking.

"Peter, promise me something."

"What?"

"I wanted desperately to avoid saying what I have to say but I think it's necessary now. You have to promise me that you'll listen and not say anything. You'll have to promise that when it's over you'll act as though I hadn't said it, that it will make no difference between us, that we'll go out to dinner and have a wonderful time, as always. Do you promise?"

"Well … I mean, I don't know what you're going to say."

"You love me, don't you?"

I said, "Yes."

"Then you can promise me."

"All right. I promise."

"Once I say this, Peter, we are both to forget what I said and that I ever said it. It's never to come between us. I am going to say this only because I don't want anything to come between us. I don't want the wonderful thing we have to be spoiled constantly by your doubts and your jealousy of Monty."

"I am not jealous of Monty."

"You're not jealous of him where I'm concerned. The jealousy is on another level. You just take it out on me."

"You're getting plenty psychiatric."

"Yes, I suppose I am.

"Well, go ahead and say what you have to say."

"Oh, Peter, I was silly. Let's forget it. I'll get dressed and we'll go out to eat. I'm famished."

She started out of bed, but I grabbed her arm. "You started something. Now finish it."

"Peter, you're awfully attractive. You're winsome and beguiling and you've become successful. It's spoiled you terribly. In a certain sense, your spoiled-little-boy ways are part of your charm. But, like a spoiled little boy, you whine and fret and are not mature enough to accept wonderful things without twisting them until you become dissatisfied with them. When you have something wonderful you feel guilty about it and think that it's not yours, that it belongs to someone else. You aren't man enough, really, to possess what belongs to you. You do the things a man does. I would be the last one to say you don't do them very well. But you always spoil the man things you do by turning whimpering little boy about them."

I sat up in the darkness, aware suddenly of my own nakedness.

"Don't say anything, Peter. Let me finish and remember what you promised. Once I've said it, we shall both forget I ever said it."

"Go ahead."

"When I'm alone, I wonder what you really think of me. I wonder what kind of woman you think I am. You accuse me constantly of mothering you and smothering you. You know yourself, Peter, how many times you've said that. And I suppose it's true. I do mother you. But I'm not that type. You've made me that type. You've forced me to play this mother role with you. I don't want to mother anyone. But it's what you want and so I play the role you want me to play so that I can hold on to you. I love you. I would do anything to keep you, not to let you get away. You've forced me into mothering you, so I do. But only for one reason, to hold on to you. Not because I am that way or want to be that way."

She was saying words and my mind was recording them, not listening to the full impact of these words now but recording them to play back later, when I was alone and could mull over each word, analyze each thought.

"I see now," she said, "that I can't hold you, that no woman can hold you until you grow up and learn to take and possess what you have; walk with assurance because you have it. It's still a mothering job I'm doing now, Peter, to make a man of you. I want to make a man of you, and then I want to be the woman that man possesses. Do you understand?"

I didn't answer.

"This is not only with me. It's with everything you do. This business with Murdick and Howell. You know you don't belong there. You've got to the top but you don't feel you belong there. You hate the Williamsburg Village you designed. It's a thing foreign to you. It's against your grain. If you had ever said, 'The Village is a piece of garbage, but I'm proud of it; it's what sells, I'm making money from it and my artistic integrity is still intact,' then I would say, 'Good for you. Stay with the firm. Keep on building Williamsburg villages. Keep on making money.' But you won't accept that. You won't accept the rewards for being a smart man who has designed what people want to buy. You're ashamed of it, you make fun of it. You sulk because you think you've prostituted yourself. So, if you feel that way, I say get away from the firm. Come to Mexico and build the kind of thing you want to build. But deep in my heart, I know you'd find a way of spoiling that, too. You'd find something to make you dissatisfied even if you were building the kind of thing you consider yourself morally and artistically qualified to build.

"You've got to learn to possess the things you have. Do you understand what I'm trying to say? You have me and you have the Village and you have money but you don't possess us. So I have to mother you. I shall continue to behave this way because it is the only way I can keep holding on to you."

There was silence for a long time. I don't know what Clarissa was thinking about. I was thinking about many things, but not about myself. I was thinking about Jill and how I felt sorry for Jill. I was thinking about Helen and how I really didn't like Helen. I began to think perhaps it was that way about Clarissa and me. She really didn't like me, not as a person. I switched then to thinking about Mitchell Swaine and how I felt sorry for him, sorry that he was all jazzed up and sorry that he was impotent and sorry that he had either the delusion or the reality of Helen trying to kill him. I even thought about home and things when I was a small boy, and about Charlie Howell, who had never wanted to make me a partner in spite of the Williamsburg Village contract.

There was this silence of unsaid words for a long time. Then I got up and dressed in the clothes Monty's tailor had made for me.

"Where are you going, Peter?"

"Away," I said.

"You'll be back. You know that, don't you?"

"I'll try very hard to stay away, Clar, but I suppose you're right, I suppose I'll be back."

"Then why fight it, darling? Why waste time between now and the time you'll be coming back to me? You'll only make yourself miserable."

"No," I said.

"I suppose it was awful of me to say what I did to you, to tell you how I really feel about you. Most of the time, I'm not aware of it, Peter. I'm not as deliberate about handling you as I make myself sound. It would have been all right if you hadn't asked me to stop comparing you to Monty. I knew you were going to ask it and I knew if you asked it I would have to say what I said. But I'm glad I did. Perhaps it will help you to understand a little bit."

"You didn't consider the possibility that it might drive me away all together."

"It's not a possibility, darling. What I said was in line with this mother role you've forced on me. I've given you a good talk-ing to, as any mother does. And you're angry and you're going to run away from home, and I'll worry while you're gone. Of course I'll worry. I won't worry about whether or not you'll come back. Certainly you'll come back. But I'll worry if you're all right, eat-ing the right things and dressing warm enough and wearing a hat when it rains."

"Shut up."

"But the point is that I'll be perfectly confident that you'll come home."

"Home," I said, "is Dubuque, Iowa."

"No, it isn't, Peter." She switched on the light, threw back the cover. "Home," she said, "is here."

"Where did I leave my shoes?"

She snaked out of bed and walked over to me. "Peter, dar-ling, let's forget all this and go out to dinner. I'm famished. You promised you'd listen and then forget everything I said. You promised."

"I didn't realize what you were going to say."

"Don't be childish. A bargain is a bargain."

"O.K., so it's childish. So I'm in character."

She put her arms around me. I held still for her but didn't move. Her hands ran up and down my back, finally making soft, mock-paddling motions. "If I could spank you and you could cry, everything would be wonderful between us again."

"It's too late for that."

"No, it isn't." She put her lips quite close to my ear so that her breath came to caress me. "Peter, let's go back to bed. Let's pretend you just came here and we'll go back to bed, and later we'll talk about silly things, irrelevant things, and then we'll go eat. I'm simply famished."

I reached behind me and took her hands away. "Sorry," I said and walked into the living room. My shoes were near the piano. Clarissa followed me. Lovely, beautiful Clarissa. As tempting as any woman could ever be.

"Darling, stop fighting yourself. Let's be what we are and enjoy what we are without fighting it, without trying to be something else."

I sat on the piano bench and watched myself tie my shoelaces. "Look, Clar, I think I believe some of what you told me. Maybe some of the things you said are true."

"Of course they are, darling. So what? So you're the way you are and I'm the way I am. So what? Frankly, darling, what's the difference? We're good for each other."

"Stop talking a minute."

"But, Peter..."

"I said to shut up." I looked up from my shoes. "What you said means one thing—you don't like me. Well, if it's true, if what you said about me is true, if I am that way, then I don't like me, either. Hell, if I thought you were dead wrong, I would have got mad, bellowed my head off. Maybe even hit you. I don't know. I know I wouldn't be pulling out on you this way. But the point is that some of it may be true. If it is, I'm damn well going to do something about it."

"But why? That's what makes you immature. You can take things as they are and enjoy them. We've been very happy together. We can go on being happy together."

"Good-by, Clar."

"You'll be back, Peter."

"Maybe."

"Sooner than you think."

"We'll see."

She turned on her tears. "It's such a foolish waste of time. We could be having a wonderful life and it'll be a foolish waste of time."

"If I come back to you, Clar, it will be for one of two reasons. Either I'll have decided you're wrong, that I'm not the way you say I am, or I'll come back if I'm beaten, beat out, if I've given up."

Through tears she said, "You never think about *me,* do you? You never stop to wonder how *I* feel, what *I* want. You only think of yourself, of *your* needs, of *your* moods. What *you* want. Do you think you have no responsibility toward me?"

"I guess you're right there, too. I haven't thought about you much except in terms of me, in terms of what I wanted from you."

"Do you think that's fair? Don't you think you owe me anything?"

"What comes next, Clar? Are you going to tell me you've given me the best years of your life?" I snorted. "Monty got those and probably a dozen other guys. How many were there, Clar, while you were married to Monty? Was I the last in a long line?"

"Peter!" This time she screamed, and this was real furor, not calculated furor. She picked up an ash tray and threw it at me. It missed.

"And while you're waiting for your little boy to come back, Clar, I'll lay you dough you're going to let other little boys take his place."

This time she just screamed, not my name, not any word, just an angry woman's scream. I left her that way, screaming. And I heard the scream out in the hall and halfway down the elevator. Even when I was out of range of the scream I was still hearing it, and I knew that nights later I would be hearing it again.

I knew what I had done. It was the first decent, manly thing I had done since Ralph Montgomery had swept me out of the drafting department of Murdick, Howell, and Maguire and into this life I was living. It was a clean, manly thing I had done. Except there was a hollowness in this clean, manly feeling. Clarissa had been right when she said we were good for each other. We were. I would miss that. I would miss that very much.

In times of stress, men go to bars. I don't know why, except that men in times of stress know that other men in times of stress have gone to bars. So I went into the first saloon I could find and I drank two drinks quickly and waited to feel lost, melancholy, ready to be telling my troubles to the bartender. But I felt none of these things, and the bartender was very busy. And I was hungry. Plain, uncomplicated hunger was gnawing at my insides. There would be other things later. I knew that, but right that minute I was hungry and I started thinking of someone I'd like to have dinner with. Jill popped into my mind right away. Poor Jill. There was so much to her and so little showed through the bleached front she had turned toward the world.

"Where's the phone?"

"Huh?"

"The phone? Where is it?"

"Down there. To the right. You want another drink?"

"No."

I phoned Jill.

"I'm so ashamed of myself for this afternoon, Petey, that I can hardly stand it."

"How about dinner?"

"I couldn't. I'm still not together. I feel sort of loose ended. I couldn't pull myself together for dinner. Why don't you come up here later? I think we are having sort of an impromptu party. It sprung up suddenly. We've been on the phone like crazy. Why don't you come? We've been careful not to invite Monty, but he'll probably show up anyway."

"Another party? But you said this afternoon that …"

"That isn't fair, Petey. You should never remind a girl that you caught her with her hair down."

"I don't understand."

"I told you that maybe all I had to do was to tell you, get it out of my system, and then everything would be all right again."

"I don't believe that. You said too much this afternoon. You can't have gone back to your place and picked up where you left off. You couldn't have."

She mumbled for a moment while she was lighting a cigarette. "You will come up later, won't you, Petey? We'd love to have you."

"This isn't real. You're talking so different from this afternoon. Why, this afternoon you …"

"Just a minute, Petey." She held her hand over the mouthpiece for a few minutes. "Sorry, darling, Andy was at the empty beer bottles and broke one."

"Did he hurt himself?"

"No, but the crashing sound frightened him. He's such a lamb."

"Jill, meet me, please. It's important."

"No, Petey, really. It wouldn't do. I've thought about it a good deal. I was silly to force myself on you the way I did; I don't know what got into me. But it's no good."

I looked around the barroom, but no one was standing within hearing distance. "But you said you loved me."

"Yes, I suppose I do, but we're not right for each other. Not yet, anyway. You're not ready for what I want, the way I want to live. You're still like Andy in a lot of ways. That wouldn't work out for us."

"You're talking a lot of nonsense and you know it."

"Is it? Is it all nonsense?" She stopped talking for a moment. "Perhaps it is. Perhaps what I wanted was you to take me in your arms and say I love you, Jill. Like in the movies. If you had done that I think I would have stayed, never come back here or to this. But you didn't say anything and so ... Well, just, and so."

"Is it too late now?"

"Yes, Petey. The mood has passed. I fed you the cue and you muffed your line. It's too late. For a while anyway, it's too late. Until the next time, until the next time I get like that and want someone to cling to so desperately. Perhaps you'll be ready then, more grown up and ready to take me as I was meant to be."

"O.K., Jill. Forget it."

"Don't be angry."

"I'm not angry."

"You're pouting."

"And whining and whimpering, too? Go ahead, give me both barrels."

"I'm sorry, Petey."

"O.K."

"Under the circumstances, maybe you'd better skip it tonight. The party, I mean."

I slammed the receiver into the cradle of the phone, went back to the bar and ordered another drink. This, I was thinking, was time for taking inventory. Everyone seemed to have been taking inventory of me, now it was time to take inventory of myself, and check my findings against their findings—against those of Jill and Clarissa and even Helen.

"You're becoming a damn introspective slob," I muttered to myself.

"What did you say, Mac?"

It was the bartender. "I didn't say anything."

He shrugged his shoulders. "I thought I heard you say something."

"No." I pushed my glass forward. "Bring me another drink."

It began again as soon as the new drink was put in front of me, this probing of myself, this trying to come to decisions about myself. I was sick of it, over my head in it. It was what I'd been doing for the past three days. The cocktail party last night was to have been an end to it. I was to wake up that morning and everything would be solved. But it hadn't worked out like that. It was worse now, more entangled, more involved.

Old man, you have nothing now. I silently said the words to myself and I was hearing Mitchell Swaine saying them to me. And they were true words; I had nothing. Not Jill, not Clarissa, not my job as it had been, not the drive to work ahead. Nothing.

"Another drink," I said, my voice showing signs of becoming thick from the drinking. I shrugged my shoulders. What the hell. Who cares?

I clutched the drink as soon as it was set in front of me. I heard myself saying, "Thanks, old man."

The bartender looked surprised. "Yeah. O.K., Mac. Anytime."

I could feel more sorry for him than I could for myself. I could feel more sorry for Mitchell Swaine. He had nothing too. He had millions of dollars and everything it could buy, including Helen. Helen was a dangerous bitch. Maybe even a madwoman. But Helen would be marvelous... I knew that now as I pictured her in my mind's eye. I saw her with a great, naked clarity. She would not be like Clarissa. Being with Helen would be like getting into a fight, knowing you're overmatched. And winning that fight and having the climaxing of the winning. Only much more than that, more potent than that.

Poor, poor Mitchell Swaine. He had nothing. Nothing. Millions of dollars and everything and Helen and yet nothing.

In times of stress, men go to bars and drink themselves into a state of not feeling. Yet drink alone will not do it. It is not enough.

So you get into a fight, messed up and mauled. But you win that fight and you feel better and you feel stronger and you have forgotten for a while that you are nothing. Or you find a woman. That was better than fighting.

I had a hard time dialing the number of the Drake Hotel. The circle was a blur, letters fusing into numbers. Finally I dialed the operator and gave her the number.

In that nasal, well-enunciated voice she said, "You are speaking from a dial phone. Please dial the letters ..."

"I can't see the letters. I'm blind."

The trained voice gave way to a twitter, and she got the number for me. They rang the room and Helen answered.

"It's Watkins," I said. "How are you?"

"I'm fine. You sound drunk."

"Not as drunk as I'm going to be. Where's your husband?"

"He's not here. Aren't you there, too?"

"Where?"

"At the party. At those girls' apartment?"

"I'm not going. I was invited but I'm not going."

"I'm not going either."

"I'm coming over there."

She was silent for a minute. "No," she said, "don't. I rather you wouldn't."

"Too good for me, huh? I haven't got enough dough."

"Look, big one, I have a feeling that you want to come here to do more than talk."

I wiped my hand across my mouth and my voice was heavy. "Yeah."

"I'd love it, but not the way you are. I don't want any slobs drowning their troubles. You'll come to me some time when you're not drunk, when you want nothing but me. I've waited this long, I can wait longer. I want you undiluted, strong and straight."

"I can sober up."

"Can you, Watkins? And when you do will you still have the guts to come up here?"

"I got guts. Plenty of guts."

She said, "You know my terms." Then she hung up.

At the bar again I was for one minute on the verge of ordering another drink. "You got coffee?"

"Yeah."

"Give me some. Lots of it."

I drank four cups of coffee, as hot as my mouth would stand them. Then I half ran the long way back to my apartment, not looking at the people I passed, not caring that they were looking at me queerly. And I wouldn't let myself think about anything, about where I was going and the complications it could lead to. I concentrated on the word sober, said it to myself, spelled it out loud, backward and forward, saw the way the word looked in print—sober. Sober. SOBER. Rebos. REBOS.

First I took a cold shower and then a hot one and then a cold one again. Still I wouldn't let myself think about anything. SOBER. Thinking the word and saying the word and seeing the word. When I had dried myself hard with a rough towel, I knew I would be all right. Sober. Quite sober.

The blue jeans and T-shirt I had worn that afternoon lay on the bed where I had thrown them. I put them on, right over my skin and stuck my bare feet into a pair of worn moccasins. There was a big trench coat I had worn in Dubuque where everyone wore trench coats. I put it on, turned up the collar and went outside. I found a cab and went to her hotel.

The door to the suite was not locked. I walked in. The foyer and living room were in darkness. A small light burned in the bedroom. I walked in quickly. Helen was standing by the bed, shaking out the flame of a match. She was dressed in the same frilled man's shirt and the same tight gray skirt. She was smiling a little. She didn't say anything. Neither did I.

I took off my trench coat, tossed it on a chair. I pulled the T shirt over my head and threw it on the floor. She watched me closely, not missing one movement I made. I kicked off my moccasins and they landed near the window. I unbuttoned the tight blue jeans and peeled them off.

Helen had not moved, not an inch, not a muscle, not even the half smile of her lips. But when I walked to her and stood close to her, my mouth close to her mouth, she moved the cigarette toward her lips. I knocked her hand away. The lighted cigarette fell to the worn hotel carpeting. I squashed it out with my bare foot.

Still neither of us had spoken. There were no words between us that needed saying. She had made her terms and I had met them. There was now only the fulfilling.

Suddenly my hand seized the ruffled front of her shirt and I pulled with all my might. She held her ground, her head high, and there was the sound of the ripping cloth. She wore nothing under the shirt. And there would be nothing under the skirt. I grabbed the flannel at her waist. My hand made the first contact with the flesh of her body.

I pulled.

There was that exquisite, exhilarating, ripping sound.

I backed up. My breathing was hard, the pulse of expectancy as alive as raw, hot wires.

Then it was her move. She came to me sharp nailed, with her hard breasts, soft tongue, and whispering voice. "I knew you'd be like this," she said. "I knew it. I knew it."

Her teeth dug into me then, hard and painful and wonderful into my shoulder. So hard I had to pry her off me and push her away. She fell, her body half on the floor and half on the bed.

Helen laughed, throwing her head back.

It had begun.

CHAPTER SIX

Conversations through a Night

I WAS WATCHING the closed bathroom door, listening to the sounds from behind it; water running, medicine chest opening and closing, Helen humming softly. I had lost track of time. We had made love without regard for time, in time only with the rhythm of our desire.

The door opened and she stood on the threshold, the light from the bathroom silhouetting her body. She was thin and tight and flat, almost no womanly curves to her. Yet I knew now how much woman she was.

"Hello," I said.

"Hello, bruiser."

I sat up a little in bed. I smiled. "Long time no see."

"You slept," she said.

"Did I? I don't remember sleeping."

"You snored."

"Did I? I don't usually, I don't think."

She walked across the room and sat in a big easy chair, crossing her legs and lighting a cigarette. "That window is open, Helen. You'd better close it or put something on. You'll catch cold."

"The air feels good," she said.

Then there was nothing to talk about. We had no common ground, no common area of experience, except, of course, the bed, and I couldn't very well say, "You're terrific. How was I?" As a matter of fact, I didn't have to ask anything. We were perfect.

There was that and it was an important thing and there was nothing else between us to talk about.

"Do you think I ought to go?"

Helen blew out a mouthful of smoke. "It doesn't matter. Do as you like."

"What about Mitch? Is he liable to walk in?"

"It doesn't matter. He won't care. He probably expected it to happen."

I remembered then that Monty had warned Clarissa to watch out for Helen, that Helen was out for me. Monty had a sixth sense, all right. I wondered if he knew how right she was for me. "Funny," I said, "everybody seemed to expect it to happen but me."

"Why didn't you expect it to happen?"

"Well ... Well, as a matter of fact, I didn't like you."

"What has that got to do with it?"

I laughed. "Not very much, I guess. It didn't seem to hamper me any, did it?"

"Do you like me now?"

I had to think about that. Actually nothing she had done had made her any different in my eyes. She was the way she had been at cocktails, the same woman. She was the woman who left the gun at her husband's bedside. "I'm not sure. I guess I still don't like you. I mean I think your attitude is lousy, and you treat Mitch pretty rough sometimes, and ..." Then I realized how I felt. "No, I don't like you any more than I did before."

"You sound so surprised, Watkins. Rather as though you expected to wake up and be in love with me."

"It's kind of confusing. I still don't like you, but it doesn't make me mad the way it did before. It doesn't mean anything except that I don't like you. I mean I know I'll want you again. I guess I'm all mixed up."

She scratched the bottom of her foot. "You're growing up, bruiser. Some day maybe you'll be a big full grown man."

"Any complaints?"

"Not at all. You were good."

I smiled, pleased with my report card.

"Then what are you giving me the growing-up routine for?"

"You see, I don't like you very much either."

I waited a minute, waited for the words to sink in. I had been through this earlier, with Clarissa. And I knew what would be coming because there would be words said that had been said before. But I knew this time there would be no anger involved. I would be feeling no anger. O.K., I thought, she doesn't like me and I don't like her. We're still good together. That was it. As far as it went. Liking and loving were another area from sex.

"All right," I said, "you don't like me. You don't have to elaborate. I get the pitch."

"Do you?"

"Yes."

"Do you remember what I said this afternoon? About your being a challenge to me, to make you like me?"

"Did you say that? I don't remember."

"You said I was a challenge, too. To crack that cold, calculating shell. You said that that was the challenge."

"I'll swing you a deal, Helen. Let's forget about challenges. Let's take what we have and enjoy it and leave it at that."

Helen stood up and walked to the window. "I'm not sure that I can."

"You'll have to." I sat straight up now and I felt fine. I was strong and sure of myself for the first time in a long time. "We don't have much to say to each other. There's only one reason we'll need one another. I don't want phone calls or pleading letters or any campaigns for love."

Quickly she said, "I never mentioned love."

"O.K., then liking. Or whatever. I guess I don't want any part of you but … Well, you know."

"What makes you so sure of yourself? What makes you think I'll agree to that?"

"You know the answer to that as well as I do. You want me as hard as I want you and in the same way."

She came over and sat on the bed. "I asked for this," she said, "by telling you about myself, the way I am. Calculating. After what I told you I'm not entitled to ask for more, am I?"

"I told you the way it would have to be."

"I'll try, bruiser." She looked straight at me and she smiled a pretty smile. "I really will," she said.

"And another thing, about Mitch... Well, I really like the guy. He's an awful phoney about a lot of things and he's plenty jazzed up but he's a sweet guy underneath all of that confusion. I really don't want to hurt him."

"You have a lot to learn about Mitchell Swaine."

"I've got a lot to learn about a lot of things but I'll learn them my own way, in my own time."

"What about Mexico now? Will you go?"

"I don't know. I'll think about it. I'll tell you tomorrow."

"What time will you be here tomorrow?"

"I don't know that either. I'll be around some time."

"You expect me to sit and wait?"

"No," I said. "I don't expect you to sit and wait. I'll call you sometime around noon. I should know by then."

She reached out and touched my arm tentatively. "I would wait," she said, "you know that."

"Yes, I know."

"Bruiser?"

"Huh?"

"Nothing. Never mind. Are you hungry? I could call down for some food."

"You think they're still open?"

"I'll try."

Helen picked up the phone and asked for room service. She turned to me and said, "They're still open. What do you want?"

"A sandwich and coffee."

"What kind?"

"I don't care. Ham. Black coffee."

As she was giving the order over the phone, I heard the front door to the apartment opening. Automatically I started up but Helen motioned with her hand and I stayed as I had been, sitting up in the bed. I pulled up the sheet so that it came to my waist.

Swaine's voice called through from the living room. "Helen?"

"I'm in here, Mitch. I'm calling down for food. Do you want something?"

"Monty is with me," he called back. I heard him ask Monty if he were hungry. I could distinguish Monty's voice but not what he said. "We just want coffee," Swaine called back in.

Helen ordered two sandwiches and four coffees. While she was still on the phone, Swaine walked into the bedroom alone. He saw me first and smiled, not surprised, almost as if he expected me to be there, where I was, in his bed. He closed the bedroom door. "Hello, old man," he said.

I started to say something but changed my mind.

Swaine kissed Helen on the cheek. Helen said, "Does Monty use cream and sugar?"

"I'll ask him," Swaine said.

"He drinks it black," I said.

Into the phone, Helen said, "All those coffees are black. Don't take too long. We're very hungry." She hung up. "How was the party?"

"Fine." He looked over at me, smiled good naturedly. "Not as exciting as last night."

"You seem sober, Mitch," Helen said.

"Yes, darling. Very sober." He blew into her face. "Pure ginger ale. Disappointed?"

Helen looked at me quickly, a moment of fright in her eyes. "No, of course I'm not disappointed in you. I'm rather pleased that you could go the whole evening without a drink."

"You know, Petey, Helen thinks drinking is good therapy for me. She encourages it sometimes, don't you, darling?"

She had walked to the closet and put on a plain flannel robe. "Under certain circumstances it's better for Mitch to be drunk than sober."

"I better get dressed," I said.

Swaine looked at me carefully. "Don't get dressed on my account. I'll go back to Monty for a while."

"Look, Swaine," I began.

"Never mind, old man. You don't have to say anything. You look terribly apologetic and you shouldn't."

"I wasn't going to apologize."

"No," he smiled. "Certainly not. You were going to explain. You're noble the way Jerry was. Jerry was so damn noble all the time. He could look so righteous when he'd done something so very wrong. So I always got the blame because I looked guilty. Some men just look guilty all the time whether they have done anything wrong or not." He walked over to the dresser and looked at himself in the mirror. "It isn't often that I can see myself this clearly, is it, Helen? And you see, even now, I look guilty, and I've been such a good chap all evening. No drinks. No passes at anyone's wife. No fights. Such a good chap and I look as though I've committed something rather deadly."

"Mitch, would you get me a handkerchief? There's one in the dresser."

Through the mirror, Swaine looked at his wife. "Which drawer?"

"The top one, I think. Yes, the left hand top drawer."

He opened the drawer and reached in. His hand stopped suddenly and his body froze rigid. "What is it, Mitch? What's the matter?"

Swaine didn't answer.

I jumped out of bed. I knew what it was and Helen must have damn well known what it was. I had put the gun in the second drawer. Now it was in the top drawer. Swaine wouldn't have touched it to move it. So that left Helen. That left Helen and her casual request for a handkerchief. I could see Swaine's face in the mirror, that hardness twisting his mouth and the perspiration beginning on his face. "Are you all right, Swaine?" I started toward him. Helen stopped me. "No, don't," she said. "Something's wrong. He's going to have a spell."

I pushed her away. "Spell, nothing. He's got the gun." I started toward him and as I came close he turned around and the gun was in his hand, not pointed at anyone but laying across his palm. "Here, I'll take that, Swaine."

Swaine shook his head. "No, don't. I've touched it now and I know how it feels again."

I kept moving toward him and he shifted the position of the gun and the barrel of it was aimed at my middle. I stopped and called to Helen. "Is that loaded?"

"I don't know," she said. "I don't know where it came from."

"Don't give me that. I asked you if it was loaded."

After a second she mumbled, "Yes."

"It's funny," he said, "to feel a gun in my hand again. It's funny, but after all these years I remember everything, learning how to shoot, how to steady my arm, how to squeeze the trigger so that I don't jerk the gun out of position."

"Put it down, Swaine."

From the living room, Monty called, "Hurry up, you two. I'm getting lonesome."

No one answered him. I whispered to Helen. "Say something."

"In a minute, Monty," she called.

Swaine was looking at neither of us but only at the gun, the gun a magnet to his eyes. "This *is* a gun, isn't it, Helen?"

Helen flopped on the lounge chair, crossing her legs, not caring that the robe flew open. "Stop behaving like a child, Mitch. You look ridiculous. You look like a bad production of Lady Macbeth. *Is this a gun?* Certainly it's a gun. It's a real, live gun and it's loaded. It shoots bullets. That's more than you can do, isn't it, darling?"

"Put it down, Swaine." My voice was tight, hard. I took a step closer and his arm stiffened, the gun coming forward. I wasn't sure if it was a deliberate gesture or not but I couldn't afford to take a chance, the set-up was too perfect; my being the way I was, undressed in his bedroom with his wife. And a witness in the next room. Monty, of all people.

She was playing a game, Helen was, a dangerous game. She was calm, cynical, disdaining of her husband. "Yes, Mitch, put down the gun. You can't shoot it. You can't shoot anything."

"You forget I'm sober, Helen."

"So what, darling? Drunk or sober you're still not capable."

The front doorbell sounded. Once and then again. Monty called in. "Should I answer it? What are you two doing in there?"

I nodded at Helen and she said, "It's room service. Let the waiter in. Give him a dollar, will you, Monty? Mitch will pay you back double." Then softer, to Swaine, she said, "You will be able to pay him back, won't you, Mitch? Of course you will. Unless you decide to turn the gun on yourself. Yes, turn it on yourself, darling, and think how nice it would feel. It would be over, everything would be over and you could be with your beloved Jerry again. You wouldn't have to spend any more time being sorry for yourself, sorry for the horrible, horrible thing you did. You wouldn't have to search constantly for his double and wind up with a cheap imitation like Peter Watkins here."

I couldn't believe it. I couldn't believe what she was doing. I shook my head to clear it, to make sure that what I was seeing and hearing was real. It was real. It was very real. More real than anything I had ever seen before.

"Yes, turn the gun, darling, and remember the words, out hunting, you and your brother. He was walking ahead of you and your gun was in your hand, the way it is now. And you hated him, really. You think I don't know that, don't you? You think I don't know that you hated him and worshipped him and were terribly, terribly jealous of him. You did hate him didn't you, Mitch, because he was so much better than you? So you followed him through the woods. You followed him, hating him, wishing he were dead. You did wish he were dead. All the time you wished he were dead. And you walked behind him and you were wishing he *was* dead and the gun was in your hand, then there was the explosion and he *was* dead and you didn't know if you had pulled the trigger deliberately or not, did you, darling? You still don't know if you're a murderer or not. Well, I can tell you. You are. Whether you tripped and it was an accident or whether you did it deliberately, it was still murder because you wanted him dead. So very much you wanted him dead."

"Stop it, Helen," I said. "Stop it." I started toward Swaine again. One step. But he turned the gun into his face. I was afraid he might pull the trigger.

Helen kept talking, the same calm way as though she were trying to argue him into going to Nassau instead of Mexico. "If you were dead, it would stop, all the torture you've been through, all the doubts in your mind. All the agony of trying to prove yourself a man, to make yourself a man again. It would all stop and everything would be very peaceful. You could be dead with Jerry and you could tell him how sorry you are and you could make it up with him instead of looking constantly for his double, to make it up to his double."

There was a knock on the door. Monty. No one moved. He knocked again. "Is everything all right in there? The coffee will get cold."

I motioned to Helen to answer him, but she shook her head. She wouldn't. Monty knocked again. "Is everything all right?"

"Get away from that door, Monty. Get away quick."

"Who's in there with you? Is that you, Petey? Was that you who just spoke?"

"Yes," I said, "it was I and I mean it. Get away."

Monty said, "Oh, this is juicy, isn't it? I'm so glad I'm here. Of course this must be old hat to you, Petey, being surprised by the husband in his wife's bed. Old hat, isn't it?"

"Get away, Monty. I'm warning you."

"You going to break my nose again, Petey?"

"Swaine has a gun."

"Oh, goody. Shoot him, Mitch. You have every right. I'll be a witness. Shoot him. It's much too good for him but shoot anyway. Shoot him, Mitch. Aim at his middle."

Helen hissed the words, "At yourself, Mitch. Pull the trigger on yourself."

Swaine was in a trance, far away. His eyes were glazed by a mist that might have been tears or the fluid of anger. The tension was too much now, it had been built so high that it had to break, it had to snap, something had to give.

His grip on the gun was becoming tighter and tighter. Helen sat forward in her chair. I was poised, ready to spring. And the silent pressure of Monty behind the door made the fourth person in the room.

Then, suddenly, blindly, moving with animal's instinct, I lunged at Swaine, at the gun. We fell to the floor, both of us struggling. But I had a piece of the gun. His grip was still on it and I felt his finger trying to edge to the trigger. With all the power that was in me, I tore it loose finally and now held the cold steel of the weapon in my own hand. Slowly, I got to my feet. Swaine lay on the floor, breathing hard, the sweat from his head dripping down on the carpeting. Helen laughed and leaned back in the chair. I opened the door and Monty fell into the room. Somehow he could even look immaculate with his nose bandaged. "Show is over, Monty. You lost."

He recovered his composure quickly. "Yes," he said. "I see you're still intact. Don't you think you'd better put that gun away?"

"I'm going to hold on to it for a while. It might come in handy."

Helen stood up. "I'm going in and eat. I'm hungry."

Monty sat down on a small chair, folded his hands in his lap. "I'm going to stay and see if there's going to be any more excitement."

"I told you, Monty, the show is over." I picked up my pants and put them on, then my T shirt, and finally my shoes. Helen had gone into the other room. Swaine was still on the floor. He hadn't moved at all. Monty was watching me, every motion I made.

"You know, Petey, I should have painted you nude. It would have made a marvelous painting. Even now I think the best thing I ever did was my portrait of you. I'm thinking of having an exhibition of my own work. Could I have it on loan?"

"You having an exhibition of your own work? I don't believe that. You're too good an art critic not to see your own limitations. If you want the painting back you can have it. You don't need a tricky excuse. It doesn't mean anything to me."

"No, I want you to keep it, Petey. Perhaps it will haunt you like a conscience. You were such a nice boy when I painted it. You were a little rough around the edges but you were nice. Eager. Do you remember how eager you were to please me, to make my store front so beautiful? No, Petey, you keep the painting and let it remind you what a nice boy you used to be and how you betrayed everyone who helped you."

"I'll burn it, then."

Monty shook his head. "Of course you won't do that. It would be like destroying yourself. You haven't that much courage."

And he was right. Monty was always right.

Swaine moved for the first time and said my name. "Petey."

I knelt down by him. "You all right, Swaine?"

"I'm sorry, old man. Dreadfully, dreadfully sorry."

"Here let me give you a hand." I helped him up into a sitting position. "O.K., now?"

Swaine saw Montgomery. "Ask him to go away for a minute, Petey. I want to talk to you."

"I'm sitting right here," Monty said. "I don't want to miss a word. It's probably going to be a touching scene between you two. I don't want to miss a minute of it."

"Scram, Monty. Give the guy a break. Go talk to Helen. She'll tell you enough to keep you interested." He made no sign of getting up. I walked toward him. "Come on, Monty, get moving."

He stood up. "Force," he said, "gives only temporary victories. In the long run, it's brainwork that wins. I yield for the moment to your superior bulk." He bowed out and I shut the door.

"Help me up, will you, old man? I feel a little wobbly." I supported him as he tried to stand up. I got him upright finally and leaned back against the dresser. "Put that away, will you?" He nodded at the gun. I had forgotten I still held it. I stuck it in the back pocket of the jeans. "I want to thank you," he said. "I didn't mean to get you into this. I tried to stay away from you."

"It's O.K. this wasn't your fault. I came here. You didn't send for me."

"I think," he said, "I would have used the gun if you hadn't taken it from me."

"On whom? You or me?"

"I don't know." He shook his head. "I'm not sure."

"You should have used it on Helen," I said. "She had it coming."

"This isn't the first time. This afternoon when I called you, that was her doing. She started me drinking deliberately. She was so nice to me, even had one drink with me and she laughed and we had such a good time and I forgot how much I was drinking until I passed out. When I woke up there was the gun waiting for me, waiting for me to kill myself."

"You want to lie down for a minute?"

"No, I'm all right. I feel better."

"If you had turned the gun on yourself it would have been murder. Helen would have murdered you just as sure as if she had pulled the trigger herself."

"Yes, I know. I tried to tell you about her before."

"I didn't believe you. I'm sorry. I should have known."

Swaine took out a cigarette and was having a bad time trying to light a match. I took the pack, lighted one and held it for him. "You know," he said, "Helen may not be so wrong in what she said about me and Jerry. I did hate him. I think all the time that maybe it was not an accident, that something happened inside me, that I went crazy for a minute and shot him purposely. I can't remember. That's the torture of this. I'm not sure. There's no way to be sure. It would be better if I knew that I was a murderer. If I was sure that I had killed him willfully that would be better. I would know what I am. But this way I'm not sure. I'm not sure either way. There is no way to be sure, is there? Do you know a way, Petey?"

"No, there's no way."

"So what do I do?"

"You get rid of Helen for one thing."

"How? She says we're married."

"Make her produce evidence."

"And then what?"

"Buy her off. Whether you're married or not, you can buy her off. A dame like that knows only one thing and that's dough. You can give her a pile and you'll never miss it."

"You don't like Helen, do you?"

"That's a great question to ask. I stand here and watch her try to get you to kill yourself and then you ask me if I like her. I didn't like her from the beginning."

He inclined his head toward the bed. "But you—"

"That's something else. That has nothing to do with liking or not liking. You told me yourself that you're ... Well, that you're impotent and that you didn't care what Helen did. I didn't want…"

"For God's sake, man, don't apologize. I told you it was all right. I expected you to lay her. You're her type. I don't mind, really." He lowered his head and kicked the carpet with the toe of his shoe. "In one way I don't mind and in another way I mind very much. I'm jealous of you, I'm jealous of any man who isn't out of whack the way I am. Particularly anyone who's been with Helen. My imagination is good enough to know that she'd be wonderful." He looked up at me. "She is wonderful, isn't she, old man?"

The taste of her was still in my mouth and the touch of her still at the tips of my fingers and the feel of her against my body. "Yes," I said, "wonderful."

"That may be the reason I won't get rid of her."

"I don't get it. I don't want to be rough on you but, what the hell, in your shape what good does she do you?"

"My shape is psychological, psychic impotence they call it. All in the mind, you know. It's all in the mind but it's a very real thing. You see, my wants are the same as yours, maybe stronger. They are stronger." He shrugged his shoulders. "But no performance, no outlet. All build up and no climax."

"It's pretty rough, I know, but it seems to me that having Helen around would be even worse. It seems that just by being near you she would tease the hell out of you and a thing like that could tear a guy's heart out."

"Unless it's already out, Petey. Unless it has been torn out before."

"Your heart can't be torn out completely. There's always some left to ache."

"You know that too?"

"Yes," I said, "I know that."

"I'm afraid if I got rid of Helen there would only be someone else like her. There were others before her, women I picked up here and there over the world. All of them were peculiar in one way or another, they would have to be to take up with me and get nothing."

"I know but you don't have to get one who's out to murder you. Get a Lesbian or something. Someone whom you like and who likes you but gets her kicks some other way. Get rid of this maniac."

Swaine turned around and looked in the mirror. He straightened his tie and smoothed back his hair. "Tell me something straight, will you, old man?"

"If I can, sure."

"If I were to get rid of Helen, buy her off if she could be bought off for money, would you take up with her, would you take her with you?"

"You think we have a deal, Helen and me? Is that what you think? You think I'm telling you this because I want Helen and your dough. Listen here, Swaine, I've tried to be a good guy with you. I've tried to level all the …"

"Don't get mad. I didn't mean that. I don't believe you planned a thing like that. I'm only asking if you would, if I were to get rid of Helen."

"No. I can tell you that right now. Definitely not. I'd probably want her again, but nothing between us could be permanent. I told you before I don't like the girl."

"You don't understand her, really. She has some good qualities. She's been good to me sometimes. I wasn't much of anything when she picked me up in Africa. I hadn't been sober in two weeks and I was undernourished and shaking from the DT's. She tried awfully hard to get me in shape. She's had bad breaks in her life. The man she was married to, the doctor, she loved him very much."

"O.K., so she loved him. Does that mean she's got to kill you?"

"No, I guess not. But you don't understand her, really."

"You must be off your rocker, Swaine. How can you feel a shred of loyalty or sympathy for a woman who ten minutes ago tried to talk you into blowing your brains out?"

"People are strange," he said. "They want strange things."

"I give up. It's beyond me."

"But you said you might want her again."

"Yes."

"And I'd be ready to have her take care of me again. You see we both need her in one way in spite of what she is and what she does." He turned back from the mirror. "I feel better now. Is there coffee in the living room? Shall we join them?"

"O.K. Let's."

When we went into the living room Monty was telling Helen a story about one of his clients who had killed her husband's mistress. Helen munched her sandwich and didn't look much interested. "Did you boys kiss and make up?" she asked.

"Is the coffee still hot?"

Helen shook her head. "Luke warm."

I motioned to Swaine. "You'd better drink it. You want half a sandwich?"

He shook his head. Without sitting down, I wolfed the ham sandwich and the coffee. "I got to get going."

Monty said, "Just like that? Aren't we going to talk this situation out?"

"You three stay and talk it out. I'm going to bed."

"Oh, but, Petey, you just got out of bed," Monty said.

"Dry up, Monty. There's such a thing as being too cute. I'm going. Anything you need or want, Swaine?"

He shook his head. "Nothing."

"Watch yourself, huh?"

"Sure, I'll watch myself."

I went back to the bedroom and put on my trench coat. Monty was standing up putting on his coat when I came back in. "Good night, Helen. Thanks for the sandwich. Good night, Monty."

"My car and chauffeur are downstairs. I'll drop you at your flat, that is if you're going to your flat. Are you through for the evening?"

"I'll walk."

"Don't be silly. It's raining again. I'll drop you off—I want to talk to you, anyway."

I shoved my hands into my pockets and started out the door. "Watkins," she called.

I didn't turn around. "What?"

"The gun. It's showing." I took it out of my back pocket and put it in the deep pocket of the trench coat and walked on out to the elevator. Montgomery was beside me before the elevator came up. We didn't speak. At the main door of the hotel I could see the rain was coming down very hard. Also I saw the glistening sleek of Monty's long black car. "O.K., Monty, let's go."

The chauffeur started up. "Good evening, Mr. Watkins."

"Hello, Herbert. Long time no see."

"Yes, sir. Long time. Where to, Mr. Montgomery?"

"We'll drop Mr. Watkins at his flat, Herbert."

"Yes, sir."

I settled down in the rubber-padded comfort of the car, huddled in my coat, my hands in the pockets, my left hand feeling the gun. Monty offered me a cigarette, but I shook my head. He didn't seem interested in talking at that point and I sure wasn't in the mood to start up a conversation. At my apartment building, Montgomery opened the car door and said to the chauffeur, "I won't be long, Herbert." He was out of the car and into the vestibule before I could object.

"Mr. Watkins?"

"Yes, Herbert."

"How is Mrs. Montgomery?"

"She's fine. She's just fine."

"Give her my regards."

"Sure."

"And when you and Mrs. Montgomery are Mr. and Mrs. and you need a chauffeur ... Well, I've been thinking of making a change."

"Thanks, Herbert. I'll keep you posted."

"Good night, Mr. Watkins."

The rain was still falling. The night was cold and penetrating. Monty said, "I could do with a drink."

"I guess there's something upstairs." When we were in the apartment I poured two straight shots. Monty held up his glass. "To your health," he said. I nodded and gulped down the hot liquor.

"Your nose," I said, "does it hurt very much?"

Monty laughed. "That's so like you, Petey, to ask if it hurts very much. It shows you have feelings. The worst kind of monsters in the world are those brutes with feeling. They're the most dangerous. Give me a plain non-sentimental ape every time. They're not nearly so treacherous as the sentimental, feeling ones."

"All right, Monty, what's on your mind?"

"It was almost a wonderful scene at the Swaines', wasn't it? I was so glad I was there."

"You didn't come back here to compare notes on what happened at the Swaines', did you?"

"No, but the best part of things like that is talking about them later."

"I'm sure you'll do plenty of that. Sit down, Monty, and get to the point."

He sat down in a small chair. Somehow he always picked the smallest chair. It made him look or feel bigger, I suppose. "I've come to make a strange request, Petey. It's something I never thought I would do."

"What do you want?"

"Not so fast. This is difficult for me. I want to make a bargain. You know me well enough to know that I don't usually make bargains or deals. I set the terms and people meet them or they don't meet them. I never budge an inch on a price or an ideal. I'm doing that now and it's very hard. You'll have to be patient with me and understanding."

"As a matter of fact," I said, "I know you so damn well, I know you're lying. You don't want to make a deal. This is all a sales talk. You've made your terms and you're going to try to make me meet them."

"I can't be angry with you, Petey. You're being smart. I taught you very well. It's rather uncomfortable for a master to realize how well his pupil has learned. Normally you would be quite right. This would be a sales talk. But there is an element concerned here that means you have to re-evaluate me, re-evaluate what I said in terms of the element."

"And the element is Clarissa?"

"Yes," he said, "the element is Clarissa, and I love Clarissa very much."

I felt sorry for him again. He was such a little man, so well trimmed and tailored, trying so hard to be something special and being nothing really, and I knew that he did love Clarissa very much. He had never been adequate for her, enough of a man for her. He knew that and I think it only made him love her more. He loved her not really as a man loves a woman but almost as a man loves a face in a picture. As a man loves an object. Clarissa, to Monty, was always a face, a Titian loveliness, a thing of orange-red and peach and flesh colors exquisitely blended. She was never a woman with the pettinesses of a woman or the desires of a woman or a woman who functioned as an animal. But he loved her and perhaps it was deeper, stronger love than loving a whole woman, body and soul at once. I flopped on the couch, kicked off my moccasins. Yes, there was that to think about, the ways in which you could love a woman.

"All right, Monty, I'll give you that. You love Clarissa. I know how much."

"Yes, I'm sure you do. You know I'd do anything for her."

"But divorce her. Don't forget you wouldn't divorce her."

"Clarissa," he said, "has been to see me."

"I asked her not to."

"Yes, she said that. But she didn't come for the reason you think. She didn't try to make me call off my campaign against you. I have a campaign against you. Quite a clever one. I haven't really begun it yet."

"From where I sit, you've made a pretty decent start."

"But nothing, Petey. Nothing compared to what I've planned. You know how I am. Remember when I was working on the Williamsburg project? That was nothing compared to what I have planned for you now."

"You think I ought to throw in the towel now, not even put up a fight."

"I always get what I want, Petey. You know that."

"Except Clarissa."

"That wasn't a question of not getting. That was not holding. Do you mind if I have another drink."

"Go ahead, help yourself."

He walked over to the built-in bar and poured a drink. "Nice decanter, Petey, Steuben?" I nodded. "Clarissa?" I nodded again. "She really has excellent taste," Monty said.

"Get to the point, Monty, I'm weary. I've been through a lot tonight."

"How was Helen?"

"Never mind the post mortems. Get down to business."

He stood over me, looking down into my face. He seemed older, tired, worn out, too. We were all worn out from existing with each other. "Clarissa is unhappy, Petey. She says you've left her."

"How could I leave her when we were never really together?"

"You had a quarrel. She wouldn't tell me what it was about. It doesn't matter. What does matter is that she's terribly, terribly unhappy. She came to me to see if I couldn't help make it right. She knows how well I know you, how well I know how your mind works. She came to me in desperation. I've never seen Clarissa desperate before. She convinced me that she loves you, deeply. I suppose she loves you as much as I love her."

"Nothing you can say or do can put us back together, Monty. You might as well forget it. If we go back together it will be later, after I've had time to work it out. Clar knows that. She knows I might go back to her."

"It would have been so simple if Swaine had shot you, Petey. You would have been so dead and Clarissa wouldn't have grieved too much because you would have been shot while being unfaithful to her. And Mitch would have been put in jail or hung, put out of his misery in one way or another, really guilty at last for something he had done. And Helen would have had his money to go back to Africa and build that hospital or whatever it is she wants."

"Helen build a hospital? You must be out of your mind. That dame hasn't got a humanitarian bone in her body."

"Well, it's some project. Swaine's money is pretty well tied up. He has plenty and it's doled out to him regularly in sizable sums but nothing in hospital-building proportion that Helen can run off with. Not unless he dies. Then she gets it all."

"To hell with Helen. Let's finish about Clarissa so I can go to bed."

"She wants you to come back, Petey. And I want you to go back to her. I never thought I would want that. I still think it's a mistake, that you're no good, no good for her. But it's what Clarissa wants so I have to want it, too."

"It's no dice. You lost your hypnotic power over me. I function now as I feel, not as you feel."

"I didn't expect you to go back to her just because I asked you to. I'm not as naïve as that. This is where the bargain comes in.

If you go back to her I'll call off my little campaign. You can stay where you are with Murdick and Howell. I'll make it right there again. And you won't be ruined as an architect because that's the final objective of my campaign. The campaign, if it is followed through, will lay waste Peter Watkins, architect."

"You've been reading too many books, Monty. It's not easy to ruin a man. Sure, you can make me well known as being a cad and being an immoral bastard. You can maybe force me to start at the bottom and build up to the top again. I'm not afraid of that. But you can't ruin me as an architect. You can't make what I design become unfunctional, you can't make it ugly and you can't make it fall apart. That is after all what an architect does. You can make it hard for me but you can't ruin me."

"You underestimate me all the time. In your heart you know I can do what I say. I've done it to other men and I can do it to you. So I'm giving you a way out. We can make a legal document out of it if you like. You go back to Clarissa and I'll stop my campaign before it really starts."

"Is that all?"

"Yes, Petey. That's it very concisely."

"Well, you tried, Monty, now go. Get out of here."

"You can have a few days to think it over."

"I don't need a few days. If I go back to Clarissa it will be because I want to, not because I was railroaded or blackmailed into it."

"I'll give you two days anyway. I know you're hot headed, quick to lose your temper and make unwise decisions. But you always come around after a while and decide that Monty knows best."

"Good night, Monty."

"All right, Petey, good night. Two days from now shall be Sunday. Shall we have lunch together?"

"Real civilized like you mean? No, Monty, it's no use. I won't change my mind. Maybe the decision is unwise. From a business standpoint it's unwise as hell. But my life is involved with this one. From the standpoint of my own happiness, I think I'm doing the right thing."

"I'll call you Sunday. Meanwhile, I'll continue with my little program for making nothing out of Peter Watkins. Enough things can happen in two days to make a man sit up and take notice. Change his mind, perhaps."

"Good night, Monty. You know where the door is."

"Good night," he said. At the door he stopped. "You know, knowing as much as I do of what is going to happen to you if you don't go back to Clarissa, I still rather envy you. I envy you Clarissa's love and I envy you your foolish, foolish courage. I would much rather be you than I. In spite of everything that I'm going to make happen to you, I would much rather be you than I. Too bad, isn't it, that I must be the way I am."

"Yeah. Too bad."

CHAPTER SEVEN

There Is Always This Morning After

THE TELEPHONE was ringing in the distance. I looked around me as I awakened, confused, not sure where I was. I had fallen asleep on the couch after Monty left and had never transferred to bed. I ran into the bedroom and picked up the phone.

"Petey, gosh, I'm glad you're there." It was Ethel the switchboard girl at the office. "Mr. Murdick wants to talk to you in the worst way. He thought maybe you'd left town again."

"No, I'm here. Put him on." I heard Murdick on the other end of the line. "Yes, Bill, what is it."

"What kind of heating pipe did you put in the Williamsburg Village?"

"Why? What's the matter?"

"Bissell of the insurance company has been on the phone. He says the specifications definitely call for copper pipe and you didn't use it."

"He's nuts. We never planned to use it. We used that Welco stuff. Everybody's using it. They guarantee it. What is he having a bird about?"

"They've had five leaks in the G development this morning. Just got through plastering and they find these leaks, ruined everything. They'll have to replaster. They had to tear open walls. Damn pipe was eaten out. Just rotted. Like acid had eaten it out. Stuff's no good. Bissell says the specs call for copper pipe and he damn well wants it."

"He's nuts, Bill. Did you check the specs on it?"

"No, I figured he knew what he was talking about. He was so sure. Wait a minute I'll get them." He called from the phone, "Miss Hedstrom, get me the overall specs on the Village." Then to me. "Just a minute I'll check them. I'm damn glad you haven't left town yet. Did you decide where you're going?"

"Not yet. I haven't made up my mind yet. Mexico maybe. Thought I might do some fishing."

"If those specs say copper," Murdick said through his cigar, "we'll all have to go to Mexico."

"It wouldn't be our responsibility anyway. It'd be the contractors."

"Sure, but think how it would make us look. We are responsible, you know. Wait a minute. Miss Hedstrom just brought them in. I'll look." He was silent a minute, turning pages. "Yes, here it is. Wait a minute. You're right, Pete, it does call for Welco. We're clear." He made a blowing sound. "I feel better."

"I'll call Bissell and tell him about it, Bill."

"No, you'd better not. He's kind of peeved at you this morning. Says that's what we get for letting a young, inexperienced man handle a job of this size. I can't understand what got into him because he really likes you. Maybe he's heard some of the scandal or something. You'd better let me call him back."

"O.K. But don't worry about it. That Welco stuff is all right."

"Send me a card from Mexico, Pete. Get some rest."

"O.K. Good-by."

I undressed, shaved, took a shower and put on a robe, went into the kitchen, made coffee and fried a couple of eggs. The phone rang again before I could sit down and eat them. It was Murdick again. "Now what?"

"Bissell says that Welco stuff is no good. He says that everybody knows it's no good. He says there's strong rumors of their going bankrupt. I checked with my broker just before I called you. He says there's several big blocks of Welco stock that some people are trying to unload."

"Relax, Murdick. I'll fix it."

"What do you mean you'll fix it? Who the hell do you think you are? Do you think you can make Welco's pipe stand up? Do you think you can stop them from going bankrupt?"

"Their pipe is fine. I can stop them from going bankrupt. You try to keep Bissell calm for a few hours. I'll phone you back when everything is all right."

"Look, Bissell will think I've gone completely out of my head if I tell him you're going to fix everything. He says he warned you about Welco and you said that you'd switch it to copper. He didn't get it in writing. He says your word was good enough for him. Now he's madder than hell at you. You ought to hear him, Pete."

"I told you to relax. It will be all right. I'll phone you later."

I called Monty at the gallery, but he hadn't come in yet. I got his new apartment phone number and called him there. He answered the phone.

"Uncle," I said.

"What?"

"I'm saying uncle. I give up. Call off the dogs."

"I told you, Petey."

"What did you use on those pipes?"

"Trade secret."

"How much Welco stock do you own?"

"Why, none. Of course, I have friends."

"Call it off, Monty. When Bill Murdick calls me back and tells me everything is all right again, I'll talk business with you."

"All right. It'll take a little time, but I'll arrange it. This is a gentlemen's agreement. I have your word that you agree to my terms."

"You have my word that I'll go back to Clarissa. Yes. You have my word on that."

"Brunch on Sunday?"

"Yes, Monty, brunch on Sunday."

"Lawyer?"

"I think we can come to an agreement without lawyers," I said.

"All right. Just the two of us. Like old times."

"And no more tricks. I have your word on that."

"You have my word."

"Hey, Monty, what did you use on those pipes?"

"Good-by, Petey, see you Sunday."

My eggs were cold but I ate them anyway. I was hungry. There were two days until Sunday, two days to think of something, to get myself off the hook, to find a way to stop Monty once and for all. I wasn't underestimating the enemy. He was clever, more clever than I and more influential and more powerful. I had only one thing on my side. I was right and he was wrong. I didn't know how much good that would do me. Sometimes being right and a nickel buy a cup of coffee, that's about all.

Also I had given my word that I would go back to Clarissa. I tried to evaluate how morally bound I was to my word when it was pledged to a man like him. It was a big philosophical question and I looked out the window and the sun was shining for the first time in a long time, shining bright to remind everyone that the weather would be nice and that after winter comes spring.

I phoned Jill. "Hi."

"Who is it?"

"Petey."

"Oh, hello."

"How are you?"

"I'm all right. I'm fine, really."

"Good party last night?"

"All right, nothing special. I'm sorry about the way I was on the phone last night. I was still a little off balance."

"All right today?"

"Yes, I'm fine."

"Do you hate Chippendale furniture again?"

She laughed a little. "I loathe it more than ever."

"I called you to ask a favor."

"What?"

"I'd like to borrow Andy for the day."

"Andy? Whatever for?"

"I don't know. It's a nice day. I feel like going to the zoo. It's no good going to the zoo without a kid. He'll get a bang out of it."

"I'm sure he will. He's ... Well, he's never been to the zoo. I'm afraid I've been rather neglectful."

"All right if I pick him up in an hour? I'll take him to the zoo and to lunch and then maybe we'll go to the movies."

"Oh, Petey, he's too young for the movies."

"Then I'll take him somewhere else."

"I don't understand all this?" She was silent for a moment. "What are you trying to accomplish?"

"I'm not sure myself. It's a nice day. I don't feel like being alone. I guess I don't know any nice adults. It'll be good to be with a kid. They're the only nice ones left."

"Andy doesn't have anything very fancy to wear. I'm afraid the best thing he has are some corduroy overalls."

"Don't worry about it. He'll look good. Kids always look good."

"All right, Petey, I'll have him ready."

We had a fine, clean uncomplicated time, me and Andy. We ate peanuts at the zoo and laughed at the animals. I wanted to buy him a balloon but it was too early in the season for the balloon man to be out selling so we made make-believe balloons out of peanut bags. We laughed a lot. He was a good kid. He held his hand tight to my hand, having to reach up to do it, but he never let go. I was his friend and he trusted me completely, and there were no secret ramifications to our friendship.

After the zoo we had lunch downtown at Fritzel's and it was a good lunch. Everybody thought he was my little boy and wasn't he cute, and it made me feel real good. Then we went to one of the department stores and Andy had a haircut on one of the wooden circus animals they used as barber chairs, and he got a free lollipop, and the barber said he thought Andy looked like me. We went from the barbershop to the toy department and had a big splurge. Andy had never seen so many toys before and he wanted everything he saw. He settled for something like thirty-one dollars' worth. I took him over to the clothing section and had the salesgirl there outfit him. He acted up a little for the first time. He wasn't interested in clothes. That tremendous package of toys was mighty tempting, distracting.

While they were wrapping the clothes I phoned Murdick at the office.

"Pete, I'm glad you called. We've been calling you at home."

"Everything is all right now, isn't it?"

"How did you do it? Even Bissell is singing a different song. He apologized, in a way, as close as a man like him can come to apologizing. I guess there were some kids or something that put slow-action acid on the pipes. They tested them and found something had been applied to them. It was all a mistake. I'm sorry I got you worked up. Boy, I hope we don't have any more of this."

"You won't, Murdick. Everything will go smoothly now."

"How did you do it? Did you know the stock even jumped a point and a half?"

"It was easy. I just had to put my body and soul in hock, that's all."

"What are you talking about?"

"Nothing. It's not important. I'll keep in touch."

"Have a good time in Mexico. Are you going alone?"

"No, I don't think so."

"You young fellows. Oh, to be young again." He made a clacking noise. "So long, Pete."

Young Andy was holding court near the wrapping desk, two salesgirls and three customers listening to him tell about the bears and elephants he had seen. When he saw me, he ran to me and crawled up in my arms. "Carry me, Petey."

"Hey, how can I carry you and all those packages?"

"Carry me, Petey," he whined.

One of the salesgirls said, "He's getting tired. He had to go without his nap to be with Daddy today, didn't he?"

"Carry me. Carry me."

"I'll carry you, Andy, but we'll have to leave all those toys here." He slid down pretty quick after that, and I loaded up and fumbled my way out of the store full of packages and one small boy.

He fell asleep in the car going home, his little arms clutching a big box. I carried him up the three flights and put him in Jill's bed. He never woke up. Then I went down and brought up all the stuff.

Jill was still in the room with Andy. Jackie helped me unload. "What the hell did you do, buy out the store?"

"Just a few things. He's a good kid."

"You look like you need a drink," Jill said.

"How do you think it'll set after peanuts and ice cream and a strawberry soda?"

"Make you feel like a new man, Petey. Say, did I tell you the story about the two Swedes at the picnic. Well, one of these Swedes, his name was Sven, he says to the other …"

"Later, Jackie. How about that drink?"

"It isn't a dirty story. It's a perfectly respectable story to tell in the middle of the day."

Jill had come in. "Go ahead, get the drink," I said.

When Jackie left, I said, "Thanks, Jill. I feel much better. He's a good boy. You did a good job with him in spite of the absence of Chippendale."

"What are in all the packages? What did you buy?"

"Toys and clothes. We had a hell of a time. I'm afraid I bought a chemistry set. You'll have to put that away for a while, I guess."

"Yes," she said, and sat down near the window. "You're funny, Petey. I don't understand you."

"What's the difference? I hope the kid doesn't get sick. I piled an awful lot of stuff into him. He got a haircut, did you notice?"

"Yes, he needed it. It's a fine haircut."

"The barber thought he was my kid, that he looked like me."

Jill smiled. "He does a little. He does look like you."

"Jill," I began, but Jackie walked in and I stopped.

"Here, Petey." She handed me a drink. She had fixed one for herself. "So this Swede, Sven, says to the other Swede. His name was Ole. He says, 'Ole, you see that girl over there?'" She went on and on. It was a funny story, I suppose. All Jackie's stories were funny, and she told them so well. I didn't laugh very hard. I wasn't in the mood for Jackie's stories, they were out of context with the day and with what I had done and how I felt. After I finished my drink, I left. Jill and I hadn't said anything to each other and as I was riding home I decided it was just as well.

When I got home, I opened all the windows in the apartment, dumped out all the dregs of the cigarettes, dusted the table tops with a pair of shorts that were ready for the laundry, made my bed and flopped down on it.

I lay there and went over things. I had found a kind of peace that day. It may have been because the sun was shining. It may have been because Monty's campaign had forced me into a decision. I would have to go back to Clarissa after Sunday. He had my word and my word was my word regardless of the morals of the man I had given it to. Yes, I would go back to Clarissa. Monty could make me do that. But he couldn't make me be in love with her again or force me to make love to her again. He could lead me to her and lock me in with her, but he couldn't make me love her again.

Nor could she.

No, she would try but she couldn't make things be the same with us again.

I phoned the Drake Hotel and rang up the Swaines' room.

When she heard my voice, she said, "Oh, hello."

"You don't sound surprised."

"That you're calling? No, I'm not surprised. You said you would."

"You didn't think that what happened last night would make any difference?"

"No. It has nothing to do with us, with what we want from each other."

"Yes," I said, "you're right. What time?"

"Mitch has been out all day. He's going to phone at six. Come over in a half hour."

"When Mitch calls, have him meet us later for dinner. Is he all right?"

"I haven't seen much of him. He seemed sober when he called."

"Disappointed?"

She said, "Where do you want to eat?"

"It doesn't matter. Arrange it with your husband."

"All right," she said.

And that's the way it was.

CHAPTER EIGHT

Evening with the Swaines

A FTER DINNER, Mitch said, "What do you two want to do?"

"It makes no difference to me," I said. It didn't. My time was to kill time until Sunday at brunch. It made no difference what I did with my time.

"What about you, Helen?"

"I'm tired," she yawned. "I'd like to go to bed."

Swaine smiled. "You must be quite a guy, Petey. Up to now I thought her appetite was insatiable, that she never was tired of it or it never made her tired. You must have something special."

Helen slicked the back of her hair. "Would it annoy you, Mitch, if I told you about it in detail? He's really quite good. He has a kind of power quite unseen. You can't tell it about him at first. You think he's going to be regular, but he's not regular or what you expect at all. He has rather more power than he looks capable of. To begin with ..."

I slammed my voice across the table at her. "Shut up!"

"Does it make you uncomfortable to hear a recap of your performance? I wasn't doing it for you, really. I thought Mitch might enjoy it. I'm awfully good at critiques of things, books and plays and lectures. Mitch hates to go to them, don't you, darling, but he loves to hear me describe them, tell about them. I don't know why this shouldn't amuse him, too."

"You have about as much feeling inside that hollow body of yours as a toad. Now shut up, and stop torturing the guy."

Swaine put a restraining hand on my arm. "It's all right, old man. Doesn't bother me a penny's worth. Embarrassing for you, though. Sorry. Every once in a while I have to apologize for Helens manners. Very sorry."

"You're a sap, Swaine, to put up with a woman like this. She's not worth anything to you. I'm telling it to you now and in front of her so she doesn't think I'm doing anything behind her back."

"I understand, Petey. Don't worry. I understand you and I understand her."

"This is gay," she said. "We're being so modern. I must say your methods are rather crude and obvious, Watkins. When you want a man's wife you don't try to tout her husband off by telling him how miserable she is. There must be a more subtle way."

"I don't want any more of you than I've had and you know it, Helen. Mitch knows it, too."

"Yes," Swaine said, "I know it, too. Surprising how much a chap can learn by staying sober for almost two days, isn't it? Do either of you want another drink, by the way?"

We shook our heads. Somehow, in spite of the complicated structure of the triangle which the three of us made, the air was clear among us; we had no need for deceit or for the playing of games which furtive lovers play. I was openly hostile to Helen, it was a genuine feeling of hatred and contempt. The supreme manifestation of that hostility was to sleep with her. We three understood that, knew it was real and the only reason for our being the way we were. We understood each other clearly, the others' motives and each one his own motive. So we could safely strip raw our words, uncoat them of social niceties which coated other peoples' words. We could be what we were and what we were to each other.

Dinner, up to that point, had gone smoothly. I had told them of my day with young Andy and my words, my way of telling it, was no different than if I had been telling it to my aunt in Kansas City or a stranger from Peru. Mitch had smiled through most of the account, being a sympathetic listener. Helen had looked bored and was genuinely bored. Then we had eaten, saying little to each other.

Helen stood up. Mitch jumped up to help her. "I'm going home. I'm tired. Are you coming, Mitch?"

"If you don't mind, I'd rather like to talk to Petey for a while. I'll put you in a cab."

She looked directly at me. Her eyes said nothing, gave away nothing of what was inside of her. "What time tomorrow?"

"I don't know. I haven't planned my time yet."

Swaine said, "I'll be gone most of the day. I have something to do. I can just as well stay out through dinner if it will make it easier for you two."

"Don't bother, Swaine. We'll work it out. So long, Helen." She didn't say anything, she just walked out with Swaine following her.

When he was back at the table he said, "I wouldn't be surprised if Helen were falling in love with you."

"Don't talk nonsense. She couldn't love anyone; she doesn't have it in her."

"You think that? You may be right. She did love someone once, this doctor she was married to in Africa. Rather an interesting man, they tell me. She never talks about him at all. She doesn't even have a picture of him. I searched her belongings many times trying to find some trace of him, a picture or a souvenir she might have saved. But she has no remnants of him at all. I wonder many times what he was like. He must have been like you, in a way, or she wouldn't be in love with you now."

"She's not in love with me. She feels the same about me as I do about her. It's pure, concentrated sex."

"Yes," he said and then he didn't say any more.

After a few, long minutes, I said, "Mitch, would you really like to kill me?"

"You must have a secret entrance into others' minds," he said. "I've been wondering that, too. Just now. Just as you were asking me about it."

"What's the answer?"

"I'm not sure. I almost killed you last night. I wanted to, you know. I almost did. I wanted to and I didn't want to. I was awfully glad when you got that gun away from me. I suppose it has something to do with whether I wanted to kill my brother or not.

"It seems to me that if I knew another guy was playing around with my wife, I'd want to kill him. Maybe I even would."

"You can't put yourself in my place, old man. That's the trouble. You don't know what it feels like to be impotent. Any man as virile as you are can't even imagine what it feels like. If I were not impotent, you see, I can imagine myself not impotent, and you were fooling around with my wife, I'd kill you."

"Look, Swaine, I'm talking about this openly, I mean about Helen, because I don't want to torture you. You know that isn't what I want. Helen wants it but I don't. I'm open about it because I want you to ... Hell, this sounds funny, but I want you to trust me. If you told me today to stop, I would stop. I'd never touch her again."

Swaine was smiling. His face looked very much the way it had when I was telling about my day with Andy. "Do you think you could, old man? Do you think you could stop now that you've started? I think she's rather like a drug in that way. Do you think you could stop just because I asked you to?"

"It wouldn't be easy, but I'd do it if you asked me to."

Swaine narrowed his eyes. "Are you asking me to ask you to leave my wife alone?"

"It does sound like that, I know." I thought for a moment, of my own motives and also of Helen. "No," I answered, "I don't want you to ask me to stop seeing Helen. But if you do ask it, I will stop seeing her, you know that."

"I know it would be a good idea, if we got the hell out of here. I'm glad Helen has bolted out on us. I want to take you some place. Perhaps several places."

"Where?"

"You'll see when we get there."

"You make it sound damn mysterious."

"Do I?" Swaine asked. "It may seem that way at first but you'll understand. You're the only one who would. Of course Jerry knew me like a book and he would … Sorry, old man, I forgot you don't like it when I compare you to Jerry."

"It's nothing personal about your brother, you understand, it's only that it makes me nervous in a way. I suppose it's jerky of me. I guess I really don't care very much any more. If it makes you feel better to compare me to your brother, it's O.K. There is a difference between comparison and identifications, though. Remember that."

"Yes, I'll try to remember." He grinned. "Have you talked about this with Helen?"

"No. Helen and I have really very little to say to each other."

"She needles me about you. She keeps saying just because you look like my brother I shouldn't kill you. She has a thing about my killing you. She's playing it the same way she plays trying to get me to kill myself. Either way it will get me out of circulation. That's her end view, to get me out of circulation."

"How can you live with her, knowing what she's trying to do to you?" I scratched my head and drank the rest of my coffee which had turned cold. "I just can't figure it. You're a bright guy, a perceptive guy. How can you just stay with her and do nothing to protect yourself?"

"You forget, Petey, that I have not been sober for very long periods. When we met at that cocktail party the night before last, I had only been in town a few days. My mind is pretty much of a blank from the time we boarded the ship in Africa until we came to Chicago. I remembered nothing, really. There were little inconsequential things I remembered but not two related events. Helen did a pretty thorough job of keeping me tanked up on that trip. But there was something important that happened on the ship, something to do with a gun and Helen trying to get me to kill myself. It didn't come into my awareness until Helen and I talked about going to Mexico. Then I remembered the incident with the gun. Nothing in detail. It's all fuzzy. At first I thought it might have been a dream or something I imagined happening. But even remembering the fuzzy pieces of it filled me with a terrible horror and fright. I knew that it must have happened. And when we talked about Mexico, I knew that her next try would be there. She was plotting it. That's why I wanted you to come."

"You don't *have* to go to Mexico. You can always say no."

"Unfortunately, that's not true. I can say no, but if I get started on liquor I won't know whether I'm traveling or standing still. She could get me to Mexico and I wouldn't know I was there."

"Why don't you join Alcoholics Anonymous or something?"

"I wish it were that easy," he said. "Yesterday when I woke up and saw the gun, I knew then that she was not going to wait until Mexico. It's important for her to get rid of me now for some reason, as soon as possible. Tempting me with a gun is such an easy way. No one would be really shocked if I killed myself. Everyone knows about me and guns. It sounds very much the kind of thing a chap like me would do."

"Then why don't you just chuck her, get rid of her? Buy her off if necessary."

"Because until today, as dangerous as she was to me, I needed her. I needed her to take care of me. She always did that very well, Petey. No matter what else she was trying to do, she always took care of me very well. Before Helen, I had landed in some bad jams, slept in some miserable gutters. But Helen has always taken good care of me. And until today I haven't stayed sober for twenty-four consecutive hours. I haven't been sober long enough to plan anything out, to realize what the situation was and how I could get out of it."

"You have a plan?"

He looked down, away from me. "Yes," he said.

"Do you think you can lay off the bottle long enough to carry it through?"

"Good question, old man. Good question. On the basis of past history, I would say no. But there is a chance. There is a chance."

"Can I help?"

"You said you couldn't afford to get involved with me. You said your own life was …"

"I know what I said. And I'm saying now that I'll help you if I can."

"Something happen to you?"

"In a way," I said, "something has happened. Some things have become resolved."

"Well, then let's get started."

"You'd better tell me where we're going."

"You'll know when we get there. Bit of mystery is good for a fellow. Keeps you on your guard."

"O.K., Swaine. You lead and I'll follow."

Swaine gave the cab driver an address on South State Street which was in a rough neighborhood; burlesque houses, show bars, and plain saloons. We didn't talk very much in the cab. I was watching Swaine. His face was all lighted up from inside, excited and expectant, like a kid's on his way to the circus.

"Mitch?"

"What?"

"What do you think you would be doing now if this thing, this accident, hadn't fouled up your life?"

Swaine had been leaning forward in the seat, his eyes reaching ahead over the shoulder of the driver. Now he looked over at me quickly, then back to the road. "Why do you ask that just at this time?"

I scratched my head. "I don't know. It beats me. I just asked it. I didn't think about it first. What would you be like now, what would you be doing?"

"It's hard to tell. I think about that myself sometimes. It would be an awful joke if I had turned out the same, still a rummy, drunken and weak and worth nothing. Perhaps I am the way I would have been if I hadn't killed my brother. Perhaps this is the way I always was and always was going to be. I think about that sometimes and I think maybe I'm right. Do you?"

"I don't know. I was just wondering.

He didn't look at me again and I didn't say any more. It was something to think about. Always before when I had known someone whose life had been ruined or changed by an external force, I could guess pretty well what they would have been like if this force had not happened to them. These people were the people whom other people talked about, saying, he would have been a great this or that *if*. Now Swaine was suggesting the idea that perhaps he would have been quite the same if nothing had happened.

And if I had not met Ralph Montgomery and if I had not met Clarissa and if. … If. Yes, I thought, there was the possibility that I would still be the way I was, worked into a similar situation, a different place, maybe, and a different cast of characters, but the basic situation the same. There was that possibility with me as there was the same possibility with Swaine. There was no way of really ever knowing.

"Right there," Swaine said to the driver, "where the big sign is."

The big sign was an amusement arcade; games, pinball machines, self-photography booths, shooting galleries, miniature bowling alleys. The works, all the lights and the noise and the music of the jive civilization. And at a time when there were few soldiers and sailors to be seen in the city there were many to be seen in the neon confines of this arcade.

Swaine jumped out of the cab. "Come on, old man, this is it."

"Are you kidding?"

"No, of course not. Hurry."

I followed him through the slow-moving crowd. He knew his direction and moved for it in a straight line, looking on neither side of him.

The man at the shooting gallery said, "Are you back again?"

In front of us was the panorama of silhouette ducks moving through cardboard grass and croaking recording croaks. Swaine picked up the gun and put it to his shoulder.

The man at the shooting gallery said, "Look, buddy, no more prizes. I told you that this afternoon. No more prizes."

Each shot that Swaine fired hit its mark, the duck falling backward to indicate the hit. His skill and aim were impressive. A crowd gathered around as he was shooting. The man in charge was hawking for others to try their skill, but no one wanted to compete with the dead eye of Mitchell Swaine.

The man said, "O.K., buddy, that's enough. Let someone else take a turn."

I interfered. "There are other guns."

"Yeah, but everybody watches him. Nobody shoots. It was the same this afternoon. The same thing. I got a lot of people but no quarters in the till. Except his."

Swaine stopped for a moment and looked at me. His face was flushed, red, beginning to perspire. "Pick one out, Petey. Pick one out and I'll hit it. Any one. Anywhere."

I pointed and Swaine hit. Time and time again. His fingers were steady, his grip was sure. There was no trace of nervousness except in his voice when he spoke. "Are you convinced? Have you seen enough or do you want to see more?"

"I'm convinced, Mitch. I'm convinced as hell. Now what?"

"Now I pay the man." He handed him ten dollars. "Keep the change," he said. "And don't worry, I won't be back again. You see, my friend here, is convinced."

"You and him have a bet?" the man asked.

"I don't know." Swaine looked straight into my eyes. "Did we have a bet, Petey?"

"I was betting on you," I said.

We stopped in at the first saloon that did not advertise music and girls. We sat down in a small booth. I ordered a drink. Swaine ordered Seven-Up. "That was good going, Mitch."

"Yes," he said. "I used to be a whale of a shot. Of course it wasn't quite fair because it's not really a gun. I mean it is a gun but it isn't really, except that I don't think it matters. I think I could do the same thing with a regular rifle or a pistol or a revolver or damn near anything. I had only to get used to the first shock of holding the gun in my hand. I used to be a good shot, really good. But then I suppose one has to be to hit one's brother so accurately through the heart."

"Cut it out, Swaine. You made a big step forward. Don't backslide. Don't feel guilty. You were good."

"It was good and it was a good feeling, a clean feeling. It was exciting. I feel alive, I mean really alive."

"That's good."

"You aren't laughing at me, are you, Petey?"

"No. Why should I laugh?"

"It's a bit of foolishness when you look at it, a grown man getting so worked up about shooting a lot of cardboard ducks, but you know what it means. No one else would know that, really, except Helen and I don't think it would make Helen very happy."

"So what happens next, Mitch? You've proved to yourself you can hold a gun again and not be afraid, not be frozen by it."

"And not feel that terrible compulsion to turn it on someone or on myself."

I laughed. "That's the big thing, isn't it? You know, for a minute you had me scared, Mitch. I thought you were going to say, you see, old man, I can hold a gun and I can shoot it and now I'm going to shoot you."

"You're getting last night mixed up with tonight."

"I hope so."

"I'm not sore at you about anything, Petey. I told you that. I'm not sore about last night at all."

"O.K., so what comes next in your life?"

He reached across the table and grabbed my arm suddenly. "Petey, you know girls. Find me a girl. Tonight. Now. As soon as possible."

"I know some numbers."

"No, I don't want that. I want a girl who will understand if … Well, if nothing happens."

It took me a long time to say it, but I had to say it. "What about Helen? That's what you have Helen for."

"Don't you see, Petey, that I can't possibly go to Helen? If I wasn't all right, it would be worse after that, worse than it is now. To defeat Helen, I have to go to her when I'm sure of myself. You can see that, can't you?"

"You feel confident now that you're O.K.?"

"I've got to find out. I've got to."

"What if things don't work out right?"

"I don't know. I can't let myself think about it. This time I know I'm all right."

But I knew what could happen if he wasn't all right. It would be worse for him, the agony would be reborn; the agony, would become a torture again, with a more tormenting, driving force. I knew I couldn't talk him out of trying but I had to make the attempt. He was appealing to me for help and the best way to help was to try to talk him out of it.

"These things," I said, "take time. I admit, being able to hold a rifle and fire it is a big step forward. But you can't get over a big illness in a couple of hours. It's going to take time."

"Don't you see that if I can fire a gun I can make good with a woman again? It fits together. It makes sense."

"Maybe on paper it does. Maybe according to logic it does. But getting over what you have to get over takes time, a lot of time. Wait a while. Don't try it yet. Wait until you're really sure."

"I'm never going to feel any surer than I am now. I hate to ask you to do this but I'm asking you to help me. I'm asking you to get me a girl who will understand and be patient. And I'm asking you to stay with me so that afterward, if I'm all right, we can go out and celebrate. Or if I'm not," he said, lowering his voice, "I may need you then, too. I know that if you're around, you'll see to it that I don't do any damage to anyone, that I don't go wild and hurt anyone."

"O.K., Swaine, if that's what you want, I'll do my best."

"You know a girl? I'll pay anything."

"You won't have to pay. The one I know will do it as a favor for a friend." I slid out of the booth, found the phone, and dialed the number. Even then I couldn't believe what I was doing.

CHAPTER NINE

This Is a Long Hour

J ILL SAID, "Sit down and stop pacing. You look like an expectant father."

"How long have they been in there?"

"Not long enough for him to get his shoes off. Sit down and relax. You're behaving ridiculously."

I sat down beside her and picked up the drink she had poured for me. "You explained it to Jackie just the way I told you to?"

Yes. She knows all about it. You're being so funny, Petey. It's almost as if you're in there instead of him."

"Don't talk foolishly."

"I don't understand it, why you're so interested in Mitch, why he means so much to you. Where do you fit into the picture?"

"I don't fit. I don't know what the hell is so peculiar about this. The guy needs a friend, he needed someone to help him. So he picked me because I look like his brother. So I'm helping him. So what?"

"But there must be more, Petey. It isn't like you to be so wrapped up in someone else. You don't give that much of yourself away for nothing. There must be something in it for you."

I gulped down the drink. "Oh, that's swell. That's a great thing to say about a guy. Don't you think I ever do anything for anybody else? Do you think it's only me, all the time?"

"You've said that about yourself, that you do things to get ahead, to make your way ahead. When you were so thick with

Monty and I warned you about him, you said you were only using him for your own purposes. And I always felt that you were using me that way, too, for your own purposes."

"That was a mutual agreement, remember? We used each other to satisfy basic needs. Those were your words, your idea. Not mine."

"Yes," she said, "those were my words." She took my hand. "I'm sorry, Petey. I'm always saying dreadful things to you that I really don't mean. You are a sweet boy, and of course you're doing it because you feel sorry for Mitch and want to help him. Rather like what you did for Andy this afternoon. You have now replaced everyone in his affections. He ate no dinner tonight. He only talked about you, how strong and fearless you are." She linked her arm through mine. "You would make a marvelous father."

"What time is it?"

"Oh, stop it, Petey, it's sickening the way you're carrying on."

"Ssh! Shut up a minute." I strained my ear toward the closed bedroom door. "I thought I heard something."

"Would you like to hear some music?"

"No."

"Would you like me to leave you alone?"

"Yes."

"I don't think I like you any more, Petey. I think you're rather a bore."

"Listen to me. There's a guy in there who wants desperately to be alive. Maybe his whole life hangs on what happens in there. This is a turning point, a big thing. I've got no patience to sit and make small talk while he's fighting for life."

Jill stood up and walked away. "You'll never grow up. You are taken in by everybody. Still the boy from Dubuque at heart. Mitch is making a fool out of you. Everyone knows he's no good. There have been doctors all over the world who have tried to help him. No one can help him. He's too far gone. He's eaten away from booze and having too much money. Do you think if he had been poor and the same thing had happened to him that he would be like this now? Of course not. You have to be rich to go to the dogs as beautifully as he has. If he had been poor, he would have had to snap out of it. He would have had to hold himself together to survive, to eat and live. He's just no good, Petey. If you're really doing this out of the goodness of your heart, you're wasting your time."

"I've wasted it before."

She turned to me, softer now and almost pleading. There was a rim of tears edging her eyes. "Is it gone again, Petey?"

"Is what gone?"

"Us. The time for us to be together. Is it gone again?"

I waited, trying to avoid an answer.

"Is it, Petey?"

"Not now, Jill. It isn't here now."

"I thought it was today when you took Andy. I watched you from the window as you left. There was the way he held your hand. And I waited at the window for two hours before you brought him home. And you carried him from the car as though he belonged to you, as though he were part of you. I thought maybe our time was back again. I was ready for you. I felt that if Andy belonged to you, I belonged to you, too. If you had said the word then, if you had given me some sign." Her head fell forward and the tears spilled out, not cried, soundless tears. "But you didn't say anything. I saw no sign."

"No."

"Are you going to marry Clarissa?"

"I don't know. That's far away."

"You still love her?"

"I don't know that either. I know I can't give her up. Not now anyway." I walked over to her and put my hands on her shoulders. "So many things have happened so quickly. You can't know them all, you can't know what they mean. Maybe later, when this is all over, I'll be able to tell you then. Maybe later when the air is all clear between us again, maybe then it will be the time for us."

"All right, Petey. I'll wait."

"It's an outside chance," I warned.

"My life has been ruled by outside chances. This is the first good one. I'll take it."

"I'm not promising anything."

"No, I know you're not. I can promise you that ..."

I put my hand over her mouth. "Don't promise anything, Jill. We're not to be tied by anything. If we get together it will be because we want to, not because we've made promises to each other."

"Yes, you're right," she said. "I think I'll put up a pot of coffee. Do I look awful? Tears louse up a girl's paint job so."

"You look fine."

Jill went into the kitchen, and I sat and waited the long interminable time. Once I heard what I thought was laughter. I froze motionless, straining to hear more, but there was no other sound. Jill stayed in the kitchen and I guessed she was crying.

When Swaine came out of the room his face showed nothing, not victory and not defeat. There was nothing but the expression his face always had, the expression of being rich and slightly disdaining. "All right, old man," he said. "Let's go."

"What happened?"

"I'll tell you later. Come on."

"Aren't you going to say good-by? I'd better say good-by to Jill."

"I'll get a cab. Meet you downstairs." He took off, fast, and I went back into the kitchen.

Jill was sitting at the porcelain-topped table, a drink in front of her, her hand supporting her tired face. "We're going," I said. "Good-by. Thank you."

"What happened?"

"I don't know. Said he'd tell me later."

"All right, Petey. And do me a favor, will you?"

"Sure. Anything. What do you want?"

"Stay away for a while. Stay away from me and from Andy and from Jackie. Just for a while. I'll tell you when it's all right to come back."

"O.K. I guess I do louse things up for you. I'm sorry."

"Good-by, Petey."

There was the sound of the shower running in the bathroom. I stood at the doorless doorway for a minute. Jackie was hidden behind the shower curtain. I started to ask her, but I changed my mind and ran downstairs, and got into the taxi which was waiting.

Swaine said, "It was all right, old man. It went all right. I came through with colors flying."

"That's fine. I'm glad."

He laughed. "Are you glad? You sound as though you couldn't care less."

"It's funny, but suddenly I don't care very much. I did, before, when I was waiting for you. The most important thing in the world was whether or not you were going to make it. Now it really isn't very important to me. I don't know why."

"Jill maybe. Huh?"

"Maybe. Maybe it is Jill. Maybe it's just that I'm bored with you and your dough and your problems and your wife and every-thing else. Maybe I'm just tired of worrying about you and get-ting involved with you. I've got problems of my own."

He hadn't even listened. He didn't care about me or my life. "This is going to make a difference," he said. "It's going to mean my whole life will be different from now on. You've got to prom-ise me one thing."

"I'm through promising things, Swaine. You're on your own now. You don't need me any more. I don't have to promise anything."

"Helen must not know. You must give me your word that you won't tell Helen that I'm all right again."

"Why not? Why aren't you going to tell her? Boy, if I were you the first thing I would do would be to go to Helen."

"Yes, I'm certain that's exactly what you would do. But, of course, I'm not like that. I have something else in mind. Give me your word, will you, that you won't tell her."

"O.K. You have my word. It doesn't matter to me any more. I'm through with her."

"Are you?" Swaine was looking at me, and I couldn't tell what he was thinking or feeling. He was something like the way he had been at the shooting gallery, a diluted version of the exhilaration which had been in him then. "Are you sure that you're through with her?"

"My only moral justification before was that you were impotent. Now it isn't true any more. So it's hands off."

"You don't have that hands-off reputation, old man. There's Ralph Montgomery and his wife."

"That's different," I said. "There was love involved in that. You know how I feel about Helen. No, you can relax. I'm through with Helen."

"She's not the kind of woman you can turn on and off like a light switch."

"I can."

"You think you can, Petey. Right now, you say you can. But when you want her and there is that terrible driving that comes from wanting a woman like Helen ... You see, I know all about wanting."

"Now you can learn something about having her, Swaine. Like I said, I'm through. I know it'll be hard. She's damn good. I hope she's as good for you as she was for me."

"You're a real peasant, Petey, full of the phoney codes of the peasants."

"Turn it off, Swaine. All of a sudden you're strutting. O.K., so you're the aristocracy with all the dough and the education and the manner of the aristocracy. This peasant came in mighty handy to you when you were in trouble. You forget quickly."

He put his hand on my arm. "Don't lose your temper, Petey. I didn't mean to tee you off on me. I didn't mean to sound the way I sounded. It's only that if I were in your position, I wouldn't even try to stop seeing Helen. I'd want to keep on seeing her and think it would be perfectly natural to go on seeing her."

"Well, that's the way you are, and I'm the way I am."

"Yes," he said, and then he didn't say any more for a long time. He looked out the window on his side and I looked out my window. Zero, I was thinking, plus zero equals zero. There was that to be thinking about and the long stretch of nothingness which lay ahead.

"Petey?"

"What?"

"I tried to give Jackie money," he said. "She wouldn't take it."

"Good for her. She's a peasant, too, with the good sound moral sense of a peasant. She did it to help you, as a favor to me. Dough isn't important to a girl like Jackie."

"While you were waiting for me, what were you thinking about, what did you want to happen?"

"I don't remember. What's the difference?"

"There's a great deal of difference. You think you can cut yourself off from Helen and me. It's not that easy, you know."

"You watch."

"All right, old man, I'll watch."

I leaned forward and tapped the driver on the shoulder. "Stop at the next corner. Let me out there." I felt like walking, like being alone, like being rid of all the Swaines and Montgomerys and Jackies and Jills in the world. West was that way, and if I walked enough in that direction there would be Dubuque and I would be that nice Watkins' boy, and maybe there would be a girl who would want nothing more than me and a little house, a house like the houses in the Williamsburg Village, and there would be all the things that the people in Dubuque do, clean uncomplicated things, easy straightforward living. If I walked far enough west there would be home and the easy, clean pace of home.

And even as I was thinking these things, I was knowing that it was not true. There were people in Dubuque basically like Helen and like Mitch and like Jackie and Jill and like the Montgomerys. They were there and if I went home again I would find them, seek them out to make myself miserable again.

The cab stopped.

Swaine said, "Good night, old man."

I didn't say anything. I started to walk toward the West.

CHAPTER TEN

Another Night

THE NIGHT WATCHMAN didn't know me. I showed my identification.

"O.K.," he said. "I guess you're Mr. Watkins all right. Got to keep out a sharp eye. Been kids around here. Vandals. Putting acid on pipes and God knows what else."

"Yes," I said. "You've got to keep a sharp eye."

"How come you want to go through the buildings this time of night? You won't be able to see much. Liable to hurt yourself with so much debris around. Want my flashlight?"

"No, thanks. I can go through the houses in the dark or blindfolded."

"O.K., but watch yourself."

I wandered through the dark, half-finished structures which would soon be homes. I had never been so clearly aware of the enormity of the monster I had created; this charming, quaint, authentic monster. I realized then how much I knew about design and space and the utilization of space and how badly my knowledge was applied here. This was Development G. There were the other developments down the line, the houses already finished, lights burning in the windows, people living in the rooms. Far ahead was the glow of the movie house, an almost exact copy of the Governor's Palace at Wilhamsburg. When it was completed, twelve thousand persons would live in this monster and breed children here.

It could have been so wonderful. And instead it was this.

I don't know exactly what I wanted to find that night in Development G of the Williamsburg Village. I went there, driving by an unknown force. Perhaps I wanted to find a shred of good in what I had done or to look at this immense project and say, good or bad, this is mine, I did this. But even that wasn't true. I had not done it. Monty had done it. I was an instrument to Monty, just as a pencil and a ruler had been instruments to me. I could not even have the satisfaction of saying it is my monster, it is horrible but it's mine, I put it across, I made money on it. I couldn't have that satisfaction. That, too, belonged to Monty.

The wind blew up suddenly, fiercely. I stood in the middle of a rutted path which would become a road and let the wind hammer at me. It was a good, clean, powerful wind. If only, I was thinking, it would blow hard enough to blow these buildings away, out of sight. For as long as they stood they would be a symbol of me, of what I was and what I could have been. But we were built to resist the power of the wind, the buildings and I, and we would have to stand and be what we were and grow old being what we were.

Coming to the Village had accomplished nothing. It only added to my feeling of depression, to my feeling of futility.

I walked a long way until I found a taxi cab to take me home. The wind had not subsided and a storm was coming. Yes, I thought, a storm is coming.

The storm came in full fury during the night. I lay unclothed and uncovered in my bed. I had not slept. I could not sleep. I listened to the storm, the great bursting claps of thunder, the crackling streaks of lightning. The wind blew the heavy rain hard against the windows. It was a night alive with noise.

Into these sounds came another sound. The doorbell. At first I didn't recognize the sound as being a sound apart from the storm. But it was there, timidly piercing these other sounds.

I slipped on a robe, pressed the buzzer which released the downstairs door, and waited, wondering who it might be.

The knock came after a few minutes. One knock. Quick. Determined.

"Who is it?"

"Let me in!"

"Who is it?"

There was a beating on the door. Fists pounding wildly. "Let me in! Let me in!"

I opened the door for Helen.

She was drenched, dripping rain. Her hair was straight, hanging in points of wetness. Her stockings and shoes were soaked through, and even her raincoat had given out to the tremendous force of the storm.

"What do you want?"

She stood for a moment, just looking at me, her eyes burning a green fire, sparkling fire into the dark of the room. Then she leaped at me, her fingernails aimed at my eyes, scratching my face, her legs kicking wildly. All this she did silently. The sounds of the storm were her words, and her actions were the movement of the storm.

She had taken me by surprise, before I could act quickly enough to ward off the attack. I felt the burn of the scratch across my cheek. I tried to grab her and hold her still. But she had a tremendous unleashed power, a wiry, catlike energy that wouldn't hold still, wouldn't be caught, wouldn't be trapped. I tried to pinion her arms, but she bit my hand. I had to hit her finally, with my open hand hard across her face, knocking her back. She stumbled, fell to the floor and lay panting there, not seeming to feel the impact of the blow on her face. Her eyes were still alive with the green fire and every breath she let out hissed the sound of this fire. All the while the raging of the storm was a background to this, a counterpart and a counterpoint to Helen, the violence of the way she was.

I touched the burning line on my face where she had scratched me. There was blood drawn. And on my hand where her teeth had sunk into me. There was blood there, too.

"I ought to kill you," I said. "Why did you come here?"

She said nothing. She didn't move.

"Get out."

Still she didn't move.

"I said get out!"

No movement. I went over to her, reached down to pull her up. But she stopped me with a gun. She had had a gun concealed in her pocket and she steadied it at me. "Put that down, Helen. You don't know what you're doing."

"Get back, Watkins. Get back." Her voice was low, shaking.

I didn't move. She started to get up. The gun came threateningly close to me. Helen was wild, mad, uncontrolled and uncontrollable. She motioned me back with the gun. This was not a sane person I was confronted with. Whatever happened to her had pushed her across the narrow border between sanity and madness. She would use the gun on me. I knew that from the assurance with which she held it. And I knew it from the way her eyes were looking at me.

Trying to appear calm and easy, I turned my back and walked slowly to the couch, sat down there, found a cigarette and lighted it. Helen had followed and stood close, with the gun pointing at my head. It was another German gun. The one Swaine had last night was in the pocket of my raincoat, hanging in the front hall. If I could get to it ...

"What happened, Helen? What did Swaine do?"

"You knew it was Swaine. You know what he did. You made him do it. I know you. I know how your mind works."

I lay back, inhaling deeply and shooting the spirals of smoke at an invisible target on the ceiling. "You don't know anything about my mind. You know how my body functions. That's all. You know that about me, that's all. Nothing else."

"What did you give him?"

"Swaine? I didn't give him anything."

"You think I'm going to kill you, don't you?"

I smiled. "No, Helen, I don't think you're going to kill me. You want me for your own purposes. I'm no good to you dead."

"Killing is too good for you. It's too good for Mitchell Swaine. But he's going to die. He's going to be killed tonight and you're going to watch it. You're going to watch him take a gun and put it against his heart and pull the trigger. Yes, Watkins, you're going to watch your precious friend kill himself. And I'm going to be laughing. I'm going to be laughing all the time the thing is happening."

"I still want to know what happened."

"You're misjudging me again, Watkins. I told you before that I am a calculator. I'm cold and as deadly as this gun."

I turned around, pushed her arm and the gun aside, stood up and walked across the room, not too certain whether or not a bullet would go through my back. "You think you're many things, Helen. You're no good, that's for sure. But as for being such a deadly, calculating bitch, I'm beginning to have my doubts. You're a kid, maybe, in over your red hair, in something over your head. So you do what a kid dreams about doing, you pick up a gun and point it at me."

Helen laughed, a snarling, grisly kind of laughter. "You're romantic, Watkins. You're a stinking, sniveling romantic. You refuse to accept reality. You refuse to accept me as I am. Because you've been with me, you're trying to make me a misunderstood little girl. I'm not that. I am what I am. And right now I'm a woman holding a gun at your back."

"You look," I said, "damn silly."

"I'm not going to kill you. I was, at first. I came here for that. But not now. I'm too smart for that."

I walked to the fireplace to look into the mirror over it. "You ought to cut your nails," I said, fingering the scratch she had made. "A fellow could get hurt in a tussle with you. I better put something on it." Through the mirror I could see her face. She was right. She was not just a kid in over her head. She was some form of animal, blazing inside with a secret wound and wanting to spit out the pus of that wound. She was a wet, dangerous animal. I started to walk to the bedroom.

"Stay where you are!"

"I'm going to put something on my face." I kept walking, through the bedroom and into the bathroom. I got some peroxide and a piece of cotton and dabbed at the scratch. Helen was there, in the doorway, the gun still leveled at my back. "We've got a thing about scenes in bathrooms," I said. "We met in a bathroom and maybe you're going to shoot me in a bathroom."

"I said I wasn't going to kill you."

"I didn't think for one minute that you were."

"You misjudged again. I came very close to killing you."

"Maybe you ought to tell me what this is all about."

"You know."

"Do I?"

"You knew what happened to Mitch. You know he's all right now."

I smiled. "Yes, I know. I didn't know you did. He told me not to tell you, and then he went and told you himself."

"He didn't just tell me."

This time I laughed. "Good for him."

"I meant what I said when I told you that you were going to watch him die."

I rinsed the bite mark on my hand and put some peroxide on it. "You still want him dead? What's the matter, isn't he any good?"

"You know, I'm deadly serious about this, Watkins. Your being flippant won't accomplish anything. I know what I'm going to do and I am going to do it."

I sat on the edge of the tub. "What is it, Helen? Why do you want Swaine dead?"

"It's my business."

"If I'm going to watch him die, it will be my business, too. Both of you have made it my business."

"You should have stayed out of it. I was so close to finishing him. Yesterday, while we were in the bar, I thought he would do it then. But you spoiled that too. You won't spoil it this time."

"Tell me the truth. Why do you want him dead? The guy is nuts about you. I don't see why, but he is. He'll give you anything you want, anything money will buy. And he's all right now. What more could you possibly want?"

"Plenty." She motioned the gun. "Let's get out of here." On our way through the bedroom, I hesitated at the bed and smiled. "Keep moving, Watkins."

In the living room I lay on the couch again, lighted another cigarette. "Come on, Helen, tell me why."

She sat on the coffee table, close to me, the gun still in position. "Do you know what love is, Watkins?"

"I don't know. Maybe I do. I'm not sure."

"I do. I know what it is to love a man with everything I have. I know what it is to love a man and respect him, not for what he can give to you but for what he is, for the work he does, for the good he does, for the integrity he has. Have you loved like that?"

"No."

"I have. I know that love. I loved a man who was worth a thousand of you and Mitch all rolled up into one."

I thought for a minute, wondering about this woman. I looked at the gun. "Maybe I wasn't so wrong about you."

"It's a matter of tense, Watkins. Present and past tense. I was all right once. I'd been knocked around plenty when I was young. I was hard and tough. But I was a damn good nurse. You had to be tough where I was and doing what I was doing. You had to be tough to look at what I had to look at and survive it. I was in

Africa and in Italy through the war. I saw them in pieces, men in pieces. Pieces of men. You had to be tough to survive that. I was built for it, all right. I was pretoughened for the job. And then I met him, the doctor whom I went back to marry."

"Yes, I know about him."

"What do you know about him?"

"Well, that he was a doctor and that you married him and that he was part Negro."

"Yes," she said. "You know all the unimportant things about him. You don't know how much of a man he was, how wonderful he was. He made me wonderful." She waited for a reaction. "Well, why don't you laugh? Go ahead, laugh."

"It's not very funny."

"Yes, it is. My being wonderful is very, very funny. He made me that way. Just by letting me be in love with him and watch him and know what he believed and how he believed, those things made me wonderful, too. You can't understand the scope of a man who is selfless. He was selfless. He lived for other people, for the good he could do for other people. All people. What they were or how much they had made no difference to him, he never thought about those things. Men were men to him. Not like you, not measuring each man by how much he can do for you or how much you might be able to get out of him."

"That's not right. You ought to know that. I helped Mitch all I could. There was nothing to be gained from that."

"You helped Mitch and you spoiled everything I planned to do."

"That's what I'm trying to find out, what were you trying to do. What did you expect to accomplish by getting Mitch to kill himself?"

"This man I was married to," she said, "was the best human being who ever lived. In a quiet way, he was a Christ, that kind of man. You know what happened to him?"

"He died," I said.

"You know how?"

"No."

"He was shot by a patient in the hospital. He was shot by a crazed, frantic man who had been committed to the hospital as an alcoholic. He was shot by a man he was trying to cure."

At last the pieces were coming together. The jigsaw events were interlocking to make the complete picture.

"Mitchell Swaine," I said.

"Yes. A no-good worthless, shell of a man took this other man's life. And it cost Mitchell Swaine nothing." She laughed instead of crying. "You know something, Watkins?" I didn't answer. I waited for her to answer. "He doesn't even remember doing it."

"He doesn't remember killing a man?"

She shook her head. "He remembers nothing."

"How did he do it? How did he get the gun?"

"Money," she said. "People in Africa are poor. An orderly who needed money. He paid five times what it was worth and got the gun. Mitchell Swaine was a pet patient of my husband's. He saw only the good in each man and he thought there was good in Mitchell Swaine. So he tried desperately to help him, and Mitchell Swaine repaid him this way."

"How did Swaine get away with it? How come he didn't land in jail?"

"My husband didn't die at once. He lay half dead for three weeks. He insisted that there was still good in Mitchell Swaine. He insisted the incident be kept quiet, that there be no prosecution of Swaine. Mitch's money helped, too. His lawyer came with money, and that money added to my husband's words kept the people in the right places quiet. I had to swear to my husband, as he lay dying, that I would fight to see that nothing happened to Mitch. He made me promise that. Technically I have kept my promise. The law has not touched him, never touched him at all."

"So you're settling this in your own way. An eye for an eye. Did you have to marry him to do it?"

"Again, you underestimate me, Watkins. To see Swaine dead would not settle the score. A thousand Swaines could die and it still wouldn't compensate for the death of one good man. I saw more than a chance to see that Mitchell Swaine died. I saw beyond that, to his money. Money means nothing to me personally. Nothing I could buy could replace what I lost when Mitch shot my husband. But if I got his money, too, that meant I could use that money to do what my husband always dreamed of doing, of building a hospital that would take care of everyone, all peoples regardless of what they were, what color they were, or how much money they had. So I picked Swaine up out of the gutter of alcohol and planned carefully what I would do. But his money is tied up. He can get it only some at a time, not the tremendous amount I need to go back to Africa to build the hospital. When he's dead, it will all be mine. No strings. And there will be a hospital and it will bear my husband's name."

"You're a funny girl, Helen. You're crazy. I mean that literally. You are as inhuman a woman as I've ever known. And yet you want to do this very human thing."

"My husband was as human as I am inhuman now. And look what happened to him. I have to be this way. I told you I trained myself to be this way. You have to be this way to survive. My husband did not survive, but I will."

I got up and walked around the room, without direction. She kept the gun aimed at me. I was in a wilderness of madmen, Helen and Swaine. Monty, too, in a way. He was out to destroy me as thoroughly as Helen was determined to destroy Swaine. Either way, Monty would destroy me. Going back to Clarissa was a destruction more deadly than Monty's attempts at destroying the Williamsburg Village and through the Village, destroying me. Clarissa was a more deadly destruction, but it would be I and

I alone who would be hurt. With the Village more people would be destroyed, innocent bystanders struck down by the madmen.

Perhaps I was a madman, too.

Helen said, "You see now why I hate you, why you've almost destroyed everything I've done. You're tempting Mitch to get well. I can't let that happen."

"No, I see that."

"I fought him tonight. I fought him as a woman fights off an attacker. Possessing my body was one thing I swore I would never let him do. You helped him get well. I fought him as hard as I know how to fight. But he had his gun and I could do nothing against him."

"It seems to me you're drawing a fine line with Swaine. You don't seem to have much respect for your body with other men."

"That's different. This was possession. You never possessed me," she said.

"No," I said. "I didn't possess you." I rubbed my eyes and looked around me to make sure what I was seeing was real, if the words I was hearing were real words or words in a nightmarish dream. The gun was very real. And if I touched Helen she would be real, too. "O.K., what now?"

"You get dressed and come with me."

"Where?"

"To the hotel. To Mitch."

"What if I refuse?"

"You won't refuse," she said.

"The gun isn't going to make me do anything. You said before you wouldn't use it."

"I might," she said. "If I have to, I will."

"You'd land in jail. You'd be hanged. You would never be able to build that hospital, if that's what you're really after."

"You forget, Watkins, that Mitch would be dead, too. Before I died. The money would go to me first, and my instructions are already drawn up for the building of the hospital. It will be built anyway. I can die knowing it will be built."

"But you don't want to die, Helen. You want to live and see it, you want to see his name up across the entrance."

"Yes," she said, "that's what I want to live to see."

"Then you won't use the gun."

"Perhaps not. But you'll come with me anyway. You'll come because you think there might be one thing you can do to help Mitch, to save his life. You won't let me kill him without doing everything you can to stop me. I'm sure of that."

"Is he at the hotel now?"

She nodded. "With two quarts of gin. He will be quite drunk when we get there."

"I wouldn't count on it."

"He'll kill himself anyway. I'll tell him what I told you. He's taken two lives so far, his brother's and my husband's. When he knows that, he'll want to die. He won't want to live."

"You've got it figured pretty good."

"Cold and calculating," she said, "even to you. You are going to try to save his life. But I want you to see him die. You are going to try to save him from me, aren't you, Watkins?"

I walked to the bedroom door. "You can put that gun away," I said. "I'll be dressed in a minute."

CHAPTER ELEVEN

There Is Night Until the Morning Comes

MITCHELL SWAINE dropped the gun on the floor. He looked at the two unopened gin bottles. "Feel like a drink?"

I shook my head.

He opened the bottle and took a long swallow. He made a terrible face and shook his head. "The first is always rough going down." He drank again. "You know, Petey, that she had to die."

I looked at the body that lay on the floor, at the face that still showed the terror that had been inside her at the moment the gun was fired. Helen. The body which had been so tight and alive now so dead. Helen. "Yes," I said, "she had to die."

Swaine offered me the bottle again. "Sure you won't join me?"

"Funny," I said, "Helen calculated so well. She figured you would have knocked off those gin bottles by the time we got here. She went wrong in her calculations all at once. She died being wrong."

"Feel nothing, you know. Third person I've killed. Feel nothing. You get used to anything. Killing, even."

"You're not a killer, Swaine. You did it in self-defense. She tried to force you to suicide. If you had kept the gun at your heart and pulled the trigger, Helen still would have been your murderer. The only way to stop her was for you to kill her. You had to turn the gun on her to save yourself. It was self-defense. I'll stand by you. I'll make a jury believe it."

Swaine ripped the spread off the bed, stood over Helen for a moment, looking at the deadness of her, then dropped the spread so that it fell over her, a swirl of satin on the worn carpeting. "Killing Helen was self-defense in a way." He drank again. "But not Jerry. And not Helen's husband."

"Do you remember it at all, killing the doctor in the hospital in Africa?"

He shook his head. "I remember very little," he said. "There was a doctor who tried to help me. I hated him. I remember that much. I didn't want to live, and he wanted me to live. He didn't understand that I didn't want to live. I hated him. But I don't remember killing him."

"Maybe you didn't."

"Yes, I did. When Helen told me the story, Petey, I knew it was true. I have done other things that I don't remember, some of them low and horrible. And I did this to her husband. I am guilty of that. And for Jerry, too, in a way. I hated him so. I hated my brother. He was everything I should have been and wasn't. We talked once, do you remember, about whether killing Jerry was an accident or murder. It was murder, in a way. I didn't have the safety on the gun. Jerry had warned me two minutes before to make sure the safety was on. I hated him telling me what to do. I left it off purposely to spite him." He drank some more. "I spited him all right, didn't I?"

"What are you going to do, Swaine?"

"In a minute, I'll call the police."

"I'll do whatever I can for you."

"What I want you to do is nothing. I want them to hang me for murdering Helen. But you and I will be the only ones who knew the real reason they are going to hang me. Only we will know whose deaths are being revenged." He held the gin bottle high. "To dying," he said. "Let's drink to dying."

"Do you think Helen really would have built the hospital?" I asked.

"You never liked Helen, Petey. You could never see her good qualities. Yes, she would have built the hospital. She was sincere in wanting that. And it *will* be built. I'll see to that. The biggest damn hospital you ever saw. You want to build it, old man? I think it's fitting that you should build it. Yes, I will leave instructions for that. You build the hospital. And do me a favor."

"What?"

"Make it a big damn thing. As big as my guilt. Build a monument to my guilt, will you?"

"I'll do anything for you I can."

"Gin is wonderful once your stomach becomes accustomed to it." He hit his stomach. "Wonderful for your guts. Preserves them. Get ulcers if you don't drink gin. Do you know that?"

"What would I build as a monument to *my* guilt, Swaine?"

"You have guilt too, Petey?"

"I could have avoided this. I came here to stop Helen from making you kill yourself. I stopped that, all right, but I couldn't stop you from killing Helen. That's my guilt."

"If you had stopped me tonight, there would have been tomorrow or the next day. I knew I was going to have to kill her, Petey. It took time for me to get the courage. You have no guilt. You only have the misfortune of getting mixed up with the Swaines. We're trouble. We *were* trouble but no more. Funny," he said, "that I should feel so free suddenly."

"Gin," I said.

He looked at me straight. A part of him was still sober, cold sober. "No, it's not the gin, old man. It's because I'm going to get what's coming to me at last." He put the bottle to his mouth again. "One more for the road, the last one."

"You'd better call the police."

"First you leave."

"No, I'll wait with you."

"No, sir. You are to stay out of this. I'll keep your name out of it. If you're smart and you keep your mouth closed, you won't become involved. I'm going to say that there were no witnesses. Be smart this time, stay out of it."

"Do you suppose, if I had stayed away from you and Helen, that this would have happened? You both warned me away, yet you both seemed to need me, want me. Do you suppose if I had stayed away, this would have never happened?"

"You were a catalyst, old man. Nothing more. Helen and I were a chemical combination that was bound to explode. You were the catalyst. You speeded the reaction. Eventually, it would have happened anyway. Nothing could stop it."

"I guess you're right, Swaine."

"So you needn't carry the guilt for this." Swaine smiled. There was a film of glassiness beginning to form over his eyes, a drooping of the flesh around his mouth. The gin was beginning to take its toll. "You will, of course, carry guilt. Jerry would have, and you will, too. You know, old man, the similarity between you two is absolutely amazing. More than a coincidence. Did I ever show you a photograph of Jerry?" He started toward the chair where his suitcoat lay. "Let me show it to you. The resemblance is absolutely amazing."

"I've seen it, Swaine. You showed it to me that first night."

"Did I?" He sat on the floor, cross-legged. "Yes, of course I did. Why don't you leave, Petey? Go away while there's still time."

"I think I'd better stay with you until the police come."

"You think I'll use the gun on myself, don't you?"

I was afraid of that. Not afraid, really, because it might have been the better way, the easier way for poor Mitchell Swaine. It would have been cheating the law. Yet either way Swaine would be dead. The end accomplished. "What do you think, Swaine?"

"About using the gun?" He shook his head. "No," he said, "I won't use it on myself. I will go through the machinery of the law ... Until he be dead."

"Who?"

He looked up at me. "Mitchell Swaine, of course."

"I'm sorry, Swaine, that it couldn't get untangled, that it had to end more fouled up than it began."

"You tried," he said. "Do me a favor and get out now, will you? I'm going to get maudlin and I like to be maudlin alone, all alone."

I started for the door. "I don't know what to say, Swaine."

"Say good night, old man," he smiled.

"You will call the police?"

"Yes, I'll call them. Now, say good night."

"Good night, old man," I said.

Swaine looked up and grinned. For that moment he was a sixteen-year-old; clean, naïve, eager, and smiling. I looked at him, then at the mound of satin over Helen, and I walked out of the bedroom, closing the door quietly.

I listened at the door. Listened and listened for some sound. It was five minutes by my watch before I heard anything.

It was Swaine's voice, sounding more sober than it had before. "Get me the police." Then a pause. "Let me talk to the officer in charge," he said. Another pause. "This is Mitchell Swaine," he said. "Listen, old man, I've just killed my wife at last."

CHAPTER TWELVE

And It Ends Here in the Light of Morning Beginning

THE KEY turned noiselessly in the lock. I called from the front door. "Clar. Clar."

It was a moment before she answered. "Who is it?"

"It's Peter, Clar."

"Oh, my God. Wait a minute. Wait there."

I closed the door and walked into the living room. The door to her bedroom was shut. The living room was a room that belonged to Clarissa, which looked like her in this beginning light of the morning. The walls were the color of her skin, and the furniture was variations of the color of her hair, all the soft and serene colors glowing quietly.

She came out, tying the sash on a pale green dressing gown. "You startled me, darling. I didn't expect you back so soon." She held out her arms. "Welcome home, darling."

I turned my back to her, walked to the window and looked out on the lake. "You know," I said, "the deal I made with Monty."

"Yes, Peter, I know." She walked to me, linked her soft arm through mine and nuzzled her head against my shoulder. "I know you didn't want me to go to Monty but I did it for you, for your good, not for me. I didn't want him to hurt you. I knew you'd come home to me eventually. And you *have* come home." She whispered in my ear, "Welcome home, darling. Welcome home."

I moved away from her. I nodded toward the bedroom. "Is there someone in there?"

"No, Peter, of course not. How could you think that?"

"It doesn't matter."

She pulled me around so that I was facing her. "Don't you believe me? What do you think I am? Go look. Look for yourself if you don't believe me. There's no one there."

"It's all right, Clar. It doesn't matter."

Clarissa threw open the bedroom door. "Go look. Look, Peter!"

I didn't bother. "A lot has happened," I began. "Many things have happened to me these last few days. You'll read about some of it tomorrow in the newspapers, I'm afraid."

"You aren't in trouble, are you, Peter?"

"No, I've been lucky. I've kept my nose clean. I've only jazzed up everybody else trying to straighten myself out. No, I'm not in any trouble."

"It doesn't matter anyway, darling. You're back with Clarissa. That's the important thing. You're back where you belong."

"Technically, I have until Sunday after brunch. Monty and I make our deal Sunday after brunch."

"Yes, and you've come here early, before you had to. I hoped you would, Peter. It's so much better this way. Beginning this minute, now, we are going to start all over again. Nothing has happened before this. Do you understand? We have no past before this minute. Only that we love each other."

"It's no good, Clar. You know the past and I know it. Not talking about it to each other won't make it nonexistent. It will always be there. Don't get me wrong. I'm going through with the bargain I made with Monty. A bargain is a bargain."

"You make it sound as though I were so much cattle."

I looked at her a very long time. "You're beautiful cattle, Clar. You're lovely, beautiful cattle. But nonetheless, it's that kind of deal which Monty and I made."

"Peter, you're saying this because you think you've been coerced. You feel that way now, but I know you better than you know yourself. You love me and you need me and you want me. After a little while, you'll be so happy you'll forget about the bargain with Monty."

"Maybe. But you don't know me better than I know myself. No longer, Clar. I've come to know myself pretty well. I wouldn't have made the deal with Monty if only I had been concerned. If the firm and the insurance company and the people who are going to live in the Williamsburg Village weren't going to suffer too, I would have told Monty to drop dead. I can stand being ruined personally. It doesn't matter to me. It's what I need, probably, to be torn down so that I can build again, build alone this time, on my own foundation, in my own way. But Monty would not only hurt me, there would be innocent bystanders. I wouldn't like that. So I made the deal to protect the innocent bystanders. I think you should know that."

"I don't want to know anything, Peter. It doesn't matter to me at all. All that matters is that you're here. I don't care how you came to be here or what the deal is with Monty. You're here, and I love you and I want you very much."

"You want me, Clar, in spite of the fact that I'm sure now that I don't want you?"

She put her hands over her ears. "I won't listen. You don't know what you're saying."

"Listen through your hands, then, Clar. Because what I'm telling you now is the truth, it is the way things are. You're beautiful and you're wonderful and you're smart and you're everything. But I don't want you. I'm a guy from Dubuque, Iowa, Clar. Have you ever been to Dubuque?" She shook her head, her hands over her ears. "When I was in Dubuque, the thing I wanted most was to get out of there, to get into this kind of life with people like you and Monty, the Swaines, the parties at Jackie's and Jill's apartment. That looked awfully good from Dubuque. It looked good here for a while. Then I found I didn't want them anymore. I'm not naïve enough to think I could go back to Dubuque and be happy there. Too much has happened for that. But I'd like to be able to live the way other people live, people with houses and kids. We could never be like that, you and me."

"You don't know what you want. You've confessed it to me a hundred times before. I know what you want, I know what you need. You need me, Peter. You want me."

"That may have been true three days ago, Clar, but it isn't true now. You wanted me to grow up, become a man. I've done that, I don't know how or why. I've been walking through a nightmare these last days and nights. I've come out of it now, the nightmare is over and I find that I have grown up, I do know what I want. At last I know."

Timidly, verging on hysteria, she said, "And you don't want me?"

"No, Clar, I don't want you. I want to finish the Williamsburg Village, make it as good as it can be, establish a reputation on it."

"But it's such a prostitution of what you believe in. It's an artistic prostitution. We've discussed this time and time again."

"Sure, but a lot of very respectable people start out as tramps. They have to, to get started. That's what I've done, I've prostituted myself, in a way, to get started. But I've built something which is solid and will sell. I have a reputation beginning, based on the Village. Maybe the next time when I get a crack at a project and I say it should be clean, straight lined, and practical they will believe me, and say this man built the Williamsburg Village. He knows what he's talking about. And if the next time they want me to make a few concessions to the straight lines, to the ideal I believe in, I'll fight, but if I have to, I'll give in and make the concessions because there will be a next time after that. Maybe then they'll do it completely my way."

"If that's what you want, Peter, I'll learn to want it, too."

"Do you like kids, Clar? Would you like to have kids?"

"Well... Of course I like children, Peter. I think children are dears. It's... Well, it's rather late for me to begin to think about having them. I'm not quite as young as you are."

"I'd like to have kids of my own, Clar."

"We can talk about that later."

"I came here, Clar, prepared to stay. A deal is a deal, even one made with a man like Monty. He has forced me to come back to you. He can force me to marry you. But he can't force me to love you."

"You do love me, Peter. You're hurt now, annoyed that you've been coerced into this. But you do love me. And after a little while you'll realize it again yourself. Believe me, darling, Clarissa knows all about you."

"No more, Clar. Maybe you did once but no more." I flopped on a big chair, loosened my tie, and kicked off my shoes. "I'll drive as hard a bargain with Monty as I can. I'll try to avoid having to marry you. I don't think he can force me to live with you. There is an ancient, corny saying, Clar, that you can lead a horse to water but…"

"Shut up, Peter!"

I took off my coat, threw it on the floor, and started unbuttoning my shirt. "There are going to have to be provisions in the agreement between Monty and me about finances, just how much of my money is going to be used and how much of yours we will require to keep us in style. I'd rather live here than in my own apartment. This suits you very well, Clar. My apartment wouldn't do very well for you. Is that all right?"

"You'll give in, Petey. You think you can keep this up, talking to me this way, feeling this way about me, as though I were a relative you had inherited and were stuck with. But you'll feel differently. You'll realize that you love me, that you've loved me all the time."

"You don't sound confident any more. You don't sound as though you believe what you're saying."

"I do believe it. I know it. I know it."

"If the situation had been reversed, Clar, how would you feel? What if something had happened that I would be in a position to force Monty to live with you, or you to live with Monty. He still loves you, Clar. He honestly believes that you still love him. What if I had the power over you and Monty which Monty has over me. Would you like to have to live with Monty again, to be with him again?"

"This is different. This is entirely different. I love you. You love me."

"No, Clar. You *say* I still love you. Monty says you still love him. But because Monty says it doesn't make it true, does it?"

She didn't answer.

"Does it, Clar?"

"No. No. I hate him. I hate him." A chill seemed to go through her, and she crossed her arms around her body, huddled against the cold coming from somewhere deep within.

"It will be," I said, "the same with me. I'll feel the way you feel now, just thinking about having to live with Monty again. Every time I touch you will be because I have to touch you, because I have an agreement that forces me to touch you."

She screamed, a long scratching scream. Her whole body tensed in the scream, her hands clenched into fists. As though she were screaming a poison out of her system. When the scream was over, her body relaxed, went limp. She seemed older then, worn out and weary. Slowly, moving with effort, she walked to the bedroom door, stood at the threshold there. "All right," she called into the room. "Come out."

Clarissa stood away from the door as we waited. It was a long wait, waited in silence.

Then there was Ralph Montgomery standing in the bedroom door, Ralph Montgomery smiling. Ralph Montgomery immaculate in a dressing gown and slippers. Even the bandage on his nose immaculate.

Involuntarily I said his name, "Monty."

He said, "The shoe is on the other foot, isn't it, Petey? Imagine you surprising another man in his wife's bedroom. Usually it's the other way around, the husband surprising you.

"You see," Clarissa said wearily, "you only knew part of the bargain with Monty. He drives a hard deal, Peter. You should have suspected it was more than just making you come back to me. I had a price to pay for getting you back. A big price in many installments. Tonight was the first installment. It would have been worth it to me, Peter, if I still believe that you would come to love me again, that things would be the way they used to be with us. I would have gladly paid the price Monty demanded. But it was so horrible. I can still feel the awful horror of it. If you really do feel the way you say, it's too big a price for me to pay. I'm too old and too tired, Petey, to fight so hard for you any more. Too old and much too tired."

"I'm sorry, Clar. I would never have permitted this, no matter who got hurt. I wouldn't have let you be hurt by Monty again in this way."

Monty was still smiling. "This is terribly touching. I wouldn't have missed it for the world. And, of course, I was the winner, after all. You two should have known me better than to think I wouldn't win. I pull the strings, make all of you move the way I want you to. You shouldn't have forgotten that."

"I never forgot it," I said. "I just never realized how really rotten you are."

"And you hate rottenness, don't you, Petey boy? You hate rotten people. That's why you're leaving Clarissa to go back to Helen Swaine. I'm sorry this couldn't have gone on longer. I really expected it would. I wanted you and Clarissa to be married, Petey. I wanted you to be married and discover me here with your wife. But this is almost as good. It would have been better if you had discovered us later, after you two were married. But this is almost as good, and I'm satisfied."

I buttoned my shirt and put on my tie, bent over and laced up my shoes. "I'm sorry, Clar, you had to go through this for me. I'm not worth it. You must know that way down deep. No man is worth it. Nothing is ever worth this much."

She said nothing. She raised her head and walked into the bedroom, closing the door after her. She had regained a portion of her majesty.

Monty was smiling. "All right," I said, "you win, Monty. You win everything but Clarissa. You'll never have her again, you know that."

"Yes, Petey, I know that. But you won't either, and that, after all, is what I was trying to accomplish. No one will ever take Clarissa away from me while I'm alive."

"You love her that much, don't you?"

"Enough so that if necessary, I suppose, I might kill to keep anyone else from having her. But with men like you, Petey, I don't have to kill. There are so many easier ways to beat you."

"You're right again, I guess. I'm a pushover for anyone and for anything."

Montgomery came over and put his hand on my arm. "Don't feel too sorry for yourself, Petey. You have some attributes, you know. There's a certain quality about you that's rather fetching. People like to take care of you. Even now, I'm standing here feeling a little sorry for you, wondering if there isn't some little thing I can do for you."

Quietly, I said, "You can get your hand off my arm, Monty."

Still smiling, he drew his hand away. "I've got rather an exciting idea for an office building, Petey. It may be up your line. I have several powerful companies who could become interested. Why don't we have dinner some time and maybe …"

"Not this time, Monty. This time you've got the wrong boy."

"It was only an idea, Petey."

I started for the door. Monty said, "My car is down in front. Use it if you want to."

"No, thanks. I'll walk."

"What are you going to do, Petey?"

"Lots of things. I'm going to build a hospital in North Africa for one thing."

"You know," Monty said, "that Jill loves you."

"Yes," I said, "I know."

"I tried to warn her against you, Petey. I told her the other night that you were ..."

I didn't hear the rest of it. I had closed the door on Ralph Montgomery and on Clarissa. The door was already closed on Mitchell Swaine and on Helen. That left what I had to build and it left Jill. There would be a time for that but it would be my time, when I wanted it and when I was ready for it. I found myself trying to remember the college song we had used to sing. It was something about the violet time.

The violet time, I was thinking, is over, and my time has begun.

THE END

www.ingramcontent.com/pod-product-compliance
Lightning Source LLC
Chambersburg PA
CBHW030124260626
47156CB00008B/2782